MW00329698

DARKNESS
BEYOND

BOOK FOUR
OF THE DUCHY OF TERRA

DARKNESS
BEYOND

BOOK FOUR
OF THE DUCHY OF TERRA

GLYNN STEWART

FAOLAN'S PEN
PUBLISHING
faolanspen.com

Darkness Beyond © 2018 Glynn Stewart

All rights reserved. For information about permission to reproduce selections from this book, contact the publisher at info@faolanspen.com or Faolan's Pen Publishing Inc., 22 King St. S, Suite 300, Waterloo, Ontario N2J 1N8, Canada.

This is a work of fiction. All the characters and events portrayed in this book are fictional, and any resemblance to any persons living or dead is purely coincidental.

This edition published in 2018 by:

Faolan's Pen Publishing Inc.

22 King St. S, Suite 300

Waterloo, Ontario

N2J 1N8 Canada

ISBN-13: 978-1-988035-39-0 (print)

A record of this book is available from Library and Archives Canada.

Printed in the United States of America

1 2 3 4 5 6 7 8 9 10

First edition

First printing: October 2018

Illustration © 2018 Tom Edwards

TomEdwardsDesign.com

Faolan's Pen Publishing logo is a trademark of Faolan's Pen Publishing Inc.

Read more books from Glynn Stewart at faolanspen.com

CHAPTER ONE

FIREWORKS FLASHED IN THE SKIES ABOVE ARBOR CITY, AND THE woman standing on the rooftop patio of the hotel chuckled to herself as cheers echoed in response.

There was always a strange tinge of irony to the celebrations of Annexation Day on the human worlds, especially for those who'd been adults on that day, twenty years before, when the battle fleets of the A!Tol Imperium had arrived and informed Earth they were under new management.

After twenty years, though, Amanda Camber could nail the guttural stop of their alien overlord's name in her head. She'd been working for them, indirectly mostly, for most of those two decades. The Imperium had done fairly by Terra, and Duchess Bond, the ex–United Earth Space Force Captain they'd made their representative on Earth, had done even better by her subjects.

There were grown adults who didn't remember a world where humanity hadn't been one race of the Imperium's twenty-eight member races; Earth one duchy of the Imperium's thirty. Amanda Camber had been a corporate spy before Annexation—and after, for that matter.

Then she'd served the Duchess as a covert agent tied up in the long-standing and messy process of uplifting Earth to Imperial technology. Now, however, she worked for the Terran Development Corporation, in a very quiet branch of their internal audit team.

The Duchy owned the worlds humanity settled...but the worlds were governed by the Imperium. It was a strange balance, and the TDC was part of the structure separating the ducal government from the new colonies. Money flowed from both the A!Tol and Earth toward the human colonies.

A lot of money. And here, on Powell, in Arbor City, a very large chunk of that money had gone astray.

Arbor City barely deserved the name. The largest settlement on the world of Powell, it held a total of fifty thousand souls, half the planet's population but still basically a sleepy backwater town to a woman who'd grown up in New York and spent the last fifteen years working out of Hong Kong.

Its Governor was an Imperial official, selected by the Empress from a list of candidates the TDC had submitted. The crow-eating, Amanda reflected, was going to be well distributed. The little scroll-like personal computer she had tucked into her back pocket contained enough data to send the Governor to an Imperial jail for a very, *very* long time.

Fifty million marks was a lot of money, but it wasn't enough to buy a blind eye from the people responsible for making sure that money had been spent building a colony.

Glancing around to make sure the rest of the guests were sufficiently distracted by the fireworks display continuing over the city, Amanda opened her communicator.

"Get me Lowell," she brusquely ordered the young man who answered. She didn't need to say more. The codes attached to the transmission would tell the young merchant officer all he needed to know.

It took a few moments to get the Captain of the ship in orbit on the line, but he sounded more amused than offended when he answered.

"This is Lowell," he confirmed. "What do you need, Ms. Camber?"

"I'm done here," she told him. "How are your 'repairs'?"

"Strangely enough, I think they might be complete by morning," Captain Nathan Lowell of the TDC transport *Pippin* told her. *Pippin* had been stranded in Powell orbit due to a power core flutter for three weeks now...exactly as long as Amanda Camber had been on-planet.

Such a strange coincidence, that.

"I'll send a shuttle down," Lowell continued. "How quiet do we need to be?"

"So long as you have a reason to have a bird down here, we'll be good," Amanda told him. "It's as bad as we feared. Possibly worse, so the sooner we move, the better."

"Give me an hour or two," the starship captain promised. "I'll have you aboard by morning and we'll 'sort out' our difficulties by then."

"All right. I'll get moving down toward the spaceport. Figure if I leave my reservation open, that'll confuse people a little longer."

"If you've got enough, we don't—what the?" Lowell cut himself off in mid-sentence, addressing his crew.

"Captain?" Amanda couldn't hear the response from his crew.

"*Kindred Spirit* just blew up," the Captain told her grimly.

Kindred Spirit was one of three A!Tol Imperial Navy destroyers patrolling the star system. Destroyers weren't supposed to just blow up, especially not modern ones! Terra had made billions of marks and paid for their own Ducal fleet by upgrading the armor and defenses of the entire Navy.

"I'm not sure what's going on," Lowell said, then paused for several seconds. "Scratch that. I have warships on our screens, coming in fast." Another pause, and an audible swallow. "*Patience* and *Corona Glare* are moving out to intercept. Orders to the merchants are to run. I'm afraid you're not getting that lift, Amanda."

Their entire carefully established plot to expose the Governor was imploding, but Amanda had always been good at improvising on her feet.

"Are they Kanzi?" she asked him. The Kanzi were the A!Tol's traditional enemies, a race of short and almost human-looking blue-furred religious slavers with matching firepower and industry.

Humans being humans, they tended to call the Kanzi "smurfs."

"I don't know," Lowell said grimly. "I don't think we're going to get away, Amanda. They're moving fast. Leave your channel open, I'm going to keep sending you all of our sensor data for as long as I can."

She swallowed and turned away from the fireworks to look out over the city. She couldn't see sirens, anything.

"Do you know if they told the Governor?" she asked quietly.

"No idea. It might have slipped the Imperial commander's mind," Lowell noted. "They are seriously outgunned here, Amanda."

"Then I'll take care of it. Whether it's slavers or someone else, we need to evacuate the city."

"That's on you," the TDC captain replied. "I'm going to try and get my ship out. Good luck, Ms. Camber."

"Good luck, Captain Lowell."

AMANDA TOOK a moment to take a deep breath and confirm that the datastream from *Pippin* was flowing properly to her communicator. Then she pulled out a digital ID badge she'd rarely had cause to use before, let it read her thumbprint to authorize the screen to wake up, and then strode over to the bouncer next to the elevator leading back down into the hotel.

"You're in charge of security here?" she barked at him.

"Ma'am." The word was a complete non-answer. "Please take concerns up with manageme—"

She shoved the ID in his face.

"Do you know what this ID card says?" she asked flatly. The bouncer was silent, staring at it. "It means I work for the Board of the Terran Development Corporation and I can arrest anyone up to and including the damn Governor—and revoke anyone's colonist license. You understand me, son?"

Amanda knew just how unkind age had been to her, regardless of the medical and exercise regimen that kept her healthy and fit and would give her about three centuries of life expectancy. She was over sixty, and unlike many of her compatriots, she *looked* like it.

"Son" was hard to avoid, even when indirectly threatening to have someone shipped back to Earth in disgrace.

"What do you need, ma'am?" the bouncer asked hesitantly.

"You need to round these people up and get them moving," she ordered. "And then you need to empty the entire damn hotel and get *them* moving. Along the way, you need to contact every other hotel in this town and get them to do the same.

"The A!Tol defense force has been destroyed and we need to evacuate the city *now*."

That was a bit of a leap. The last data she'd seen had the two surviving destroyers charging the unknown ships...but given that even with *Pippin*'s sensors, Lowell had been reading at least one *battleship*, the destroyers were doomed.

She was expecting to have to argue, to spend precious seconds convincing the security guard that she was who she said she was and had proof of what she was saying.

Instead, he took one long look at her face, swore, and grabbed his communicator.

"Rogers, Melliam, Young, Wu," he barked names into it. "Protocol Orange. I repeat, *Protocol Orange*." He paused. "Yes, boss, I know what Protocol *fucking* Orange is. Powell is under attack."

He leveled a gaze on her as he overrode the elevator.

"Car will go all the way to the main floor, then run back up so we can start running the evac," he told her. "Nearest police station is two blocks north; you should be able to make it at a run faster than you can grab a car. They can relay to the rest of the cops."

Amanda blinked, then nodded firmly.

"Thank you."

"I can only save this one hotel, ma'am," he told her. "*Go!*"

AMANDA WOULD FREELY ADMIT she was chubby and graying, but she'd stayed physically fit regardless. The two-block run to the police station was enough to leave her breathing heavily but still able to speak.

The city wasn't really reacting yet. The hotel had been stirring behind her, but the news hadn't made it down to the surface. She couldn't blame the Imperial commander, really. They'd probably assumed that the merchant ships would let the surface know—and the civilians had assumed the Imperials had let them know.

It wasn't as if there was a lot of time. Ships under interface drive moved at half the speed of light or more. The picket was going to get obliterated and they were going to get obliterated *quickly*.

Amanda didn't have time for delays or bullshit, which left her completely ignoring the looks her sweaty state was getting her. It was sufficiently mid-festival that there was already something of a line to talk to the officer at the desk, and she walked right past it.

"Ma'am, there is a li—"

She slammed her Board ID down on the officer's desk.

"And all of their problems have become irrelevant," she snapped. "I need to speak to your boss, and *you* need to get on coordinating your officers to arrange an evacuation of Arbor City."

"You can't just march in here and—"

"I work for the Board and the Duchess," Amanda barked. She spent so much time keeping her true employers quiet that it felt weird to be leaning on them like this...but she had a *bad* feeling about what was going to happen if they didn't get everyone out.

"I bloody well have the authority and there's a hostile *fleet* in this star system, so we all bloody well have the need. *Move*, Officer."

The hard-bodied woman behind the desk hesitated for a moment longer, taking a second to scan the digital ID card on her desk, then nodded and hit a command under her desk.

"Through that door, second door on the left," she told Amanda. "He's been buzzed, though he won't be expecting this."

"Get these people moving," Amanda replied grimly. "Their lives may depend on it."

She didn't wait for a response from the front desk officer, following the directions to barge into the precinct chief's office.

"What the hell is going on?" the burly man behind the desk demanded. He looked like he was around the same age as Amanda, which meant he could have anywhere up to fifty years on her at this point.

"The A!Tol picket is currently charging a force with stealth fields and at least one battleship," Amanda said flatly. "*Kindred Spirits* was ambushed and destroyed. I'm getting a feed to my communicator from a ship in orbit, but it doesn't look like any of the civilian ships are going to get out either."

The precinct chief stared at her...but was pulling up his own link to the orbital sensors while he was doing it.

"Son of a *bitch*," he cursed. "We need to evacuate the cities."

"*Thank you*," Amanda breathed. Then she saw his screen—just as the Imperial Navy destroyer *Patience* vanished from the scans. A second battleship appeared from stealth as its weapons fired, complete overkill against the much smaller ship they'd just obliterated, and swung around at *Corona Glare*.

Neither the feed from *Pippin* nor the orbital sensors really had the resolution to tell Amanda what happened next, but it was over very quickly.

"This is my job now," the chief told her quietly. "You're getting a feed from one of the transports?"

"I am," she confirmed.

He handed her a datachip.

"This will link you to the orbital sensors for as long as they're intact," he told her. "We have an airpad on the roof. You're on the first flight out, ma'am."

"I can't do tha—"

"Evacuating the city is my job now. Your job is to bear witness," the police chief said flatly. "You can't do that if you're dead."

THE POLICE AIRCRAFT that Amanda was led onto was a familiar vehicle. The model was standardized across most of the Imperium, a modular tilt-rotor designed to be able to handle a number of roles from aerial pursuit to search and rescue to prisoner transport.

This time, there'd been no time to install modules. Every space that could be emptied had been emptied, and everyone who'd been in the police station except the officers themselves had been crammed in.

It had been a good night to decide to complain about the neighbor's party.

Amanda made her way into the cockpit as the engines spun up and the aircraft lifted from the roof of the precinct station. Now the city was more awake, and they were far from the only vehicle in the air or on the roads as police and security detachments across the city pressed any aircraft they could find into evacuation duties.

She tried to check the progress of the battle in orbit and inhaled sharply. She was no longer getting a feed from *Pippin,* and there was no way Captain Lowell had got his ship far enough clear to enter hyperspace.

Pulling up the police sensors proved her worst fears. A rough shell of new ships had appeared, presumably dropping stealth fields as they opened fire. It wasn't a solid shell and they weren't big ships, destroyer equivalents, but it was enough that every civilian ship had been intercepted.

And destroyed. She couldn't see any captive ships on the tiny screen of her communicator. The strangers had blown up every ship in orbit, and even as she watched, icons for orbital infrastructure began to disappear as the two battleships came into orbit.

"Fly faster," she told the pilot grimly. "They're taking out the orbitals."

Her screen went blank as the last sensor platform went down. Her briefing suggested there had been about five thousand people living in orbit. The dozen civilian ships in orbit had probably had another thousand crew aboard, and the destroyers had carried a hundred sentients apiece.

They were all dead.

"Hang on," the pilot suddenly barked, hammering the controls to maximum power as he dove for the surface. Amanda wasn't sure what he'd seen until the shockwave washed over them.

"My god," someone said behind them. "That was the *city*."

"Sensors aren't clear," the pilot reported to her quietly. "At least four kinetic strikes. Maybe more. Arbor is *gone*."

They were flying close to the surface now, barely skimming the trees and unable to see any other aircraft. Behind them, another pillar of fire plummeted from the sky.

Amanda didn't need the pilot to tell her there wasn't a city where that one had hit. The aliens had just used orbital bombardment to wipe out a *farm*.

Which meant...

"Do we have coms with the rest of the evacuation?" she snapped.

"Most of 'em; why?" the pilot asked. "Everyone is running as hard as they can."

"Because they need to *stop*," Amanda told him. "We need to land *now*—they're targeting power signatures, and every aircraft on the planet is going to stick out like a sore thumb."

THEY LEFT the shuttle behind at a run, enough of the people aboard the police aircraft listening to Amanda and chivvying the rest along to keep them safe.

The irony wasn't lost on her that most of the people she was using to keep order were probably the criminals who'd been in the station's cells, but with the police aircraft landing, she suddenly found herself responsible for four or five hundred people...with ten pilots for support.

They managed to get everyone about a kilometer away from the aircraft before their cooling power plants attracted the attention Amanda expected. It was, thankfully, a *small* kinetic strike as things went.

She was flung to the ground by the shockwave, the breath knocked from her lungs, and then silence took over the night as she waited. Ten seconds. Fifteen.

Whatever power sources they had with them weren't enough to attract fire from on high. They were okay...for now.

"Check in on everyone," she ordered. "Get a tally of the injured and of what supplies we have, then see if we can get everyone under whatever's left of the trees for shelter."

She looked around grimly.

The police aircraft had been stuffed with people, not food. They'd assumed—as she would have, if she'd thought about it—that they'd be able to rely on the farms for food and shelter.

Except those farms were now craters along with Arbor City.

"What do we do in the morning?" the pilot from her aircraft, a young man whose name she still hadn't picked up, asked.

"We survive," she told him grimly. "And we wait for the Imperium. Those destroyers had hyperfold communicators. Someone *will* be coming."

She hoped.

CHAPTER TWO

EVEN ABOARD ORBIT ONE, THE PRIMARY ORBITAL STATION FOR the Duchy of Terra Militia space fleet, there were parties celebrating Annexation Day. Most of the partiers were in uniform, however, which meant that they could only get so out of hand.

MPs who had drawn the short straw kept watch on everything, and a pair of the white-helmeted troopers escorted Lieutenant Commander Morgan Casimir through the throng. Both were older than the blonde Militia officer, but they treated her with a degree of deference that left her swallowing her irritation.

Morgan knew lecturing the Corporal and Private would be both inappropriate and a waste of everyone's time—and they'd *probably* fall back on the logic of "respect is due an officer." She just knew perfectly well that the deference *she* was getting was less to do with her lofty new O-4 rank, still so fresh it squeaked, and more to do with the fact that her stepmother was Annette Bond, the Duchess of Terra.

"*Bellerophon* is this way," the Corporal told the young officer, leading the way off the main thoroughfare into a somewhat quieter section of the station. The battleship Morgan had been assigned to was being kept away from any area where civilians might wander into —and a guarded checkpoint stopped them before they entered the docking arm.

"Identification, please," the Ducal Guard Sergeant told them. The woman clearly recognized Morgan but still insisted.

Morgan passed her digital ID over with an approving nod.

"Lieutenant Commander Morgan Casimir, reporting aboard *Bellerophon* as an emergency replacement for Lieutenant Commander Alex Yu," she said crisply.

Alex Yu had been in a shuttle accident two days earlier, forcing the Militia's newest battleship to delay her departure while they found an officer qualified to serve as her assistant tactical officer and cleared to know everything about *Bellerophon*.

Given that Morgan's father, Ducal Consort Elon Casimir, had been instrumental in the design of the ship and her stepmother ran the planet, she had the clearance. They'd decided she could be spared from her *utterly critical* logistics role.

"You're on the list," the Sergeant replied with a salute. "Congratulations on the promotion, Lieutenant Commander."

"Thank you, Sergeant. Am I clear from here without escorts?"

"Only people past here are *Bellerophon* crew," the MP told her. "Last I heard, Captain Vong was holding the ship until morning to allow them the celebration, since they were held up anyway."

Morgan nodded. She'd moved as fast as she could, but the Militia had decided to bump her promotion up and move her aboard only ten hours before.

"Then we can let Corporal Winton get back to keeping an eye on the party," she said with a chuckle. "My thanks, Corporal. I think I can find my way to the only starship on the dock from here."

"Of course, sir." The MP saluted. "Our pleasure."

With a nod to both her escort and the checkpoint guards, Morgan stepped forward into the secured dock. Her second-ever starship assignment awaited.

THERE WAS a gallery about fifty meters short of where the directory said the main accessway to *Bellerophon* was, and Morgan couldn't help herself. She stopped there, stepping up to the abandoned window—she could hear the party going on in the main open area of the dock, but it hadn't spread out here—and looked out over the warship that would be her home for at least the next year.

Her last shipboard assignment had been aboard the destroyer *Ottawa*, one of the *Capital*-class ships that had been the Duchy's first refits for their own service. She'd spent two years as the most junior person in their tactical department, learning the ins and outs of the Ducal fleet.

The distinction between *Ottawa* and *Bellerophon* was huge, and it wasn't just size. *Ottawa* had been half a million tons and just over one hundred fifty meters long. A!Tol-designed, she was built around a central hull with sweeping nacelle arches that held her antimissile turrets and heavy proton beams. Once the arches were taken into account, she was almost as wide as she was long.

Bellerophon was not so evenly proportioned. Massing ten point five million tons, she was just over eighteen hundred meters long and only six hundred across at her widest point. Her core hull was a double-ended spindle showing her Terran ancestry, but heavyset "wings" at her rear spread her main weapons systems away from her hull, while arched nacelles in the A!Tol style stretched her defensive armaments out.

It was an awe-inspiring mix of Terran and A!Tol design paradigms, and Morgan Casimir thought the ship was gorgeous, and not just because it was as much a child of her father and stepmother as her twin sisters were.

Turning to resume her journey toward the battleship's boarding tube, she realized she was no longer alone. A tall and well-muscled man with dark hair and brilliant blue eyes was looking down his nose at her.

Her noting of the man's features and attractiveness came to a sharp halt as she recognized the gold circle and triple bars of the man's insignia and the shoulder patch of *Bellerophon* on his Militia uniform.

"Sir," she greeted the Commander with a crisp salute.

"Do you *enjoy* having the most powerful vessel in the Militia held up on your arrival, Lieutenant Commander Casimir?" the officer asked her in an acid English accent.

"No, sir," Morgan replied crisply, resisting the urge to dissolve into her shoes.

"Then why, Lieutenant Commander, did you decide that 'with all urgency' did not apply to *you?*" he snapped.

That had been the exact phrasing in her orders, yes. A phrasing she'd heeded in leaving even the limited possessions of a Naval officer behind and reporting aboard Orbit One with literally the clothes on her back.

"Wanted to see the ship, sir," she confessed. "No excuse, sir. My apologies."

He grunted.

"Commander Chin Masters," he introduced himself. She'd missed the Asiatic cast to his features, but the first name brought it to her attention. "*Bellerophon*'s tactical officer and your new boss. Your effects?"

"Going into storage on Earth," Morgan responded instantly. She tapped the small bag she was carrying. "This is all I'm reporting aboard with."

He eyed the bag with suspicious eyes, then shrugged.

"There may be some hope for you yet. Let's get aboard, Lieutenant Commander. We're already two days overdue, so you have very little time to learn before we head for Rimward Station."

MASTERS LED the way aboard the battleship with a practiced gait. He clearly knew the ship and the dock like the back of his hand, in a way Morgan had only begun to master aboard *Ottawa* at the end. Apparently, practice made that easier.

She was able to keep track of where they were going and what deck they were on, however, and realized they were heading to the tactical officer's office before they got there. Masters, it seemed, was planning on starting her off immediately.

The trip to his office, however, was silent and he gestured her to a seat wordlessly as he poured two glasses of water without asking what she wanted.

"Lieutenant Commander Casimir," he stated. "Promoted less than twelve hours ago and assigned to what many would regard as *the* premier O-4 slot in the Militia. Lieutenant Commander Yu *earned* his rank and his place in this slot, Casimir. Why do you think *you* got it?"

"I got this slot because someone at HerCom decided that it was easier to accelerate my promotion than to read someone else in on Gold Dragon clearance and bring them up to speed on *Bellerophon*," Morgan told him.

HerCom was the Human Resources Command. HerCom, along with her last group, LogCom—Logistics Command—ShipCom—Shipbuilding Command—and RadCom—Research and Development Command—made up the ground-support contingent of the Duchy of Terra Militia.

"You already *had* Gold Dragon clearance?" he demanded.

"I spent the last year of my pre-Academy education living on DragonWorks Station because of a security threat," Morgan said quietly. "I spent my weekends doing grunt admin for the team working on *Bellerophon*'s power systems to earn spending money."

She didn't like to think of the *reason* she'd ended up living on the secret research station hidden inside Jupiter's atmosphere, not least because the threat had only been declared credible after her girl-friend at the time had taken a bullet meant for her.

Josephine had survived. Their relationship, understandably, hadn't.

The shooter had confessed to being part of an anti-Imperial organization targeting the Duchess's family. Since the Duchess couldn't disappear, the kids had. The twins, being the actual Heirs, had to occasionally appear, but no one had questioned Morgan vanishing for a year.

"Since I had that clearance already, I was working on *Bellerophon*'s logistics needs," she continued. "I assumed that my familiarity with both the class and the ship herself were the reason for my assignment."

Masters grunted. Morgan suspected *his* interpretation of her getting the position involved more nepotism.

"Lieutenant Commander Yu and I had been working together to get this team up and running for six months," he told her. "We've had the tactical department complete and doing exercises for a month."

She nodded. She wasn't quite stepping into a dead man's shoes, but it was pretty near. Lieutenant Commander Yu had nearly died, and reconstruction was going to take months. Months *Bellerophon* didn't have to wait, not for one relatively junior officer.

"You're going to be the odd one out for a while and you need to keep my department together," he continued. "Think you can manage not to screw this up?"

"Believe me, sir, if I screw this up, my stepmother will *never* let me live it down," Morgan told him with a moment of fervent humor that extracted a grin from her new boss.

It wasn't a bad start. She was going to have a long time to work on him, after all.

CHAPTER THREE

VICE ADMIRAL HAROLD ROLFSON LOOKED AT THE SOMEWHAT disastrous aftermath of the party with a huge grin.

"I think that went well, don't you, love?" he asked his wife. It was rare for Ramona Wolastoq to have much time to spend on his ship. He commanded Rimward Station for the Ducal Militia, and his wife was humanity's preeminent xenoarcheologist.

She was down to spending only a third of her time buried inside Jupiter these days, but a good chunk of what was left was going through ancient ruins. The colony in the Lelldorin System had found the wreckage of an industrial civilization that appeared to have actually committed humanity's old nightmare: nuking themselves into the Stone Age.

They'd done it long enough ago that the nuclear winter had passed, leaving the planet Arend perfectly habitable for humanity but with some fascinating ruins. Ramona had stopped by on her way through and found herself commandeered to help host the Admiral's party.

"You put me in a dress and made me make nice to people," she complained, only partially joking. "It went all right for that. I didn't punch or stab *anyone*."

Harold chuckled. His wife was from the Algonquin First Nation in North America, and she was often abrasive to those who didn't respect her achievements or her. She was a tall woman, with broad shoulders and tanned skin, more than able to intimidate anyone who got on her bad side.

When they'd first met, she'd intimidated *him*, and Harold had at least fifteen centimeters on his wife and the bulk to go with it. Reputation and tradition had stuck him with the massive red beard he'd had when Annette Bond's ship had fled the A!Tol conquest of Earth.

He'd grown the beard when there'd been no real rules enforced on *Tornado*'s crew. That leeway had survived the end of their mission, and the beard had become part of his reputation.

The remaining members of *Tornado*'s crew were given a certain amount of leeway...leeway that Harold had found was its own kind of trap, eventually.

Fortunately, he liked having a beard and the *Majesty*-class super-battleship *President Washington* had plenty of space for the larger-than-life personality expected from him. Even as he was joking with his wife and helping the stewards start to clean up, he kept one eye on the wallscreen showing his fleet.

Rimward Station of the Duchy of Terra Militia orbited the planet Isaac in the Asimov System. Two super-battleships, *President Washington* and *Indira Gandhi*, hung at the core of the picket, with six *Manticore*-class battleships orbiting them.

Two squadrons of *Thunderstorm*-class cruisers and a matching number of destroyers brought the picket to seventy-two ships total. It was the single largest Militia presence outside Sol. It was also, so far as Harold could tell, the single largest deployment of a Ducal Militia outside their home system in the Imperium.

The Imperial Navy regarded the Ducal Militias with a degree of condescending benevolence in the main, but the Navy *also* knew that the *Terran* Militia was being used as a testing ground for an entire generation of new technology.

As the stewards ushered Harold away from the mess, his wife stepped up next to him and leaned over to kiss his cheek.

"You put me in this dress," she purred throatily, clearly not caring if the stewards heard her. "I hope you have plans for getting me *out* of it."

He wrapped an arm around her and grinned brilliantly.

"As it happens, my love, I—"

His communicator was between them, which meant they *both* felt the harsh buzzing of the high-alert communication. With an apologetic look at Ramona, Harold pulled the device out.

"Admiral Rolfson," he answered it shortly. "What is it?"

"Sir, we have an incoming hyperfold distress signal," his staff communications officer told him. "We're still decrypting, but it came in under an Imperial Navy code. I think you need to see this."

"I'll be right there," he promised, then looked at Ramona. "Sorry, my love."

"You're as married to your ships as I am to my ruins," she told him. "We both knew what we were getting into."

PRESIDENT WASHINGTON'S flag bridge was an efficiently laid-out space, designed to allow an Admiral with a staff of about a dozen to command an entire fleet. Most of that efficiency was built into an impressive suite of communications tools that allowed each member of the flag staff to easily coordinate up to a hundred more crew.

The Rimward Station fleet wasn't large enough to require that, but the design was still useful, as it meant that Harold could gather his people and have access to the primary holographic tank that filled the central section of the room.

"There's few details in the message," Commander Yong Xun Huang told Harold grimly. Like many of the first generation of the

Militia's officers, he was Chinese—originally a member of the secret fleet the China Party had prepared in case the old United Earth Space Force had turned on them.

When the newborn Duchy had needed crews to field a fleet against the Kanzi, the China Party's people had volunteered. In an inevitable, if unplanned, exchange, Chinese officers made up a notable plurality of the senior personnel of the Militia.

"No details?" Harold asked. "But it's a fully encrypted distress signal, correct?"

Harold could remember a day when a system like Powell would have had no way to communicate with his fleet. The massive starcom installations that still formed the backbone of the communications infrastructure of the Imperium were expensive and took forever to build.

Even Asimov, the central military posting in the Imperium's new human colonies, didn't have a starcom. What they all had, however, were hyperfold communicators. The technology had been given to the Imperium in exchange for favors done for one of the galaxy's elder races, the Mesharom.

Hyperfold coms had a range of roughly ten light-years, with a transmission lag of about an hour per light-year and a drastic fall-off in bandwidth at a distance. Most of the Imperium had been seeded with hyperfold relays now, but this message was direct from the Imperial picket at Powell.

"It is," Xun Huang confirmed. "But...it was an *automatic* transmission."

That sent a chill down Harold's spine. There was only one automated and encrypted message that an Imperial Navy ship would send via hyperfold communicator.

"It's a Code Omega," Harold stated aloud. "Which ship?"

"*Corona Glare*," his coms officer reported. "There's not a lot of data attached, but what is attached suggests that both *Patience* and *Kindred Spirit* had already been destroyed. There is no secondary telemetry."

"But if we didn't get Code Omegas from them..." Harold's operations officer, Captain Nahid Ling Yu, trailed off softly. The Chinese-Iranian officer looked sick, yanking on her shoulder-length black braid as the conclusion sank in.

"They had to have been destroyed before they could send even an automated transmission," Ling Yu continued after her pause. "How much data *did* we get?"

"Automated Code Omega sends us a short-range sensor snapshot," Xun Huang told them. He threw it up in the hologram. There wasn't a lot of detail or information—there was only so much the limited-bandwidth emergency transmission could include.

It was enough to make the battleship looming over *Corona Glare* very clear.

"Impossible to tell if there's more ships in the system," Ling Yu said, her voice very level and slow. "But if they ambushed a destroyer with a *battleship*..."

"Then we have to assume that they had more than one," Harold finished. With a grim shake of his head, he reached the only decision he could have made and kept his stars—or his soul.

"Get me Rear Admiral Sun," he ordered. "I'm going to hold his squadron and one of the destroyer squadrons here with instructions for Captain Vong and *Bellerophon* once they arrive. The rest of us are going to Powell."

And *he* was going to have to explain to his wife that their limited interlude had just come to a sharp end and send her on her way to her expedition.

Damn it.

CHAPTER FOUR

The super-battleship *Indira Gandhi* led the way into the Powell System, her exotic-matter emitters sufficient to open a portal out of hyperspace well over thirty kilometers wide. *President Washington* brought up the rear of the formation, her emitters holding the portal open as the rest of Harold's task force passed through.

Hyperfold coms didn't work across the hyperspace barrier—another disadvantage that kept the starcoms in use—but regular radio did. By the time *Washington* carried Vice Admiral Harold Rolfson into the star system, he knew what was waiting for him in terms of enemies: nothing.

That also summed up the amount of orbital industry and civilian shipping visible in the system, both of which should have been present.

"We're running a cross-collation from all task force sensors," Ling Yu reported. "But...initial scans show no power sources in the system. At all."

Two gas giants, both of which should have had cloudscoop stations. One major and two minor asteroid belts, all three of which should have had small to medium mining operations. Five rocky uninhabited worldlets that *should* have been dark.

And then Powell itself. A colony world with a population of over a hundred and twenty thousand sentients, over ninety-eight percent human, with three major power installations and almost as many minor power sources as people.

"Nothing on the colony?" Harold asked, making sure he understood.

"Nothing," Ling Yu confirmed. "We'll resolve more data as we close, but even at this range, our sensors should be able to pick up even mid-sized generator facilities."

Even Harold couldn't force cheer in the face of that news. There were no ships, friendly or hostile, in the system, and all of the power sources that *should* have been present were gone. There was an easy answer for all of that and he did *not* like it.

"We're already moving in, I presume?" he said, as lightly as he could.

"All ships have reported in and we're moving towards Powell at point four light." She shook her head. "Sir, it..."

"I know what it looks like." Harold stepped away from her to study the plot in the hologram tank. "Split the destroyers off," he ordered. "Send them on a sweep of the outer system. Some of the asteroid miners or cloudscoops may have gone dark and avoided notice. Even in the worst case, some may have made it to escape pods."

Ling Yu nodded and began to give orders as her Admiral continued to stare at icons that should have been lit up.

One hundred and twenty thousand sentient beings. People in his area of responsibility, that he'd been supposed to protect.

What the *hell* had happened there?

BY THE TIME they reached orbit, Harold had part of an answer and he didn't like it.

"We're running debris-pattern analysis, but it looks like every spaceside installation was destroyed by interface-drive missiles," Ling Yu told him. "Anything that might have had a sensor package sufficient to give us any data was blown to pieces.

"Then they went hunting through the asteroid belts and the gas giants." She shivered. "Captain MacArthur reports they *are* finding escape pods from the mining facilities and cloudscoops. Some were destroyed, others managed to hide."

The attackers had fired on escape pods from civilian installations. Harold understood his operations officer's shiver. He could, just barely, see a logic behind firing on civilian installations or firing on military escape pods. Shooting up civilian escape pods, though...that was just vicious.

"And the planet?" he asked.

"Kinetic bombardment," she stated in a toneless voice. "Not interface-drive weapons, not energy weapons. Probably specialized kinetic munitions, but I can't be certain, as that's outside our design paradigm."

The gravitational-hyperspatial interface momentum engine didn't play particularly fair with Newtonian or Einsteinian physics, and humanity's scientists hadn't fully worked out how it worked before the A!Tol arrived and they got handed somebody else's textbooks.

The current standard interface-drive missile of the A!Tol Imperium, though, accelerated to point eight cee in just under two seconds. Planets didn't survive being hit with that. On the other hand, the interface drive didn't handle atmosphere very well, and missiles were even worse for it. The safety protocols built into Harold's missiles to prevent accidentally hitting planets were simply an augmentation of an existing "flaw" of the system.

"We don't go in for mass bombardment," he agreed quietly. "Any sign of life on the surface?"

"Nothing. The three major settlements are just craters. It looks like every farm or moving vehicle got a smaller kinetic strike. If there was a power source, it got blown up."

"Genocide," Harold concluded. "Someone just wiped out one of our colonies. A hundred thousand souls. The *fuckers*."

His curse echoed in the stunned silence of his flag bridge. The world in the holographic tank *looked* mortally injured, too. "Nuclear" winter was well on its way to taking hold. Life would probably survive, life tended to do that, but anyone who'd managed to survive this atrocity was going to face an uphill battle to *stay* alive.

"Keep the destroyers on the search for survivors from the outer installations," he finally ordered. "But get the cruisers moving back into hyperspace. We won't get much useful data from four or five light-days out, but we will get *some* answers."

His gaze remained focused on the dying world beneath him.

"And if I know my Duchess and my Empress, they are going to want those answers. More, they're going to want a *target*."

And so did Harold Rolfson. Someone was going to burn for this.

CHAPTER FIVE

Amanda Camber watched the night sky carefully. Her mental math suggested that a Militia force should be arriving around now, but...with no telescopes, no communications and no power, she had no idea.

"Do those look like new stars to you, Kyle?" she asked the big guy leaning against the tree next to her.

Kyle McDermott was at most half her age. She'd confirmed that he had been in the precinct station cells, though she hadn't asked why as the big man had turned out to be essential to keep everyone alive.

There were a few hunters in the group, but McDermott was both a hunter *and* a professional chef. He'd helped the others find animal life and edible plants in the forest where they'd ended up and had known how to turn freshly hunted animals and gathered plants into real food.

"I'd say they were satellites," he replied as he looked at the night sky with her. "Except we haven't had satellites since we ended up out here. So, yeah, new stars. Ships?"

"I'm hoping," Amanda admitted. "Go keep an eye on everyone. I'm going to try and call up."

"And what happens if they're *not* friendly?" he asked.

"I get blasted from orbit and the rest of you better hope the next ships along do low-altitude surveys," she told him with forced cheer. "Now get out of the blast radius, Kyle."

He snorted and gave her a mock salute. She waited for him to get off the hill and head down toward their crude camp in the valley below, under the shelter of a convenient mountain. The hope was that the mountain would protect them from detection and kinetic strikes.

None of that would help once she turned on her communicator with enough power to reach orbit.

Once her helper was out of sight, she pulled the device out. She hated risking it. Her communicator currently held the only copy of the sensor records. She'd checked—no one else among her collection of refugees had a communicator or computer with enough memory space to hold a copy.

Unfortunately, no one else had a communicator that could reach orbit. With a sigh, she pulled the scroll-like device open and turned it on, ordering it to full power and to try and ping the Militia network.

And then she closed her eyes and waited for hell to fall from the sky.

Nothing happened. She kept her eyes closed for a few more seconds, and then checked the screen. She had a contact. A Duchy of Terra Militia code was responding to her ping.

"Militia ships in orbit, this is Director-at-Large Amanda Camber from the Terran Development Corporation," she said crisply. "I am approximately sixty kilometers from where Arbor City was, with just over five hundred survivors.

"We have limited food and water and require immediate aid. Please con—"

"This is Vice Admiral Harold Rolfson," a familiar voice cut her off. "We are deploying shuttles to your beacon immediately. Are you in need of medical assistance?"

She breathed a long sigh of relief.

"No, Admiral, everyone we pulled out is physically fine," she told him. "I'd suggest you find every damn counselor you have in your fleet, though, as these people are pretty shaken up."

Rolfson snorted.

"Everyone up here is pretty shaken up, so I can guess," he agreed. "Ms. Camber...do you know what the hell *happened*?"

"I know a bit. I also have full sensor records from the orbital network and a TDC transport." She paused. "People died to get that data, Admiral. Please tell me it'll be worth it."

"A lot of people died," he said grimly. "I don't think anything will ever be worth it, but if we can ID the bastards who did this, they're going to pay.

"Shuttles are less than five minutes out. We're sweeping for other survivors, but..."

She winced.

"Anyone?"

"Looking like another five hundred from the belt and cloud-scoops," he said gently. "Otherwise..."

"I got everyone evacuating during the attack," Amanda whispered. "At least some should have abandoned their vehicles, but they can't be far from the cities."

"That's...useful to know," Rolfson told her. "I'll pass that on to our shuttle pilots. You have my word, Amanda. If anyone survived, we will find them."

AMANDA WENT STRAIGHT from the shuttle bay to the super-battleship's tactical analysis center. From the harried expression of the Arabic-looking staff Captain who arrived shortly after she did, the Admiral's staff hadn't realized she knew the layout of the ship that well until the Marine escorting her had called in.

"Ms. Camber, I am Captain Nahid Ling Yu," she introduced

herself. "I'm Admiral Rolfson's operations officer. You said you had scan data?"

Amanda gestured to the screens around them, where *President Washington's* tactical department was already pulling the data from her personal communicator.

"From the TDC ship *Pippin* and from every satellite feed that the Arbor City Police had access to," she confirmed. "Reading all of this is mostly beyond me, I can basically say 'this is a starship, right?' and probably be right."

Ling Yu chuckled and stepped over to study the displays as the analysts worked away to assemble a complete sequence of events.

"We're lucky you got this," she noted. "The bastards who attacked blew up *everything*. All we have from the space installations is escape pods, and no one thought to grab sensor records in the rush to survive."

"Thank Captain Lowell and precinct chief..." Amanda paused, then swore as she realized she'd never even learned the name of the man who'd got her out of the city. "They got me the links," she said quietly. "I'm just a messenger. I'm here to bear witness."

"I understand," Ling Yu told her, putting a hand on Amanda's shoulder. "There are no words for this, Ms. Camber. You need to make sure that you meet with one of the counselors as well. Everyone we're pulling off of Powell is going to need all of the help we can give them."

Amanda nodded, then shook herself. The Militia officer was at least twenty years younger than her. When the woman had been born, Amanda had been digging her way through the ugliest mid-Asian genocide of the last two hundred years to break into an abandoned corporate research facility.

She'd seen worse. This was, at least, an impersonal slaughter.

That didn't really seem to help.

"I want to see your results of the data analysis," she finally told the operations officer. "You can check my file if you like; I'm cleared for it."

She had just enough clearance to know that there were multiple levels of Dragon clearances above her, and that the Duchy shared those clearances with the Imperium. Her own work with the Duchess, however, meant she was cleared for anything less-classified than that.

And Amanda Camber *needed* to know who the sons of bitches who'd bombed a world around her were.

MORNING BROUGHT an invitation for her to join the Vice Admiral and his staff for a briefing. Amanda wasn't military and never had been, but she understood what an "invitation" to join an Admiral entailed.

Plus, it was what she had requested.

It was the first time she'd seen Vice Admiral Rolfson in person, and she was surprised to see how closely his image hewed to his reputation. He wasn't a massive man, but his long hair and massive beard, both still bright red, lent him a larger-than-life feel.

His face looked like he was used to smiling and laughing...but he was doing neither today. Today, the Vice Admiral in command of the Duchy of Terra Militia's largest out-system deployment was leaning on the arm of his chair, his chin resting in his hand as he studied the holographic display at the front of the briefing chamber.

"Now that the good Director has joined us, can you lay it out, Captain Ling Yu?" he asked, his voice tired.

Amanda started to apologize for being late, but he cut her off with a wave of his hand.

"You're not late, Ms. Camber. I'm just impatient and angry. Someone is going to pay for this, and I very much want to know who."

Ling Yu sighed and tapped a command, bringing a ship into the middle of the holoprojector for everyone to study.

"We don't have enough information to get hard IDs on anything," she admitted. "What we do have, however, is a lot of suggestive data —and a solid visual on the ship that destroyed *Patience* and *Corona Glare*. This is what they look like."

Camber studied the ship, but she knew that she wasn't exactly familiar with starship taxonomy. It was roughly shaped like a pair of stacked horseshoes, with four prongs reaching forward from a blocky base. It rang a bell, but...

"The design paradigm is Kanzi," Ling Yu concluded aloud. "Stealth fields are not a known development of the Theocracy, but they're not blind to the massive technological advancements the Imperium has been undertaking.

"Multiple factors of the ship and the incident do not align with known Kanzi technology or general Kanzi methodology," she continued. "Most of the factors are easily being explained by this being a new class of battleship. The devastation of the local population, however, is *very* unlike the Kanzi."

"That would depend on their goals," Rolfson said. "If they have a covert stealth fleet, they may well be attempting to use it to draw the Imperium into an overextended position hunting a 'mystery enemy' while they prepare their regular fleets for outright war.

"While they would prefer to take slaves, the Theocracy Navy is willing to make many sacrifices at their High Priestess's command. Massacring a population they could sell for money would be a small demand."

Rolfson's voice was utterly flat. Cold. His tone said everything he needed to say about the concept of slavery or mass murder.

"What happens if it is the Kanzi?" Amanda asked.

"War," Rolfson replied. "We will send all of our data to the Sol starcom via hyperfold relay for transmission to the Empress. The full response to this is the Imperium's business."

He shook his head.

"There does not appear to be anything more we can do here," he concluded grimly. "Ms. Camber, we will be transferring you and the rest of the survivors to two of our cruisers. They will carry you all back to Asimov.

"I'll have some personal messages for you to deliver as well, but we owe all of the survivors safety and protection."

"What about you?" she asked.

"This Fleet will proceed to Lelldorin and the other colony systems closer to the Kanzi border," he said grimly. "We will make certain no other world suffers Powell's fate, and we will demand answers from the Kanzi.

"One way or another."

CHAPTER SIX

"Attention! Terra arriving!"

None of the Imperial Marines lining the path between the space shuttle and the exit deeper into the space station were human. The officer snapping orders was one of the A!Tol, a massive female towering over two and a half meters tall in her heavy power armor.

The troops themselves were a mix of Tosumi and Yin. Both species were avian in appearance, though the Yin were taller and generally more human-looking despite their fine blue feathers. The Tosumi were squat creatures with vestigial wings, but they were also one of the Imperial Races—species the A!Tol had learned uplifting on.

The Imperial Races' original cultures hadn't survived. Outside of the inevitable differences around sexuality and relationships, the Tosumi functionally had the same culture as the A!Tol.

The A!Tol might forgive themselves for the destruction of those cultures. Eventually. Maybe.

Duchess Annette Bond wasn't taking bets on when. She returned the salutes of the Imperial Marines as she walked forward into DragonWorks Station, a quartet of the Ducal Guard following her off the shuttle in their own power armor.

She'd had access to Imperial-level medicine since well before she'd returned to Earth and, despite being closer to seventy than sixty, felt healthier than she had at forty. The pair of fifteen-year-old twins causing havoc back on Earth spoke to her health in her fifties, if nothing else.

That thought brought a smile to her face and carried her to the end of the ceremonial guard, where three people were waiting for her. The central figure was a glittering-carapaced sentient that resembled an upright scarab beetle. Standing to the right of the Laian station head was a human in a business suit, managing to look both neatly dressed and awkward in a way she'd only ever seen engineers master.

To the Laian's left was a young human in the uniform of the Imperial Navy, with the simple silver circle insignia of a Lesser Commander. That was a new rank since the last time she'd seen him, and she gave them all a smile.

"Dockmaster Orentel," she greeted the Laian. Orentel had once served as the senior shipyard manager for the semi-pirate Laian group that ran the station the humans called Tortuga. She and her mate, somewhat ostracised by their people due to monogamy being out of the norm for Laians, had led the portion of the exiles that had immigrated to Earth.

"Dilip." She turned to the engineer. Dilip Narang had worked for her husband for decades at Nova Industries and then been poached by the Imperium and the Duchy to help run DragonWorks.

Her brightest smile, however, was directed at the young Japanese man in the Imperial uniform.

"Lesser Commander Tanaka," she greeted him. "It's good to see you, Hiro. How's your mother?"

Harriet Tanaka, once a battleship commander for the United Earth Space Force, had been the first human officer to put on an

Imperial uniform. She'd done it to get treatment for then-ten-year-old Hiro Tanaka's rare cancer.

Somehow, no one had been surprised when the son had followed the mother into Imperial service.

"She's doing well," the younger Tanaka told her. "She sends her regrets for not meeting you in person, but given the circumstances, she didn't want to leave her flagship."

The vestige of pleasure and humor Annette had summoned fled her and she fell back into her "iron-faced ruler" mode as she nodded and glanced at the two sentients who ran the research station.

"Let's get to your confidential meeting room," she ordered. "Harriet and I need to make sure we're on the same page here, and I want to pick the DragonWorks' collective brain."

If history had taught her anything, it was that there was never only going to be *one* crisis.

ANNETTE STEPPED into the conference room and stopped short. Despite everything going on, the view from the window that covered one wall of the room was still jaw-dropping.

DragonWorks Station didn't orbit Jupiter. DragonWorks Station was *inside* Jupiter, in a ten-thousand-kilometer bubble of space held open by the application of massive shield generators. The gas giant's famous Red Spot was around and above them, swirling storms of gas and energy that shone a blood-red light through the window.

Taking a deep breath, she stepped over to the end of the long wooden table and waited for everyone else to be seated. A faint haze shimmered over the window as a privacy shield engaged, and a new figure appeared in one of the empty chairs.

Fleet Lord Harriet Tanaka was present only by hologram, but she gave Annette an abbreviated bow and nodded firmly to her son.

"This is your meeting, Duchess Bond," Tanaka said calmly, the petite Japanese woman still looking as young and healthy as ever.

Annette envied her. Medical care or no, she was certain *she* didn't look as good as the Imperial officer did.

"And we're here to make sure you're involved," Annette told her. "There are Gold Dragon–secured rooms on Earth, but none of them have the communications infrastructure to reach your flagship."

Tanaka nodded. Her super-battleship flagship—indeed, the entire Imperial Seventy-Seventh Fleet—was hidden in the pocket with DragonWorks Station.

"This meeting room is now secured under Gold Dragon protocols," Dilip Narang announced, the dark-skinned and graying engineer looking tired. "We've all been briefed on the basics of what happened at Powell, so as Fleet Lord Tanaka pointed out, this is your meeting, Duchess."

"Powell was a fucking massacre," Annette said flatly. "I have a TDC team currently reviewing if the impact winter is going to be minor enough for it to be worth returning anytime in our lifetimes, but..." She shook her head. "That's a secondary concern.

"As we speak, Empress A!Shall has summoned the Kanzi ambassador to demand answers," she continued.

"And all Navy stations are on full alert," Tanaka told them. "Squadrons are being deployed forward to the border. The Imperium is preparing for war."

"Are we ready?" Annette asked. "I know *Bellerophon* is the only fully Gold Dragon–equipped ship we have, and she's Militia still."

"It's been twelve years since we rolled out hyperfold coms to the entire Navy," Orentel reminded them with a shrug of her multiple shoulders. "We've quietly deployed many of the Green Dragon systems through the fleet. The *Vindication*- and *Integrity*-class ships are fully equipped with hyperfold beams, and we've deployed almost sixty of those two designs across the Imperium.

"Few of the Black Dragon systems are worthwhile on their own." The Laian spread her claws wide in acceptance. "The Imperium is not prepared to embrace weapons systems that reduce their pilots' life expectancies by years for every hour they're deployed. Starfighters will remain a Wendira innovation."

Annette nodded. That had been the expectation, but after the Alpha Centauri incident, the Imperium had had vast quantities of sensor data on the Wendira attack parasites and a number of mostly intact samples. Humanity was close enough to their carrier and jet-fighter days that she knew her people had pushed hard to try and find a usable space fighter.

The three tiers of work done at DragonWorks were Green, Black and Gold Dragon. Green Dragon was the tech everyone knew the Imperium was working on somewhere, evolutions of the hyperfold coms the Mesharom had given them and similar next-generation systems.

Black Dragon systems were the systems their closer enemies and allies probably guessed they were working on. Matter-conversion power technology, stolen from the Reshmiri. Starfighter technology, stolen from the Wendira. Hyperspace missile and tachyon sensor technology, stolen from the Mesharom.

Gold Dragon was the tech they hoped even the Mesharom didn't know they had, the systems and science based on the survey and samples of the Precursor ship humanity had given up to that ancient race.

"So, we have Green Dragon tech available to most formations, but not Black or Gold," Annette concluded. "Do we know anything about the weapons systems and stealth fields used at Powell?"

Narang shook his head.

"No, and that's weird," he told them softly. "We don't have a lot of data, but we should be able to at least ID the systems. Beyond the use of point eight five interface-drive missiles, we can't."

The Imperium had upgraded to a point eight cee missile in the last decade. Point eight five was the theoretical maximum, currently a Core World exclusive—though DragonWorks was working on that.

"The records are pretty close up to the destruction of several of the orbital platforms," Tanaka pointed out. "We should know what was used there."

"And we don't," Narang repeated. "It was outside our experience. Outside *any* Imperial record."

That sent a chill down Annette's spine. Something sounded familiar there, but she couldn't place it.

"I guess that's a problem for the Navy," she said quietly. "What about the other *Bellerophon*s?"

"*Herakles* and *Perseus* are beginning their trials as we speak," Orentel told her. "We can accelerate them and have them ready for deployment in a week or two, but that is a risk."

"They're Militia ships, not mine," Tanaka said. "The decision is yours, Annette."

"Accelerate them," Annette ordered. "We'll hold them in Sol for the moment as we try and work out what the hell is going on. Rolfson may need more support than even our worst fears; having another pair of Gold Dragon battleships ready to back him up is the best we can do."

"What about *Bellerophon*?" Tanaka asked. "We can reach them via the starcom. Do we brief Captain Vong, at least?"

"He'll have twice the detail we can send him by starcom from the hyperfold network as soon as he arrives in Asimov," Annette pointed out. "That's less than a day. I trust Vong's judgment."

She might not be willing to influence Morgan's career, but she'd still be *damned* if she'd let her stepdaughter serve on the ship of someone she *didn't* trust.

"So, we wait?" Narang asked.

"We wait," Annette confirmed. "We see what Rolfson finds at Lelldorin and we see what the High Priestess and the Empress discuss.

"We wait," she echoed. "And we prepare for war."

CHAPTER SEVEN

"BATTERY CHARLIE-SIX IS *STILL* LAGGING BEHIND EVERYONE else," Morgan reported crisply. She stood in front of Commander Masters's desk as they went over the daily report. She'd been invited to sit, but she actually thought better standing.

"That's four of our hyperfold cannons," Masters pointed out. "Even a few seconds off sequence could undercut a bombardment intended to bring down a target shield."

"Depending on which tests we're looking at, they're as much as five seconds off," she told her boss. The numbers were being projected on the wall, but she wasn't looking at them. She'd written the report summarizing the last three days' worth of tests that she'd supervised, plus the two weeks before she'd arrived.

"They're the last to arrive after general quarters and take a noticeably longer time to respond to commands from the bridge," she continued. "Ninety-plus percent of the time, the battery is firing in central control and it won't matter, but...the other ten percent of the time, Charlie-Six could get us in serious trouble."

Masters nodded, the tanned officer studying her levelly.

"You've been running the tests these last few days and you have Yu's notes," he said. "What do you think the problem is?"

Morgan looked back at her boss and snorted.

"I think you already know the answer," she told him. "But it wasn't in Yu's notes."

The Commander chuckled.

"I have my own suspicions, but I want to hear what you think," he replied.

"Petty Officer Stevens is making no attempt to cover up her team's shortfall," Morgan said. "She honestly seems more frustrated by the problem than I am, and her previous record is impeccable. Normally, I'd expect a problem like this to be the PO."

"Not the battery crew themselves?" Masters asked.

"While I'm sure there is theoretically such a thing as a bad crew, my experience is that a good noncom can get acceptable work out of even the worst teams," she told him. "None of the files for Charlie-Six's crew suggest the kind of endemic discipline or training problem that would explain this kind of shortcoming."

"So?"

"I went and physically watched them for the last scramble drill," Morgan said. "Charlie-Six is at the rear of the ship, positioned in the rear armament arch." She shook her head. "Those crew were coming in at an outright run, sir, trying to make the time. That battery is the most awkwardly positioned weapons position on the ship, sir, with the only nearby ship transit car crossing through all of Engineering.

"Unless PO Stevens's crew were literally sleeping at their guns, they couldn't man the battery in time. I double-checked their detailed scores—they *start* every exercise behind but catch up to the standard by the end. They're out of breath, sir, from running to try and make the scramble time."

Masters laughed and clapped gently.

"I didn't even think of the possibility that they were out of breath," he admitted. "I'd run the ship schematics and realized the scramble problem. So, Lieutenant Commander Casimir, what would you recommend?"

"There's a limit to what we can do without building a new transit tube," Morgan told him. "We can do some rerouting, but I ran some models and they don't buy the crews enough time. Looking at the schematics, there's a *reason* the tubes run that way, but I think the engineers need to get that fixed for the next generation of the ships."

"Put together a proposal and we'll make sure it makes it back to DragonWorks," Masters ordered. "We're not far from going into mass production on the class, so let's make sure our ships are worth their weight when we piss off *everyone*."

Morgan chuckled. Commander Masters had clearly been briefed on the degree to which the Gold Dragon–level technology had been stolen, hidden or otherwise acquired in ways that were going to anger the Core Powers once unveiled. She doubted he really grasped the true depth of it. *Morgan* wasn't sure she grasped the true depth of it, and she'd listened to her stepmother and Admiral Rolfson discuss how to keep the Precursor tech underlying some of *Bellerophon*'s systems secret from the Mesharom.

"That doesn't help us for today, though," she noted. "We need that crew on their guns in under ninety seconds and we need them there without having to sprint." Morgan smiled. "Fortunately for everyone, there's a set of engineering rating berths at the base of the rear armament arch. I'm relatively sure we can move those crew to somewhere they can still reach their stations in time...and if we put Charlie-Six's crew there, they should be able to make their stations from their racks in under sixty seconds.

"*Without* running."

Her boss considered her in silence for a minute.

"Show me," he ordered. "I'll raise it with Commander Nguyen. We need that scramble time, Casimir. Let's make it happen."

That was the first time he'd called her by anything except her rank. She hoped that was a good sign.

BACK IN HER QUARTERS, Morgan took a deep breath as she checked the time. In theory, she was supposed to have a minimum of twelve hours between shifts. In practice, well, those rules applied as well for starship officers as they'd applied for officers of any stripe in history. Regs kept at least sixteen hours between her bridge watches, but given the number of other duties the second-ranked officer in a battleship's tactical department had...

She was due on the bridge in six hours, just before they arrived in Asimov. The siren call of sleep, however, was interrupted by a notification on the console in her quarters. Mail call.

Bellerophon, like every other capital ship in the Imperium, had both hyperfold communicators and a starcom receiver. Without a transmitter, the starcom could only receive messages, but that meant that they could get mail from home, even if they couldn't easily reply to it.

Morgan hit the command to play the message without checking to see who it was from and then inhaled sharply as the pale skin and red hair of her girlfriend, Christie Torres, appeared above the hologram projector.

"Hi, Morgan," Christie said. "I got your note. Really?"

Morgan didn't even need to wait for her girlfriend to continue before she winced.

"Almost a year we've been together," the redhead noted. "A year, and all I get before you're aboard ship and headed out-system is a fucking *text message*?" She shook her head. "I would think I deserved better than that, but it's pretty typical of you, isn't it? I didn't get treated much better when you were aboard *Ottawa*, did I? Guess I was just too shiny-eyed then."

The naval officer lowered herself into her chair gingerly as Christie continued. She wasn't going to pretend she didn't deserve the lecture. Their relationship had been shaky for a while, and Morgan knew damn well it was her fault.

This time, it had been outside her control. She couldn't say the same for the other times she'd done something similar.

"We're done, Morgan," Christie told her. "When I actually get to see you, you're great, and there's definitely a charm to dating the Duchess's stepdaughter, but...fuck, woman, you are the most frustrating lover I've ever had.

"We're done," she repeated. "I'll mail the shit you left at my apartment to your parents. Somehow, I'm sure I can find the address. Don't contact me. I won't answer."

The hologram froze as the recording ended, and Morgan sighed. She stared at the image of her now ex-girlfriend for several seconds, then disappeared it with a wave of her hand and went digging into the drawers for the medkit.

She wasn't going to sleep without help after that, and, well, she was due on the bridge in six hours.

CHAPTER EIGHT

MORGAN HAD SEEN MORE HYPERSPACE EMERGENCES THAN SHE could count, as a passenger in her teens and then as an officer aboard a patrolling destroyer. There was still something awe-inspiring to her in the sight of the exotic-matter arrays lighting up with power and tearing a hole back into reality.

Hyperspace was an ever-fluctuating gray nothingness to human eyes, but the bright blue Cherenkov radiation from the hyper portal still lit it up. Reality was visible through the highlighted portal for the handful of seconds before the ship slipped through the hole it had torn in hyperspace.

Then *Bellerophon* was in the Asimov System, the battleship swinging toward her destination and bringing up her interface-drive systems.

"Helm, what's our ETA to the Rimward Station docking facilities?" Captain Vong asked.

"Forty-two minutes at point five cee, sir," the officer holding down navigation replied.

"Tactical, anything unusual on the screens?"

Morgan was already pulling and cycling the data, but it was

Masters's job to reply to the Captain. Her job right now was to make sure that her boss had the right data...and while there wasn't anything unusual on their sensors, there was definitely something *missing*.

"The fleet is gone," she murmured, highlighting the orbit where Vice Admiral Rolfson's capital ships should have hung. "Half the cruisers and destroyers are left, but the capital ships have moved out."

"Well, Tactical?" Vong repeated, and Morgan realized the Captain had probably heard her muttering to Masters.

"Lay it out, Casimir," her boss ordered, staring at the screen. "You spotted it first."

She swallowed and turned to look at the Captain. The older Chinese officer looked down at her from his command chair with a gentle smile.

"The Rimward Station Fleet has deployed, sir," she said crisply. "One of the cruiser squadrons and one of the destroyer squadrons remained behind to protect the system, but the capital ships and half the escorts have left the system, presumably under Admiral Rolfson's command."

As she spoke, she was highlighting data and transferring it to the main screen. Masters was adding his own notes and data to it as she did so, but he let her explain it to the Captain.

"Thank you, Lieutenant Commander," Vong told her. "Well caught. Helm, bring us up to point six cee, if you please. I'd like to know what's going on sooner rather than later."

Bellerophon's regular "flank" speed was point five five lightspeed. She had a point six five lightspeed sprint mode that she could sustain for up to ten minutes. More than that, however, risked both ship and crew.

Point six wasn't full sprint, but it was definitely hustling for the big ship. Captain Vong was worried.

"Coms, what do we have incoming?" he asked.

"Rimward Station will be aware of our arrival in about fifteen minutes," the communications officer replied. "I imagine we'll have hyperfold coms with them shortly afterwards. Vice Admiral Rolfson will almost certainly have left..."

"Lieutenant Commander Antonova?" Vong asked into the sudden silence.

"We just picked up a hyperfold transmission coming into the system, directed towards Rimward Station Command," the young woman replied. "It's not coming through our relay network and I'm not familiar with the protocols, but...I think it's Mesharom?"

"Mesharom?" Vong sounded surprised, which was reasonable. The Mesharom and the A!Tol Imperium got along reasonably well, but the galaxy's oldest species and greatest Core Power didn't like each other, let alone anyone else.

"I think it's Frontier Fleet," Antonova replied. "I'm not familiar with Mesharom communications."

"Damn. Do we have anyone who is?" Vong asked.

Morgan swallowed, then slowly raised her hand.

"I've worked on Mesharom diplomatic communiqués," she noted slowly. "I...I've also met Mesharom Interpreters."

The Captain laughed.

"That would make you the *only* person on this ship, Lieutenant Commander Casimir," he pointed out. "Antonova, send Casimir the transmission and keep decrypting it."

The data flowed across Morgan's screen and she studied it for several seconds. There were patterns to the Mesharom hyperfold protocols. The Imperium and the Duchy of Terra had a lot of the coms protocols, but identifying which one wasn't... There it was.

Morgan tapped in a series of commands and the communication resolved.

She inhaled sharply as she read the headers, then looked up at the Captain.

"Captain Vong, it's a Frontier Fleet message, all right," she confirmed. "It's a distress signal, requesting immediate assistance from any A!Tol Imperial Navy units."

Her CO shared her hard swallow as he met her gaze.

"You know the Mesharom better than me," he admitted slowly. "Is this as strange as I think it is?"

"To my knowledge, sir, the Mesharom Frontier Fleet have *never* sent a distress signal to an Arm Power military."

AN HOUR LATER, *Bellerophon* rested in orbit above Isaac as replenishment vessels from the support stations swarmed over her. With all of the messages from Admiral Rolfson received, Morgan Casimir found herself unexpectedly pulled into a senior officers' meeting.

Sitting next to Commander Masters, she calmly concluded that it was in her best interests to sit down, shut up and pay attention. She was pretty sure she knew why Captain Vong had pulled her into the meeting, and her part to play would come.

Vong himself was standing at the front of the conference room, next to a large wallscreen like a stereotypical twentieth-century teacher with a blackboard, studying the information laid out on it with a hawk-like gaze.

"All right, people," he greeted them without turning around. "We now have all of the information we're going to have." He tapped the astrographic chart on the wallscreen, and a three-dimensional version of the local stellar region appeared above the main table.

"Vice Admiral Rolfson left the Powell System for Lelldorin three days ago," Vong noted, highlighting the two systems in green with a line between them. "Hyperspace currents being what they are, he is anywhere from twelve to seventy-two hours out from Lelldorin.

"He's been out of communication with the hyperfold relay network, however, for three days, which means we are more up to date on Lelldorin's status than he is," the Captain concluded grimly. "There haven't been any Code Omegas, but no one in Asimov has heard a peep out of the system in two days. It's not looking good."

Morgan hadn't heard that part yet and managed to not audibly react. Lelldorin was slightly less developed than Powell, but still...if the same level of devastation she'd seen in the reports from Powell had been carried out, then another hundred thousand innocents were dead.

"Our orders," Vong told them, "are to remain here in Asimov and secure the system against any possible threats. That said, my orders are clear that I am not being placed under the command of Rear Admiral Sun and I am to exercise my judgment as to the deployment of *Bellerophon* until we can hear from Admiral Rolfson."

He let that sink in. Morgan didn't even need to look up the rank tables to know that Vong was senior to any of the Captains commanding the cruisers and the destroyers. Rear Admiral Sun commanded the cruiser squadron and the Rimward Station, which would normally put *Bellerophon* under his command.

"This communication from the Mesharom, however, throws everything out of line," he concluded. "Lieutenant Commander Casimir has personally interacted with the Mesharom and made a study of the Core Powers in general during her time at the Academy. She's the closest thing we have to an expert on the Mesharom in the system, so I want her to lay out the situation as she understands it. Lieutenant Commander?"

Morgan swallowed, glancing over at Commander Masters who gave her an encouraging nod.

"The background is probably known to everyone," she said quietly. "There are a number of powers in the Galactic Core who have a significant technological edge over the star nations in the galactic arms. Our own Gold Dragon programs are intended to level that playing field, mostly with stolen technology.

"We believe the Mesharom at least suspect the existence of the Gold Dragon programs, but they're also the ones we've been hiding them from," she continued. That piece probably wasn't known to most of the people in this room, and she couldn't clarify beyond that. *She* knew that a good chunk of the Gold Dragon tech was based on Precursor systems.

That, however, wasn't even classified Gold Dragon. Classifying it would require the Imperium to admit that piece of information *existed*.

"For various reasons, including—as we learned at Centauri—the search for Precursor artifacts and the enforcement of the Kovius Treaty Zones, the Mesharom maintain Frontier Fleet forces throughout the galactic arms. These are usually between two to six Mesharom battlecruisers."

She flipped the specifications they had on the latest-generation Mesharom ships onto the holographic display.

"While the other Core Powers often go in for much larger ships, a Mesharom battlecruiser remains, ton for ton, the most powerful warship in the known galaxy. They do not ask for help. They do not, generally, *need* it.

"But they sent a distress signal to Asimov. They specifically requested A!Tol assistance. I...don't know if even *Bellerophon* is a useful reinforcement to a Mesharom squadron, but they asked for our help."

"Much of the Imperium's survival and strength has been built upon our relationship with the Mesharom," Vong reminded them all. "We have reason to believe that the Mesharom are responsible for several of the interventions that staved off the Kanzi invasion of Sol seventeen years ago, and they helped defuse the Alpha Centauri incident.

"We owe them. As Lieutenant Commander Casimir notes, *Bellerophon* isn't a match for a Mesharom battlecruiser—but she's closer than anything else in the A!Tol Imperium. Therefore, I'm returning command of Rimward Station to Captain Tongue and taking *Bellerophon* to the coordinates provided."

He smiled grimly.

"I expect, Lieutenant Commander Casimir, that you will be pressed into service as our de facto expert again at that point," he warned her. "So, I'm going to make your life suck. Everyone: please consult with Commander Casimir for any information you believe you will need on the Mesharom. Sorry, Lieutenant Commander, we're not cutting the rest of your duties."

She hadn't expected anything else and nodded calmly.

"I live to serve, sir."

She couldn't give another answer, after all.

MORGAN HAD BARELY MADE it to her office when Victoria Antonova followed her in, the willowy blonde communications officer smiling apologetically as she did so.

"You've actually *met* a Mesharom?" she asked as the two young women took seats. "That's...well, that's freaking cool."

Morgan laughed. Victoria Antonova, like her, was part of the new generation of officers who'd grown to adulthood in the Duchy with a full knowledge of the galactic scene. She was two years older than Morgan herself and was another rising star of the Militia, from what Morgan could tell.

"You wouldn't say that if you'd done it," Morgan told her with a chuckle. "How do you feel about millipedes?"

The communications officer shivered and Morgan chuckled again.

"Me too," she confirmed. "Now imagine a three-meter long hybrid of a millipede and a fuzzy caterpillar. That's a Mesharom. They're big, they're fuzzy, and they have enough legs and arms to start a shoe store."

Antonova chuckled herself.

"I've seen pictures. They're intimidating, but...I'm told they're occasionally difficult to communicate with? I'm going to be responsible for talking to them when we get to the rendezvous, so I'm hoping you can help me out."

Morgan nodded. A ship's communications officer was often the most junior of her senior officers, which meant that while Antonova only had a year's seniority on Morgan, she was in all of the meetings like the one Morgan had just been dragged into.

"You won't be talking to them," she told the other woman. "That's the biggest thing to realize. At no point will you be directly communicating with a Mesharom. Everything will go through an interpreter AI, and their coms to us will be short, potentially rude by our standards. They don't *like* people."

"I keep hearing that about them, but I'm never quite sure what that means," Antonova admitted.

Morgan considered how best to phrase it.

"At their default state, a Mesharom communicates with other Mesharom in short sentences, preferably shouted from a distance," she explained. "Electronic communications were the best invention ever, and their civilization *survived* by passing notes for millennia.

"Mating, children, all of this is very formalized and organized because they don't *like* being around each other. Take your worst moment of stage fright ever, layer in that you were actually going to have to do it naked, and then multiply by ten." Morgan shook her head. "That's about their baseline."

Antonova looked perplexed.

"Always?" she asked.

"*Always*," Morgan confirmed. "Now, you're never going to deal with a normal Mesharom. Any of them aboard their ships can at least stand other Mesharom for extended periods, but they also use a *lot* of robots to make up for how few of them can be on a ship."

"So, we can talk to the shipboard ones?"

Morgan chuckled and sighed.

"No. Even the ones that make up their starship crews can't really deal with aliens. In desperation, they *can*, but they usually have an 'Interpreter' aboard. An interpreter is, by Mesharom standards, extra-ordinarily brave. By our standards, they're shy and often abrupt.

"But the Interpreters *can* talk to aliens, so they do. One alien at a time, please and thank you, and only in person, but they're the key to Mesharom interactions with the rest of the galaxy."

"So, we talk to machines mostly, and then we may talk to a specially trained ambassador type?"

"Exactly. The Interpreters are entirely reasonable to deal with in my experience, but I've only ever met two," Morgan admitted. "I don't feel qualified to be an expert."

"That's two more than the rest of the ship combined," Antonova pointed out. "But..." She glanced around, as if making sure they were alone in Morgan's office. "Can we really help them? They're the *Mesharom*."

"We're supposed to conceal a lot of our capabilities from them." Morgan shook her head. "If we stick to protocol, we might not. If we go all-out, though...*Bellerophon* is one of the few ships in the galaxy that might qualify as being in the same weight class as a Mesharom battlecruiser."

"That makes no sense," the other officer said.

"There are reasons. Even I only know some of them. I leave that kind of shit to my parents."

"Most people would if they had *your* parents," the other woman agreed. "Hell, *I'd* leave that kind of thing to your parents too."

They laughed together, sharing a grin.

"It's a good thing they're the ones who have to deal with it, then, isn't it?"

CHAPTER NINE

SOMEHOW, EMERGING FROM HYPERSPACE INTO THE EMPTY space between the stars was different from jumping into a regular star system. There was a chilly silence on *Bellerophon*'s bridge as she emerged at the coordinates the Mesharom had given them.

"What have we got?" Vong asked into the quiet as Morgan and Masters ran through the sensor data.

"We're nine light-years from Asimov, just over four light-years from the nearest star system," Masters said aloud. "I'm...not detecting much of anything out here, sir."

"The Mesharom wouldn't have called us out here as a prank," Vong pointed out. "I guess they could be hiding under stealth fields?"

"Or damaged or otherwise not emitting an energy signature," Masters replied grimly. "What I can tell you for certain is that there's no active ships out here."

Morgan was already tasking active sensors to pulse specific zones and laying in patterns for drones. She flipped the pattern to Masters for approval. The Commander glanced over the screen, poking at a few sections of the plan, then hit Activate.

At ten point five million tons, *Bellerophon*'s immense mass didn't even tremble as two dozen drones fired from her missile tubes. They flashed away from the battleship at sixty percent of the speed of light, hyperfold communicators sending their data back to the mothership near-instantaneously.

"Any communications, Commander Antonova?" Vong asked.

"Negative, sir." The blonde Russian shook her head. "Com channels are dead. No radio, no hyperfold except our drones. From the amount of chatter out here, we might have dropped out into a completely random patch of nowhere."

"I don't think we did that," the Captain replied. "So, where *are* our caterpillar friends?"

Morgan swallowed hard as the data started to feed back from the drones. Multiple angles of active radar and lidar pulses gave her the answer to Captain Vong's question, and she didn't like it.

"Here," she said quietly, flashing an icon on the tactical display. "And here. And here." Six separate icons appeared on the display. "Dispersal patterns suggest at least thirty-six hours from destruction, which would align with the distress signal we received."

Nine hours for the message to reach Asimov. Five for the Duchy of Terra warship to get moving. Twenty-one for them to get to this abandoned patch of space.

"My god," Vong murmured. "Six ships destroyed. All Mesharom?"

"Hull spectrography suggests so, yes," Masters confirmed. "No other debris, sir. Just...six Mesharom battlecruisers that somebody blew to hell."

"There's no way someone punched out six Frontier Fleet battlecruisers without taking a scratch," the Captain objected. "There's got to be more debris out here, even if they were careful to clean it up. Casimir, Masters—find it."

He shook his head.

"Someone just killed six Core Power warships. We need to know who. If the Mesharom are at war out here, that's one problem. If it was the damn Kanzi...it's an entirely different problem."

"THAT'S IT," Masters said several hours later, his voice half-exhausted. "It's good to know the fuckers didn't get it all their own way."

"I'd have been happier if they hadn't been willing to vaporize any of their own survivors that happened to be aboard their wrecks," Morgan pointed out.

They'd managed to pin down the distinct patterns of vapor that showed where the Mesharom's enemies had destroyed their own wreckage. They hadn't cared about the Mesharom wrecks, but they'd used what looked like massive antimatter warheads to obliterate the remnants of their own ships.

"They may have evaced before they wrecked the ships," her boss said. "But it doesn't look like it. The only way we're getting any data here is to jump out and get old light."

She snorted. It was doable, but the resolution sucked—and that was assuming that you calculated your jump close enough to make a useful scan in a reasonable time frame.

"I just can't shake the feeling that the Mesharom wouldn't have sent that distress signal without a plan," she told Masters. "That they sent it at all tells me they were losing and they knew what was going to happen to them. They had to have planned *something*."

"Got any inspiration?" he asked. "Because in the absence of a brilliant idea, I don't see any choice but to tell the Captain we're done here."

She nodded, studying the wreckage.

"Antonova," she called, turning away from the tactical department to look at the coms officer. "We've got Mesharom contact protocols on board, right?"

"Yeah, but there's nobody out there to talk to," the other woman pointed out. "We'd be shouting into the void."

"Would we?" Morgan murmured, looking back at the screens. "Have we been post-processing for stealth fields?"

Masters blinked.

"You would have been the one doing it," he pointed out.

The A!Tol Imperium knew more about stealth fields than they once had, but they still couldn't detect them quickly. What they could do was go over several hours of scanner data and look for the recurring "glitches" that showed a stealth ship *had* been there.

"If I had Core Power tech and I were building escape pods, I'd build in the best stealth tech I had," Morgan said aloud. "If we can't see them, we can still *talk* to them."

"And if they're hiding, they're sure as hell not dropping the stealth fields without some sign there are friends out here," Antonova replied. "I can pulse a general hello and identifier. See if anyone responds."

"Please, Lieutenant Commander," Morgan asked. "If there's anyone left out there, we need to help them."

MORGAN WASN'T QUITE HOLDING her breath as the radio messages swept the wreckage. She was hoping that someone had survived and presuming that they had some way to receive the transmissions that *Bellerophon* was sending out.

The casualty list for a Mesharom detachment was shorter than it would have been for an equivalent Imperial formation. Each of the battlecruisers had only carried between sixteen and twenty Mesharom, with most of the "hands" that crewed the vessels provided by complex robotic drones.

Of course, the Mesharom had one of the slowest population growth rates in the galaxy—and none of the advanced races were reproducing particularly quickly. The hundred or so dead represented by the wrecked fleet were a painful loss to their species and especially to the much smaller portion of their race that could tolerate space travel.

If someone had survived, though... the Imperium might be able to find justice for them.

"Nothing," Antonova noted. "Assuming they're in the debris field, we should have a response by now." She shook her head. "I don't think anyone made it out."

Morgan nodded stonily.

"It was a long shot," she admitted. "Thanks, Antonova."

"Wait," Masters suddenly barked. "Vector one-seven-zero by oh-four-five. Out eleven million kilometers. What have we got there?"

Morgan tuned the scanners to the point her boss had flagged and saw the same thing he had. There was something new on the screens, something that hadn't been there.

"Revectoring drones," she said quickly. "Looks like something just dropped a stealth field but has a radar-absorbing hull. Trying to get a visual."

The bogey started moving before her drones reached it, glowing on their screens as it brought up an interface drive and shot toward *Bellerophon* at half of lightspeed.

"Any response to our hail?" Morgan asked.

"No...wait," Antonova said, echoing Masters's earlier interruption. "I've got a text note requesting an interception and docking protocols." She shook her head.

"And then they're asking for one individual to board the pod for 'diplomatic discussions.'" The coms officer met Morgan's gaze. "You guessed right, Casimir."

"Well done," Masters told them both. "I'll contact the Captain, but I can guess what his orders are going to be. Go make sure you're checked out on the emergency hazmat suits, Casimir. I think you're up."

Morgan swallowed hard but nodded.

It looked like she was going to meet her third Mesharom ever.

If only she felt qualified to have that conversation.

CHAPTER TEN

THE POD RESTING IN THE MIDDLE OF ONE OF *BELLEROPHON*'s small craft hangars looked huge. Almost forty meters long, the stark white ship filled the central space of the hangar, locking a third of the battleship's assault and transport shuttles in while they worked out what to do with their new passengers.

"There's no access we can see," the Ducal Guard Sergeant leading the security detail told Morgan. "Sensors say the hull is active microbots?"

"Yeah, same thing *Bellerophon* uses as a support for her compressed-matter plates," Morgan told the trooper. "They do the same thing but with smaller plates. Can't tell where the CM ends and the microbots begin."

She looked around the hangar. There were two dozen Guards in a rough encircling pattern around what she was pretty sure was an escape pod, plus several techs poking at the smooth white hull. She sighed.

"What part of 'send one individual' is so hard for us to grasp?" she asked rhetorically as another tech helped her into the skintight hazmat suit. She nodded her thanks and zipped up the transparent second skin over her uniform, leaving the hood and face cover unsealed.

"Let's clear the hangar, people," Morgan ordered. "Our *best* case here is an experienced Interpreter, used to aliens but not necessarily enthused with their job. In any case, the sentient we're dealing with is going to be extremely stressed.

"Let's not push it. I'll meet them alone."

"Lieutenant Commander, that's not sa—"

"Sergeant, that's a Mesharom escape pod," she cut off the Guard NCO. "Our intel suggests her power source is a small matter-conversion plant. If the Mesharom wants to kill us, they overload that plant and *Bellerophon* is history. Let's not fool ourselves as to our safety, all right?"

The Guard swallowed but nodded her acquiescence. Troops and techs started to move out, and Morgan waited until the hangar was empty except for her and the pod. Then, closing up the face and head cover of the hazmat suit, she stepped over to the white ship and rapped on the hull.

"I am Lieutenant Commander Morgan Casimir of the Duchy of Terra Militia," she said loudly and clearly. "I've been designated as our point of contact with your Interpreter. May I board?"

There was no audible response, but a portion of the hull a meter or so over from where she stood began to flex and run, almost as if melting, to uncover a standard-looking airlock hatch.

With a deep breath, Morgan crossed to the hatch, which swung open as she reached it. The airlock was large enough for a Mesharom, which made it extremely roomy for a human, especially a relatively small one like Morgan.

She stepped inside and the door slid shut behind her. The Mesharom was in *Bellerophon*'s hands for safety...and now Morgan Casimir was in the Mesharom's hands.

THE OTHER SIDE of the airlock opened into a cavernous space that likely formed most of the pod. Although it was large enough for thirty or forty humans, Morgan suspected it was designed to hold a single Mesharom. Maybe two.

A pair of worm-like segmented robots were waiting by the airlock door. Serpentine constructions built of flexible plates and a smoothly flowing black fluid she guessed to be similar to the hull, they were identical to the robots Morgan had seen before.

Even Mesharom escape pods, it seemed, came with servitors.

"This way, please, Lieutenant Commander," the left robot told her. "Interpreter-Lieutenant Coraniss awaits."

There were no subdivisions inside the ship, though Morgan thought she could pick out several lumps of microbots that could be used to divide the pod into individual rooms. As it was, however, she could see their rescuee from across the ship.

Interpreter-Lieutenant Coraniss—a First-Seeder, if Morgan remembered the cultural rules around Mesharom names and their seven genders correctly—was a three-meter-long fuzzy millipede with orange and blue markings. Dozens of long feelers, both hands and feet depending on the Mesharom's desire, fidgeted nervously with a computer panel while Coraniss focused away from Morgan.

The robots stopped her about two meters from the Mesharom, who was clearly very unsure of themselves. Morgan knew it was dangerous to project human emotion onto even bipedal aliens, let alone something as different as a Mesharom, but she had the strong impression that Coraniss was terrified.

"Are you okay?" she asked before she could even think about it.

The fur and legs rippled in a way that gave Morgan a moment of nausea, then the Mesharom pulled back from the computer. They still didn't look at her as they considered the question.

"No," Coraniss finally replied. "I appreciate the concern, and no, I am not 'okay.' I was the most junior Interpreter of the Fifty-Third Flotilla, the only officer who could be spared. I was not consulted.

Not advised. I was delivered into this pod and fired into space without warning."

The alien shivered.

"I am not okay," they repeated. "But I have a task, Lieutenant Commander Casimir, and I will see it done."

"We received a distress signal from your flotilla," Morgan told them. "We arrived as quickly as possible. Too late to save your people."

"Such was expected," Coraniss admitted. "The hope was not to save the flotilla. The hope was to save the one selected to bear witness. To save me...and the data I now possess."

"You have records of the ships who attacked you?"

"I do. They are...strange," the Mesharom told her. "I will provide you with all of the information I have and will assist your efforts against them as best as I can. A vessel will be sent to pick me up, but it will take some weeks to arrive."

Morgan swallowed.

"Has...has a Frontier Fleet Flotilla ever been destroyed like this?" she asked.

"Never."

The word hung in the pod for several seconds, and Coraniss turned to level their massive crystalline eyes on Morgan.

"Never," they repeated. "Few powers in the galaxy would dare such. Fewer still would succeed." They gestured to the computer.

"All of my records have been transferred to your ship. My servitor should be able to direct your crews as to how to interface with this vessel to provide air, power and food supplies, if you would be so kind."

"Of course," Morgan promised. "We will do everything in our power to see to your comfort."

"My comfort is most easily seen to by remaining aboard this pod," Coraniss told her. "I do not doubt that you would do all within your power, but I would not be comfortable aboard your vessel."

"We can keep your pod aboard and inside our defenses while

providing hookups, at least," the human said. "We will keep you safe."

"It is appreciated. You will hunt the killers of my crew as well?"

Morgan grimaced, then realized the alien probably wouldn't understand the gesture.

"The decision is not mine," she admitted. "But I do not know why we wouldn't. We value our relationship with your people...and you were attacked in our space."

———

THE DATA DUMP from the Mesharom pod was huge, but it turned out to not have any real answers. Morgan stared at the ships that had emerged from nowhere in frustration.

The six battlecruisers had been hanging out in the middle of nowhere. How exactly they expected to know if they were needed was unclear, though Morgan guessed that they had a hyperfold relay network stretched through the area and spies everywhere.

Then, without any warning according to the files the Mesharom had given them, a hyper portal tore itself open in the middle of the Frontier Fleet formation. Twenty ships, each over twice the size of the ten-million-ton Mesharom battlecruisers, emerged in knife-fighting range of the Mesharom and opened fire.

There were data codes in the exchange of fire that the Mesharom hadn't bothered to provide explanations for, but what the human officers could decipher told them it had been a brutal exchange of close-range fire. Proton beams, hyperfold cannons, interface-drive missiles and at least three weapon systems the humans had no basis to identify filled the space between the two fleets.

"No wonder they didn't ask Coraniss's permission," Morgan observed as they played the battle again, at one third speed so they could go over it in detail. "I make it less than thirty seconds from the portal forming to their captain firing them into space."

"And less than sixty seconds from the portal forming to the

complete destruction of the Mesharom fleet," Masters agreed. "The bastards bled for it, but they wiped out the only major Core Power formation out here."

Twenty ships had emerged, each a twenty-million-ton-plus behemoth equipped with weapons *Bellerophon*'s computers couldn't identify from the Mesharom data. Six had survived.

"The post-battle data is less clear," Morgan observed. "Looks like it's just from the pod's sensors, through the stealth field. But...they didn't even try to check for survivors. They just closed in and blasted their wrecks into vapor. If any of their people survived the fight, they killed them themselves."

"There's nothing about these ships that matches any of our files." Her boss shook his head. "It's hard to judge a lot of their tech level, though, since it's not like we have solid files on the Mesharom's ships."

Morgan ran the post-battle data on her own screen while several of the analysts started running the battle again, at one-tenth speed this time. It still wasn't going to take very long to run.

"I don't know who they are," she said slowly as she looked over the data and ran another progression.

"But?" Masters encouraged.

"I think I know where they went." Morgan turned her screen, showing the projection to him. The vector the strangers had left on intersected with a major hyperspace current less than a day's travel away. It didn't lead anywhere the Imperium had noted as being of worth...but there were two stars and a black hole along its route.

"*Well* done," her boss said with a broad grin. "All right, Casimir. Package it up. You and I get to go talk to the Captain."

Morgan swallowed.

"Yes, sir."

CHAPTER ELEVEN

HAROLD COULDN'T QUITE HELP HIMSELF. WHEN HIS FLEET made the jump into the Lelldorin System, he closed his eyes and half-held his breath. He was hoping against hope he was wrong, but he suspected he knew what he was going to find.

"EM radiation is dark," Ling Yu stated flatly in the silence of the flag deck. "We have no radio signals. No energy signals."

He opened his eyes.

"What should we be seeing?" he asked.

"There was an Imperial destroyer echelon posted here," she replied. "Eight ships. We had a *Thunderstorm*-class cruiser, *Katrina*, positioned here as well. No cloudscoops, but there should be at least one major mining platform in the belt.

"Plus, well, an orbital refinery complex and several transshipment platforms and two major fusion power centers on the surface."

"All gone," Harold concluded. He was studying the screens now. Lelldorin had six planets and an asteroid belt, but his eyes were only for the inhabited second planet, Arend.

"We're launching probes to sweep Arend," Ling Yu told him.

"But all evidence suggests that Lelldorin suffered the same fate as Powell."

He nodded.

"Take the fleet in," he ordered. "We'll send down the shuttles and survey drones. If there are any survivors, we need to know."

He shook his head.

"How long until the ships we sent to grab old light at Powell catch up?"

"Twenty-four hours," Ling Yu confirmed.

"Then we have twenty-four hours to search for survivors," Harold told her. "Then I'll make contact with the Imperium and request orders." He checked a chart on his own seat's screens and shook his head.

"From here, we have a few options," he concluded. "We can check out Xīn Táiwān or..." He considered the map for a long moment.

"Or we can move to Alstroda and demand answers from the Kanzi."

"That would be war, sir," Ling Yu pointed out. She wasn't arguing, just stating the facts. Alstroda was the Kanzi equivalent to Asimov, the primary anchorage for their Rimward security forces.

"If the Kanzi are behind this, we're already at war," he told her. "And if they think they can kill a quarter million people and we'll let it slide, I have an epiphany waiting for them."

The guttural growl from his flag bridge crew told him everything he needed to know. His crews and his officers would back him if he went for Alstroda. He'd start a war...but for some reason, Harold Rolfson wasn't sure he cared.

AREND DIDN'T LOOK any better from orbit. Neither of the two main settlements had approached the size of Arbor City on Powell, but that didn't make the ugly bombardment scars that should have been the homes of eighty thousand people any less hideous.

"Same pattern," Harold concluded aloud. "They hit the population centers with heavy saturation bombardment, then orbited sweeping for power sources and hit anything they could detect with a small-scale kinetic."

"Shuttles, farms, hell, even road trains," Ling Yu confirmed. "Captain MacArthur is reporting no luck in the asteroid belt."

Harold's destroyer squadron commander was probably going to need a stint in counseling after this mission, the Vice Admiral reflected. They all would, but Captain Leah MacArthur was the one taking sixteen ships into an asteroid belt that *should* have had three or four thousand people and finding nothing but silent tombs.

"And no convenient TDC agents with sensor data, either," Harold said. "Not much point in scanning for old light."

"I doubt we'll find anything different than we did at Powell," Ling Yu confirmed. "*Lightning* and *Cyclone* should be arriving in the next few hours, we'll learn more about what happened at Powell then."

"Will we?" he asked. "We already know a lot from Camber's data. Captain Lowell took his ship right at the bastards when he realized he couldn't run. We owe that man a lot."

"We made at least a partial payment by getting Camber and the survivors to safety."

The two Ducal officers studied the data.

"What do we do, sir?" she finally asked.

"We wait for Captain Ryan and Captain Siobhan to return," he told her. "We go over every piece of data we have and send it all back home. After that..." Harold sighed. "After that, it's the Empress's call, I suppose. Much as I want to go knocking on some Kanzi doors with antimatter weapons, starting a war is above my pay grade."

THE ARRIVAL of the two cruisers and their data didn't give Harold much relief. After going over everything with his staff, he retreated to his office to consider what he knew and decide just what to do next.

The data from the old light aligned with what they had from Camber. They had a bit more time frame, since Camber's data had ended with the destruction of the local sensor platforms, but that was all.

The hostiles hadn't even left in a useful direction, though their vector had been close enough to a direct route to Lelldorin that Harold was grimly certain they'd gone straight there. They could sweep for old light and try to locate where the enemy had gone from there, but the timing made it useless.

It would take at least a day or more to identify the direction the attackers had gone, and he was already running four days, at least, behind them. He needed to know where they were going or where they were coming from, and he didn't know that.

He didn't even know *who* they were. The data suggested Kanzi, but that didn't add up either. The Imperium had a pretty good idea of what the Kanzi Theocracy was up to in terms of weapons research.

Right now, intelligence said the Theocracy was just rolling out a plasma lance and desperately trying to duplicate the Imperium's hyperfold communicators. They were behind the ball technologically and falling further behind by the year. They might have had a black project, much like DragonWorks, for secret development...but that wouldn't produce entire fleets clearly more advanced than the Theocracy was supposed to have.

And then there was the Mesharom distress signal that *Bellerophon* had received. His latest updates from Captain Vong warned of the annihilation of an entire Mesharom Frontier Fleet squadron, by ships entirely different from the ones that had shown up in Powell or Lelldorin.

It was possible that the two sets of incidents were unrelated, but that struck him as unlikely.

With a sigh, he brought up his console and settled in to face the camera as he recorded a message. Hyperfold coms were fast, but they weren't instantaneous. His transmissions would travel at about a light-year an hour to Sol.

They'd then be relayed to A!To instantaneously by the Sol starcom, and Annette Bond could have a live discussion with A!Shall. Harold could not.

"This message is transmitted priority alpha-one," he said calmly to the camera. "I see no choice but to declare Code Tsunami-Maximum. Two star systems have been devastated by an unknown attacker with casualties estimated at over two hundred and sixty thousand. Imperial ships assigned to defend those systems were destroyed to the last. A lack of Code Omega transmissions from the majority of those vessels suggest surprise attacks carried out with stealth fields and overwhelming firepower.

"I am attaching all sensor data we have from Powell and Lelldorin, but my own assessment is that we are faced with a hostile operation intended to draw our forces out of position in preparation for a large-scale invasion, most likely by the Kanzi Theocracy.

"I intend to proceed to the Xīn Táiwān System in the hopes of heading off an attack on the only remaining secondary colony in this area," he noted. "I request any and all available reinforcements be deployed to meet me there, and reiterate Code Tsunami-Maximum. All stations should go to maximum alert and the Imperium should prepare for war."

He paused thoughtfully.

"The only caution I can include is that we never did learn who the Kanzi at the Alpha Centauri Incident were," he reminded his listeners. "There is a possibility, however slight, that the Kanzi attacking our systems are from the same rogue group.

"The sheer scale of the attack, however, leads me to conclude that only the Theocracy could possibly be responsible for these attacks.

"If I do not locate a hostile force at Xīn Táiwān, then I intend to proceed to the Alstroda System and demand answers from the Fleet Master there."

He cut the recording and hit Transmit, swallowing hard as he did. Bond or the Empress could order him off, still, but his intention was in the message. Remembering the Alpha Centauri Incident meant he had to *consider* the chance it wasn't the Theocracy, but he wasn't sure he believed that himself.

Someone had killed a quarter-million innocents.

He was going to make them pay.

CHAPTER TWELVE

ANNETTE BOND STOOD SILENTLY AT THE FRONT OF THE conference room with her Council as Rolfson's message stopped playing, waiting to see if anyone said anything.

Only about half of her Council, the appointed officers of her government who helped her run Earth, were physically present in the luxurious space at the top of Wuxing Tower in Hong Kong. Hologram emitters in the chairs of the missing individuals showed their link-in, however, and she studied them each in turn.

Her two eldest biological children, the twins Leah and Carol, sat at the opposite end of the table. Despite their inherently chaotic natures, they were her Heirs and had been sitting in on Council meetings for over a year. They understood that they were there to listen and learn, not command.

They did not yet realize that their untainted perspective had a value all of its own.

Most of the other faces around the table hadn't changed since she'd assembled the group eighteen years before. Li Chin Zhao was still overweight, his health starting to deteriorate as the health issues that *kept* him overweight began to take a more obvious toll. The former ruler of China and current Councilor for the Treasury still had a mind as sharp as a whip and was her strong right hand.

Opposite him was her Councilor for the Militia. The gaunt and white-haired form of Jean Villeneuve belied the physical and emotional strength of the man who'd fought two desperate battles in Earth's defense. He'd lost the one against the A!Tol—but he'd carried the one against the Kanzi.

She'd finally convinced him to retire five years earlier. Sitting next to Villeneuve was Elon Casimir, her Ducal Consort and the man who'd made that convincing possible.

Between them, Zhao, Villeneuve and Elon were probably more responsible for the success of the Duchy of Terra than anyone else alive—and Annette didn't exempt herself from that assessment.

"Admiral Rolfson's Code Tsunami-Maximum has already been relayed to A!To," Annette told her allies, agents...and friends. "The final decision as to what we will do is up to Her Majesty and the Houses of the Imperium."

There were plenty of humans *in* said Houses at this point. One each in the Houses of Races and Duchies, and then twenty in the House of Worlds. Two of those last now represented dead worlds, and Annette had to admit she didn't know how that was treated under Imperial law.

"For us, however, we will likely be called upon to move ships to protect our colonies alongside whatever forces the Imperium sends."

It would probably be Tanaka, and Annette had every intention of sending *Herakles* and *Perseus* with her. *Bellerophon* was now tied up in her own mission, but her two sister ships would be a useful reinforcement to Tanaka's fleet.

"What do we have to spare?"

"We can free up a capital ship squadron relatively easily," Villeneuve said instantly. "With appropriate escorts, roughly comparable to what we had at Rimward Station. That would reduce Sol to a single squadron of capital ships, however, and we only have so many ships we could pull in from elsewhere."

The entire Duchy of Terra Militia had four squadrons of capital ships, thirty-two *Manticore*-class battleships, sixteen *Duchess of Terra*–class super-battleships and sixteen *Vindication*-class super-battleships. That made them one of the most powerful Ducal Militias in the Imperium but still left only so many resources they could send out to defend the TDC colonies.

"Set it in motion," Annette ordered. "Elon, make sure the *Bellerophon*s are ready to go as well. We'll send them out, too. I expect to be reinforcing Tanaka, but we also need to remember that we are the most industrialized system out here.

"If someone is trying to stab the Imperium in the back, we're the biggest target on the board. We'll need to coordinate with Tanaka and Fleet Lord !Olarski at the Kimar Fleet Base."

!Olarski had four capital ship squadrons under her command, plus escorts. If she could send even half of her force forward to Sol, Annette would feel a lot more comfortable. On the other hand, the A!Tol had a hundred-light-year chunk of the Kanzi border in her area of responsibility.

She might have other priorities, and Sol was well defended on her own.

"What about the Yards?" Elon asked.

"We keep our security perimeter outside them," Annette told him. The Raging Waters of Friendship Yards complex was the largest military shipyard and refit facility in the Rimward third of the Imperium. It was the beating heart of the Duchy of Terra's local economy and contribution to the Imperium, both in terms of money and military strength.

"But if it comes down to it, we defend people over hardware," she continued. "Hopefully, !Olarski can reinforce us if Sol comes under threat. Most likely, however, this is intended as a distraction while the Theocracy prepares a sucker punch closer to the Imperium's core systems. I don't expect to see us come under direct attack."

"And if we do?" Carol Bond asked from the far end of the table, the fifteen-year-old blonde looking surprisingly calm at the prospect.

"What happens if we strip our defenses to support the colonies—the ones the *Imperium* is supposed to protect—and then we are attacked?"

At least if her daughters were going to ask questions, they were good questions.

"The Imperium is *also* supposed to protect us," Annette reminded everyone. "And if anyone thinks this system is defenseless because three-quarters of the Militia's capital ships are elsewhere, well, we have some surprises for them!"

THERE WERE a dozen secured conference rooms in Wuxing Tower that had links to the starcom orbiting Earth, but Annette Bond was all too aware of how vulnerable even the Imperium's best cyber-security was to penetration by the Core Powers.

For ninety percent of her communications, it didn't matter. For the remainder, however, she had a space aboard the starcom station itself. Behind air gaps and vacuum gaps and dozens of power-armored Ducal Guards and Imperial Marines, she settled herself into a plain desk and made the call only she could.

Empress A!Shall had apparently been waiting. A hologram of the A!Tol ruler appeared across from Annette. Most A!Tol wore their emotions on their skin, unable to conceal their feelings from anyone.

A!Shall did not. Annette had seen her Empress lose emotional control twice in twenty years, but normally, the A!Tol female was a steady gray color.

Today it was clear she was close to the edge of that control, flickering patterns of green and black flashing through the gray as A!Shall faced the Terran Duchess.

The A!Tol was a rough bullet shape with four large locomotive tentacles and sixteen manipulator tentacles that allowed her to use technology. A!Shall was small for a female of her race, roughly one hundred and eighty centimeters tall at her full height.

She was also young for her rank. An A!Tol female could expect to live five or six hundred long-cycles—roughly two hundred and fifty to three hundred years—but A!Shall was only a hundred and twenty.

Roughly sixty years old. Younger than Annette herself, in fact.

"My dear Dan!Annette," A!Shall greeted her, using the prefix that designated Annette's rank. "It seems you are once again at the heart of our affairs."

"I liked the thirty long-cycles where everyone forgot we existed," Annette replied. "It was much quieter."

"For us all, Dan!Annette. Your assessment of this news?"

"War," Annette stated. "It has to be the Kanzi. There's no one else in play."

"I have spoken to the Priest Speaker," A!Shall told her. "Directly. He swears 'upon the Face of God' that they have not ordered such an attack."

"The High Priestess has lied to the Kanzi she sends to us before."

"She has," the Empress agreed. "I hesitate to believe him. I also hesitate to launch a war that will kill billions without certainty."

Annette winced.

"And those who have already died?" she asked.

"Will be avenged," A!Shall snapped, the harsh cracking of her beak cutting through her translated voice like a knife. "This will not stand, Dan!Annette. You have my word."

"So, what do we do?" Annette asked levelly.

"We prepare to defend our borders. Tan!Shallegh has taken command of a Grand Fleet and is moving to the Sontar System."

The Sontar System had been the scene of a dozen or more battles between the Kanzi and A!Tol—and Tan!Shallegh was the Empress's nephew as humans counted family, the original conqueror of Earth and one of the Imperium's premier fleet commanders.

If he was taking a Grand Fleet—more than ten squadrons of capital ships, at least three hundred and sixty battleships—to Sontar, then the Imperium was preparing an invasion of Kanzi space.

"I will not—I can not—commit the Imperium to an offensive war against the Kanzi," A!Shall told Annette. "But I will not allow *anyone* to bombard our worlds and slaughter our citizens. We have taught the Kanzi Clans that we will not tolerate slave raids across our borders. Now we must teach the galaxy that we will meet atrocity with flame and the sword."

Annette bowed her head in mute apology for misestimating A!Shall.

"Encrypted orders are being relayed to Fleet Lord Tanaka," the Empress continued. "She will deploy her entire fleet forward to rendezvous with Rolfson. Any reinforcements you can spare will be appreciated, and I will make certain that additional forces are moved forward to protect DragonWorks and Sol.

"I will not open a war without reason, Dan!Annette Bond. I also will not permit massacre to go unpunished. We will have justice for our dead and I will have my answers—even if I must send Fleets to Arjzi itself."

CHAPTER THIRTEEN

"WELCOME ABOARD *VINDICATION*, YOUR GRACE."

Annette Bond tolerated the formal ceremony from Admiral Pat Kurzman for all of fifteen seconds. Then she pulled the senior officer of the Duchy of Terra Militia's space forces into a tight embrace.

Pat Kurzman had been her executive officer when she'd taken the cruiser *Tornado* into exile as a privateer for Earth. He'd backed her then—and backed her again when she'd finally knelt to Earth's conquerors.

Vindication was named for how the various people who'd "collaborated" felt about the relationship with the Imperium now. The super-battleship was the largest warship the Imperium had ever built, an eighteen-million-ton behemoth almost three kilometers long and wide. Clad in Terran-built compressed-matter armor and shielded by Terran-designed antimissile systems, her class represented the current top of the line in the Imperial Navy.

And the first ship of that class was now the flagship of the Duchy of Terra Militia.

"You realize you don't get to command this deployment yourself, right?" she told Kurzman bluntly as she let him go. Before he could respond, she embraced Kurzman's husband, General Arthur Wellesley.

The men were a study in contrast. Wellesley was a product of both the British nobility and the Special Space Service, the elite troopers who had served the United Earth Space Force as boarding soldiers. He was tall and slim and, even with gray beginning to sneak into his hair and neatly trimmed beard, made for perfect recruiting-poster material.

Pat Kurzman was a product of Manchester's industrial districts, a broad-shouldered man gone gray far before his time. He remained well muscled and physically fit, but he'd gained extra pounds around the edges with age.

Not that his husband seemed to care. The two traded looks as Annette let Wellesley go and then met her gaze calmly.

"I know," Kurzman allowed. "But *Vindication* was my flagship, so I figured I'd come along and see Tidikat off."

Annette blinked.

"Tidikat?" she asked, making sure. Vice Admiral Tidikat was the senior officer of the Laian exiles, Orentel's mate. He was also the *only* nonhuman flag officer in her Militia, though there were other Laians working their way up the ranks.

"Rolfson is already out there, Amandine is holding down Alpha Centauri, and you'd have my husband chain me to a wall if I tried to command the deployment myself," Kurzman said with a chuckle as he listed off the other Vice Admirals. "I'm keeping Van der Merwe here in case I go senile and you need someone to back me up, so that leaves Tidikat."

Four capital ship squadrons called for four Vice Admirals, and that was all the Duchy had. Annette had assumed Kurzman would send Vice Admiral Patience Van der Merwe, but Tidikat also made sense.

"It's your call," she assured him. "What are we giving him?"

"He commands First Squadron," Kurzman reminded her. "Didn't see a reason to change that; just need to get my staff off before he leaves the system with *Vindication*. Conveniently, someone else brought *Tornado* along."

Annette chuckled.

"No one is letting *me* leave Sol anymore," she pointed out. "Certainly not to go to war, anyway!"

She didn't entirely approve of the ridiculous degree of overprotectiveness her entire Duchy seemed to take toward her, but she could understand it. And live with it. Leah Bond was fifteen. In a best-case scenario, she'd be into her second century before she took over from her mother.

In a worst-case scenario, Annette would still prefer that Leah was at least *twenty* before she had to run a planet.

"That's what you have us for," Wellesley confirmed, the General smiling calmly at her.

"*You* don't get to leave the system either, *General*," she told him. "I may not let you run my personal guard anymore, but I still feel more comfortable knowing you're watching my back."

Wellesley took a very obvious glance past her into the space shuttle behind her, currently occupied only by four of his power-armored Ducal Guards.

"Looks okay right now," he told her. "But we should get moving. It's not that long a flight to Jupiter these days."

COVERING for all of the traffic that needed to go to Jupiter had proven more of a concern than Annette had originally anticipated. The first shipments and the station itself had jumped into hyperspace near Earth and then emerged near the gas giant and disappeared.

As Sol had become more industrialized, however, there was enough civilian shipping of various sorts throughout the system to make ships emerging from hyperspace at Jupiter visible. A Militia observation post had covered things for a little while, but that hadn't been enough.

To help make the area closed to civilian traffic, the observation post had added a cloudscoop. Then a zero-gee training facility. Then a Guard training facility on the surface of Ganymede, which had rapidly transitioned into a joint Guard-Marine training facility.

The Jupiter planetary system was now a military reservation, the rings and moons forming the gravitational anchor for a dozen different facilities necessary to the functioning of a star system's armed forces. There was even a small secondary shipyard, which had officially built almost four times as many ships as its pair of capital ship slips could have produced—the yard making a good cover for ships built at DragonWorks itself.

The presence of the entire First Squadron of the Duchy of Terra Militia was unusual, but every one of the *Vindication*-class ships that made up Tidikat's command had been there before.

"We have confirmed the no-fly zone is clear," the human operations officer on *Vindication*'s flag bridge reported. "There are no prying eyes within the planetary system, and we have cleared the emergence zone."

"Understood," Tidikat replied, his translator running a smooth baritone over his own chittering voice. "Inform Jupiter Control we have confirmed clearance. Fleet Lord Tanaka should be able to move out."

Annette kept her hands calmly behind her back as she stood next to Admiral Kurzman and watched Tidikat work. She didn't need to be there. Neither did Kurzman or Wellesley, and yet...

They had yet to do anything that risked revealing the existence of DragonWorks quite this badly. With dead worlds and dead innocents, however, secrecy was a far lower priority.

"Tanaka confirms," a communications officer reported brightly. "Seventy-Seventh Fleet is commencing exit operations."

Even interface-drive ships couldn't move *through* a gas giant's atmosphere at any significant speed. The trip from DragonWorks' bubble, some two thousand kilometers below the Red Spot, to the surface took Tanaka's ships almost five minutes.

There was no warning from any of the sensor officers, though Annette suspected their scanners did show the ships coming. One moment, the Red Spot continued to roil along as the storm had done for a thousand years.

The next, the massive form of an A!Tol super-battleship emerged from it. And then another one. And another.

A stream of massive warships emerged slowly and carefully from Jupiter's atmosphere, *Vindication*-class ships leading the way. *Glorious*-class ships, the old top of the line, followed. Two full squadrons of Imperial super-battleships, thirty-two ships in all, emerged from the spot.

And then their escorts followed, smoothly moving up to quadruple the number of cruisers and destroyers attached to the joint fleet.

"Fleet Lord Tanaka, this is Vice Admiral Tidikat," Annette's Laian subordinate greeted the Imperial officer. "First Squadron has been seconded to your command. We await your orders."

A holographic image of the delicately featured Japanese woman appeared in the flag bridge's main holotank, a small smile playing around her face.

"It's good to be back in open space with a fleet again," Tanaka admitted. "I acknowledge command of the Duchy of Terra's First Squadron, Vice Admiral. My operations people will get you your slot in formation; we'll be moving out immediately."

The Fleet Lord turned her attention to Annette and her companions.

"Duchess, Admiral, General," she said with a nod. "You have my word. We will find the bastards responsible for these atrocities and we will bring them to justice with fire and sword. That is the Empress's order...and it is *my* word."

"I know," Annette told her. "I have faith in your sword arm, Fleet Lord Harriet Tanaka. We'll keep the lights burning while you're gone."

"You'd better," Tanaka replied firmly. "I saw *Tornado* hanging out with First Squadron; I'm guessing she's your ride home?"

"As always," the Duchess confirmed.

Tornado had been Earth's first hyperspace-capable warship; the starship Annette had taken into exile as a privateer and the key to how all of this had begun. Originally an experimental test-bed, her modular design had lent itself well to upgrades, so the cruiser remained Annette's personal transport even as a revolution in weapons systems quietly swept the Imperium.

"Then I suggest you transship, Your Grace. The sooner the Seventy-Seventh is on our way, the sooner we can end this nightmare."

CHAPTER FOURTEEN

Xīn Táiwān—New Taiwan in English—was the newest colony under the authority of the TDC. There was, Harold understood, one newer colony in the Imperium, a Frole world some sixty light-years spinward, but Xīn Táiwān was the newest human world.

Once Harold had the Governor on a holographic communication, the young-looking man looked absolutely terrified at the presence of a full task force in orbit.

"I am Governor Hymie MacChruim," the dark-skinned and red-haired official introduced himself. "I'm...not sure why your fleet is here, Vice Admiral. We don't generally see warships at all here in Xīn Táiwān."

"Aren't you supposed to have an Imperial picket?" Harold asked. "We've seen multiple colonies come under attack from an unknown force and are investigating."

"We're supposed to *receive* an Imperial picket, yes," MacChruim replied. "Eventually. Right now, though, we don't even have the infrastructure to keep a destroyer in orbit supplied, so we are left to ourselves."

The Militia Admiral sighed.

MacChruim wasn't paying attention, though.

"What do you mean, colonies have come under attack?" he demanded. "We don't have a reliable link into the hyperfold relay network or a starcom receiver. We're out of touch."

"Powell and Lelldorin have been destroyed," Harold told him flatly. "I'm waiting on Imperial reinforcements to rendezvous with me here. We don't need resupply, but if there's somewhere I can send crews for shore leave...say, well away from the settlements, it would be appreciated."

Harold *trusted* his people, but his fleet had almost fifty thousand people aboard. There were only about fifty thousand people on Xīn Táiwān. Shore leave was, by necessity, something to be done on nice beaches a long way away from the locals.

"We have very little in terms of amenities, but if you can bring them with you, I think my staff can recommend a beach or two," MacChruim said slowly. "Are we in danger, Admiral?"

"Frankly? I don't know," Harold admitted. "You and Asimov are the next-closest colonies, and Asimov is quite secure. I intend to remain here until Imperial forces arrive, which should take a week or so."

"Depending on the currents, *aber sicher*," the Governor agreed. He shook his head. "We will provide what assistance we can, Admiral, but...understand that we are a very young colony." He smiled. "Which means, for example, that I need to go shovel out my cattle barn this afternoon. Myself."

Harold laughed.

"I promise you, Governor MacChruim, we will keep you and your cattle safe!"

"SHORE LEAVE? With everything going on right now?" Xun Huang asked as Harold's staff gathered in the conference room. "That seems...a strange choice."

"That, Commander, is because I have ulterior motives," Harold told his communications officer. "Surgeon-Commander Tran, how many of our doctors are qualified to do psychiatric assessment and counselling?"

Dieu Tran was used to going almost unnoticed in staff meetings, and the Vietnamese woman started at being called upon, before narrowing her eyes thoughtfully as she pulled on a long black ponytail.

"Every one of our doctors is qualified to do assessment and at least basic counseling," she noted. "We only have about fifteen fully qualified psychiatrists, though. We've been keeping our medical staff busy in the aftermath of Powell and Lelldorin."

"You have," Harold agreed. "And we've assessed less than ten percent of our crews." He leveled his gaze on his people. "Our people have arrived too late to the massacre twice now. That...grinds on the soul.

"*We* know what's being done about it, what we're planning, how we're preparing to hammer those responsible. Only a tiny portion of our crews can say that.

"So, the first people we're dropping on that beach are going to be our doctors and they're going to get set up before anyone else arrives," he instructed. "We're going to cycle as many of our crew through at least a single day's shore leave as we can—and every person who goes down to the surface talks to a counselor."

Tran nodded thoughtfully.

"We need it," she said calmly. "It's hard on the doctors as well, but I'm guessing that they'll be on the surface the entire time?"

"They'll be spending their days treating everyone we can spare, but they'll get a few hours of beach relaxation in themselves, I hope," Harold confirmed. "I know what I'm asking of them, but I hope they'll understand."

"They will," his chief medical officer said flatly. "And if any of them don't get it, I will educate them. It's a good plan."

"We've got between six and ten days before Fleet Lord Tanaka arrives," Harold reminded his staff. "We need to make as much use of that time as we can. Starting a war is above my pay grade...but it most explicitly is *not* above Lord Tanaka's!

"We'll cycle ten percent of the crews down to the surface each day. They get one day and one night on a beach that is, apparently, free of bugs that like to eat humans. We'll use a random lottery system to select who goes, but make it clear to the Captains: mission-critical personnel *will* go down in the first five days."

"What about officers?" Ling Yu asked. Her question might have been interpreted as hopeful, but her tone was flat.

"Rank hath its privileges," Harold said sardonically. "Today, those privileges include missing shore leave because we need the fleet ready to go into action if our strangers show up."

SOMEHOW, Harold wasn't surprised when Tran showed up at his office several hours later. The fleet's chief medical officer didn't even bother with waiting after knocking; she just opened the door and set herself in a chair in front of his desk, eyeing him with level dark eyes.

"Doctor," he greeted her after a moment. "How can I help you?"

She snorted.

"You just ordered a setup that will bring every other officer and crew in this fleet in to see one of my doctors," she pointed out. "And when are you planning to see a counselor yourself?"

He sighed and slid his communicator across the desk.

"As soon as I'd received a message like this...or the alternative," he told her. The message on the communicator had just arrived through the hyperfold relay network—from Ramona, telling him that her expedition hadn't left for Lelldorin yet and she was safe.

"If I'd received a message telling me that my wife's expedition had been on Lelldorin, this conversation would involve me informing you that I was surrendering my command out of concern for my mental state," he admitted flatly. "One fiancée lost to war was enough for one lifetime, and at least she was a starship captain. We knew what we were getting into then."

"I'm glad she's okay," Tran agreed as she slid the communicator back across the desk. "I'll admit, I had forgot she was supposed to be on Lelldorin. I'm still concerned about your mental state, Vice Admiral."

He smiled thinly.

"Because everything I said about our crew applies to me?" he noted. "Because the man who made the decisions that delivered us to those systems too late was me?"

"What else could you have done?" she asked.

"Nothing. Believe me, Dr. Tran, I know that," Harold said. "I left Earth behind once. That was harder, in many ways. I don't think you'll find many veterans of the original *Tornado* mission who are particularly mentally fragile, Doctor."

"There aren't many veterans of that mission left, Vice Admiral," Tran pointed out gently. "A lot of them are dead. Most of the rest retired, and with good reason. So, just because you faced one horrific tragedy and survived, a new one shouldn't bother you?"

His laugh was short and bitter as he leaned back in his chair and studied her.

"I wouldn't go that far, Dr. Tran," he admitted. "I'm shaken, yes. A lot of people died and I'm damn angry about it. Nothing I could have done short of outright prescience could have saved those worlds or those innocents.

"But I will be *damned* if I will fail the next ones. If I have to start a war, if I have to shatter the Theocracy, to protect our remaining colonies...I will.

"I don't know what you want me to say, Dieu. I'm going to do my job and I think I'm capable of doing so. What more do you want from me?"

She chuckled.

"Not much," she agreed. "I just needed to get a feel for where you were at, Vice Admiral. I'll admit I was more concerned about you ordering retaliatory strikes than breaking."

"That would *be* breaking," Harold said, his voice quiet in shocked horror. "Worse than. No, Dr. Tran, I will not be launching my own atrocities against the Kanzi. Too many questions in play still.

"But I will get answers. One way or another."

CHAPTER FIFTEEN

"SET CONDITION ONE THROUGHOUT THE SHIP. REPEAT, SET Condition One throughout the ship. All hands to battle stations. This is not a drill. All hands to battle stations, set Condition One throughout the ship."

If there was anyone aboard *Bellerophon* who wasn't already at their battle station, Morgan would have been stunned. The estimated arrival at the black hole had been public knowledge for over a day. The entire bridge crew had drifted in over the last hour as the clock ticked down.

Technically, Morgan was the tactical officer on duty, but Masters had showed up about twenty minutes earlier. Instead of taking over the main console, however, he'd tucked himself into one of the petty officer stations and pulled out a book, very obviously *not* relieving her.

As Captain Vong walked onto the bridge, exactly five minutes before the scheduled emergence, and the battle stations announcement rang through the ship, Masters carefully put his bookmark in the book, closed it and walked over to the main station.

"Lieutenant Commander Casimir," he greeted her. "I relieve you. Report to your battle station."

"I stand relieved, sir," Morgan said brightly, rising and taking exactly six steps to the assistant tactical officer station. There was, as she understood it, a continuing discussion over whether or not the new warships should have a secondary bridge.

Human design philosophy called for redundancy—but A!Tol design philosophy was based around a combat environment where a ship was either fully functional or mission-killed. There wasn't much in between, even with compressed-matter armor. A!Tol designs buried the bridge at the absolute center of the ship, and modern designs had a second shell of compressed-matter armor around it.

But still no secondary bridge, which put the assistant tactical officer just to the tactical officer's right.

"Readiness report?" Masters asked her.

"All batteries live and green," she confirmed with a quick glance at her console. Enough of the crews had already been at their stations that the batteries had all checked in within thirty seconds.

Bellerophon was ready for war.

Her boss nodded to her, then turned to Captain Vong.

"Captain, all weapons systems and batteries are live and green," he reported. "We are ready for battle."

"Let's hope we won't be fighting one," Vong told the bridge. "Bring shields and sensors to maximum power. Time to emergence?"

"Seventy seconds and counting," navigation reported.

Morgan ran over the detailed assessments for the ship's guns. There were no warning signs hidden behind an overall green status indicator. The ship's missiles, hyperfold cannons, proton beams and plasma lance were all ready for battle.

A notification popped up on the corner of her console and she concealed a smile. Interpreter-Lieutenant Coraniss might be one of the few among their people who could talk to non-Mesharom, but the young alien still vastly preferred text communication to speaking in person.

Watch safety margins, the note told her. *Interface-drive interactions with gravity singularities are different than initial calculations suggest. Margin for ship of this mass potentially twice your expectation.*

Use this calculation set:

The email devolved into math. Morgan could follow it, and some of her smile slipped through as she did.

"Navigation, I'm forwarding you some information from our passenger," she announced. "New calculations for interface-drive interactions with singularities."

The bridge was quiet for a moment as the navigator processed the data.

"Damn, if these calcs are right, we could have accidentally trapped ourselves, easily."

"I'm not betting *against* Mesharom calculations," Morgan said.

"Lieutenant Commander, please forward those calculations to my station as well," Captain Vong said evenly. "And perhaps archive them for our R&D teams?"

"Forwarding now. Already archived, sir," Morgan replied, while sending a quick *thank you* back to Coraniss.

The Mesharom Interpreter wasn't a scientist or an engineer—Coraniss was a navigation officer, if Morgan had understood their conversations correctly—which meant they wouldn't necessarily realize they'd just handed over the key to one of the Imperium's recurring engineering problems.

The Imperium knew that the Mesharom, like the Precursors before them, used a gravitational singularity to power their ships, an even more efficient prospect than the matter-conversion plants concealed deep inside *Bellerophon*'s hull.

All of the Imperium's attempts to duplicate a singularity plant had, however, failed as soon as any kind of interface drive became involved. In the interests of keeping their ride safe, Coraniss had just handed Casimir a key calculation needed for the next generation of power plants.

"Emergence in five seconds," the navigator reported. "Opening portal...now."

THE PORTAL TOOK them into deep space for only the second time in Morgan's experience, and to a black hole for the first time in the experience of any officer aboard. The Duchy of Terra Militia had kept most of its operations close to home, and the A!Tol Imperial Navy gave black holes a massive safety margin.

Morgan's scanners had software written by the A!Tol, and they were *not* happy to be surveying a black hole from this close in. She had to mute four critical-danger alerts just to get a clean sweep of the accretion disk.

Once she'd done so, however, answers started to fall into place with surprising speed.

"I've got definite radiation trails from large-mass interface drives," she reported. "With the background rads from the black hole and the accretion disk itself, I can't give you definite numbers, but I'd say a group of at least six heavy warships came through here."

That would line up with the number of survivors from the clash with the Mesharom Frontier Fleet. Working out where their targets had gone from here, however, was going to be harder.

"They definitely dove into the accretion disk," Morgan concluded aloud as she continued to review the data. "They were hiding their trail."

Like diving through a river on a planet, the accretion disk would hide the signs she was using to track them. They could circle the disk, looking for the point where the alien fleet had left, but that could take days. Weeks.

Possibly months. The accretion disk was just over a light-day thick and two light-days across, a collection of debris being slowly consumed by the black hole at its center. That was a *lot* of volume to scan for an exit point.

"I hate clever enemies," Vong said aloud. "Anything you can find for me, Casimir?"

"Our drones might have more luck covering space than we will," she admitted. "I'm not sure what else to suggest." She glanced over at Masters. "Commander?"

"We'll deploy drones and sweep the exterior of the accretion disk," Masters confirmed. "The drones' scanners, however, don't have enough power to punch into the disk itself. Only *Bellerophon* can do that—and we may find some more clues in there if we look."

"Agreed," Vong said. "They didn't just stop here to hide their trail, people. I want to know what they came here for—every piece of data we learn about them gives us another piece of the puzzle."

He smiled thinly.

"And the sooner we solve *this* puzzle, the sooner we go back to dealing with the *people* who blew up two of our colony worlds."

They were close enough to the relay network to get updates whenever they came out of hyperspace, and Morgan agreed with the Captain. *Bellerophon* wasn't going to be missed in the search for Powell's murderers—but that didn't mean her crew didn't want to be there.

Politics and promises would keep them here for now, however. Humanity owed the Mesharom too much to leave the destruction of a Frontier Fleet squadron as an unanswered question—and they couldn't take the chance that the two attacks were unrelated, either.

MORGAN HAD SPENT a year of her life on DragonWorks, surrounded by scientists and engineers by the hundreds. During that year, she'd learned the oft-repeated phrase that no great discovery was ever announced by "Eureka." They were announced by studying the data and saying "huh, that looks funny."

That phrase was definitely on her mind as she studied the data from the sensors. The Imperium had enough scans of black holes that she knew roughly what she was looking at and how difficult it was going to be to identify the trail of an interface drive through the accretion disk.

The oddity she was looking at didn't belong. It wasn't an interface drive, but it was some kind of trail cut through the disk. It looked funny.

"PO Maki," she called one of her noncoms over. "Take a look at eight four point six by thirteen point three three, out just over a hundred million klicks. What do you see?"

The Japanese Petty Officer fed her coordinates into his console and looked over the area.

"Huh. That looks funny."

Morgan chuckled.

"I know," she allowed. "It's not an interface-drive trail, but *something* is cutting a hole through the accretion disk. Guesses?"

Keane Maki swallowed and glanced over at Commander Masters, who was paying attention to the drone sweeps. Morgan wasn't putting him on the spot, but she was curious what the NCO thought.

"It *could* be a ship," he suggested hesitantly, then shook his head. "No, sir. It's not a ship. Too big. That's... I think that might be a planet."

"That far out in the middle of nowhere?" Morgan asked, but she was already feeding that assumption into the scanners and adjusting her sweep toward the end point of the trail.

"Yep," she answered her own question a moment later as they localized the ship. "Well, calling it a *planet* is being extraordinarily gracious, PO Maki, but it's definitely a big honking rock of some kind. I make it twenty-five hundred kilometers across and clearing itself a path through the dust and debris. Can you confirm?"

"I get the same," Maki replied a moment later. "Small planet, big asteroid, either way it's probably the single biggest piece of real estate in the accretion disk."

"Which makes it the most likely landmark for if you had a rendezvous point, doesn't it?"

Morgan didn't wait for Maki to reply before pinging Masters.

"Sir, PO Maki found something," she told her boss. "We think it's a planetoid...which makes it the most likely place for our friends to have rendezvoused with somebody else."

"Nice catch, both of you," Masters said as he began to go over their data. "Let's get one of the probes lined up for a dive into the disk and then I'll get the Captain involved. This might be the breadcrumb we're looking for."

THE CURRENT GENERATION of sensor drones carried by the Duchy of Terra Militia were equipped with a widely varied suite of systems, including light shields and a hyperfold communicator.

The combination was enough to allow Morgan to watch her probe take a hit from a piece of debris that overwhelmed both the shields and the inherent anti-debris properties of an interface drive in real-time. She had enough warning to see the rock coming and not enough warning to save the ten-million-mark probe.

"I don't think probes are going to cut it in the accretion disk," Captain Vong noted drily as he saw the results. "Commander Masters, will *we* have any problems if we head in?"

"No," Morgan's boss said instantly. "Our shields are more than powerful enough to withstand random debris. The probes are really only shielded against normal space debris, not an accretion disk."

"Commander Hume," the Captain continued. "Do you have Commander Casimir's planet in your charts yet?"

"We do," Kumari Hume, the Indian-born navigator, told them. "ETA is just over eleven minutes at full speed, but..."

"Let's take it a bit slower than that, Hume," Vong agreed. "Twenty-five percent of lightspeed, if you please. Commander Masters, Lieutenant Commander Casimir—keep your eyes peeled.

Feel free to use the proton beams or the Sword suite to keep our space clear."

Morgan began running a basic defensive program into the computers as the battleship dove toward the accretion disk. The Sword antimissile suite should suffice to protect the ship from most debris, and she brought that online in automatic tracking mode.

The proton beams were a secondary weapon, but they'd still suffice to take out any natural debris heading their way. The Swords' drone sisters, the Bucklers...weren't going to be safe to deploy.

"I recommend against deploying the Buckler drones," Masters told Vong, echoing Morgan's thoughts. "We'd lose them far too quickly even if we aren't engaged. That leaves us vulnerable if we do find an enemy in here, Captain."

"I ran the same numbers, Commander," the Captain replied. "Interface missiles are going to have a hell of a time in this mess. If we are attacked, you are cleared for Green Dragon engagement protocols."

That meant everything the Imperium officially admitted to having—the newest generation of Sword and Buckler, the heavy plasma lance, and the point eight cee interface-drive missiles—was clear for use, as well as the new-generation shields and the hyperfold cannons.

"And if those aren't enough?" Masters asked quietly.

"We have a Mesharom aboard, Commander," Vong replied. "I'd rather not flaunt this vessel's true power in front of the people we stole pieces of it from." Morgan spotted his familiar thin smile reflected in her console as he spoke.

"That said, I will authorize escalation to Black and even Gold Dragon protocols if needed to defend this ship. Is that sufficient for you, Commander Masters?"

"Yes, sir."

"Good. Commander Hume? ETA to the disk?"

"Twenty seconds to entry," the navigator confirmed. "This is going to be a bumpy ride."

BUMPY WAS OVERSTATING THINGS A BIT, but *terrifying* was bang on.

From the moment *Bellerophon* entered the debris field, Sword was alive. Lasers flickered out at larger chunks of rock and ice as they approached, reducing them to vapor and gravel that pelted the battleship's shields.

Then there was the vapor and gravel that had already been present. Here, in the accretion disk of a significant black hole, Morgan finally saw conditions that rivaled what entertainment liked to present asteroid belts as.

Their speed was the main issue. Point two five cee was slow for an interface-drive ship...but that was the only standard you could say that in.

At a quarter of the speed of light, *Bellerophon* smashed through the accretion disk like a belly-flopping swimmer. There was no subtlety or stealth to their approach. Even a stealth field couldn't have hidden someone moving through the debris field, let alone someone moving at their speed.

Morgan watched the patterns around them like a hawk. Half of her attention was looking for larger debris, chunks of rock too large for the Sword turrets' lasers. Those she tagged for the proton beams.

The rest was watching for a trail like theirs. The most likely situation was that their prey had moved on, and their best-case scenario was finding an abandoned fueling station or some such.

If the warships that had attacked the Mesharom were still there, however, then *Bellerophon* was screaming her presence for all to see. They weren't going to turn that down.

She checked the status signals on her standard missile launchers —her Alpha and Bravo series batteries—and her hyperfold cannons— her Charlie and Delta series batteries. The proton beams—the Epsilon batteries—were live, firing at her targets as she flagged the debris.

Currently, those were the only batteries her console was showing. Her Foxtrot, Golf and Hotel batteries wouldn't even show up on her systems unless the Captain authorized higher-tier engagement protocols.

All of the weapons systems Green Dragon protocols gave her were green and live, and she returned her attention to the space around her ship.

"Any sign of company, Commander Masters?" Vong asked.

"Nothing so far," the tactical officer replied. "Should we bring up a marching band as well?"

"We're all on the same page, I see," the Captain noted with a chuckle. "I don't think the band would make much difference, but give me a maximum-power radar pulse at that planetoid, please."

Morgan was already on it. Emitters across the battleship's hull adjusted and then pulsed.

They were getting a lot of garbage returns. There was a *lot* of debris out there, but...

"I have movement!" she barked. "Unknown contacts, in the lee of the planetoid. Interface drives coming online and heading in our direction."

"I see we have their attention," Vong said calmly. "Commander Antonova, send the standard challenge, if you please. This is Imperial space.

"Commander Masters, Lieutenant Commander Casimir...stand by to engage the enemy."

CHAPTER SIXTEEN

ONE MOMENT, MORGAN'S CONSOLE HAD AT LEAST BASIC ACCESS to all of *Bellerophon*'s weaponry. The next, that entire screen shut down, and she barely stopped herself from whipping around to glare at Masters as he yanked offensive control from her station without a word.

"You're on scanners," he ordered dismissively. The tone was very different from all of their interactions since the very first few. "Find me targets."

Swallowing her personal reactions, she realized that the split made some sense. It was just a surprising shift from how things had been operating even a few moments before. She pulled in the sensor feeds, cross-referencing to make sure she had the unknown ships locked in.

"I have one super-battleship that matches the Mesharom sensor data, three ships in the battleship-mass range that energy signatures suggest are logistics ships, and four destroyers," Morgan reeled off as her team crunched through the analysis.

Then something flashed on her screen, a small note as a program she'd forgot to turn off came back with a result, and she stared at the icon for a long moment.

"Commander Masters, Captain—we have a warbook entry for those destroyers," she reported. She was distracted as she dove into the data and found its source: a series of scans from the *Thunderstorm*-class cruiser *Liberty*.

"What do you mean?" Masters demanded. "They don't match anything I've ever seen."

The difference in tone between the cooperative relationship they'd been building and his suddenly harsh attitude as they neared combat grated on her nerves, but it could easily *just* be combat... combat and the nerves of a twenty-four-year-old.

She swallowed and transferred the data on her screen to her boss.

"The Alpha Centauri Incident began with a four-ship formation of strange destroyers with unknown, Core Power–level technology and a fundamentally Kanzi design," she explained aloud. "They were trying to steal the Precursor ship and landed Kanzi troops.

"Those destroyers are over a ninety percent match to the ships over there. If they're not the same class, they're from the same designers with the same tech base."

"Kanzi," Captain Vong said slowly, clearly listening in. "Like the battleships at Powell."

Morgan nodded.

"Similar, sir. Kanzi-style designs but built around tech the Kanzi don't have." She was pulling more data as she spoke. "The troops they landed were definitely Kanzi but had a degree of ritual scarification and other body mods the Kanzi Theocracy would not tolerate."

"Fifteen years and we don't hear a peep from these strangers, and now they're blowing up worlds and Frontier Fleet battlecruisers," Masters said thoughtfully. His harsh tone toward Morgan had faded again, back to something closer to the professional evenness she'd grown used to.

"Indeed." Vong leveled his gaze on the hologram tank. "Lieutenant Commander Antonova?"

"Sir?"

"Any response?"

"Nothing," the blonde Russian officer confirmed.

"The super-battleship is a definite match for the Mesharom data —and she and the destroyers are maneuvering in our direction," Morgan reported. "That's a response of one kind, I suppose."

"Yes."

The bridge was silent for several seconds and Morgan studied the incoming ships. They'd brought their own drives up to point two five cee, clearly agreeing with *Bellerophon*'s crew on the safety of the debris field.

The three logistics ships were going in the other direction, but five warships were heading their way.

"Let's not play games with these people," Vong finally concluded. "Commander Masters, Black Dragon Protocols, if you please. Confirm our hyper missile status."

Morgan swallowed as a new set of batteries appeared on her screens. "Batteries" was a misnomer for the Golf series, though. There was only a single weapon in each of the twelve Golf batteries, a vertical cell-launched missile twice the size of *Bellerophon*'s assault shuttles.

"We have twelve Black Dragon III dual-portal hyperspace missiles," Masters said levelly. "All are reporting green and ready to deploy."

"Target the destroyers with two apiece, plus one each on the logistics ships and the lead unit," Vong ordered. "Let's clear the pawns off the board, people."

THE SAME ALPHA Centauri Incident where humanity had seen these alien destroyers before, three of the Core Powers had also ended up engaging each other. The Mesharom were long-standing informal allies, but they had hard rules on tech transfer.

The Laians were now formal neutrals, using that nonaggression pact to enable their war against the Wendira, who were arguably informal enemies of the Imperium. Their presence at Alpha Centauri, however, had been because of old Laian technology that had ended up in human hands.

Alpha Centauri had been humanity's first colony and, even before that, had been a logistics depot for their privateering campaign against the A!Tol. By the time everyone had decided to fight over the Precursor ship there, the Duchy and the Imperium had had the system completely wired up with scanners of every type.

The Mesharom had intentionally sold the Imperium hyperfold communications technology in exchange for the Precursor ship on Hope, the colony in Centauri. They'd hinted at how to build the hyperfold cannons that formed the backbone of *Bellerophon*'s armament.

Morgan was relatively sure they hadn't expected humanity to manage to reverse-engineer their hyperspace missiles from the scan data, and to be fair, humanity hadn't. DragonWorks was an Imperial project, with scientists and engineers from all twenty-eight species of the Imperium and access to every scrap of data and technology the Imperium had ever acquired from the Core Powers.

The Black Dragon III was an exact duplicate of the Mesharom weapons deployed at Alpha Centauri in *capability*. In order to cram in the ability to generate an entry and exit portal from hyperspace, a twenty-gigaton antimatter warhead, and even the relatively weak and short-lived interface drive they had, however, the Imperium's weapon was over *twenty times* the size of the Mesharom version.

Bellerophon massed over ten million tons. She carried exactly twelve of the weapons, and Captain Vong's orders sent every one of them into space.

They appeared on the battleship's scanners for several seconds as their launchers blasted them into space and they cleared the shields. Then twelve relatively tiny hyperspace portals tore through the accretion disk and the missiles vanished.

They were still over two light-minutes from their targets. The sensor solutions Morgan was providing for the targeting data were that far out of date...but the weapons themselves would arrive almost instantly.

It took almost two minutes, even with the closing velocity involved, before *Bellerophon*'s crew saw the results of her missiles, and Morgan barely suppressed a victorious whoop at the sight.

"Destroyers one, two and four are down," she reported. "Two of the logistics ships are gone; the third is crippled." Her elation faded as she studied the data. "It doesn't look like we even penetrated the super-battleship's shields."

"I didn't expect to," Vong admitted. "Commander Hume? Bring us to combat speed, if you please. Commander Masters...deploy the Bucklers."

"We're going to lose them fast," the tactical officer warned.

"That is what they exist for, Commander," the Captain reminded him. "ETA to interface missile range?"

"At full speed, assuming they don't adjust to match, one hundred thirty seconds," Masters said. "Cut thirty seconds off of that if they accelerate to point five as well. Assuming they have the same missiles as at Centauri, they outrange us."

"Understood. Hyperfold cannon range?" Vong asked.

"Forty seconds after missile range. Lance range ten seconds after that, proton beam range ten seconds after that." Masters shook his head. "At some point in there, they're going to try and break off."

"Perhaps not," Vong murmured. "Lieutenant Commander Casimir, what was the effective range of the weapon the aliens used against the Centauri picket?"

Morgan checked the neatly summarized data in the warbook.

"One light-second, sir."

"Commander Hume, we don't know how fast our friend actually is," the Captain said conversationally, "but consider yourself authorized to use every scrap of sprint speed and maneuverability we have to keep us at least one million kilometers from the enemy.

"There's going to be more surprises today. Let's make sure the ones they give us aren't fatal."

THE ENEMY CAPITAL ship increased her speed as *Bellerophon* charged toward her, stabilizing at point six cee. The Terran battleship could match that, but not for extended periods. The increasing velocities meant that the distance between the two ships was evaporating like snow in a desert.

"Drive metrics and hull design match Kanzi standards, like the destroyers," Morgan reported. "She's three million tons bigger than even their *Grand Protector*–class ships, though, and the *Protector* can only make point four eight cee."

"Keep that surviving logistics ship and the damaged destroyer dialed in," Vong ordered. "We're going to want to board them when this is over."

Assuming they survived. Morgan wasn't sure that was a reasonable assumption. *Bellerophon* was the most powerful battleship the A!Tol Imperium and its Duchies possessed, but the strange Kanzi ship outmassed her two to one and had a clear speed advantage.

Then her musings were interrupted and training took over.

"Vampire!" she snapped. "Target has opened fire at one point two light-minutes. Missiles incoming at point eight five cee. Defenses engaging!"

At eighty-five percent of lightspeed, the gap between the light of the missile launch reaching *Bellerophon* and the missiles themselves arriving was measured in seconds. Their active missile defenses were designed for this environment, though, and the Buckler platforms were already out.

Lasers lit up the darkness as Morgan's computers struggled to resolve individual missiles and parcel them out to her defensive systems. She'd loaded in the parameters and would adjust as they got more data, but there was only so much human intervention possible in ten seconds.

The numbers were terrifying. The hostile ship had launched over a hundred and fifty missiles at *Bellerophon*. A dozen Buckler platforms swung into the path of the weapons, lasers firing in rapid sequence to reduce their numbers.

Sword turrets mounted on the battleship's hull followed suit, but shields still glittered under the impact as the tsunami of fire smashed through the debris field.

"Return fire as soon as you have the range," Vong said calmly as a second salvo came crashing toward them.

There was no noticeable sensation when *Bellerophon* fired. Morgan didn't feel anything, but one moment, the screen only showed Bucklers and incoming missiles. Then next, ninety-six green icons lit up on the screen as their own interface-drive missiles launched into space.

At point eight cee, the new missiles were significantly deadlier than the ones the Imperium had brought to the Alpha Centauri Incident. The enemy missiles were still more powerful.

"Commander Hume, get us to hyperfold cannon range as soon as you can," Captain Vong asked calmly.

Morgan wondered just how he could sound so calm, so level, as dozens of missiles slipped past their active defense screen to hammer into the shields. *Bellerophon*'s shields could take dozens of these missiles, but she could see weak points starting to appear.

She moved Bucklers and reprioritized Sword targeting to keep those weak spots covered. Engineering officers moved power around as well, and the weak spots began to recover as she made sure missiles hit elsewhere.

The missiles were *damn* fast and damn smart. Her ECM didn't seem to be doing much of anything, though her Bucklers and Sword turrets were massacring the incoming fire. There were still too many making it through for her peace of mind.

"Enemy performance aligns with the strangers at the Centauri

Incident," Masters observed as the results of their first salvo came back in. "No active defenses, but powerful shields." He paused. "Our new shields are comparable."

"Bogey is continuing on a direct course for us," Morgan said. She winced as debris took out one of her Bucklers, tapping commands to deploy a new unit—and then two more as stray missiles hammered into her defense platforms. "Thirty seconds to one light-second."

"We'll end this first," her boss promised. "Hyperfold cannon range!"

A hyperfold transmitter was almost instantaneous inside a star system, but the amount of power that could be transmitted fell off rapidly. In communications, this translated to bandwidth. A hyperfold com would allow a real-time video transmission inside a star system, but at the ten-light-year range used to build the relay network, it was far more restricted.

If you built a powerful-enough transmitter, however, and ran enough energy through it, you ended up with an overpowered maser that reached its target instantly at about ten light-seconds.

Each of *Bellerophon*'s six Charlie and six Delta batteries held four hyperfold cannons. The big ship passed that line in space and all forty-eight of the energy weapons spoke in anger for the first time.

Their targeting data was out of date, but it was accurate *enough*. Morgan couldn't tell how many of the maser strikes hit, but the battleship's shields clearly fluctuated. She wasn't sure if they'd punched through the shields, but if they did, they didn't pierce the armor underneath.

The range was dropping fast now, and all of *Bellerophon*'s different weapons systems were in play. Masters was continuing to run them all himself and Morgan could *see* the reduced efficiency from that. She wasn't sure why he wasn't trusting her, but he also wasn't trusting the Chiefs whose job it was to take that load off his console.

More missiles and hyperfold cannon shots blasted across space, and Morgan found herself deploying a second wave of Buckler drones to try and buy the battleship time. So far, the only weapons the enemy had deployed were regular missiles—but at a range rapidly dropping toward two million kilometers, point eight five missiles were bad enough.

"Does this asshole have anything other than missiles?" Masters asked.

"I'm guessing he has whatever hell weapon the strangers had at Centauri," Vong pointed out. "Where's my plasma lance, Commander?"

Morgan blinked. They'd crossed the range line for the massive weapon that ran the length of the battleship's hull and Masters hadn't fired it. He'd been distracted managing the hyperfold guns and the missiles.

"Commander?" Vong repeated a second later—and then Morgan's screen lit up with the controls for the big gun.

"Take it over, Casimir," Masters snapped. "Don't fuck it up."

The enemy was evading more now, trying to dodge the hyperfold cannon blasts that were materializing around her. Between missiles and maser bursts, she was in serious trouble—but she was continuing to blast a hundred and fifty-six missiles at *Bellerophon*.

Both ships still had their shields. Whatever fire had made it through on either side had failed to penetrate the heavy compressed-matter armor. The bogey's additional mass and firepower wasn't making up for *Bellerophon*'s active defenses...yet.

Setting up the lance took her less than a second. Morgan had already been feeding Masters the targeting solution; he just hadn't used it.

This time, the entire ship *did* vibrate. Powerful electromagnets ran the length of the battleship, gathering superheated, still-fusing plasma from the fusion cores and pulsing it toward the enemy at near-lightspeed. The pulse followed a magnetic channel that latched on to the enemy and held on through their maneuvers until the round impacted.

The lance shattered the enemy's shields. Hyperfold cannons and missiles hammered home, sending energy and explosions glittering across the enemy hull. For a moment, Morgan thought they'd got her.

But the enemy ship was *huge*. She took the pounding for ten seconds. Fifteen. Twenty—and then her shields flashed back up and she was blasting away from *Bellerophon* at sixty-five percent of the speed of light.

"Break off, Hume," Vong ordered.

Morgan swallowed an objection, looking at the screens to see what the Captain saw. *Bellerophon*'s shields were still up...barely. If they pressed the encounter at this range, it wouldn't take "hell weapons" for the strange Kanzi ship to take them down.

Interface-drive missiles could more than handle *Bellerophon*.

With the black hole and its accretion disk in the background, the two massive ships broke away from each other at nearly the speed of light.

Even Morgan, though, was grimly certain this fight wasn't over.

That had just been round one.

CHAPTER SEVENTEEN

"Status report," Vong ordered as the ships finally drew out of missile range of each other.

"Shields are intact," Morgan reported immediately, having spent the withdrawal consulting with the engineers. "We'll be back to full power within two minutes. No critical hull damage; the new armor-support matrix seems to have helped absorb the impacts."

The support matrix was a Gold Dragon tech, subtle enough to go unnoticed even as a layer of active microbots—based on the Mesharom technology—absorbed impact and moved support as necessary.

Point eight five cee missiles could dent compressed-matter armor, but the support matrix had prevented that. It also helped avoid the usual problem of CM armor, which was plates detaching from each other under impacts.

"We've fired off our entire stock of dual-portal hyper missiles and roughly ten percent of our interface-drive missiles," Masters reported. "Plasma lance is fully recharged and the hyperfold cannons performed roughly as expected."

"We will have a conversation about that later," Captain Vong said calmly, and even Morgan winced. The Duchy of Terra Militia had learned many of its traditions from the particular habits of Admiral Jean Villeneuve—among them the simple dictum of "praise in public, criticize in private."

Vong's statement was as close as any Militia officer would come to criticizing a subordinate in public.

"Hume?"

"Engines are running without issue; we didn't use our sprint capacity, so Engineering tells me the capacitors are still at full strength," Hume reported.

"And what about them?" the Captain asked.

Morgan looked at Masters, who gave her a go-ahead gesture. His expression was odd...was he actually looking *guilty*? Just what had been going through the tactical officer's head when he tried to run the ship's entire armament himself?

"We hit her pretty hard," Morgan said slowly. "Her shields were down for almost thirty seconds, during which we hit her with roughly a hundred and eighty missiles and a similar number of hyperfold cannon blasts.

"She's *huge* and her armor took most of that," she warned. "There was some outgassing and vapor trails before the shields went back up. I'd guess we separated at least a few CM plates, but she didn't fire while she retreated. We can't judge the damage to her armament, though I would think we'd done some."

The strange Kanzi ship outmassed them two to one, but it was *Bellerophon* that had landed the hardest hits. The enemy's missiles were better, but *Bellerophon* had entire weapons systems they didn't appear to.

"What about our friend's logistics ship and destroyer?" Vong asked.

"The logistics ship is headed toward the black hole," Masters reported. "I'd say she's trying for a slingshot to make up for her lower interface-drive velocity."

"At a third of the speed of light, that requires going *damn* close,"

Hume noted. "It's almost suicide at that speed. Any faster...it *would* be suicide for us."

"But we can still get closer to the singularity than she can," Morgan's boss replied. "We can still catch her. The super-battleship is moving to cover her."

"I'm seeing the destroyer falling behind," the Captain noted. "Let's vector in on her, see if we can catch up and board her befo—"

The holographic plot flashed white and Morgan swallowed as she focused her screen on where the destroyer had been.

"Self-destruct," she concluded, somewhat uselessly. "Implosion-explosion sequence." She ran the sensor data backward and shook her head. "It's like they compressed the entire ship into a cube about a meter across and then the antimatter reacted to the rest of the ship."

Masters shook his head. "I don't suppose our Mesharom passenger would know what is going on there?"

"I can ask," Morgan offered. "I suspect they're going to have some pointed questions about the hypermissiles."

"That was inevitable with Black Dragon," Vong told her. "Touch base with our guest via email; we're going to go after that capital ship again.

"We needed the breather as much as they did, but now I think we want to pin her against the black hole and pound her into pieces. I want that ship intact enough for us to board the wreckage, people. If they're going to blow themselves up, I don't expect prisoners...but at this point, I'd settle for *autopsies*."

Morgan couldn't help but nod in agreement. There were too many questions still unanswered here.

YOUR POD HAS SENSORS, I know. Are you watching? Morgan asked. The bustle of the bridge was continuing around her, and it seemed she'd been left with control of the Charlie through Foxtrot batteries this time. That gave her the hyperfold cannons, the proton beams and the plasma lance.

Whatever bug had crawled up Commander Masters's rear seemed to have been kicked out by the Captain.

Given that the weapons she was in charge of were the shorter-range systems, however, she had time to communicate with Coraniss.

Yes. Fascinating. My briefing was incomplete; I was not informed of hyperspace weapons in your arsenal.

Morgan concealed a chuckle, glad the Mesharom couldn't see her. That was the advantage, she supposed, of dealing with a very junior officer. Coraniss didn't know that the Imperium wasn't supposed to have hyperspace missiles at all.

Of course, they'd hand their data over to their superiors once *Bellerophon* got them to safety. No one expected differently. Some of the Imperium's secrets had been given away today.

They are crude things, but they work. Did you see the destroyer self-destruct? The effect was outside our experience. Do you know what happened?

Morgan would have hesitated to be so frank with a more senior Mesharom, but Coraniss, by their own admission, didn't know what the Imperium was supposed to not know. They might well answer questions they shouldn't.

Implosion of a singularity power core. Ugly way to die.

"*Fuck* me," Morgan snapped aloud, then swallowed and looked over at her boss apologetically.

"I'll forget I heard that if you tell me what caused it," Masters told her.

"Coraniss says the destroyer had a singularity power core," she replied. "Presumably backed by antimatter secondaries, given the explosion, but..."

"Well, that explains the shields," her boss said thoughtfully. "They don't necessarily have more advanced shield *technology*; they're just pushing a *lot* more power through it."

One of the reasons that *Bellerophon* could carry more weapons than her older *Manticore*-class sisters was her power supply. The *Manticore* class used antimatter and fusion power cores to meet their energy needs.

Bellerophon used a pair of reverse-engineered Reshmiri matter-conversion power plants, doubling the power output of the older battleship in less than a fifth of the space.

Of course, if the Rashmiri ever realized the Imperium had outright stolen one of their matter-conversion plants to dismantle and duplicate, there would be hell to pay. That particular Core Power, however, was a long way from A!Tol territory.

DragonWorks's current holy grail was a singularity power core. These strange Kanzi apparently had them.

"It also explains why they managed to get their shields back up so quickly," Morgan agreed. "That super-battleship has a *lot* more power to play with than we do."

"I'll brief the Captain," Masters promised. "You see if Coraniss knows anything else." He paused. "Once you're done with them, check on the Hotel batteries. *Quietly*."

She swallowed and nodded.

The Hotel batteries were the last offensive secret they had left, the key weapons system concealed behind the Gold Dragon clearances. If Masters thought they might end up deploying them...he was nervous.

Which was fair. Morgan herself was *terrified*.

"HE'S TRYING TO EVADE," Hume noted aloud. "Pushing point six cee while he covers the logistics ship."

Apparently, their enemy wasn't *completely* cavalier about the lives of their fellows. They might have blown up the surviving destroyer, but they were trying to protect the remaining supply ship.

Though that, Morgan reflected, might be more of a reflection of a need for those supplies versus any concern for the lives of the ship's crew. Certainly, if these were the Kanzi from the Centauri Incident, they had never shown concern for their people's lives before.

"Well, let's give our new friend a choice," Captain Vong ordered. "Commander Hume, direct course for the logistics ship, if you please. Commander Masters—I want her intact. Casimir—can you tell if the logistics ship has a singularity power core?"

Morgan studied the screens. *Bellerophon* had a massive suite of sensors, but they'd never scanned a ship they *knew* had a singularity core before. She had the data on the destroyers and the super-battle-ship. How close were those to the logistics ship?

She ran the comparison and then gestured one of the NCOs over.

"Maki, do you see what I see?" she asked quietly. The noncom leaned over her shoulder and looked where she was pointing.

"Looks like it, sir," Maki replied. "It might be something else, but it's in the right place."

"Lieutenant Commander?" Masters asked. "Would you and the PO care to share?"

"There's a trio of unusual gravity signatures on the super-battle-ship, similar to a strange signature on the destroyers," Morgan reported. "They're muffled and shielded, so they didn't trigger as significant on our initial scans, but I'd guess they're the singularity cores.

"The freighter doesn't have one. I'm reading radiation signatures to suggest antimatter and fusion cores, but no singularity."

"Well done," Masters allowed.

"Can we target the antimatter plants?" Vong asked. "To take that ship intact?"

"Not from any significant range," Morgan told him. "We could program the targeting data into the missiles, but that's a fifty-fifty chance at best. If we got within hyperfold range and...had live targeting data, we might be able to do it."

Their sensor probes couldn't get close enough to provide that data, though she could use them to cut the communication loop. There *was* an option, but it was Gold Dragon tech.

The Captain knew what she meant but shook his head.

"We'll try for a conventional disabling pass, then," he ordered. "What are our friends doing?"

"Logistics ship is pushing closer to the black hole," Masters reporting. "Trying to force a tighter slingshot...I don't know if she'll make it. The battleship is turning back towards us."

"I want a salvo with disabling programs loaded fired at the freighter the moment we have range," Vong ordered. "Otherwise, we'll fight that battleship. There's no retreating this time, people. When this is over, we're going to leave her falling into that black hole.

"Am I clear?"

The bridge crew's response, including Morgan's, was unquestionably a growl.

CHAPTER EIGHTEEN

THE KANZI SUPER-BATTLESHIP RECOGNIZED THE CHALLENGE implicit in their charge and came to meet them. Their course, however, showed their conflicting priorities. The battleship commander was clearly hoping to use their superior speed to keep in their missile range and outside of *Bellerophon*'s range.

The logistics ship, however, wasn't fast enough to evade the Terran ship. She was diving deeper and deeper toward the black hole, and Morgan was starting to wonder if the Kanzi ship would make it under any circumstances.

"I'm not sure we're going to be able to catch that freighter, even if we disable her," she said aloud. "She's cutting the line damn close as it is."

"And the battleship is being damn clever," Masters agreed. "Unless that freighter has another five percent of lightspeed in reserve, she's already doomed."

"Let's not assume the enemy is incompetent," Vong said. "If nothing else, the super-battleship can tow them out if she wins this fight."

"We'll be in their missile range in fifteen seconds. From there, it depends on what they do," Hume reported.

"They're going to turn," the Captain concluded. "They've come in at a course that gives them that option, but they have to let us close on the logistics ship to do it."

"Sir, I have to register my protest at getting this close to a black hole," the navigator replied. "That logistics ship is already doomed. I'd rather not follow her in, even if I trust the Mesharom calculations to tell me how close I can get."

A distance, Morgan knew, that was easily half again what they might have guessed earlier. Only the fact that she had confirmed the presence of singularity cores on the Kanzi ships left her figuring the enemy had the same calculations.

"I'm not counting on that ship to fall in on her own, and I'd love the chance to examine her," Vong replied. "We'll close with her and see what she does as we get close enough to send boarding shuttles over. Casimir, Masters—get the Bucklers out and keep those missiles away from my ship!"

Morgan was already on it. At some point soon, she was going to run out of defensive drones, but she had a full shell out between them and the Kanzi warship as they dove closer to the black hole.

"Well, Lieutenant Commander Casimir, welcome to what is *probably* the craziest maneuver you'll ever see in your career," Masters murmured to her. "If you get a clean shot with the hyperfold cannons on that freighter, take it."

The first wave of missiles hit the outer perimeter of the defensive drones before she could reply, lasers lighting up the debris field around them as the Kanzi tried to make the most of their range and speed advantages.

Bellerophon crashed out of the accretion disk into the "open" space around the black hole. They were into space now where anything without an interface drive—or a velocity best measured in fractions of light, anyway—was already sucked into the singularity.

"Range on the transport. Firing."

Masters's words echoed on the bridge as the three ships danced through the terrifying "surf" of the black hole.

"Enemy salvo defeated, no leakers," Morgan reported. The range was too long. The extra handful of seconds were more than enough for a defensive system designed to hit at least *some* missiles with fractions of a second's warning.

"He has to either close or leave the transport to us," Vong said with satisfaction. "Major Phelps—prepare your shuttles. We might actually get a chance to board this bastard."

"His big brother is making the same call," Masters warned. "He's stopped playing games and he's coming straight for us. Point six cee."

The Captain snarled. "Major, can your shuttles make it from here?"

Morgan couldn't hear the response from the Ducal Guard commander. She could hear Vong's orders, though.

"Whether you're on that transport or drifting in space, we *will* come for you, Major. On the honor of the Empress."

A few seconds later, new green icons speckled the charts as a dozen assault shuttles blasted clear of *Bellerophon*'s hull. In the chaos, Morgan slipped a probe in far closer than she should have.

For a handful of seconds, the hyperfold coms from the sensor probe gave her near-real-time targeting data on the ship. It was long range for the hyperfold cannons...but she didn't actually want to do that much damage.

Six batteries, including the now-much-better-rested Charlie-Six, came to life and twenty-four hyperfold cannons spoke. The freighter had four antimatter cores and Morgan ripped all of them open to space in a single moment of violence with only half of *Bellerophon*'s guns.

"Target shields are down; interface drive is flickering," she reported a moment later. "Antimatter pods are venting into space. She isn't self-destructing anytime soon, folks."

The transport was also now *definitely* doomed, though. Either of the capital ships fighting over her could pull the wreck out of the black hole's gravity well. Without the more powerful ship's engines, however, that logistics ship was only going to one place.

Hell.

THE TWO CAPITAL ships continued to close, rushing toward each other at an incomprehensible speed. Missiles flashed across space, the Buckler drones cutting the Kanzi salvos down to a manageable size as the enemy ship continued to take most of *Bellerophon*'s missiles directly to their shields.

Then there was a gap in the enemy's fire, and Morgan swallowed a curse as she realized what they'd done.

"Sir, they've fired on the logistics ship! Less than thirty seconds to impact."

There was no time for using their missiles as countermeasures. No time to try and interpose the Buckler drones. Under the current rules of engagement, they couldn't intervene...and they had over a hundred Guards already aboard the Kanzi ship.

"Go Gold Protocol," Vong snapped. "Casimir, take those missiles down! Masters, *kill that bastard.*"

New options and commands appeared on Morgan's screen, and she hit a command she'd never actually seen used outside of simulations. All of the tests of the system had taken place in buried spaces they were certain the Mesharom weren't watching.

A new set of exotic-matter emitters, completely different from anything else aboard the battleship, came to life. Energy cycled down the arrays and converted into new particles, tachyons pulsing from the negative mass of the strange arrays in super-lightspeed streams.

Five seconds after Vong gave the order to go Gold, Morgan Casimir had a real-time image of everything within thirty light-seconds of *Bellerophon*. Perfect targeting data.

Five seconds after that, her hyperfold cannons opened fire. Even with live data, she wasn't hitting with every shot, and she was trying to shoot down a hundred and sixty missiles with forty-eight guns.

The geometry gave her less than fifteen seconds, enough time to cycle the hyperfold cannons five times at minimum power.

It was enough. Two missiles made it through her fire, diving toward the logistics ship...and missing to fall into the black hole, their targeting systems fried by approaching too close to the singularity.

"Hotel batteries are live," Chin Masters reported as the Kanzi missiles died. "Internal hyper portals open. Firing."

The Mesharom built their hyperdrive missiles to be independent entities, capable of entering and leaving hyperspace under their own power. That required a lot of exotic matter, which was always in limited supply in the Imperium, and a lot of space and power.

Testing at DragonWorks had discovered, however, that exiting hyperspace actually took less power and exotic matter than entering it. A *lot* less. A missile that only needed to *leave* hyperspace could actually be built into a platform only three times the size of a conventional interface-drive missile.

Bellerophon had four Hotel batteries. Each contained one hyperspace-portal generator and six missile launchers—and all of them were buried deep inside her hull. There was no need for a single-portal hyperspace missile to be launched from the exterior of the ship.

Twenty four missiles screamed into hyperspace at point eight cee, crossing the space to the Kanzi warship in fractions of a second and plunging back into reality under their own power. The same tachyon scanners that allowed Morgan to protect the freighter also gave Masters real-time targeting data for his attack.

Sixteen of the missiles emerged next to the Kanzi super-battle-ship, slamming into her shields with the full force of a modern interface-drive missile loaded with a twenty-gigaton antimatter warhead. The shields flickered and collapsed...but it didn't matter.

The last eight missiles had appeared *inside* the shields, punching through compressed-matter armor to deliver their deadly payloads into the enemy capital ship.

"Target destroyed," Masters reported with grim satisfaction. "Single-portal hypermissile magazines at ninety percent."

"Lock them back down," Vong ordered. "Return to Green Dragon protocols." He shook his head. "Let's hope our Mesharom friend thinks we just had better luck with the second round of dual-portal missiles."

The single-portal missiles were in many ways a more advanced weapon than the Mesharom used...and they were made possible by shielding technology learned from the Precursor wreck humanity had sold the Core Power.

Technology the Imperium wasn't supposed to have access to anymore.

CHAPTER NINETEEN

"The Kanzi are lying to me."

The recorded communiqué from Empress A!Shall sounded tired. Harriet Tanaka *felt* tired, the Fleet Lord run ragged by taking her fleet outside of Jupiter for the first time in five years.

"It's strange," A!Shall's recorded presence continued. "I'm not certain they're lying to me about attacking our systems. That's sufficiently out of character that I'm prepared to consider other possibilities, however unusual.

"But they are definitely lying to me. Ships are moving, fleets being assembled. If they're not moving against us, I'm not sure who they are moving against."

The communique was mostly informational at this point, though Harriet was getting a personal message from the Empress since she was heading to the flashpoint.

"I want to tell you to refrain from starting a war," A!Shall concluded, a flash of sadness tinging her skin despite her iron self-control. "I cannot. If it is the Kanzi burning our worlds, crush them. You have my full backing.

"If it is someone else..." The Empress shivered, tentacles flickering. "You have my full backing," she repeated. "You are a Fleet Lord of the Imperium. That grants you authority and I will not restrict it."

"Hyperspace being what it is, I'm not sure how long it will be before you arrive in Xīn Táiwān. Keep us advised via the hyperfold relay. You are authorized to use any systems up to Black Dragon in the conflict with the Kanzi."

She paused.

"I understand that two of the *Bellerophon*–class ships are with you. I trust your discretion on the Gold Dragon systems, Fleet Lord, but I would prefer that the Kanzi not become aware of our possession of tachyon sensors or single-portal hyperdrive missiles."

The Empress shivered again.

"I know better than to control distant tides via a one-way communication link, however. I trust your discretion," she echoed. "Your service does honor to the Imperium.

"Avenge our dead, Fleet Lord."

HARRIET HUMMED SOFTLY to herself as she entered her flag bridge. Her staff and their supporting teams were busily working on managing the thousands of details and tasks required to run an entire fleet.

Her Seventy-Seventh Fleet was still half a day out of Xīn Táiwān, and her staff was already looking overwhelmed. She made a note to see if she could coopt more of the squadron-level staff—or Rolfson's people, for that matter—to make sure her own people weren't overwhelmed.

Her Fleet, after all, was "merely" thirty-two super-battleships, thirty-two cruisers and sixteen destroyers. Adding the Militia's second squadron, she was up to forty-eight super-battleships, two *Bellerophon* battleships, forty-eight cruisers and thirty-two destroyers.

Rolfson's fleet would add another sixteen cruisers and destroyers, ten more battleships and two super-battleships. She wasn't up to the strength of the Grand Fleet that Fleet Lord Tan!Shallegh was mustering against the Kanzi core worlds, but the fifty-plus capital ships still made up a powerful force for this far out on the frontier.

"Fleet Lord," her chief of staff, Sier, greeted her. The tall blue-feathered and black-beaked Yin had been with her since her first cruiser in the Imperial Fleet, rising from her First Sword—executive officer—to her flag captain and now to Division Lord and the effective second-in-command of her fleet.

"Any news from the fleet?" she asked.

"Two hundred and sixteen minor disciplinary complaints, sixty-five engineering issues, twelve promotions and one enlisted sentient locked in irons," he reeled off. "A quiet day. None of that really requires the Fleet Lord's attention."

A hundred and thirty ships, including three squadrons of super-battleships, represented the best part of three hundred thousand sentient crew. That *was* a quiet day.

"Any intelligence updates?"

Sier shrugged, a gesture his race shared with humanity.

"Nothing meaningful. Imperial Intelligence is still chasing wing shadows to find the flock. There's something there, but..."

"That's much what the Empress said in her communique," Harriet told him. "I want you to start a new series of training exercises across the fleet." She hummed thoughtfully for a moment, then smiled wickedly.

"I want us to exercise our ships against a 'conceptual enemy' based off the *Bellerophons*' Gold Dragon tech," she told him. "Someone with an optimal combination of Core Power tech, the most advanced enemy we can conceive."

Sier blinked slowly, his eyes meeting hers in a manner that sent atavistic shivers down her spine. The Yin had evolved from large predatory birds. His thoughtful expression reminded her ancestral monkey of an attacking eagle.

"What are you expecting to fight, Fleet Lord?" he asked.

"I don't know, but my hunch is that either we aren't fighting Kanzi, or the Theocracy has some secrets we all missed!"

"ATTENTION TO THE FLEET LORD," Sier called out as Harriet entered the room. A long table in the center of the space contained her officers as well as the Captain of her flagship, *Justified*. A virtual table continued off into the "distance," containing *Justified*'s XO—currently physically on the super-battleship's bridge—and the rest of her Captains, XOs, Division Lords, and Squadron Lords.

Only the people physically present were actually expected to stand, but all of her officers made at least an attempt at whatever their species used as an at attention pose until she waved them all back to their seats.

"All right, people," she greeted them. "We are currently twelve hours from Xīn Táiwān. If anyone has any concerns about the fighting capabilities of their ship or their formation, I better already know about them!"

The warm silence that answered was what she expected. Seventy-Seventh Fleet hadn't deployed in years, but the command staff had been together for ten long-cycles. They'd had months and long-cycles to get their ships exercised together in the shelter of the shielded spot in Jupiter—and many of the virtual exercises had included the Militia officers represented by Vice Admiral Tidikat's First Squadron.

"We'll get a more up-to-date reporting on the local situation once we drop out of hyperspace and can link into the hyperfold network," Harriet continued. "What we're getting by starcom is about twenty-five hours out of date right now. We should be hearing from *Bellerophon* shortly, given the estimate Captain Vong provided when he entered hyperspace, but we'll get that via hyper-fold first.

"What we do know is that it's been a quiet week. Our genocidal strangers appear to have disappeared from our space, which makes me nervous," she admitted as her officers started to look more relaxed.

"I'm happy to see our worlds and people spared their visits," she agreed with her people's unspoken comment, "but I worry about where they may have gone. The force that attacked the Mesharom was of a similar style but deployed ships quite unlike those used in the attacks on our systems.

"We have very little solid intelligence. We *do* know that the Kanzi appear to be maneuvering as well, but many of our usual assets in Theocracy space have been unusually quiet. The Emancipators are keeping the Imperium up to date on deployments around the usual flashpoints, but they're not talking about movements out here."

Harriet had few positive impressions of the Kanzi, which meant it had been quite a shock to realize that the Theocracy actually had a live and vibrant, if officially proscribed and occasionally actively purged, abolitionist movement.

Like the American Confederacy in Earth's past, the Theocracy's economy was utterly dependent on slavery. Harriet had little hope that the Emancipators would actually change anything, but to be fair, neither did the Emancipators.

They didn't make up the majority of the Imperium's intelligence assets in their nation by accident, after all.

"I want to split up Division Lord Peeah's squadron," she noted, with a nod to the Pibo officer in question. Pibo were one of the Imperial Races and resembled nothing so much as the Grays of human UFO mythology. Peeah was a lesser-male, a four-foot-tall humanoid with massive black eyes and dark gray skin mottled with spots of orange.

He also commanded her most modern destroyer squadron.

"Peeah, I want you to deploy your platforms in a scouting pattern along the border," she told him. "And by 'along the border' I mean 'inside Kanzi space.' If the Theocracy has a significant naval force in the region, I want to know where they are before *they* do; is that clear?"

"As summer waters," Peeah confirmed. "We will detach from the fleet immediately."

"The rest of us are going to take up a nodal defense position at Xīn Táiwān," Harriet continued. "We'll absorb Vice Admiral Rolfson's task force and remain above our most vulnerable colony until we have more data. Once Peeah's initial scouting sweep is complete, we will reassess the situation."

She smiled grimly.

"My current tentative plan is to proceed to Alstroda and neutralize any potential threat from the Theocracy," she admitted.

"Whether by diplomacy or violence will depend on them."

CHAPTER TWENTY

BELLEROPHON SHIVERED AROUND THEM AS KUMARI HUME TOOK the Terran battleship deep into the gravity well of the black hole. Systems across the bridge were screaming a dozen alerts, and even Morgan's tactical console was warning her that half of her weapons weren't going to work properly.

"Contact in thirty seconds," Hume reported. "Please tell me no one over there has guns left. This could get really, really bad."

"We're in control," Major Phelps reported grimly. "I'll give you the rest of the details once we're all back aboard, but it's not pretty. But we *are* in control of the bridge, the remaining fusion cores, and the maneuvering jets.

"No one over here is going to be trying to ram *Bellerophon*."

"Oh, good," Morgan murmured. Her own focus was on the hyperfold-equipped drones still surveying the accretion disk. It didn't *look* like there were more ships out there, but these strange Kanzi had already surprised them more than once.

"Contact...now."

A soft tremor ran through the entire battleship, and Morgan joined in the general sigh of relief.

"We have hull contact. Engineering is deploying tow cables and I'm extending the interface field," Hume reported. "At least five minutes until we can move out, but I think I've got the descent arrested. Nobody is falling into the singularity now."

"Time dilation?" Vong asked softly.

"Twenty-six percent," Masters reported. "We've been in tau factors for about forty-five minutes, and real-world time has been about fifty-two minutes. If we pull up in five minutes, we'll have lost about twenty all told."

"Could be worse," the Captain said. "Any problems with the tow cables?"

"Nothing," Hume replied. "Proceeding per plan."

Morgan, like most of the bridge crew, found herself half-holding her breath for the five minutes it took to hook the wrecked transport up to *Bellerophon*. Eventually, however, the two ships began moving away. Slowly at first, then faster and faster as Hume grew more confident in the connection.

With the accretion disk, it would be over an hour until they were in clear space, but the worst was over. They'd danced with the edge of a black hole and come away alive.

MORGAN WASN'T ENTIRELY sure *why* she was in the Guard debriefing once the troopers started returning aboard the battleship—at least not until Major Alexander Phelps approached her and grabbed her hand in his own.

"Thank you, Lieutenant Commander," he told her fiercely as he shook her hand. His beaming smile flashed white teeth in dark skin, and his skin was warm against hers. For a moment, Morgan found herself mildly distracted by the man's athletic build and bright blue eyes, but then she forced a smile and met his gaze.

"For what, Major?" she asked slowly.

"The bastards tried to blow every damn thing they had that could wreck the ship or kill us," Phelps told her. "If you hadn't taken out their antimatter plants, we'd have been vaporized when we tried to board."

A shadow passed over his face.

"It was bad enough, Casimir," he admitted. "But without you, we'd have all died. I owe you. My *Guards* owe you."

"Major Phelps asked that you be in this briefing so he could thank you personally," Vong interjected from behind them, and Morgan almost jumped. She'd focused on the Guard more than she'd meant to—a bad habit to get into.

"And given that you and Commander Masters are going to be dealing with many of the consequences of what the Major has discovered, it seemed wise," the Captain continued, a twinkle in his eye suggesting that he'd caught Morgan's distraction.

"Come, Casimir. The poor Major is going to have to brief us all, and none of this is pretty."

Morgan fell into line behind the Captain with a final nod at Phelps, who returned the gesture with a brilliant smile before crossing to the front of the room.

"All right, everyone," he said firmly. "We've still got teams on the wreck going over everything, but Captain Vong asked me to give an initial 'what the hell happened' briefing on what we found."

A rough schematic of the ship appeared on the wall behind Phelps as Morgan and the senior officers took their seats.

"We are forwarding this briefing to our Mesharom guest," Morgan warned everyone. "I'm not sure if Coraniss will be watching this live or in recording; it will depend on how they function with it best."

She figured everyone got her meaning: Dragon-classified items were off the board as much as possible.

"Well, hopefully, they'll know something we don't," Phelps replied. "These people were complete fanatics. I've fought Kanzi raiders and pirates, and I've read the files on Imperial Marines going up against their Theocracy counterparts.

"The Kanzi field ground troops with strong religious fervor, but only a few key units are true zealots," he noted. "These grunts were fanatics to a smurf.

"We boarded the ship in the face of heavy resistance and intentionally targeted the fusion cores," he continued. "That turned out to be a *damned* good plan. At least one core was already in overload by the time my Guards got to it, and we only barely managed to short-stop it.

"After that, they flooded a significant portion of the ship with the hydrogen fuel for the cores and ignited it."

Morgan winced at the image of hell that brought to mind.

"We lost seventy-six Guards and have a hundred wounded," Phelps said levelly. "Most of those were when the bastards lit off the hydrogen. Once we'd seized the cores, Life Support and Engineering, resistance...stopped."

"They started surrendering?" Antonova asked.

Morgan had looked up the files on the Alpha Centauri Incident. She guessed what had actually happened even before Phelps shook his head.

"No. We have no prisoners, at all. No survivors. Once they realized the ship was lost, they started suiciding—many with poison, some with bombs as they tried to take my Guards with them.

"They killed themselves to a one to avoid capture."

The briefing room was silent for several long seconds as that sank in.

"That is not very Kanzi of them," Vong finally said. "I thought the main Kanzi faith was against suicide?"

"It is," Morgan confirmed. "What worse way, after all, to end the life of a perfect mirror of God?"

She tried to keep her tone level, but she suspected more of her opinion of the Kanzi's insane religion slipped through than she meant to.

"It's also against scarification or body mods," Phelps pointed out. "And these smurfs were scarred, tattooed and pierced like nobody's business. Patterns, runes, imagery...none of it lines up with our files on the Kanzi."

"That is weird," Masters said. "I thought the Kanzi had unified their languages?"

"More so than humanity, but fringe languages exist and the Theocracy's insistence on the official 'Tongue of God' means we don't have translator code," Morgan explained. She then shut up, realizing that she probably shouldn't be answering questions in this meeting.

Instead of complaining, however, Captain Vong chuckled.

"For those who weren't aware, Lieutenant Commander Casimir's Academy curriculum was tactics and xenoanthropology. She quite possibly knows more about our enemy than most of us."

"The weird thing, though, is that we could talk to what was left of their computers," Phelps said after a few moments of quiet. "The dialect was archaic and the software was strange, but all of the interfaces were in the usual Kanzi language."

"Anything else we need to immediately know, Major?" Vong asked.

"These guys may *look* like the smurfs, Captain, but...they don't seem to think like them. I've fought them and now I'm wondering just what we're missing!"

AFTER THE STAFF MEETING, Morgan found herself pulled into a private meeting with Commander Masters in his office. Her boss looked tired as he gestured her to a seat.

"I think better standing," she reminded him.

"I know," he allowed. "On the other hand, I'm tired and my neck hurts, so how about you *don't* make me crane it to look at you?"

It didn't take a great deal of crankiness on the part of a superior officer to make a question into an order. Morgan sat, folding her hands into her lap as she carefully studied Chin Masters.

"I owe you an apology, Lieutenant Commander Casimir," he admitted.

"I believe it is a basic principle of any military force that no superior ever owes an apology to a junior, sir," she offered carefully. She wasn't sure just what had been happening on *Bellerophon*'s bridge during the battle with the Kanzi, but she was sure that a fight with her boss was not the solution.

"It is an even more basic principle, Casimir, that when the ship's Captain calls you into his office and spends forty-five minutes explaining how you have been failing to do your damn job, that said Captain is correct," Masters said flatly, then sighed and rested his face in his hands.

"I owe you an apology," he finally repeated after a few moments. "I assumed you had this position from nepotism, and almost everything I've done since you came aboard was, at least on my side, classed as 'giving you enough rope.'"

Morgan swallowed. She thought they'd been building a good working relationship, getting past that initial friction. Apparently, she'd been wrong.

"You kept doing a damn fine job," he admitted, "but part of me wanted the damn assistant tactical officer *I* chose and had been working with for six months. I wasn't setting you up to fail, I wasn't that far gone, but I sure as hell wasn't expecting you to succeed.

"And when you did succeed, I chalked it up to luck and 'gave you more rope.'" He tapped a command on his desk and a machine started to whir away, making coffee. "And because I'd been thinking that way, I failed to notice that my top subordinate was doing her job just fine, even with only half-assed support from me."

"And then we ended up in a battle," Morgan said quietly.

A panel slid aside and the coffeepot rose out of the desk. Masters pulled out two cups and poured coffee for them both, clearly marshaling his thoughts.

"Then we ended up in combat," he agreed. "And however good a job you'd been doing, my brain was still seeing it as giving you rope, so I panicked at the thought of you in command of a battleship's weapons in combat.

"That was *not* a response you deserved and far from the response you'd earned," Masters said flatly. "I failed you. I failed this ship. I failed *myself*. And because I was so busy failing to lean on the strong right arm I didn't see that I had, I failed to fight my Captain's ship."

He took a long swallow of coffee. Morgan waited. There wasn't much to this self-flagellation that she could contribute to. It seemed Captain Vong had already done his part, and Morgan didn't figure her O-4 opinion was really needed.

"I realized that much on my own," Masters said after a moment. "What the Captain pointed out to me was how badly I had failed in my duty as your superior, to support you, train you and recognize the work you were doing.

"Like I said. I owe you an apology."

"Apology made and accepted," Morgan said firmly. "I don't think that harping on the past is going to improve things, do you?"

Masters paused, carefully taking another sip of coffee.

"Perhaps not," he allowed.

"I may not be Annette Bond's biological daughter, Commander, but she is still my mother," Morgan told him. "She'd say we have a job to do and going forward is the only way to fix it. I've been doing my job, best as I can, and honestly, sir, I've never been an ATO before. I didn't know this wasn't how it was supposed to be!"

Masters barked a bitter laugh, but his smile was genuine. It reached into his eyes and sparkled for a few delightful seconds.

"Well, it's not," he told her. "So, we're going to do better...first and foremost, you should be in the senior officers' briefing. You're a line officer—you're ahead of, say, Lieutenant Commander Antonova in the chain of command and you *need* to know what's going on!"

CHAPTER TWENTY-ONE

SUPER-BATTLESHIP AFTER SUPER-BATTLESHIP FLASHED through the hyper portal into the Xīn Táiwān System. Harriet's flagship led the way, all sixteen of her *Vindication*-class ships forming an armored spearhead in case the worst had happened—and the odds were that no one would have even noticed the two *Bellerophon*s that slipped through the portal right after them.

The *Vindication*s had been built from the ground up with hyperfold cannons and plasma lances, and the older ships had been refitted with hyperfold coms and cannons.

The *Bellerophon*s were her snipers, carrying twice as many hyperfold cannons as any of her super-battleships and concealing almost her entire hyper-drive missile armament.

Thirty-two more super-battleships followed, interspersed with dozens of cruisers and destroyers. Harriet Tanaka's fleet carried more *humans* than lived in this system, and less than five percent of her crews were human.

"We have the Rimward Squadron on scanners," Sier reported. "Xīn Táiwān remains in Imperial control."

"That's fascinating," Harriet murmured. "No evidence of a combat action at all?"

"Nothing," her chief of staff confirmed. "We've linked with Admiral Rolfson's force and are downloading updates. No one in Xīn Táiwān has had so much as a sniff of the enemy."

"Then where did they go?" she asked aloud. "One week they're smashing along our Rimward frontier, killing hundreds of thousands. The next they're gone. What am I missing?"

"At least some of them went and interrupted the Mesharom's lifting wind," Sier reported. "We have a full report from *Bellerophon*. She engaged a Kanzi super-battleship in a black hole system."

The Yin paused, clicking his beak sharply in the gesture his people used in place of a shake of the head.

"They had to go full Gold Dragon to carry the day," he noted. "With a Mesharom aboard."

"Well, there goes *that* set of secrets," Harriet sighed. "We'll keep that in mind. A Kanzi ship?"

"Captain Vong says yes, but that they *also* encountered destroyers that matched up with the vessels that began the Alpha Centauri Incident."

"Make sure Admiral Rolfson has every piece of data Captain Vong has on those ships," she snapped. "He's the only ship commander who survived that fight. If the destroyers are the same... he'll know."

"He should have everything *Bellerophon* sent us," her subordinate pointed out. "They are a Militia ship, after all."

"Get us into orbit and schedule a meeting with our Lords and Vice Admiral Rolfson," Harriet ordered. "We'll go over everything we know while we wait for Division Lord Peeah to report in. There were no super-battleships at Powell, Sier. It's entirely possible we have two enemies in play, and I don't want to miss a move by the Kanzi because we're watching our back for the bastards who took on the Mesharom."

"And if we do find out who killed the Frontier Fleet squadron?" Sier asked.

"The priority is the people who murdered our citizens. But once we've dealt with them, I have every intention of finding the people who attacked Frontier Fleet and...expressing the Empress's displeasure."

ONCE THE RIMWARD SQUADRON'S eight capital ships were absorbed into Harriet's Seventy-Seventh Fleet, the skies above Xīn Táiwān's single habitable planet were witness to an awe-inspiring collection of firepower.

Shuttles flickered between the behemoths at carefully controlled speeds. With the entire fleet occupying a space barely fifty thousand kilometers on a side, their usual speed of around half of light would be a disaster waiting to happen.

Those shuttles delivered each of Harriet Tanaka's senior subordinates aboard *Justified*, with Vice Admiral Rolfson arriving last and providing a textbook-perfect salute.

Of course, that textbook was the United Earth Space Force's, not the Imperial Navy's or even the Duchy of Terra Militia's. It was closer to the latter than the former...but it was also the salute that Harriet Tanaka had originally trained with.

She returned it, then switched to the Imperial Navy's hand (or equivalent tool-using limb) to heart gesture.

"Welcome aboard *Justified*, Admiral Rolfson. It's been a while."

"That it has," he agreed. In truth, Harriet didn't believe she'd ever met the man in person, but they'd been on various conference calls and exchanged emails by the thousand over the years.

Meeting in person wasn't really required to know someone anymore.

"Did I spot a pair of *Bellerophons* hiding in the shadow of your super-battleships?" Rolfson asked.

"You did," Harriet confirmed. "You were briefed on *Bellerophon* herself's encounter?"

"Yeah," he said quietly. "Sounds like our Gold Dragon protocols may be wrecked with regards to the Mesharom—and they were who we were hoping to hide it from!"

"Let's just hope they don't put the pieces together," she told him. "Or if they do, they don't see any sense in crying over spilt beer."

He snorted.

"We have more immediate problems," he noted. "I'm guessing you plan on briefing everyone together?"

"Indeed. Is there anything you need me to know before we get in with everyone?" Harriet asked.

"The ships *Bellerophon* fought? They were the same as the ships at Centauri," he told her, confirming what she'd suspected. "That had me take a second look at the data from Powell."

"And?"

"I don't know any more about the ships than anyone else does... but the beams they took *Patience* and *Corona Glare* out with?" Rolfson grimaced. "They're the same guns the bastards took out Centauri Station with during the Incident.

"I don't think we're facing the Theocracy, sir. These guys are smurfs, no two ways about it, but I'm not sure the High Priestess knows any more about them than I do."

Harriet snorted.

"It's possible," she allowed. "But if they make a wrong move right now, I'm not going to hesitate to punch their blue faces all the way back to the High Priestess's own damn house."

"And I'll be with you the whole way," Rolfson confirmed. "Never did like having slavers for neighbors, after all."

WITH HER SQUADRON commanders gathered in the briefing room, Harriet took a moment to wonder at the complexity of the

Imperial command structure. She had three Imperial Squadron Lords, two Terran Vice Admirals, three Imperial Division Lords—commanding squadrons of lighter units—and three Terran Rear Admirals.

Including her, there were six humans in the room. All three of the Militia squadron commanders were human, as was Vice Admiral Rolfson. One of her Division Lords was a human, one of the still-small handful of human flag officers in the Imperial Navy.

Tidikat was the fifth Terran officer, the Laian looking perfectly comfortable in his oddly tailored white Militia dress uniform. Harriet's own subordinates included a Yin, a Frole, a Rekiki, and two Indiri.

She was waiting on a response from her Pibo flag officer, but the collection of strange species in the room was impressive. Division Lord Iffa, her Frole cruiser squadron commander, was an ambulatory mushroom. The Indiri were wide-faced, red-furred frog-like amphibians, and the Rekiki was a large crocodilian centaur.

It was an odd collection, but they were all professionals and she knew the skills of both groups of officers perfectly well. Her Seventy-Seventh Fleet had been lurking inside Jupiter for ten long-cycles at this point.

"As of today, we have exerted levy right on the Duchy of Terra's Rimward Squadron and absorbed Vice Admiral Rolfson's command into Seventy-Seventh Fleet," Harriet told her people. "His units will continue to report to him going forward, to avoid confusion, but this is now a single combined force. One of the largest ones to ever be deployed this far out on the Rim."

She shook her head.

"Unfortunately, our best efforts have left us with few answers as to what is going on out here," she admitted. "The evidence is such that I am inclined to believe the Theocracy's protestations of innocence: it definitely appears that the rogue Kanzi who attacked Hope thirty long-cycles ago have shown up again.

"On the other hand, I *don't* believe that the Kanzi don't know anything," she continued. "I forwarded the diplomatic briefing package I received from A!To to all of you. Did everyone have a chance to review it?"

If anyone had somehow *failed* to review the documents the Fleet Lord had sent over, they didn't admit it. It hadn't made for enjoyable reading.

"Imperial civilian communication with the Kanzi is limited at the best of times, but it has been completely shut off now," Harriet noted. "Getting data from our agents inside the Theocracy has apparently proven more difficult than usual, but we have confirmed a significant movement of Theocracy Navy units around their territory."

"Doesn't that suggest that the shadow-lichen *are* up to something?" Iffa asked. The translator converted their voice into something intelligible, but the original sound of their speech was still audible. Frole spoke by emitting gases from multiple different orifices on their body, creating a rather odd cross between speaking in tongues and fart humor.

"And that is part of why I think they know more than they're telling us," she said grimly. "We know even less about what they're doing than usual, but..."

"I've reviewed all of the data we have," Rolfson said into the silence. "There's no question of it: the destroyers that *Bellerophon* engaged are identical to the ships that attacked Centauri. The rest of the ships, from the battleships at Powell to the super-battleships that attacked the Mesharom, are of a similar ilk. Kanzi design but not Kanzi technology."

"So, who are they?" Tidikat asked. "These strange Kanzi are not known to either of the peoples I have served, and most organizations that crawl in shadows have been to *Builder of Sorrows*."

Tidikat was an exile from exiles, and the main block of Laian Exiles were clustered around what had once been a major mobile shipyard for the Laian Ascendancy. Known to humanity as Tortuga, *Builder of Sorrows* was a major pirate and smuggler port.

If these strangers hadn't been to Tortuga, then they almost certainly weren't hiding in Theocracy space.

"I think these people, whoever they are, are coming from beyond known space," Harriet said quietly. "Beyond the Rimward of both the A!Tol and the Kanzi there is space we have scouted—but beyond that, there is only darkness and best guesses."

"They come from the darkness beyond our known stars," Iffa agreed. "I wonder, Fleet Lord...if perhaps we are not even the main target of their attack."

"Explain," she ordered.

"They are Kanzi...but not from the Theocracy. Is it not possible that we were simply targets of opportunity as they went for their own people?" the Frole asked.

Harriet tapped a command, opening a holographic chart of the region, highlighting the now-devastated human worlds.

"It would explain why Xīn Táiwān went unattacked," Rolfson pointed out as they all looked at the star chart. "If they were heading...here, they'd have passed by Lelldorin and Powell but not New Taiwan."

"And their force that took on the Frontier Fleet would likely have been able to rendezvous with them there, using the black hole as an easy reference point for changing their course," Tidikat added.

"When would they have reached Avida?" Harriet asked, letting her subordinates run the numbers. Avida was the Kanzi colony next along the line that ran through Lelldorin and Powell.

"Fifteen cycles ago," Iffa concluded. A little over two weeks.

Harriet nodded, starting to hum softly as she thought and studied the map.

"What about Kanda?" she asked.

When humanity had joined the Imperium, the Kovius Treaty that both the Imperium and the Kanzi recognized—mostly because the Mesharom Frontier Fleet existed to enforce it—had declared a forty-light-year radius of Sol to be human territory. Which meant, now, Imperial territory.

A chunk of that sphere had cut through space the Kanzi had regarded as theirs, and they'd had a few colonies beyond that sphere.

Kanda was the largest, a thriving world of two hundred fifty thousand Kanzi and four hundred thousand slaves.

It was also further Rimward on the line drawn through Avida, Lelldorin, and Powell.

"They don't have hyperfold coms and we're not scouting their distant colonies," Rolfson said quietly. "They might know if something had happened, but we wouldn't."

Before Harriet could finish her thought, an emergency alert pinged on her com. Not much would get to her in this meeting, and she suspected she knew what she'd see even before she opened the device.

"Division Lord Peeah has made contact," she told everyone. "The Kanzi have left Alstroda."

A HOLOGRAM of the smooth-skinned gray Pibo appeared in the middle of the table, replacing the astrographic chart. The image was aligned toward Harriet and Peeah saluted crisply as the recording began.

"Fleet Lord Tanaka, we may have a problem," he said calmly. His natural voice was inaudible to human ears, but the translators picked it up. "One of my destroyers did a scouting run of Alstroda. The entire mobile fleet positioned there is gone—only the fixed defenses remain in place."

He blinked his large black eyes three times in rapid succession, a sign of discomfort.

"Per the last intelligence assessment I have access to, Fleet Master Shairon Cawl should have at least four squadrons of either super-battleships or battleships, plus escorts. None of those ships are at Alstroda.

"Reviewing long-range anomaly scanner data from my other

ships, we believe we have confirmed that Fleet Master Cawl has deployed to the Avida System," he continued. "I am moving half of my squadron to shadow him while the remainder spreads out to watch for further Kanzi movements.

"While Avida is Theocracy space, I must note that it is also extremely well positioned to enable strikes against Asimov or Sol. The deployment of forty capital ships this close to the border is a clear violation of the treaties."

The Theocracy used a ten-ship squadron instead of the sixteen-ship formation used by the Imperium and its Duchies. Peeah wasn't wrong...except that Seventy-Seventh Fleet was even *more* powerful... and was equally close to the border.

"I will attempt to have one of my ships drop out of hyperspace every quarter-cycle to check the hyperfold relay network for updates," he continued. "We will keep you advised of Cawl's movements."

The recording ended and Harriet shook her head slowly and thoughtfully.

"That lines up with our own guesses," she noted aloud. "But it is also a threat we have to respond to. Cawl has forty capital ships. We have sixty. The odds are in our favor, but there is now no other force in this region that can oppose him."

That the Theocracy position out here had out-gunned the official Imperial presence a thousand to one had been a known factor. Fleet Master Cawl had, in fact, been deployed to keep the local Clans in line after they'd run their fleets into a joint Imperial–Duchy of Terra meat grinder at Asimov four long-cycles earlier.

Unofficially, the counterweight to his presence had been the Terran Militia and Seventy-Seventh Fleet. The Imperium had refused to publicly move forces, but Harriet had seen her reinforcements tick up...and she also knew that the Imperium had paid for the first run of *Bellerophon*s. All of which were entering Terran service.

"If these strangers hit Avida, then Cawl is responding to them just as we are," Rolfson noted.

"That is true," Harriet agreed. "But since the Kanzi won't *talk* to us, they knew we were moving here and they did us no such courtesy.

"No. We have no choice. All ships will report readiness within the twentieth-cycle and we will proceed from there. Barring unexpected news or readiness issues, this fleet will deploy to Avida within a tenth-cycle."

And that was that. Harriet Tanaka had committed her fleet to move in a little over two hours—and even if everything the Kanzi were doing was above board, she might have just ordered the beginning of the war the Imperium had dreaded for longer than humanity had known either alien nation existed.

CHAPTER TWENTY-TWO

"Thank you for coming to me so quickly," Coraniss told Morgan.

The big caterpillar-esque alien still hadn't shown their face to Morgan. Like the previous times Morgan had visited the Mesharom aboard the pod, Coraniss faced their computer monitors while speaking.

"We've communicated mostly by text," Morgan reminded the alien. "A request to visit was unusual enough to bring me quickly."

Masters had honored his commitment to bring her into the loop and give her the level of involvement in shipwide affairs she should have had. The extra work, of course, was leaving her *completely* swamped. His support had helped mitigate the impact, at least, and she was feeling mostly in control of her duties.

She was still missing a drill of the plasma lance crew to be here.

"That is fair," Coraniss admitted.

"Is there anything you need?" Morgan asked. One of the reasons she'd rushed down was concern that the Mesharom might be missing something key to their health or the pod's function.

"No, the connected umbilicals have served perfectly," the alien confirmed. "Universal Protein is no more pleasant for me than any other race, but it serves. I have information to pass on."

Morgan took a seat in the chair one of Coraniss's worm-like segmented robots placed for her and waited patiently.

"Information?" she asked carefully.

"I am linked into the hyperfold relay network for the Frontier Fleet," the Mesharom told her. "My superiors have been receiving my reports, but I have not received more than basic acknowledgement."

Morgan couldn't see Coraniss's front, so she was spared the full effect of the multi-limb shiver that was their shrug. She'd seen it before, however, and recognized it.

"I did not expect more until a ship was dispatched to retrieve me."

No human would have been nearly as calm when faced with the lack of communication, but Mesharom weren't human.

"So, a ship has been dispatched?" Morgan asked.

There was a chittering sound. It took Morgan several seconds to realize Coraniss was laughing—it wasn't a sound she'd heard from Mesharom before, and it was out of character for most members of the race. It wasn't that they didn't have senses of humor, but they were very restrained by human standards.

"That was all I expected, but I did not consider context," the Interpreter admitted. "With the data on your engagement with the strangers, the decision has been made to intervene directly."

A chill ran down Morgan's spine. They'd demonstrated a lot of technology they weren't supposed to have in that fight. An "intervention" could just as easily be intending to bring the Imperium back into line as anything else.

"A full task force of the Frontier Fleet is on its way," Coraniss told her. "Elements of the Core Fleet are also being deployed, but they will take time to arrive. They are not close."

Morgan wasn't even certain what a "full task force" of the Frontier Fleet would entail. The Imperium certainly didn't have records of more than single six-ship squadrons getting involved in anyone's affairs.

And the Mesharom Core Fleet? They weren't even in the records. The Core Fleet was a *legend*. A myth, not a real force.

"How long?" Morgan couldn't keep herself from asking.

"Approximately sixty-three days for the Frontier Fleet," Coraniss told her. The actual phrase they used, Morgan realized, was "quarter-orbit." The Mesharom homeworld was closer to a duller sun than Earth, orbiting in just over two hundred and fifty days, but the translator software turned that into something its audience would know immediately.

"One hundred twenty-six days for the warships of the Core Fleet."

"Warships?"

"Of course," Coraniss confirmed. "Frontier Fleet's ships serve many purposes. Only the Core Fleet contains the Mesharom's true warships."

THE BRIEFING ROOM was silent as Morgan reiterated Coraniss's words to the rest of the senior officers aboard *Bellerophon*.

"If what we've seen of the Mesharom aren't warships, what *are* they?" Antonova asked, the blonde communications officer looking concerned.

"Patrol ships, basically," Morgan told her. "Definitely *military* ships, armed craft...but not true warships. Coraniss didn't give me much on what their warships actually look like, beyond 'much bigger' than their battlecruisers."

She sighed.

"I don't get the impression that Coraniss has ever actually seen a Core Fleet deployment," she continued. "Certainly, I checked the records. There hasn't been a Core Fleet deployment in at least two or three centuries, and that was on the opposite side of the galaxy from us against a Core Power we know almost nothing about."

"The Anditch," Vong confirmed. "I checked the files myself. We know at least the physical appearance and size of territory of most of the Core and Arm Powers. We *don't* know that about the Anditch, only that they challenged the Mesharom and are no longer a player in Core politics."

A shiver ran around the room. The Mesharom were slow to develop tech and slow to respond to provocation. They were losing their edge over the other Core Powers with each passing decade—but three hundred years ago?

"We do know that they still *exist*, right?" Antonova asked. "The Mesharom didn't...exterminate them?"

"Imperial Intelligence doesn't think so, but a lot of our usual sources for background data dry up rapidly when the Anditch are mentioned," Vong told her.

"All of this, however, is thankfully a problem for later. We can look forward to Frontier Fleet reinforcements in the medium-term future, and if things *truly* go to shit, these Core Fleet 'warships' may come along in time to save our hides.

"For now, however, we need to consider the enemy in front of us," he concluded. "Surgeon-Commander Miyamoto, if you can brief us all on the results of your autopsies, then Major Phelps will fill us in on what we've learned of their tech."

Surgeon-Commander Masuyo Miyamoto looked like there was a sumo wrestler or twelve in his background, a heavily over-weight man who moved with a delicate grace and had some of the longest and most careful hands and fingers Morgan had ever seen.

"My and Major Phelps's people pulled physical samples from two thousand and eleven individuals," he said in precise, Japanese-accented English. Everyone aboard *Bellerophon* had the same trans-lator earbuds as the Imperial Navy, but the Militia still tended to insist on English for all communications.

Just in case the Imperial-built translation hardware and software failed.

"When we did our autopsies and genetic analysis, however, we had to go back and reverify all of our samples," Miyamoto told them. "Because on initial examination, it appeared that we only had samples from seventeen individuals."

"I wondered why you asked," Phelps interjected, the Marine looking concerned. "I don't think my people messed anything up."

"They did not," the doctor told him. "Neither did mine. Two thousand and eleven separate individuals. Seventeen unique genetic codes. Some minor variations that we detected once we looked deeper, but at the core: seventeen genomes."

"I don't understand, Miyamoto," Captain Vong admitted.

"They're clones, Captain. We examined over two thousand clones based on seventeen individuals." The surgeon shook his head, his jowls wobbling. "Mass-produced spacers, I would guess. It would explain the enemy's cavalier attitude towards their personnel's lives."

Morgan swallowed hard. Clones?

"I didn't think that even Imperial technology was up to mass cloning," Masters pointed out. "Is this a Core Power thing?"

"We retrieved several functionally intact corpses for more detailed examination," Miyamoto replied. "All of them show signs of accelerated growth. At least one of the corpses we examined was a full adult, but examination of bone growth patterns and musculature suggested that the individual was less than five Terran years old.

"That kind of forced growth is beyond any known technological base," he concluded. "Yesterday, I would have told you that mass-producing trained adult soldiers in five years would be impossible.

"Today...today I must admit that it has happened. They are Kanzi, not human...but Kanzi and human biology is as similar as any two species from different worlds can be."

"My god."

Morgan wasn't sure which of the officers had muttered. It might have even have been her.

"Appropriate," Miyamoto stated. "Whatever technology is behind this is nearly godlike so far as we are concerned. We can make no assumptions on enemy population or resources. If they can mass-produce spacers, what is to say they cannot mass-produce miners? Farmers? Scientists?"

"It has to be Precursor technology," Morgan said into the silence that followed. "An intact Precursor facility, clearly fallen into the wrong hands."

"What do we do?" Masters asked slowly.

"We fight," Captain Vong told them all grimly. "We have seen their limits. *Bellerophon* can demonstrably fight them at a two-to-one tonnage disadvantage...though that may not be enough, given what Dr. Miyamoto just described.

"Major Phelps? What do we know about the enemy technology?"

"Masters and Casimir might be more helpful than me," the Marine told them all. "Examining the freighter didn't tell us much we didn't already know. In many ways, she was crude and old-fashioned. You can clearly see the Kanzi derivation in her design and tech, but the language used was antiquated and a lot of the systems were even more so.

"And then there were pieces like nothing I'd ever seen," he continued. "Their hand weapons are comparable to ours, but their squad support weapons are hell. Whatever they hit just...disappears."

Phelps shook his head.

"We've reviewed the sensor data, and it *looks* like they're managing to transport the target into hyperspace...but not any layer of hyperspace we're familiar with. Mechanical or organic, nothing survives the process."

"Masters?" the Captain asked.

"That aligns with what our records show of their short-range energy weapons," Morgan's boss confirmed. "Anything they hit is simply obliterated. A transfer into an unstable hyperspace layer would...fit.

"Their longer-range weaponry is based around much the same

base principles as the Core and Arm Powers. They possess a point eight five cee interface-drive missile that is notably smaller than ours. They don't seem to have any weapon between those two in range, though given that they appear to have a perfect defense against proton beams..."

"Our *Bellerophon* outmatches them," Vong concluded. "But the rest of the Imperial Navy is only barely up to their weight class at best. And we have no idea how many ships they may have."

"So, what do we do?" Masters repeated.

"We make sure everyone knows what we've learned and that the Imperium is ready for what's lurking beyond our borders," the Captain told them. "Then we move to Asimov and dig in."

He shook his head.

"This enemy seems to have moved out of our space, but I can't risk expecting that to last."

CHAPTER TWENTY-THREE

THERE WERE FEW THINGS IN THE GALAXY THAT WERE ALLOWED to interrupt the limited family time that Annette managed to squeeze out with Elon and their children. She and Elon were both swamped with work at the best of times, and the current crisis didn't alleviate that.

Leah and Carol, the older twins, shared the general status of "Heirs," even though Leah was the older by several minutes and was actually Annette's designated successor. They were hip-deep in an intensive pre-college prep program—by their own choice, to Annette's surprise—*and* spent much of their free time shadowing one or the other of their parents.

The two younger girls, at ten and eight, weren't being dragged into any of that yet. Megan Bond was just old enough to understand that something was currently *very* wrong in the galaxy. Alexis Bond, however, was not.

She was also too young to really understand the board games the rest of her family might prefer and had insisted on Monopoly. Which, despite Elon's success in the real business world and her elder sisters' training in economics, she was cleaning up at.

"That's Boardwalk, Mom!" she crowed. "You owe me fourteen hunned!"

Annette's sparse pile of brightly colored currency didn't stretch to that, and she turned her gaze to her equally sparse collection of property to see if she could mortgage anything—and then her communicator buzzed.

Elon and the twins froze. *They* understood what it meant for someone to interrupt the four-hour Sunday evening block the Duchess of Terra had fought to keep open for her family through thick and thin, peace and war.

"Well? Where's my money?" Alexis asked brightly.

"It'll have to wait a moment, love," Annette said quietly. "Elon, I think I'm bankrupt anyway. Can you take over foreclosing me for Zhao's future replacement?"

Her Consort chuckled, but it was forced.

"Of course."

Annette stepped out of the room, a chill in her heart as she opened her communicator.

Maria Robin-Antionette had been her personal secretary for over fifteen years and was married to Annette's press secretary. The two gorgeously attractive women were about the only thing keeping Annette from going insane dealing with Earth's press and bureaucrats—and the Robin-Antionettes were a large portion of *why* she got her family evenings.

"What is it, Maria?" Annette asked, the chill expanding to consume any anger she'd felt at the interruption.

"We received a starcom request from a Mesharom AI," her secretary told her. "No specification on *who* is asking, but they've requested a live starcom channel with you *immediately*."

Annette considered all of the things they'd done that could have pissed the Mesharom off, and sighed. *Bellerophon* had done exactly what they needed to, but there were going to be prices to be paid for what the Imperium had done to be able to build her.

"Can we relay to my secure office or should I be grabbing a shut-

tle?" she asked. She trusted Robin-Antionette to know what was
needed.

"The only people we directly use the starcom to hide from *are* the
Mesharom," her secretary pointed out. "I'll have them make the
connection to your office once you initiate the lockdown protocol."

"You know what you're interrupting," Annette said. "I hope this
isn't as bad as it could be."

"Good luck, Your Grace."

THERE WAS STILL some dim evening light shining into the office
when Annette entered, and she took a moment to look out over Hong
Kong's skyline before she activated the lockdown.

She'd needed a city the whole world knew to act as her capital,
and her own status as an American had meant that choosing New
York would have been favoritism. That had left her with only a
handful of options, and Hong Kong had fit their needs well.

Wuxing Tower, the main center of the Duchy's government, was
easily visible from her penthouse apartment. Several smaller towers
around the city had been absorbed into the government now as well.
Annette's determination to maintain a lean government had collided
with the sheer necessity of governing a planet of some eleven billion
people.

The Terran Development Corporation took up almost as much
space in Hong Kong as the Duchy did, with its *just*-sufficient separa-
tion of authority from the Duchy to meet the Imperial standard. The
Duchy owned every world and star system within forty light-years of
Sol—that was how the Imperium met their Kovius Treaty obligations
—but those worlds were governed by the Imperium.

That over half of the Board of Directors of the TDC were also
members of Annette's Ducal Council was an expected reality of that
situation.

With a sigh, she pressed the button next to the window that took her office into lockdown. Heavy shutters closed over the doors and windows, and a dozen other less obvious security measures took effect.

Sitting at her desk, she made sure the channel linking her to the starcom station in orbit was active and encrypted, and then waited for the Mesharom to make contact.

Thankfully, she didn't have to wait long. Within a minute of her signaling that she was available to the AI setting up the call, the half-scale holographic image of a Mesharom appeared in front of her desk.

The shrunken caterpillar-like creature was familiar, and she inclined her head.

"Interpreter-Captain Adamase," she greeted the alien. The Mesharom final-bearer had led the flotilla that had intervened at Alpha Centauri.

"Interpreter-Shepherd Adamase," the Mesharom corrected calmly, and Annette nodded in understanding. Adamase, it seemed, had gone up in the world since the Centauri Incident.

They'd traded long-range emails and such since, but she hadn't had a live conversation since then, and she hadn't known they'd been appointed Shepherd of their region.

Shepherd was an odd title. The religious overtones of the English translation weren't quite right, but it got the message across. A Shepherd was assigned a region of space outside Mesharom territory that they were responsible for. They commanded the intelligence networks and Frontier Fleet units in that area and generally acted as an ambassador slash sector governor.

For a region the Mesharom didn't control.

"How may I assist you, Interpreter-Shepherd?" Annette asked carefully.

"You could speak truth, which it seems you have not done in some time," the Mesharom told her.

Annette sighed and laced her hands together on the table as she met the alien's multifaceted eyes.

"Why don't you tell me what you think I've lied to you about?"

she asked. "I am the leader of a world, director of a corporation that is developing a dozen more, and direct vassal to the Empress of a thousand stars. There are a thousand things I can't tell you about and a thousand more I would be required to lie to you over."

"You dance well, Duchess, but the game is over," Adamase told her. "I now possess the sensor records from our escape pod of the engagement between *Bellerophon* and the Unknown warship. Hyperspace missiles? Tachyon sensors? Self-motile armor?" The alien's limbs snapped back and forth sharply, creating a nerve-wracking chittering sound.

"How much of the Precursor ship did you steal?"

Annette paused to marshal her thoughts, then shook her head at them.

"We duplicated tachyon sensors based on scans of your own ships," she pointed out. "The concept of a self-motile matrix to support our armor was taken from the Precursor ship, yes, but we developed our own technological basis for it. We based the hyperspace missiles on scans of your weapons in action, and our comparable weapon is *immense*."

"And your *other* hyperspace weapon?"

It seemed all of their secrets were out. Annette sighed again.

"The Gold Dragon missile system did require technology based on the Precursor ship, yes," she admitted. "We failed to duplicate the gravitational singularity plant, but we managed to find a comparable form of shielding that allowed us to create a contained hyperspace portal.

"The only physical component of the Precursor ship we kept was a small sample of the hull matrix. We did keep all of our scan data on the vessel. We promised you the *ship*, Shepherd Adamase.

"We did *not* agree to hand over our data and samples. You took it upon yourself to destroy those...and we took it upon ourselves to protect them."

"The destruction of *all* data from the Precursor ship was an assumed part of the deal," Adamase replied.

"Then you should have included that in our discussions," Annette replied. "We have scans of the ship, yes. We also have scans of you, the Laians, and the Wendira in action. Alpha Centauri was and is home to a massively powerful distributed sensor system.

"Those, combined with other scraps of technology acquired by the Imperium over the decades, allowed us to build *Bellerophon* and her sisters. We did not break our agreement, Shepherd. If there was an instruction we were not given, whose responsibility was *that*?"

The dangerous chittering accelerated.

"You *know* why we guard the technology of the Precursors," they snapped.

"Yes," she agreed. A long, long time ago, the Mesharom had had a relationship with the Precursors equivalent to the relationship humanity had with the A!Tol. Then the Precursors, in a grandly misguided attempt to make their ships more efficient, had built a device that had broken the laws of physics. All of their technology had failed...including the ubiquitous neural implants the Precursors and their thralls had used.

Annette had been sworn to secrecy on that and had kept her oath.

"I know why," she repeated. "And I gave our scientists enough information for them to know we could not rely on any of their tech to work as we had seen it. Since we had to rebuild from sensor data and base principles, I can guarantee you that none of our new technology is a close-enough match to theirs to risk the death of worlds or stars."

She was glaring at the Mesharom now.

"The research was in *my star system*, Adamase. How insane do you think I am?"

The chittering had slowed.

"You should not have done it," they told her.

"That is not your decision to make. It is not your directive to give. The A!Tol Imperium *must* guard our borders, must protect our citizens. The Laian and Wendira attack on Alpha Centauri only proved that we needed the strength to stand against the Core Powers. We are not your toys or your children."

Adamase was silent now.

"What you have done is sufficient for me to order the destruction of your research facility," they warned her after several long seconds. "Research into the Precursor technologies is forbidden. It is what the Frontier Fleet exists to stop."

"We didn't research Precursor technology," she pointed out. "We researched our *own* technology to see if we could duplicate effects the Precursors once commanded." Annette snorted. "We weren't successful on a lot of things. I know your ships have singularity cores, Shepherd, but we have not mastered that yet.

"And we now face an enemy who has. Did you see the latest report from *Bellerophon*?"

"I have," Adamase allowed.

"Can any of the Core Powers duplicate what these rogue Kanzi have done?" she asked.

"No."

The translated word hung in Annette's office like an anvil.

"Could the Precursors?"

"I don't know," Adamase admitted. "It is...possible that such might have been within their capabilities. It is possible that such a technology could still function after all they did...and, perhaps, be repairable by people who had studied Precursor tech."

"Wait." That rang a bell in Annette's mind. "Didn't the Kanzi fight a civil war? One where *you* provided the A!Tol a star killer to make sure one side was defeated... because they were studying Precursor tech?"

"Yes." Adamase considered. "That would...compute, Duchess Bond. But for your sake, I hope there is another answer."

"Why?"

"The Kanzi would *rule* all other races that match their image of God. The Taljzi planned to *exterminate* them."

"Would you let them?" she asked.

"Whoever these Unknowns are, they have destroyed a Frontier Fleet squadron and are clearly abusing Precursor technology," Adamase told her. "All that I can authorize has already been done. The First Triumvirate must now decide our final course."

"And what have you recommended?" Annette swallowed her fear. The First Triumvirate ruled the Mesharom, three individuals with the combined authority to commit the entire Core Fleet to war.

It had *never* happened. If the Mesharom went to war, the galaxy would change forever.

"For now, that we deploy limited elements of the Frontier and Core Fleets," Adamase explained. "We must know more of these strangers before we go further...but I have also recommended that we begin awakening the Reserve.

"If they are the Taljzi and they have the force to threaten the galaxy again, then aid and allies will not be enough. In the hands of the Taljzi, Precursor technology is an untold danger."

Every claw snapped shut on Adamase's legs with a single harsh snapping sound.

"We have not watched the galaxy dig itself out of the Precursors' ashes to watch it be burnt down by murderers. We *will* act."

"I WANT Fleet Lord Tanaka informed that the Mesharom are fully aware of just about everything we were hiding under the Dragon protocols," Annette told an emergency gathering of her Council later that evening.

"Shouldn't we run that by the Imperium?" Villeneuve asked. The gaunt old Admiral remained, as always, the voice of reason on her Council.

"We will *also* inform A!To, but I am not giving the Fleet Lord orders," Annette pointed out. "Using the Gold Dragon–tier technology aboard the *Bellerophon*s with her is at her discretion. This information simply changes what might qualify as 'her discretion.'"

"I agree. I just want to be sure we're not pissing off our superiors as well as the Mesharom," her old friend told her.

Annette chuckled.

"I believe we have accrued an account of sufficient depth with A!Shall to protect us from most issues there," she pointed out. She looked around at her Council.

"The Mesharom are more concerned about what Vong's people found aboard the stranger ship than with our own games around the Precursor ship," she told them. "I was hoping to buy us some grace with *Bellerophon* having partially avenged their ships, but it was easier than I expected."

"The cloning process we're postulating is crazy; I can see why the Mesharom think it's Precursor tech," the petite white-haired Asian woman at the far end of the table from Annette told them all.

Doctor Her Royal Highness An Sirkit was the Councilor for Health Affairs. The job had been unkind to her, and the Thai princess looked like she'd aged forty years in twenty. She'd also managed to get Imperial medical technology distributed to every part of the globe...a success generally credited with *keeping* An Sirkit merely a princess and not Queen of Thailand.

Her parents, after all, were far older than she was.

"Some of the Core Powers could, *maybe*, do some degree of mass-production cloning," she continued. "None of them have done so, because it's not a particularly efficient technology. No one has ever, in the literature we have access to, force-grown a clone to adulthood in five years."

"The closest thing I'm aware of is Wendira drones, who normally mature in about seven years."

"Without knowing what kind of technological platform they have access to, we don't know how powerful this enemy could be," Zhao said slowly. "Even from a small base population, that kind of technology would have allowed them to grow immensely. And we don't even know what they started with."

"Adamase has a suspicion," Annette told them. "He mentioned the Kanzi civil war and a name I'm not familiar with: the Taljzi."

"Minds of God," Leah Bond interjected. The Council had been called by hologram, but Annette's Heirs were there with their parents.

Everyone looked at the teenager, who flushed but continued at a gesture from Annette.

"Kanzi means 'faces of God,'" she explained. "Taljzi means 'minds of God.' They were a splinter sect of their core church, three hundred and some years ago. They managed to push a reform movement, similar in public impact to the Protestants in our own history."

"I'm guessing it didn't end as well," Zhao noted.

"They fought a civil war. At the same time the Taljzi picked a fight with the A!Tol. We decided we didn't want a genocidal army as neighbours and deployed a star killer at their core shipyard system, wrecking the balance of power and allowing the Kanzi to defeat the Taljzi."

Leah shivered. Unlike the rest of the Council, she had been born after the Annexation. Her use of "we" referring to the A!Tol Imperium didn't even sound off, even if it was something the older members of the Council probably wouldn't do.

"Anyone who wouldn't convert was killed," she said quietly. "Some must have fled, if Adamase is worried."

"Genocidal?" Sirkit asked.

"That's what Adamase said as well," Annette agreed. "That the Kanzi seek to conquer but the Taljzi seek to destroy."

The room was silent.

"What do we do?" Carol asked from beside her sister, her voice very small and very young.

"We prepare for war on a scale I hoped would never be seen in your lifetimes," Annette replied. "Elon, Villeneuve—how many single-portal HSM launchers do we have in Sol?"

"We have sixteen *Thunderstorm*-D–class cruisers, each carrying a single S-HSM battery. One portal, six launchers," Villeneuve said calmly. "All of our *Bellerophon*s are currently deployed forward. A resupply of S-HSMs is on its way to Asimov to meet with *Bellerophon*.

"We also have twenty-two automated defensive platforms based around the same S-HSM battery, scattered throughout the system," he continued. "We have approximately, I'd have to confirm the numbers, two thousand D-HSMs in our stockpiles. We don't have very many launchers for them, but most of our ships can strap a D-HSM or two to their hull, or we can simply launch them from deep space."

"That's it," Annette concluded. "Twenty-eight top-line weapons, two thousand second-rate missiles. The rest of our arsenal isn't meaningless, but the ability to shoot our enemies before they reach us is important."

She looked at Zhao.

"Zhao, how much money can we actually field if we need to?"

The massive Chinese treasurer grinned at her. Despite the grin, he looked exhausted. Annette realized she'd probably woken him from resting after one of his intermittent seizures and shook her head apologetically at him.

"We are a Duchy of the Imperium," he noted. "Which means that not only do we have access to our own resources, but we have access to the Imperium's resources. Not, perhaps, immediately—but sufficiently that no one is going to argue if I start borrowing money with a pledge of Imperial reimbursement.

"I'm not sure what you're thinking, Your Grace, but I guarantee you we'll run out of industrial capacity we can redirect before we run out of money to spend."

Annette laughed quietly and nodded.

"Thank you, Li Chin Zhao," she told him. "As always, you enable me."

"I enable what needs to be done," he replied. "You always seem to know what that should be."

"Elon." She turned to her husband. "I need you to get on the channels with Raging Waters and DragonWorks. Every empty slip, every construction yard we can throw together needs to have a *Bellerophon* keel laid in it by the end of tomorrow. How many can we start?"

He looked thoughtful.

"I think we have ten slips in the system that are empty right now," he admitted. "That doesn't sound like enough to me, so I'll get in touch with my people. We may be able to repurpose a number of the battleships under construction to be basically *Bellerophon*s, though they may look a bit odd.

"Some of those ships are on order to the Imperial Navy," he warned.

"Most of the ships we're about to build are going to *go* to the Imperial Navy," Annette replied. "If it's Imperial and we can recut it to become a *Bellerophon* or a *Thunderstorm*-D before completion, do it.

"From this moment forward, we do not lay a keel in this star system that is not going to carry tachyon sensors, hyperfold cannons and S-HSMs, people. We need to start mass production of those systems, because as much as possible, I want them retrofitted into every ship under construction—ours, the Imperium's, hell, even the ships for the other Duchies.

"*Nothing* leaves Sol that cannot fight these Taljzi—if that's who they are—toe to toe. We've been hiding our upgrades for a decade. That stops now. If an enemy is going to come at us from nowhere with Core Power–level tech, then I will do *everything* in my power to meet them with Core Power–level tech."

She smiled fiercely.

"A!Shall says humanity was one of the best things to ever happen to the A!Tol Imperium. Let's remind the galaxy why you do not *fuck with our friends*."

CHAPTER TWENTY-FOUR

PRESIDENT WASHINGTON WAS IN THE SECOND WAVE OF SUPER-battleships to enter the Avida System, which meant that Harold Rolfson already knew what was waiting for him when his flagship entered normal space in Kanzi territory.

It was a familiar darkness, every electromagnetic signal gone silent in death. He'd seen it in Powell and in Lelldorin. Now he saw it in Avida...and he really, *really* wanted a drink.

"My god," Ling Yu breathed. "The planet...it's *burning*."

Harold followed his ops officer's gaze and swallowed. Avidar, the sole habitable planet in the Avida System, had been a world of some five million souls, about half and half Kanzi and slaves. Intelligence said the world had been marginally habitable when the Kanzi had arrived, but the cataclysm that had destroyed much of the biosphere had also created deep layers of petroleum.

Avidar was effectively a planet-wide tar sand, and even a modern galactic economy had a billion and fifty uses for hydrocarbons. Most of those uses were far more valuable than merely *burning* the stuff, so Avidar had been about half mines and half refineries, producing vast quantities of plastics and other products for the Kanzi Theocracy.

Those mines and refineries were gone now. The planet itself had been bombarded hard enough to expose hydrocarbon layers across most of its surface...and then they'd been ignited.

Eventually, the fires would run out of oxygen. A habitable planet had a *lot* of oxygen though, and by the time the fires on Avidar died, the world would be permanently uninhabitable.

"That wasn't an accident," Harold pointed out as he studied the wreckage that had been a living, if unpleasant, world. "They targeted fracture lines and hydrocarbon deposits with intent. Someone came here to end a world and kill five million people."

He had more sympathy for the slaves than for the smurfs, but the world beneath him had been home to more people than any of the human colonies he'd seen burned to ashes. There was also at least the possibility of innocent Kanzi, he supposed.

"Link our sensors into the rest of the fleet's and keep everyone updated," he ordered. "Maybe someone will see something I don't, but it sure as hell doesn't look like the Kanzi fleet is here."

He shook his head.

"I guess the only real question is if they died here."

***

AVIDA HAD BEEN HOME to a massive amount of spaceborne heavy industry: asteroid mining facilities, orbital ore refineries, cloud-scoops, the works. The system hadn't been a major supplier to the Theocracy, but it had been wealthy enough to register on the government's radar.

That was all gone now. Every station, habitat and industrial plat-form was debris now, along with the civilian shipping that had served them. The backdrop of a burning planet made the mess harder to sort out, but Harold's people were good.

"There were two squadrons of escorts here," Ling Yu finally concluded. "Ten attack cruisers, ten destroyers. It doesn't look like they took any of the attackers with them."

"Any sign of where the attackers went?" Harold asked.

"Possible someone else in the fleet has sorted it out, but I can't," she admitted. "Give me a bit more time and I think I can pick out where the *Kanzi* went, but the only way we'll dig up the attackers is old light."

"The Kanzi may have already done that for us," he mused. "Tanaka's scheduled a briefing shortly. We'll see what the rest of the fleet has dug up. Do we have anything useful?"

His ops officer snorted.

"Nothing the rest of the fleet won't have passed up the chain already. There isn't much to see here, boss. Just another dead system—this one isn't ours, but that doesn't make it much less depressing."

Harold nodded. He'd seen the aftermath of enough Kanzi slave raids that his opinion of the blue-furred bastards ranged between disgusted contempt and utter hatred. Five million dead sentients, however, was a tragedy no matter who they were.

"We need to find these people," Harold said. "Find them and burn them to ashes."

"Sir!" Xun Huang's shout echoed through the flag bridge. "Warning signal from the outer system scouts—we have a hyper emergence!"

"Do we have an ID?" Harold snapped. "Is the tactical network up?"

"Not yet and yes," Xun Huang reported. "Nahid?"

The Chinese-Iranian ops officer was already linking in to her systems.

"The Rimward Squadron is ready for action; no orders from the flag," she reported.

"Hold off on Buckler drones for now, but bring all ships to battle stations," Harold ordered. "Best case, we need the practice. Worst case..."

Worst case, the strangers were back. That seemed unlikely—the most likely scenario was...

"We have an ID," Xun Huang barked. "It's *Dark Sun*, Division Lord Peeah's flagship."

SOMEHOW, Harold wasn't surprised when the all-captains briefing was accelerated after *Dark Sun*'s arrival. Within twenty minutes of the destroyer making contact, Fleet Lord Tanaka had pulled every ship commander and flag officer into a single massive holographic briefing.

Few of the people in the briefing were in rooms together. Most were in their own offices, but the software linked them all into a single massive virtual table, automatically focusing on whoever was speaking at the moment.

"As we speak, movement orders are already being sent to all of your navigation departments," Tanaka advised them all as the last PRESENT flicked on. "Division Lord Peeah has brought terrifying news: most importantly, units of his squadron have been shadowing Cawl's fleet since they left Avida, and there is no doubt as to his destination now:

"Fleet Master Cawl has violated Imperial space and is en route to the Xīn Táiwān System."

She grimaced.

"That is an act of war...but it's one that we are also guilty of. I hesitate to prejudge the Fleet Master's actions without more information. Nonetheless, we have no choice but to pursue. We have better charts of this region than he does, but that won't be enough for us to beat him to Xīn Táiwān.

"We will arrive within thirty-six hours of the Kanzi. Depending on what we find, I intend to give Cawl one opportunity to explain himself and find a peaceful resolution. If his explanation is unsatisfactory, we will engage the Alstroda Fleet."

"What about the strangers?" Harold asked before he could stop himself. That had...terrifying implications.

From Tanaka's expression, she understood them as well.

"The most likely scenario I can see is that the Kanzi are pursuing the strangers who attacked Avida, in which case the survival of the colony at Xīn Táiwān is very much in danger. We are already moving as fast as we can, and I have instructed Captain Vong to meet us there.

"*Bellerophon* is closer, so I hope that she can arrive before Cawl. Her qualitative advantage, however, is unlikely to suffice to engage an entire Kanzi battle fleet. Vong's orders are to observe and harass, and *not* to risk his ship."

"What if the colony is in danger?" Tidikat asked, the Laian officer clearly willing to state what the rest of the Militia officers—almost all humans—couldn't bring themselves to.

"His orders are not discretionary," Tanaka said in a stony voice. "If I thought, for even one second, that *Bellerophon* could save Xīn Táiwān from the Kanzi fleet, I wouldn't hesitate to risk Vong's ship.

"Against that kind of numerical advantage, however, even *Bellerophon* cannot carry the day, and I will not permit Vong to sacrifice his vessel...however much I understand the urge to do so.

"Whatever will happen in Xīn Táiwān is no longer in our ability to prevent. We must make certain that we are in position to *avenge* it."

No one had argued to leave a detachment behind to protect Xīn Táiwān. They'd been so confident they'd projected the enemy's course, and the strangers had left Imperial space. They'd thought the system was safe.

That certainty might have cost Governor MacChruim and his people their lives.

CHAPTER TWENTY-FIVE

THEY'D BARELY EVEN LEFT THE HYPERSPACE PORTAL INTO Asimov before Captain Vong ordered the engines cut. He disappeared into his briefing room, leaving Masters in command of the ship while Morgan and Antonova traded confused glances.

"Any idea what's going on?" Morgan asked the communications officer.

"*Something* came in on the hyperfold relay, maximum priority," Antonova replied. "Imperial encryption, Captain's-Eyes-Only."

The tall blonde shook her head.

"We'll find out soon enough, I suppose," she allowed. "Speaking of finding out, what's this I hear about you and Major Phelps?"

Morgan paused in astonishment.

"I don't know what you've heard," she admitted. Phelps and his blue eyes were definitely featuring in her thoughts of late, but he was hardly the only workplace crush Morgan was ignoring. Antonova's own grace and lithe athleticism were a more regular problem for Morgan, if only because she tended to share a shift with the senior communications officer.

"Rumor has it that you and the good Major have been making

googly eyes at each other at every opportunity," Antonova replied. "At least a few folks have put pieces together and figured you were making time off-duty."

Morgan chuckled.

"I don't recall making obvious 'googly eyes' at *anyone*," she replied. "Phelps is pretty, yes, but I haven't had much of a chance to get to know the man. Listening to rumors will get you in trouble, Lieutenant Commander."

The other woman chuckled.

"That they would. I mean, there are similar rumors about you and me!"

From the warmth in her ears and the way Antonova continued chuckling, Morgan was pretty sure she was blushing.

"Sorry, Morgan. I was just teasing," the coms officer told her. "We all know better than to chase crushes on a warship; there's only so many of us aboard. Phelps *is* dreamy, though."

"That he is," Morgan replied, latching onto a *mostly* safe observation. "You never know with Marines, though."

"Captain on deck!" one of the Marines at the back of the bridge suddenly barked as Captain Vong strode onto the bridge, a grim look on his face.

"At ease," he ordered before anyone finished rising. "Masters, I have the con."

"You have the con," the tactical officer agreed, crossing the bridge to his station between Morgan and Antonova.

The bridge was silent as everyone waited to see what the Captain had learned.

"Commander Hume, set a maximum-velocity course for Xīn Táiwān," he ordered quietly. "Use our sprint capacity as much as you can. We need to be there *yesterday*."

Somehow, the silence deepened.

"Commander Antonova, make contact with Rear Admiral Sun," he continued. "He is supposed to have deployed several units in that direction already. We'll need their planned courses to make sure we catch up if we can. They *should* be his *Thunderstorm*-Ds, so we'll be trailing them, but every extra launcher is going to count."

He smiled sadly.

"Get me an all-hands channel first, Victoria," Vong ordered. "Everyone needs to know what's going on."

Morgan swallowed, watching in silence as her friend gave the Captain a thumbs-up.

"All hands, all hands, this is the Captain speaking," Vong said calmly. He easily projected his voice across the bridge, and Morgan knew the internal communications system would carry it to the rest of the ship.

"We have an update from Fleet Lord Tanaka. She has entered Kanzi space to challenge the maneuvers of their Alstroda Fleet.

"Unfortunately, she has not found the Alstroda Fleet and has instead found dead worlds and shattered space infrastructure, all too familiar to Seventy-Seventh Fleet now," Vong told them grimly.

Morgan couldn't help swearing under her breath, and she wasn't the only one. A wrecked Kanzi world changed the nature of the game...a lot.

"Seventy-Seventh Fleet has also confirmed that Alstroda Fleet left Kanzi space several days ago, heading for the Xīn Táiwān System. We and the cruiser echelon that Admiral Sun deployed are the only ships that can potentially beat them there, so that is what we are going to do."

The silence that spread through the ship now contained a frozen chill.

"The Fleet Lord suspects that the Kanzi are pursuing the same people who attacked Powell and Lelldorin, and the Xīn Táiwān System may be in danger. My orders are clear: I am not to risk *Bellerophon* in an unwinnable contest with an entire Kanzi battle fleet.

"If, however, I regard *Bellerophon*'s intervention...indeed, *Bellerophon*'s *sacrifice* as having the potential to save the fifty thousand civilians in that star system, I do not intend to obey those orders.

"We are already underway. Depending on the fates, we may either beat Fleet Master Cawl to Xīn Táiwān or we may arrive shortly after him. No matter, we will do our duty."

BY THE TIME they reentered hyperspace, Morgan was done with her bridge shift and back in her office. It was hard to focus on the minutiae of her job with the Captain's words hanging over her head, but she tried.

The email chain between her, Masters and about seven of the engineering officers over whether they'd be able to fabricate single-portal hyperspace missiles aboard *Bellerophon* kept dragging on. She'd already accepted the reality: they could make everything except the hyperdrives in their onboard machine shops, and the only real impediment to the hyperdrives was a lack of exotic matter.

The *engineers*, on the other hand, were still trying to brainstorm a solution. Morgan had already added a note to her file of "recommendations for the next generation of *Bellerophon*s" to "include an exotic matter allowance in supplies."

Being able to replace their own munitions was handy. It wasn't essential, not when the Militia was never supposed to operate far from their bases and the Imperial Navy rarely deployed battleships without a fleet train, but it was useful.

Skimming through the details of the engineers' suggestions had her blinking against exhaustion when her door buzzer sounded.

"Enter," she said instantly. Any distraction was worth it right now!

She was surprised, however, to see Major Alexander Phelps step into her office. He wore an informal gray uniform and gave her a swift salute and a smile.

"How may I help you, Major?" she asked.

"I'm off duty," he replied. "This isn't actually a business visit. I can come back later if this is a bad time?"

Morgan sighed. Victoria Antonova, it seemed, wasn't the only one listening to rumors. She wasn't entirely sure how she felt about this.

"Now's as good a time as any, I suppose," she allowed. "What's up, Major?"

"Please, call me Alexander," he asked. "I was...wondering if you would be willing to join me for dinner in the officer's mess."

She considered, then gestured him to a seat.

"You realize that mixing work and emotions is a bad idea, yes?" she asked.

"Yup," he agreed cheerfully. "On the other hand, I heard the Captain's speech. Sounds like I might not get another chance—and it's not like we're in each other's chains of command."

"Even putting aside who my parents are," Morgan said, "this would *still* be a bad idea. And even if it wasn't..." She sighed and shook her head. If Antonova had presented this scenario to her, she'd have figured she'd leap at it, but the reality was different.

"I got dumped by email when I reported aboard *Bellerophon*, Alexander," she told him. "Trying not to let that get to me, but I don't think I'm ready to walk that particular path again just yet. You're a sweet man, you probably *are* my type...but it's the wrong time.

"Even if we may not get another chance," she conceded with a grin. "It's not you, Alexander; it's me."

He chuckled, but there was a bitter undertone to it.

"I think we've all heard that before," he said, slowly rising. "I won't take up more of your time, Lieutenant Commander."

"Alexander..." She stopped him with a gesture. "I'm saying no *today*. Not no forever, understand?

"So, I have to insist: please, call me Morgan."

CHAPTER TWENTY-SIX

IN NORMAL PRACTICE, *JUSTIFIED*'S SHIP'S DAY RAN, LIKE ANY flagship, on "the Admiral is up." Or the Fleet Lord, in this case.

Since Harriet Tanaka was suffering from an ugly round of insomnia, however, she was staying inside her quarters during what would normally be ship's night. She had an office there, and so long as she was only reading emails and reports, not sending them, no one would know the Fleet Lord was up.

Well, no one except her long-suffering Tosumi steward, who calmly delivered a pot of green tea to her elbow with a silent flutter of yellow feathers and vestigial wings.

"Thank you, Ortal," she told the alien. "I'll be up for a bit, but you don't need to watch me."

"The claws of my tasking say differently," Ortal on Varas replied with a cluck of her beak.

"Go rest, please," Harriet said with a smile. "I'm fine, just having trouble sleeping."

"The tea won't help," on Varas pointed out, and Harriet chuckled.

"I know. I'm giving up for now; allow an old woman her vices."

On Varas clucked disapprovingly—with the new medical sciences, Harriet probably had well over two centuries left in front of her, so "old woman" was a poor descriptor—but disappeared out of the Fleet Lord's quarters.

"Ask me for anything but time," Harriet murmured once she was alone. The wallscreens in her office showed the table of organization of her fleet, ship by ship, on one side and the astrographic charts around Xīn Táiwān on the other.

She had no way of knowing when *Bellerophon* had received her orders. The hyperfold communicators' inability to talk to ships in hyperspace was a major obstacle. It was far too easy to get used to near-instant communication across any distance and then lose it when they needed to travel.

If Xīn Táiwān had a hyperfold communicator, she'd have known more when she left Avida. She'd have been able to order an evacuation.

The communicators remained a government and military exclusive, however, and even the civilian ships there couldn't have received her messages.

It wasn't even like she had a decent ETA to the threatened system. Her fleet was following a current, a denser portion of hyperspace, that the Kanzi didn't know about. That would let her arrive sooner than the Kanzi could guess...but it still didn't let her predict her arrival with accuracy.

Hyperspace didn't *work* that way. It wasn't a consistent, easily calculated thing. The trip from Earth to Centauri was usually only a day or two...but could occasionally be a week. The trip from Earth to A!To was somewhere between four and seven months.

The Mesharom and other Core Powers had some tricks that DragonWorks had failed to duplicate. According to what the Mesharom had told the Duchess and *Bellerophon*, it would only take them a bit over four months, two-thirds of a long-cycle, to move a Core Fleet formation from Mesharom territory to Asimov.

Right now, Harriet Tanaka would have voluntarily sacrificed a limb to be able to move her fleet that fast. The decision to abandon Xīn Táiwān had been hers...and despite the front she'd put on for her people, she was grimly certain that Cawl was chasing the enemy.

Which meant that it was entirely possible fifty thousand people had already died for her mistakes.

CHAPTER TWENTY-SEVEN

THERE WAS A DEATHLY SILENCE ON *BELLEROPHON*'S BRIDGE AS the seconds ticked down. Every hand on the battleship was at general quarters, every weapon system armed, every sensor prepared to seek out the secrets of the system.

There was no holding back. Captain Vong had already ordered Morgan to use the tachyon scanners to get the most up-to-date information. Given that they knew Coraniss had reported everything they'd seen to their superiors, there was no point in holding back now.

Especially not if fifty thousand lives were in the balance.

"Emergence in sixty seconds," Hume reported. "Our escorts confirm formation and emergence time."

According to the reports Morgan had seen, *Bellerophon* wasn't going to be able to use her sprint capacity again anytime soon. Her engineering section was going to have to rebuild the wrecked capacitors that had fed that system from scratch.

But they'd caught up to the echelon of *Thunderstorm*-D–class cruisers Rear Admiral Sun had sent on ahead, which tripled the number of S-HSM batteries at their disposal. Twelve launch portals and seventy-two hyperspace missile launchers weren't much, but Morgan suspected they'd be enough to give the Kanzi a bad day.

"Forming hyper portal. *Shadow* and *Fallout* are leading the way."

The eight cruisers accompanying *Bellerophon* were the most modern ships in the Militia's arsenal and a quarter of the vessels of their class in existence. They had sacrificed the earlier *Thunderstorms*' proton beams entirely and given up a third of their conventional missile armament to squeeze in sixteen hyperfold cannons, an upgraded plasma lance, and the S-HSM battery.

Unlike *Bellerophon*, they'd done it with conventional fusion and antimatter power cores, too.

"Emergence."

The single word hung in the bridge like a suspended anvil as Morgan set to work. Tachyon emitters came to life, pulsing their impossible progeny across the star system. Receptors for a thousand mundane and exotic particles across her ship's hull drank deeply of the detritus of a star.

They found only silence, and Morgan felt a heavy weight settle in her chest.

"We're alone," she reported aloud. "No Kanzi ships. No...civilian shipping. No station." She swallowed. "No power signatures from the planet. Xīn Táiwān is dark."

The silence seemed to consume the entire bridge, reaching around to eat people's voices and thoughts as awareness of Morgan's report rippled outwards.

"Did we..." Vong coughed, swallowing to clear his throat then continuing in a more level voice. "Did we beat the Kanzi here? Or..."

"All calculations suggest they shouldn't have made it yet, and I'm not picking up anything to suggest a major presence of un-stealthed ships," Morgan said slowly. "I think...I think this was our strangers again. Attack from stealth, blow up...everything."

No defenders. Nothing had been stationed there yet, and both the Imperial Navy and Morgan's own Militia had decided the system was safe.

They'd been wrong.

"Get drones into space," Vong finally ordered. "Sweep every square centimeter of this star system. If there is *anyone* out there—survivors, stealthed enemies, *anyone*—we need to know."

He shook his head.

"Then get us into orbit. The Kanzi are still coming, and I have every intention of asking just what the *hell* they think they're doing when they get here."

MORGAN DREW the short straw of the watch-qualified officers and remained on the bridge as *Bellerophon*'s crew slowly stood down from battle stations and settled into orbit of Xīn Táiwān. The cruisers were sweeping the rest of the system, but it wasn't like there'd been that much industry to start.

If there was any positive to the whole mess, it was that the colony had been small enough that the kinetic bombardment didn't look to have set off a nuclear winter. It was a small blessing, given that the single settlement and its surrounding farms had been blasted into a giant crater.

Morgan hadn't visited the planet before this, but she knew Seventy-Seventh Fleet had. She wasn't looking forward to the Fleet returning—the survivor's guilt this was going to engender would be brutal.

"*Bellerophon*, this is Shuttle Six."

Eight of the battleship's shuttles were flying a survey over the wrecked colony. Their search was probably futile, but none of *Bellerophon*'s crew could leave without at least searching.

"Six, this is *Bellerophon*," Morgan confirmed. "What do you need?"

"I got a blip on my scanners, but then it went dark," the pilot replied. "Might be nothing. *Might* be a stealthed power source."

"What kind of power source, Six?" she asked.

"Not a damn clue, sir." The pilot paused, then continued in a firmer tone. "Requesting aerospace drone deployment for a low-altitude survey. This is a messy set of mountains; I don't really want to take a shuttle in."

"But if there's a power source, there may be people," Morgan agreed, bringing up the sensor panel and checking her stock of the class VI autonomous multi-environment sensor drones. "I've got three AMESDs dropping now; switching them to your control for a close survey."

The robotic craft fell away from *Bellerophon*, letting gravity do most of the work of delivering them into the atmosphere before bringing up their drives and diving toward Shuttle Six.

"I've got them; I'll let you know what I find," the pilot promised.

"You're the only one who's found *anything*, Six," Morgan told her. "Good luck."

She watched the drone sweep for a minute or so, but it would easily take hours to search the mountain range above the Xīn Táiwān colony for people.

The battleship was the center point around which they were rotating their entire operation in the system. The cruisers were spiraling outward from the planet, with hyperfold com–equipped drones leading the way.

Morgan wasn't sure what Captain Vong had hoped to find, but she was the officer of the watch and the one responsible for those drones. At this point, she could basically program a sweep pattern in her sleep, but that would be somewhat irresponsible.

If anything strange happened, after all, she'd have to account for it and adjust the sweep pattern. Right now, she was just going over the data and ordering occasional post-processing checks for stealth ships.

They couldn't pierce a stealth field in anything resembling real time. What they could do was dedicate a significant portion of *Bellerophon*'s computing power to go over a five-minute section of sensor data looking for the oddities that would confirm a stealth field's presence.

It took about thirty minutes, and the area she could do it over was relatively small. She could run a full ninety-minute post-process on *all* of her sensor data—and she'd started doing just that sixty minutes before—but that data would be so out of date by the time it was done, it was almost useless.

"Huh. That's funny," she murmured to herself. There was *something* in the asteroid belt. It was almost too much to be a stealth-fielded ship, though it wasn't like they knew the full details of the stranger's stealth systems.

"PO Maki, can you redirect drones E-17 and K-9 towards two-thirty-two by one-sixty-five, thirty-two million klicks out?"

"On it," the noncom replied, his focus on his console as he got to work. "Huh. That's funny."

"That's what I said," Morgan said with a chuckle. "Now let's get past 'funny' and see just who our joker is, shall we?"

THEIR "JOKER" reacted to the drones before the drones were close enough to give Morgan any clear data on them. Interface-drive missiles erupted from the blip that Morgan was tracking, flashing toward the drones at point eight five cee.

"Tachyon scanners live," Kami reported. "We've got a clean look at the bugger. Looks like three to four megatons, Kanzi attack cruiser or A!Tol battlecruiser size."

Twice the size of the *Thunderstorm*-Ds but less than half the size of *Bellerophon* herself. A big escort, much bigger than the destroyers they'd seen the strangers using so far.

"Is she Kanzi?" Morgan asked.

"Not sure," Kami admitted. "Her interface drive is up; she is maneuvering for clear space. She's running, sir."

Morgan ran the numbers. The cruiser was already at point six cee and was at most two light-minutes from space where she could open a hyper portal. None of the Militia ships could range on her with interface drive missiles or even hyperfold cannons.

Bellerophon and four of the *Thunderstorm*s could range on her with the S-HSMs, but Morgan wasn't supposed to deploy those on her own authority. Captain Vong was asleep. She *might* be able to get approval before the enemy fled, but she couldn't rely on that.

She was the officer of the watch.

"Stealth field suggests the strangers," she said aloud. "Which means that this is one of the sons of bitches who've killed four worlds we know of. She is *not* getting away. Kami, vector in more drones, get her in tachyon range and give me live targeting data.

"On it!" the PO snapped.

Morgan sent an alert to the Captain's cabin, but it was almost an afterthought as she plugged into the codes to bring the Hotel batteries online. Twenty-four missile launchers and four contained hyperspace portals came online while Kami got her the targeting solution.

"Sixty seconds to hyper portal range," Kami reported. "We have live data."

"And we have launch," Morgan replied as she hit a command. The batteries pulsed, flinging their missiles into hyperspace, and she issued a shutdown command.

She wouldn't get a second salvo. The *Thunderstorm*s might get a round of their own in, depending on who was on their bridges, but she wouldn't. Even with the hyperspace missiles, it was a twenty-second flight time.

The stranger "knew" she was outside range of anything the Terrans possessed. She was running fast and straight toward open space...until she seemed to run into a wall in space.

Half of Morgan's missiles missed, their twenty-gigaton warheads lighting up tiny suns around the enemy ship. At this kind of range, even live targeting data at launch couldn't guarantee a hit.

Eight bracketed the enemy ship, dumping massive quantities of energy into her shields and shattering her forward momentum. Those eight might have been enough, the ship writhing in the antimatter explosions.

It didn't matter if they were. The last four missiles emerged *inside* the stranger's shields, one of them literally inside the ship itself. When those explosions faded, there was nothing left of the running cruiser.

"Compressed-matter armor doesn't help against that, I suppose," Morgan said quietly. "We won't be able to do that very often before the enemy learns better."

CHAPTER TWENTY-EIGHT

FIVE MINUTES LATER, CAPTAIN VONG ENTERED THE BRIDGE, and Morgan rose to salute her superior. Vong was in full uniform and walking at a leisurely pace. He'd clearly seen the situation resolved before he'd been able to react and had chosen to take his time getting to the bridge.

"Lieutenant Commander Casimir," he greeted her. "Report."

"We detected an anomaly in the asteroid belt, sir," she reported. "We vectored drones for confirmation, which were destroyed by missile fire revealing what appeared to be a stealthed heavy cruiser. Missile speeds and stealth field suggested one of the strangers, so I concluded we didn't want to allow them to escape.

"They were well beyond conventional weapon range, so I authorized the deployment of a salvo of single-portal hyperspace missiles. The target was destroyed."

Vong nodded and stepped up to the command seat.

"I have the con, Commander," he told her.

"You have the con." She rose, stepping away nervously as she waited to hear what Vong had to say.

"You are aware of the level of secrecy around the Gold Dragon systems," he said calmly. "While the fact that the Mesharom are now aware of our possession of those systems has increased our discretion, that discretion is explicitly given to *Captains*, not to assistant tactical officers, correct?"

"Yes, sir."

"So, you took it upon yourself to deploy weapons systems you were *not* authorized to fire. Why?"

"The enemy scout could have reported on our presence, the presence of the inbound Kanzi fleet, or the presence of Seventy-Seventh Fleet once they arrive," Morgan replied. "We also may have found survivors on the surface, and the cruiser may have been able to launch a long-range bombardment to threaten those survivors once revealed.

"The decision was mine and I take full responsibility for it," she concluded.

Vong chuckled.

"That it was, that you do, and so I will make sure is reflected in your record," he confirmed. "Probably under sections labeled things like 'takes appropriate initiative' and 'damn fine shot.' You made the right call, Casimir. I'd have done the same, but I wasn't here, so let the record show that I fully endorse your decision."

She exhaled a breath she hadn't realized she was holding.

"Now, from the sound of it, we need to get in touch with our shuttles again. Survivors?"

"SHUTTLE SIX, this is *Bellerophon*, what is your sweep status?" Morgan asked.

"We've got something, *Bellerophon*," the pilot replied. "AMESDs have located what looks like a concealed low-yield pebble-bed reactor buried *deep* in a cave. We never would have found it if they hadn't had to vent just as we were flying over.

"The drones have triangulated the actual reactor, but we've basically landed the damn things. If the goal was to be invisible from orbit, someone gets an A."

"Can you make contact, Lieutenant Pearson?" Vong asked, cutting into the channel. "If there's survivors down there, we need to know."

"Trying to localize an entrance now, but it looks like the mountains are a bit of a warren," the pilot admitted. "AMESDs are mapping with ground-penetrating radar. I think we're looking at a natural complex, but at least some prep work was done."

"How much prep work?" Morgan asked. "Are we talking Farmer Joe and his family or..."

"Sir, I'd hate to give false impressions...but I think that's the colony's backup power plant in there. We may be looking at an impromptu survival bunker for the whole settlement."

Morgan was silent and Vong shook his head at her.

"I think you understand me, Lieutenant, when I say we need to find that entrance ASAP," he told the pilot. "We'll get off your shoulder. Happy hunting."

"I don't think I've ever been happier to hunt for a needle in a haystack, sir!"

"YOUR PEOPLE GAVE us one hell of a heart attack when they parked that shuttle in the main entryway," Hymie MacChruim told the bridge crew of *Bellerophon* two hours later. "*Oy vey*, we thought the damn bastards had found us."

"Came out to meet us with a dozen hunting rifles," Lieutenant Jeff Pearson confirmed, standing next to the Governor. "Never seen a happier bunch of guys pointing guns at me."

"We'd buried the reserve plant back here since folk were nervous about a fission pile," MacChruim told them. "After everything we heard about Powell and then Lelldorin, well, I figured 'God helps those as help themselves' and started moving food and other supplies in.

"We had an evacuation plan, horses, cars, other things that couldn't be scanned from orbit. Soon as there was even a blip on the scanners, we got folk moving."

He shook his head.

"Not everyone listened," he said sadly. "But...some, Captain Vong. Some listened. We don't have food for long, maybe another couple of weeks...but I've got fifteen thousand souls in these caves."

"And they owe you their lives," the battleship Captain confirmed. "We're going to drop a chunk of our reserves of Universal Protein and medical supplies, as well as at least a couple of doctors. We'll make sure you're dug in for the long haul, but...for now, we're going to need to leave you in there."

MacChruim looked surprised but fatalistic.

"It's not over yet, is it?" he asked.

"No. There's a Kanzi fleet heading this way," Vong told him. "We beat them here by a day at most. I want you to take the supplies we're going to drop to you and pull your heads back into your hole.

"If the worst comes to worst, Fleet Lord Tanaka is only a day behind the Kanzi. She'll dig you out then."

Vong smiled grimly.

"You already saved yourselves, Governor. I'm going to make sure you *stay* saved."

CHAPTER TWENTY-NINE

THE ARRIVAL OF THE KANZI FLEET WAS A SPECTACLE LIKE Morgan had never seen. She hadn't been present for the Grand Fleet arriving in Alpha Centauri after the Incident there or for Tanaka bringing her fleet out of Jupiter. She hadn't been old enough to really pay attention or understand when the Imperial fleet arrived to annex Earth or later to relieve them from the Kanzi.

When the Alstroda Fleet arrived in Xīn Táiwān, however, not only was she present and paying attention, but she was one of those responsible for developing a countermeasure. She wasn't sure she saw one.

Twenty attack cruisers led the way, the three-megaton ships sweeping the system with their scanners as they looked for the enemy. A solid phalanx of ten super-battleships, a full Kanzi squadron, followed on their heels.

Twenty six-hundred-thousand-ton destroyers came next, spreading out at sixty percent of lightspeed to open up the fleet's sensor horizon as the rest of the capital ships began to come through.

The portal was wide enough that even the battleships and super-battleships were coming through five across. Another twenty super-battleships and then twenty battleships emerged, followed by twenty more attack cruisers and thirty standard cruisers.

Fifty capital ships was more than Tanaka had warned them to expect. The escorts alone would probably have been enough to take down *Bellerophon* and her single eight-ship echelon of cruisers.

There wouldn't have been much *left* of the Kanzi fleet, given the advantages of the Gold Dragon ships, but they'd have overwhelmed the Militia. The battleships and super-battleships wouldn't bleed as hard to take down the Militia ships, but it wouldn't go all their way, either.

"Kanzi fleet will enter hyper-missile range roughly a minute after they head our way," Morgan reported. "*Thunderstorm*s are returning to orbit at sprint velocities; we should have consolidated our forces inside five minutes."

"Thank you, Casimir," Vong replied. "What's our munition status on the S-HSMs?"

She checked the numbers.

"We have sixty-six missiles in each battery magazine, eleven per launcher. Just under sixteen hundred total," she reported. "The *Thunderstorm*s haven't fired off any of their HSMs, but they only had ten each to begin with. Forty-eight launchers, four hundred and eighty missiles there."

"And how many missiles do you think it would take to disable the Kanzi fleet?" the Captain asked.

So far, the Alstroda Fleet hadn't moved in-system. They were assembling their formations at their emergence point—and they'd emerged unusually far out.

"We'll have probes at twenty light-seconds to provide real-time tachyon scanning in just over three minutes," she noted. "Given that real-time data, I think we can probably guarantee the destruction of a battleship with a full salvo from *Bellerophon*'s batteries, and be reasonably confident in the destruction of the destroyers with a single battery salvo."

The cruisers she'd probably want to hit with twice that, either half of *Bellerophon*'s armament or two *Thunderstorms*—and the super-battleships would take twice the firepower of their lesser sisters. The numbers didn't look pleasant.

"At least three thousand hyper missiles," she concluded. "And that's assuming they made no attempt to adjust for the new threat environment. If we were lucky, we could probably destroy the super-battleships before they reached their weapon range of us."

At which point, the battleships and escorts would have a roughly ten-to-one advantage over *Bellerophon* and her escorts and would crush them. Thirty super-battleships for one battleship, however advanced, and a sparsely populated star system...that was a trade a lot of people would make.

"Well, then, I think we should make sure we have those drones in position," Vong told her. "But we will not commence firing until we've had a chance to communicate."

He smiled sadly.

"And let's give them the chance to do that first. Every second they delay is one less second we're waiting for Fleet Lord Tanaka."

TO MORGAN'S SURPRISE, the Kanzi stayed right where they were. The formation they took up was a defensive one, not an assault pattern. Some of the destroyers moved deeper into the Xīn Táiwān System, but they were clearly acting as drone tenders, allowing the Kanzi equivalent to her AMESDs to study the star system.

"We've got drones heading for us and the planet, sir," she reported as the Kanzi sweep continued. "We can take them out, but..."

She studied the drones. That didn't look right.

"But what, Lieutenant Commander?" Masters asked sharply.

"We can take them out *way* too easily. Their stealth systems have been turned off. The only way they could be more obviously asking permission would be if they, well, asked permission."

"I'd prefer it if they did," her boss noted. "Captain? That sounds like more of a command decision."

Vong snorted.

"Let them scan the planet. Blow anything that comes within a light-second of our ships."

"Yes, sir."

Even the Sword turrets were powerful enough to destroy the incoming drones. It took Morgan a few seconds to program the limit the Captain had set into their systems. A single Kanzi drone crossed that line and disappeared in a ball of fire.

Two more died before the robots picked up on the perimeter and followed their instructions, sweeping around the Terran ships to scan the world behind them.

"What are you thinking, Mr. Smurf?" Morgan murmured. "You know you can take us, so what game are you playing?"

"Captain!" Antonova turned in her chair, the coms officer looking surprised. "I have an incoming transmission from Fleet Master Cawl!"

"Well, that's unexpected," Vong replied. "Let's see what the blue bastard has to say. Put him through."

The Kanzi were far enough away that the transmission was a recording, probably sent as soon as their drones had reported in on the status of Xīn Táiwān.

Cawl, like most Kanzi, looked like a petite fourteen-year-old human with blue fur. In his case, the fur was some of the darkest Morgan had seen in pictures of his race, a navy blue so deep as to be almost purple.

His fur had once been a single solid color, also unusual among his race, but age had taken its toll. Streaks of a grayer blue were scattered through his fur, and the white splash of growth over a scar crossed his face and his right eye. The eye had been regrown since, but the scarring remained.

"Imperial Militia warship, I am Shairon Cawl, Fleet Master of the Kanzi Theocracy and commander of the Alstroda Fleet," he said calmly. "I apologize for my violation of your borders, but I arrive in the direct trail of the monsters responsible for the destruction of multiple systems and the deaths of millions.

"My scans show that they have brought their horror here and I offer my condolences for your losses. I am *not* here to threaten your worlds or your ships. If at all possible, I would speak with your local military commander directly.

"It seems that for the first time in some lifetimes, our two nations share an enemy. We both have a duty to act on that."

CHAPTER THIRTY

FLEET LORD HARRIET TANAKA PROBABLY SHOULDN'T HAVE BEEN in the first wave out of hyperspace. There were arguments both ways, but the Imperial Navy tended to prefer that its flag officers lead from the middle, not the front.

With a planet at risk because of her decisions, however, *Justified* led the way out of hyperspace with her entire squadron, followed almost immediately by Vice Admiral Tidikat's First Squadron.

The thirty-two *Vindication*-class super-battleships were the armored gauntlet at the heart of her fleet, and she entered the Xīn Táiwān System prepared to challenge any enemy.

What she found was entirely different.

"I have the Alstroda Fleet on scanners," Sier announced. "Four light-minutes away at eighty-five by thirty-six."

That was odd. That put them in almost perfect parallel with her fleet's emergence point and well away from any position where they could attack anyone. They might have been trying to ambush her, but that would imply more information than she hoped they had—and they'd got it wrong.

"Bring the Fleet around," Harriet ordered. "Defensive formations; super-battleships will cover the emergence of the fleet."

The Kanzi were out of weapons range right now, but the Imperial Fleet couldn't move the hyper portal. They could close the distance in minutes, well before she could finish deploying her fleet.

"Sir, they're in a defensive formation," Sier reported. "Other than basic in-place evasive maneuvers, they're not moving. They're...waiting?"

"Hyperfold transmission from *Bellerophon*! Captain Vong is requesting to speak to the Fleet Lord immediately."

"Put him through to my seat," Harriet ordered. Hopefully Vong had *something* resembling answers.

The Vietnamese Terran Militia officer looked surprisingly unstressed for having an entire enemy battle fleet in the star system. He didn't look *good*, he still looked exhausted and strained, but not nearly as bad as Harriet would have expected from someone who'd been under threat for at least twenty-four hours.

"Fleet Lord Tanaka, I must urge you *not* to engage the Kanzi fleet," he said quickly. "Fleet Master Cawl entered Xīn Táiwān in pursuit of the people who destroyed Avidar. He and I have had some limited discussions, but since I knew you were on your way, I wanted to leave any serious negotiations to you."

Vong shook his head.

"He didn't get here in time and neither did we," he admitted. "The strangers arrived and bombarded the colony. The locals, however, were smarter than any of us gave them credit for and had thrown together an improvised emergency bunker.

"Governor MacChruim didn't save everybody. But he got over a quarter of his people to safety, sir. That's better than we had any right to expect."

Harriet felt like she'd been punched in the stomach. *She* had been the one to withdraw her ships from Xīn Táiwān. MacChruim had reduced the impact of her mistake, saved thousands of lives that she'd condemned, but tens of thousands had still died because of her.

Their deaths were a drop in the bucket compared to what had been lost to these bastards so far, but they were *her* fault.

"It was," she finally allowed. "Have the Kanzi given you any trouble?"

"None at all," Vong said. "I was hoping to scare them off with a demonstration of the hyperspace missiles, but they haven't threatened us at all. Cawl wants to speak to you, since we share an enemy."

He grimaced.

"I'm not sure if the smurf knows more about these people than we do, but he seems just as determined to see them stopped. He's not talking about what the Kanzi have lost, but we *know* about Avidar, sir.

"That's a lot of dead. More than we've lost."

"We share an enemy, as you say, Captain," Harriet agreed thoughtfully. "I can't afford to *fight* Cawl, not if there's still a genocidal enemy fleet on the loose, so I may as well hear what he has to say."

She considered the situation.

"Do we know where the bastards went from here?" she asked.

"We didn't have the hulls to sweep for old light," Vong admitted. "Cawl *may* have; I'm not certain."

"Then I will need to speak to Division Lord Peeah before I speak to Cawl," Harriet concluded aloud. "Even a truce with the Kanzi won't help us if we can't find these murderers."

"FLEET MASTER SHAIRON CAWL, I am Fleet Lord Harriet Tanaka of the A!Tol Imperium," Harriet said calmly into the recorder. "Your presence in this system is arguably an act of war, but we both know we're far enough out on the edge of nowhere, the normal rules don't really apply.

"The same people that attacked your Avida System have attacked several A!Tol systems—and a Mesharom Frontier Fleet Squadron.

All evidence we have suggests that they are Kanzi, which makes your presence here something of a problem."

She smiled grimly.

"I have enough evidence to suggest that they are *not* Theocracy, however, which means I'm prepared to at least let you explain your presence here. If you know something about these attackers that I do not, I would appreciate the explanation.

"As things stand, I am prepared to tentatively extend a one-cycle truce to allow for this discussion. At the end of that cycle, if your fleet does not withdraw from A!Tol space, I will be forced to destroy you."

She settled back in her seat to see how the Kanzi replied. She had more capital ships than the Kanzi and a lot more super-battleships. That wasn't even taking into account the dual-portal hyperspace missiles all of her capital ships had stored in their shuttle bays, or the three battleships and sixteen cruisers carrying S-HSM launchers.

If she decided to fight the Kanzi, she had a decent chance of annihilating Cawl's entire fleet before he could even get into range of her. That would require her expending her entire long-range firepower, though, and she suspected she was going to *need* those hyperspace missiles when they caught up to the real enemy.

The Kanzi didn't have hyperfold communicators, so her message would take a while to wing its way over to the other fleet, and their response would take just as long to come back. She wasn't used to having to wait this long for messages anymore, but she was prepared to be patient.

It was better than killing people, even if those people were smurfs. There weren't many people in the Imperium with a lot of sympathy for the Kanzi.

"Incoming transmission, sir."

"Play it."

The Kanzi that appeared on Harriet's screen was probably the oldest individual of that race she'd ever seen, though Kanzi medicine was up to Imperial standards. That told her a lot about the injury that had claimed Cawl's eye at one point and left the scar behind. Even the eye was fixed, but it was hard to completely remove scars.

"Fleet Lord Tanaka, I appreciate your tolerance," he greeted her. The underlying sound of his voice under the translation was fascinating to Harriet, a series of purring meows that had a calming effect on her nerves. If she understood Kanzi as well as she thought she did, Cawl was *trying* to be conciliatory.

A good chunk of what humans portrayed in tone the Kanzi portrayed in different levels of, well, purring or hissing along with their speech. Cawl probably wasn't as calm as he was projecting, but he was at least trying to be friendly.

"You are correct both in that the creatures that have bombarded our worlds are *biologically* Kanzi," he allowed, "and that I know more of what we face than you do. I do not understand *how* these creatures exist in such numbers or have access to such firepower, but I know who they are.

"You mourn a pair of worlds and a few hundred thousand. I mourn a claw's worth and *millions*, Fleet Lord Tanaka. Our blood has been shed even more freely than yours, but I know my enemy now. If they have made themselves your enemy, that is not a blade I shall toss aside lightly.

"I would meet with you in person, Fleet Lord. Neither of us would be able or willing to meet aboard the other's flagship, but I *do* have several unarmed logistics ships with decent facilities for such a discussion."

He smiled. Like most Kanzi gestures, it was *very* human.

"I would, of course, gladly meet aboard one of your ships if that is your preference. I have little to hide in terms of technology or munitions, however, and I am not certain the same is true for you these cycles.

"I await your response, Fleet Lord."

He bowed and the message ended, leaving Harriet with even more questions than she'd started with.

"You can't seriously plan on agreeing to that, can you, sir?" Sier asked.

"I don't see a choice, Division Lord," she told her chief of staff. "I *am*, however, going to require that we meet on his unarmed ship, between our fleets...with an Imperial destroyer standing by, in case he gets clever."

CHAPTER THIRTY-ONE

HARRIET WAS MORE THAN A LITTLE SURPRISED BY THE readiness with which Cawl agreed to her terms. Within two hours of her return to the Xīn Táiwān System, she found herself approaching an unarmed Kanzi logistics ship aboard the destroyer *Impulsive*.

Regardless of what Cawl thought, *Impulsive* and her Rekiki crew weren't the biggest threat the Kanzi freighter faced. Vong and his cruiser escorts had now joined up with Seventy-Seventh Fleet, and they'd adjusted the screen to put all sixteen of the S-HSM armed *Thunderstorm*-Ds on this side of her fleet.

That single squadron of Militia cruisers could probably take on half of Cawl's fleet on their own. Punching out the single freighter wouldn't even register as a task.

"We are at the agreed distance, Fleet Lord," the Rekiki Captain Ikoto told her. The crocodilian centaur was of her species' noble caste, looming well over not only Harriet but also most of her Rekiki crew.

"Your shuttle awaits."

"Thank you, Ikoto," Harriet replied. "Are you ready if something goes wrong?"

"We're localizing her power plants now," Ikoto replied. "My Marines are standing by, in their power armor and locked into their shuttles. If the Kanzi wish to play, we will play."

"Let's hope this goes more smoothly than that," Harriet murmured, "but it's good to know you are standing by. Thank you for the ride."

"Always a pleasure."

More power-armored Marines fell in around Harriet as she left the bridge and headed for the boat bay. From the moment she'd put on a Captain's uniform in the Imperium's service, her bodyguards had been Tosumi.

Now, almost twenty years later, she understood just what message assigning guards from one of the Imperial Races to the newest Captain from the newest member species of the Imperium sent. The only stronger sign of support would have been to assign A!Tol guards—and *that* would have been favoritism.

"We've confirmed Cawl is aboard," her senior bodyguard told her as they reached the shuttle. "Are you sure this is safe, Fleet Lord?"

Harriet chuckled.

"No, Initiate," she told the Marine. "I don't think it's safe. But if we can make sure that both of our empires have their fleets pointed at the people *bombarding planets* instead of at each other, I think that's worth the risk."

"It comes with the job."

"You're the Fleet Lord. We will protect you."

Harriet nodded her understanding to her Marines and hummed thoughtfully to herself as she boarded the shuttle.

A meeting like this was almost unheard-of—but unheard-of actions tended to have unheard-of results.

THERE WAS an honor guard of Kanzi ground troops waiting for Harriet as she stepped off her shuttle. She'd never even been this close to Kanzi of any stripe before, and the almost-human blue-furred troopers set her on edge.

The guard was carefully chosen too. They were all within a couple of centimeters of each other's height, about a hundred and forty centimeters tall. They had slightly different facial patterns, but the rest of their fur was invisible beneath black ceramic body armor.

It wasn't power armor, but it would probably shed a plasma bolt or two. The twenty Kanzi troopers, however, had made the same concession to diplomacy as her four Tosumi power-armored guards: none of the troops were armed.

Shairon Cawl stood at the end of the line, and Harriet was surprised to realize the Kanzi couldn't stand unassisted. Even in his black leather uniform, the exoskeletal brace he wore around his right leg was clearly visible, and even with it, he was leaning on a silver-topped black metal cane.

Nonetheless, he came forward to meet her, his movements slow but smoothly practiced. Whatever had limited the old Fleet Master's mobility had happened long ago.

"Greetings, Fleet Lord Tanaka," he told her, offering a gloved hand. "It is an honor to meet one who has met the challenges of race and station as thoroughly as you have. May the Light of God shine upon us in our discussions today. We have much to speak of."

Harriet shook Cawl's hand, studying the Kanzi with careful eyes. He looked and acted like a kindly grandfather in two-thirds scale with blue fur, but she knew the reputation of the sentient across from her.

Cawl had earned a reputation as one of the Theocracy's better tacticians in several short and sharp wars with species that had discovered interstellar travel before the Kanzi found them. They hadn't been even fights, but Cawl had concluded them with a deadly efficiency that had probably saved lives on both sides.

He'd then solidified his reputation in a punitive campaign against one of the Kanzi Clans that had overstepped its boundaries. The Clans were only *semi*-independent—in many ways, the Duchy of

Terra had more independence than a Kanzi Clan—and one had pushed too far.

Shairon Cawl had commanded properly-escorted battleships where the Clan only had cruisers, but he'd had a tenth of their hulls and a fifth of their tonnage. He'd crushed them in sixty days, before his reinforcements even had a chance to arrive.

Somehow, that both did and didn't contradict the calmly confident little blue alien in front of her.

"It is in the interests of both of our masters to see those responsible for these atrocities taught the error of their ways," Harriet told him. "I would be doing less than my full duty were I not to hear what you have to say."

"That is His Light speaking, not your people's anger," Cawl replied. "Come, Fleet Lord. I have laid in refreshments that will be safe for both you and your Tosumi guards. There is no point in us having our discussions standing around in the shuttle bay, after all."

Harriet inclined her head in acceptance. She had very little enthusiasm for *anything* to do with the Kanzi version of a god, but there was no point in being rude.

CAWL LED the way deeper into the ship, dismissing his own guards while allowing Harriet's to accompany her. Despite his limp, cane and mechanical walking aid, he still managed to move surprisingly quickly.

She was still moderating her pace so as not to accidentally charge ahead of him and couldn't help studying him from the corner of her eye. For that level of disability, combined with the scarring on his face, he had been *very* badly injured at some point.

Eventually, he led her into a conference room of sufficient size to hold an organizational meeting for an entire convoy. It showed clear signs of being rapidly redecorated to a less-austere level than its original standard, with scuff marks on the floor where a table had been pulled out and a new one dragged in.

Whoever had done the redecorating job had done amazing work. The table was clearly undersized for the room, but it was a rich dark red wood unlike anything Harriet had ever seen before, with the stylized flame of the Kanzi Theocracy inlaid into it in gold and silver.

Blue hangings, with the same gold-and-silver flame stitched into them, had been hung around the room, and a sideboard of the same red wood had been added with a carafe of some dark blue liquid and multiple glasses.

Without asking, Harriet's Tosumi bodyguards pulled the hangings back to make sure there were no concealed assassins or doorways. Once that was confirmed, the birdlike aliens pulled back to the door.

"Your guards may remain if they wish," Cawl told her as he stumped over to the sideboard. "I have few secrets of my own at this stage in my life, and no secrets of my government's that I would unveil to you that I would not unveil to them."

Harriet snorted and gestured for the Marines to rest at ease. Cawl seemed likeable enough for a slaving, mass-murdering smurf, but she wasn't going to trust him, either.

"Please have a seat, Fleet Lord," he told her, offering her one of the glasses of blue liquid. "The drink is pila fruit juice. It is not an intoxicant and is safe for your race, though I suggest you check it with your scanners."

Her communicator contained a tiny sensor for exactly that purpose. Like the translator earbuds she was wearing, that kind of scanner was ubiquitous in galactic society.

The juice checked out, as did the small tray of cookies that the Fleet Master delivered to the table before taking his own seat. As a bonus, the scanner would also detect almost all poisons, so Harriet took a careful sip of the juice.

For the first time since learning the Kanzi Theocracy existed, Harriet truly regretted the tensions between them and the Imperium.

The flavor that danced across her tongue was softly sweet with notes she'd never tasted before. In the absence of the continuing cold war, it would have been one *hell* of an export, at least to humans.

Of course, it was also grown by slaves. She couldn't forget that.

"The niceties are all well and good, Fleet Master, but we are not here to make friends," Harriet told him. "What do you know about these attackers?"

Cawl's responding snort reminded her of nothing so much as a kitten's offended *mewp*.

"*You* may not be here to make friends, Fleet Lord Tanaka, but I feel it is my duty to provide a counterpoint to the rather harsh image of my species I know your people have acquired," he told her. "We have a thousand other reasons to be here, but His Light demands that I at least make the attempt."

She arched an eyebrow at him, wondering if he would catch the skeptical gesture, and he responding with a chuckling purr that was *very* clear in the emotions it conveyed.

"I will deny neither my people's reputation nor the actions that led to it," he said. "But remember that those you have met do not define all of my species, please."

He sighed.

"And I must beg of you not to judge us by this newest branch of my people you have encountered."

"The Taljzi," Harriet hazarded. That was the name the Mesharom had used. "Kanzi with ceremonial mutilations and brands, and a genocidal impulse towards everyone?"

Cawl blinked once. That was the extent to which he displayed his surprise, but it was enough for Harriet to pick up on it.

"The Taljzi," he agreed. "The 'minds of God.' I would have other names for them myself, but I cannot deny that is the name they gave themselves."

"Who are they?" Harriet demanded. "We know they were a faction in your civil war, but not much more than that."

"They are heretics," Cawl stated. "Understand me, Fleet Lord:

for all that our faith may seem a monolith from the outside, we tolerate many sects and differences of opinion within that structure. There are many disagreements of just what many of the commandments of God mean, and many arguments. There are reformers who would change how the Kanzi interact with each other, with other races, with the galaxy. These are tolerated, to a point.

"It is *difficult* to earn the title *heretic*," he concluded. "So, the Taljzi had gathered the governments of entire worlds, entire sectors, to their banner before they became so clearly lost that the High Priestess of the time proscribed them."

"And so you had a civil war," Harriet said.

"And so we fought them. And we fought the A!Tol. And the A!Tol gutted the Taljzi home systems...and we finished the job."

Cawl shook his head.

"From what you say, you have recovered bodies or video of them. We have little of the same, but enough to know who we face. They are the Taljzi and they have burned *five* of our worlds, Fleet Lord. Ten million dead.

"They have come from nothing to destroy everything...and I would have said this was impossible."

Harriet took a few moments to process what Cawl was telling her, quietly sipping the fruit juice as she marshaled her thoughts. If the Kanzi had lost five worlds, their neat line through space hadn't covered everything. They already knew there'd been two fleets— destruction of more Kanzi systems suggested a third.

How many ships and soldiers did these people *have*?

"You understand, Fleet Master, that it is obviously not impossible," she finally said. "Clearly, they have set up a new territory somewhere beyond both of our Rimward borders and have now decided it is time to strike back."

"That is clear, yes," he agreed. "And yet..." He sighed. "Let me show you something, Fleet Lord."

He placed a small holographic projector on the table and tapped a command. The image of a Kanzi with pale blue fur appeared above the screen. Scars had been burnt into her face and breasts, swirling patterns that were wide enough that the fur had never regrown, and she wore only a black leather kilt and a harness with a steel dagger pinned to her left shoulder.

"I took the liberty of translating the recording, as the dialect she is speaking is both archaic and not one the Imperium would be familiar with," Cawl noted. "I will provide you the original so you can validate it.

"This was transmitted to every ship and city in the Kanda System. One ship, a fast courier vessel, managed to escape." He grimaced. "I suspect, now, that she was *permitted* to escape."

The recording started.

"I am the First Return of the Mind of God," the Kanzi said harshly. "You who cast us out and denied the will of the divine have now been judged. The unending legions of the holy will drive you from the worlds and stars you have falsely claimed, and you will share the fate of the false children.

"We bring you the divine will of the Mind of God. Kneel and you will die quickly. Challenge His will and you will die painfully."

She smiled, baring canines that had clearly been sharpened.

"Please, challenge Him. I will *enjoy* instructing your worlds with fire."

The image froze.

"That was it," Cawl told her, his voice edged with a hiss under the translated speech. "That is *all* that our lost kin said to us before they started bombarding worlds and murdering innocents."

"That doesn't leave much interpretation, does it?" Harriet asked. "Am I to presume that the 'false children' are..."

This time, Cawl *definitely* hissed. It was a wordless expression of anger and disgust.

"What my High Priestess would call 'lesser children,' yes," he confirmed carefully after a moment to regain his composure. "Non-Kanzi who bear the form of the divine. Like yourself."

What his *High Priestess* would call lesser children? Harriet noted the evasion and wondered just what the being she was sharing drinks with would call her. Now was not the time for that question.

"So, if they are here, why do you say this is impossible?" she finally asked.

"Because the proscription was complete," he replied. There was a low growling hiss underlying his words. "Those who did not forswear their heresy and accept sterilization were put to the sword and the flame. Our Church does not proclaim heresy lightly...and applies the full penalties allowed to Her Holiness even more rarely."

"You killed them all."

Harriet's words hung in the conference room for a long time before Cawl bowed his head.

"Yes. It was before my time, but I had ancestors who served in those fleets," he told her. "I will claim no innocence. My own campaigns against our rebels in this time have been informed by that war—the sooner I ended the conflicts, the safer those who challenged His Will were from that level of retribution."

"Clearly, some escaped," Harriet pointed out after the silence grew unbearable.

"We have gone over all of our files and we believe we have identified the group that escaped," Cawl told her. "But it makes no sense. Perhaps as many as ten ships, at *most* twenty thousand Taljzi, escaped the proscription. I would accept that they survived, that they founded a colony...but to field fleets of battleships with more advanced technology than the Theocracy after a mere few hundred orbits?"

He shook his head.

"It makes no sense."

"It also isn't important," Harriet pointed out. She was beginning to have an idea of what had happened now, but she wasn't going to tell Cawl about the clones and the evidence of some kind of Precursor facility in Taljzi hands.

"No," he agreed. "I know where their fleet went from here, Fleet

Lord Tanaka. They will not find their next destination defenseless... but I fear that Fleet Master Oska may fail and Alstroda will fall."

"Shouldn't you be there, then?" Harriet asked.

Cawl grimaced.

"I can't make it in time," he confessed. "They lured me out of position, but Oska should have arrived at Alstroda with four more squadrons of capital ships before they get there. I cannot warn her, though, and I fear for my people."

"What do you want, Fleet Master?" Harriet asked.

"I have a limited ability to communicate with Her Holiness," he pointed out. "I have broad authority to negotiate on behalf of the Theocracy. I wish to negotiate a temporary pact of nonaggression and agreement of mutual support against the Taljzi.

"I do not know how they grew their strength or where they hide, but I fear this is only the *First* Return and that more fleets are coming. My nation cannot stand against them while yours sharpens its knife against our back."

"I can't negotiate that," Harriet replied. It wasn't entirely true, but there were limits.

"Yes, you can," he said with another chuckling purr. "You can't sign a final agreement, but you and I can agree on at least the principle of nonaggression until we fully understand the threat."

"There are concessions my government will demand for that," she warned him.

"I know," Cawl agreed. "That is above my level. It is my duty to make sure my nation can fight this war."

"I have to consult with my superiors," Harriet told him. The Kanzi had to be aware that she could do so, so it wasn't like she was giving up any great secrets. She smiled grimly as she thought that.

"What I *can* do, right now, is use one of my destroyers that is scouting Alstroda to warn this...Fleet Master Oska, was it?" she continued. Somehow, she wasn't worried about admitting to the violation of Kanzi borders with a scouting flotilla while Cawl had an entire *battle fleet* in Imperial space.

CHAPTER THIRTY-TWO

MORGAN WATCHED ON THE SCREEN AS *BELLEROPHON* SLID INTO formation with her sister ships. *Herakles* and *Perseus* were barely out of the yards, and she wouldn't have been surprised to find that they still had work crews aboard.

From what she understood of their orders, Vice Admiral Rolfson was concentrating their S-HSM armed ships into a single formation. A full squadron of *Thunderstorm*-Ds had taken up formation around the three battleships.

Unless Morgan was badly off on her estimates, that meant Seventy-Seventh Fleet had every S-HSM armed capital ship in existence and half of the escorts. That was assuming that no one else had an equivalent weapon, but the Mesharom's response suggested that was unlikely.

The weirdest part to the whole situation, though, rested roughly three hundred thousand kilometers to *Bellerophon*'s starboard flank. That was where the *Kanzi* formation began, with their own neat ranks of starships.

This was the closest she'd ever been to a Kanzi ship of any kind, and she studied the vessels with fascination. The Kanzi went for a blocky inverse U-shape as their base hull, spreading their defensive weapons apart much as the A!Tol did but without the fragile—and hard-to-armor—swooping nacelles humanity's overlords went in for.

It ended up with a cruder-looking ship, but Morgan wasn't inclined to be fooled. The Kanzi didn't have hyperfold communicators, hyperfold cannons, or hyperspace missiles—but they'd rolled out their own active laser-defense systems, a new generation of shields, and even faster missiles over the last fifteen years.

Intelligence suggested that the Kanzi were definitely behind the curve versus the Imperium, but they were determinedly advancing their tech to close the gap. The Kanzi battleships nearby were no equal to *Bellerophon*, but the super-battleships could probably give her a run for her money.

Assuming, of course, that they knew all of the new ship's tricks.

Morgan smiled coldly. The first Kanzi super-battleship to tangle with her baby was not going to know those tricks—and was going to have a *very* bad day.

"LIEUTENANT COMMANDER CASIMIR, a moment of your time, please?"

It was never a good sign, however confident you were in your recent work, when the Captain asked for a moment of your time. Morgan swallowed and looked up at Captain Vong with a forced cheery smile.

"Of course, sir. How can I help you?"

"Step into my office with me, please."

Hiding another nervous swallow, Morgan followed Captain Vong into his office. His wallscreens showed much the same data as she'd been viewing on her own console, with rows upon rows of Terran, A!Tol and Kanzi warships.

"Mind-boggling, isn't it?" he asked quietly. "Commander

Casimir, I wanted to get a feel for how the younger officers feel about this situation."

"Sir?" she blinked confusedly. "I'm not sure what you mean."

Vong sighed.

"Commander, I fought the Kanzi," he reminded her. "I held the role you do now when a Kanzi fleet tried to assault Earth, and I saw a lot of my friends die aboard warships pressed into action against an enemy we knew wanted to enslave us.

"I had friends who were caught up in the kidnappings on Earth that were intended to be sold to the Kanzi, too." He shook his head. "Duchess Bond saved them from that. That's why I volunteered for the Militia the day it was announced."

"I'm still not sure I understand, sir," Morgan said carefully.

"Morgan, every officer in this Militia—hell, in the Imperial Navy, too—has been trained and prepared for war with the Kanzi. The older officers, however, like myself—like Vice Admirals Rolfson and Tidikat—we've *fought* the Kanzi. I was at Asimov when the Clans showed up to try and take slaves and ran into our battle squadron."

He shook his head again.

"The smurfs are slavers, murderers and *scum*—and even the fact that these Taljzi have burned millions of them doesn't exactly make me weep for them. I don't hate them, not really, but the thought of working with them makes my skin crawl."

"And you want to know if the officers who *haven't* fought them feel that way?" Morgan asked carefully.

"Yes," he confirmed. "This...alliance, or whatever it ends up being, may decide whether or not our remaining colonies out here survive. I won't—I *can't*—let my own prejudices get in the way of that."

"To us, sir, the Kanzi are the bogeyman," Morgan said slowly. "We've trained to fight them, we've seen video of their slave raids, but it's not personal to the younger crew the way it is for the senior people.

"We can work with them. Hell, we can honestly mourn their

dead—no one deserves what the Taljzi have done to these worlds. I don't know if that's what you want to hear..."

"It is," Vong said with a sharp intake of breath. "I need to know, Commander Casimir, that my subordinates are *not* blinded by prejudice. There's going to be enough of that in my colleagues...and in my mirror."

"We'll try to yank you up short politely if it looks like you're going off the deep end, sir," Morgan promised.

The Captain chuckled.

"God willing, it will never come to that. I just don't trust these people as far as I can throw *Bellerophon*."

CHAPTER THIRTY-THREE

"You have *got* to be kidding me."

Annette let her words hang in her living room. This wasn't even a meeting of the kitchen-cabinet portion of her Council. This was Li Chin Zhao, an old friend, visiting her at home while she and Elon dealt with a sick eight-year-old.

Alexis Bond had had every immune booster vaccine, nanotechnology, and medical science the galaxy could offer. She was still an eight-year-old child attending a school full of other eight-year-old children, a situation generously referred to as a plague breeding pit.

And even the A!Tol Imperium hadn't managed to come up with a vaccine that covered every strain of the common cold. Alexis had worn her nose red with sneezing and tissues, and while her caretaker had been with the family since before Annette had married Elon, sometimes a little girl just needed her parents.

"I'm not," Zhao insisted, passing a box of tissues over to Annette. "Fleet Master Cawl has the authority to commit the Theocracy to at least some of that. Anything he promises is preliminary until verified by actual plenipotentiaries at one of the capitals, but his word *does* bind the High Priestess."

"A nonaggression pact and potential alliance," Annette considered. "With slavers."

A hand half-consciously traced the thin line across her face. She'd lost an eye to a slaver once, and her crew had been short enough on regen matrix that scarring had been unavoidable by the time they'd fixed her up.

She'd seen Kanzi try and conquer her world. She'd seen Kanzi kidnap and attempt to rape her crew. She *knew*, despite everything she and the Imperium had done, that there were human slaves in the Theocracy now.

"I think Cawl knows what the price of admission is," Zhao reminded her. "The Imperium has always been clear: we will *not* negotiate anything with the Theocracy while any sentient from a member race of the Imperium is a slave in Kanzi space.

"To even start talks beyond this preliminary promise of nonaggression will require them to free tens of thousands of our people. I don't know if the High Priestess will go for it...but that alone might be worth it, Annette."

Alexis sneezed and her nanny swept in with a damp cloth to clean her face—and the Duchess of Terra's suit.

"They're terrified," Annette finally said as Alexis's sneezes dissolved into soft crying on her mother's shoulder. "These Taljzi... they really have the Kanzi scared."

"Cawl is afraid, yes. And one of their best tacticians," Zhao agreed carefully. "I think he knows his enemies."

Annette didn't miss the plural. She stroked the tiny blond head resting against her as she met her treasurer's gaze.

"What are you implying?"

"Our files say Cawl is an Emancipator," Elon said bluntly, dropping onto the couch next to her and offering Alexis a cup of steaming tea. "Or at least a sympathizer. Part of that branch of their religion, if not actually part of the movement itself."

"You two think he's using this as a lever against his own nation?" she asked. "My read of his file says he's loyal."

"He is. He won't betray the Theocracy...but he may try and lever some reformations into it," her consort told her. "It's up to you, my love."

"It's A!Shall's decision," she pointed out.

Elon shook his head as he gently extricated Alexis from Annette, coaxing her into his lap to take a sip of the tea.

"You know damn well she'll listen to you if you have an opinion, especially if you speak in favor of it," he pointed out.

Annette sighed. He wasn't wrong. And she couldn't turn down the chance to make sure they didn't accidentally stab each other in the back while facing an unknown enemy.

"I'll talk to her," she concluded. "You can watch Alexis?"

Her husband chuckled. "That's part of the job description included in *daddy*, I believe. Go, my love. Find out what new surprises the galaxy has in store."

WITH HER OFFICE locked down once again, Annette connected into the starcom and made the request to speak to A!Shall. It seemed that she was on a high-priority list, as the Empress was on the line within a minute.

"Dan!Annette," A!Shall greeted her. "You have news."

It wasn't a question.

"I do. Thirty hours ago, Fleet Lord Tanaka made contact with the Alstroda Fleet under the command of Fleet Master Cawl. They did not engage each other, and Fleet Master Cawl has offered a temporary nonaggression agreement to allow us both to focus on the Taljzi."

There was a flash of color across the Empress's controlled gray skin, over so quickly Annette didn't catch the hue.

"That is quite the offer," she concluded. "Does Tanaka trust him?"

Annette chuckled.

"I don't think many of our military officers would trust a Kanzi

Fleet Master, no matter what," she pointed out. "Tanaka believes he is serious, though, and concerned about the return of the Taljzi.

"Our attackers apparently had at least two, potentially three fleets moving through our space and Kanzi space. They have communicated with the Kanzi, which is more than they've done with us or the Mesharom, but the Kanzi don't know about the cloning factor."

Annette grimaced. The concept of mass-producing soldiers made her skin itch.

"So, they have no idea how a handful of fleeing ships turned into an attacking armada. They may still be underestimating their old enemy."

"I am not," A!Shall said grimly. "Are we certain of this, though? This could all be a trick."

"The Mesharom told us the same story," Annette reminded her Empress. "The evidence pulled from the ships *Bellerophon* engaged also support it. We have data suggesting the Kanzi are moving their fleets—and the fact that the Emancipators aren't updating us on those movements suggests that *they* believe there is a real threat to their people."

"I've heard nothing from Arjzi," the Empress noted. "The High Priestess and her ambassadors are being very quiet these days. It worries me."

"I think they're terrified, Your Majesty. The Taljzi want to exterminate them." Annette shivered. "Unless I'm misunderstanding both the information Cawl provided and my conversation with Adamase, the Taljzi want to exterminate *everyone* who isn't Kanzi—potentially even all of the non-Taljzi Kanzi, at this point."

The channel was silent for almost a full minute.

"!Olarski is already on his way to Sol with his fleet," A!Shall finally said slowly. "More ships will follow. I will not redeploy Tan!Shallegh and the Grand Fleet, not yet, but we will begin to assemble a *second* Grand Fleet at Sol."

"We are already mass-producing S-HSM batteries, tachyon scanners and hyperfold cannons," Annette promised. "We can refit at least a portion of the ships as they arrive."

"Your Consort will have to see to that," her Empress told her. "You should prepare for a long swim, Dan!Annette Bond. I may have a new task for you."

"My liege?"

"Someone must go to Arjzi and negotiate with the High Priestess," A!Shall explained. "We shall speak with their ambassadors here to confirm the preliminaries, but if they are prepared to meet my price, then you will travel to Arjzi and speak with them.

"I must send someone I can trust and..." The Empress allowed a flash of blue and red to flush over her skin, showing a testing amusement. "I must send the Kanzi someone who can lie if needed. I *want* true peace with them, Dan!Annette.

"But you know my price. I do not believe the High Priestess will pay it—but I think they will work with us for this war. And who knows? Perhaps the tides will stop."

Or the horse will learn to sing.

The A!Tol Imperium would never truly make peace with Kanzi until they gave up slavery.

CHAPTER THIRTY-FOUR

EVEN WITH THE HYPERFOLD RELAY NETWORK, A RESPONSE FROM the Imperium would take over two days. The initial decision to agree to Cawl's offer of nonaggression and working together was on Harriet Tanaka, and she made the only decision she could.

"Fleet Master Oska has received your message," she told Cawl. "Our destroyer *Underwater Shining* will remain in the system to relay communications and keep an eye on affairs."

The old Kanzi in the hologram shook his head.

"Days away, and you can talk to him in a ten of spans," he noted. A span was roughly a quarter of a Terran hour. "There's a reason I was sent out here to prevent more provocations. Did Oska send a message to me?"

"There is an encrypted package attached to Captain Leeare's message, yes," Harriet confirmed. "It should already have been forwarded to your flagship."

She didn't need to tell Cawl that her Pibo officer had copied the message and decrypted it before forwarding the original encrypted version. There was nothing in the message that was unexpected—and for that matter, she was certain both Oska and Cawl had assumed anything they sent via the Imperium's hyperfold communicators was being read by their not-quite-enemies, not-quite-allies.

"Depending on what routes they took, the Taljzi may be arriving in Alstroda at any time in the next turning," Cawl warned. "Oska's fleet is not as weak as I feared, but our intelligence suggests the Taljzi have multiple squadrons of battleships and their technology is superior."

"If all of the forces we know of have combined, there are least five super-battleships on top of that," Harriet warned. "Those would be the survivors of the force that attacked the Mesharom."

Cawl visibly shivered, then ran one furred finger down the scar on his face.

"I do not even understand what they were thinking, to provoke the Mesharom," he admitted. "Our own nations are mighty enough; why would they challenge the oldest and greatest of the Core Powers as well?"

"The Taljzi do not seem particularly bothered by who they provoke," she said. "I think with the Mesharom, they wanted to destroy the local Frontier Fleet before it could get involved. There are no other Mesharom fleet units nearby, though forces have been deployed to counter this invasion."

"Invasion." Cawl let the word hang on the channel. "Invasions seek to conquer, Fleet Lord Tanaka. The Taljzi seem to seek only to destroy. Their goals, their old mission, would be to at least conquer the Kanzi and change our minds to match theirs. Instead, though, they have simply burned worlds and murdered millions."

If Harriet's math was remotely correct, the Taljzi had killed far more of their distant cousins than they had of any other race. She doubted that was unintentional—and she wondered if the aliens' apparent access to Precursor technology was part of that.

If they could clone and raise programmed children who they *knew* would believe as they did, why convince anyone? Why bother talking at all when you could level worlds and repopulate them with indoctrinated clones?

The sheer callousness with which the Taljzi seemed to treat *all* lives—their own as well as their enemies'—was utterly foreign to Harriet. They seemed determined to leave entire swathes of the galaxy in ashes.

"I do not pretend to understand what they are thinking or what they want," she finally told Cawl. "They are, at least biologically, your species, Fleet Master—and I am not under the impression that *you* understand them.

"I will settle for grasping their objectives so I can counter them."

Cawl raised his cane in a vague salute.

"I agree," he said. "I don't know what cruelty, what evil has warped their minds. I only know that to serve *my* oaths and *my* people, they must be stopped."

"HOW CONFIDENT ARE we in Fleet Master Oska?" Rolfson asked at the flag officer meeting a couple of hours later.

Harriet shook her head.

"We don't know much about her, unlike Cawl," she noted. "Kailur?"

Her Tosumi intelligence officer, Division Lord Kailur Fo Nadit, shook his feathered head.

"Our last information on Karilee Oska has her as a *Guard* Master commanding a small task group on their spinward flank," Fo Nadit told them all.

Guard Master was equivalent to an Imperial Echelon Lord or a Terran Rear Admiral. Fleet Master was equivalent to Harriet's own Fleet Lord or a Terran full Admiral.

"How old is that?" she asked Fo Nadit.

"Four long-cycles," he told her. "If she's a Fleet Master now, she's almost certainly freshly promoted and has advanced rapidly over those four long-cycles. That suggests either victories, unlikely to have occurred on one of their quieter borders, or a high level of political and religious reliability."

"Which raises a fascinating question," Sier pointed out. "Was she coming to support the wind under Cawl's wings...or steal it?"

"Reading between the lines of my conversations with him, he's regarded as politically reliable but a religious outsider," Harriet replied. "He hasn't talked about Oska like she was sent out to replace him, but I could see her being sent out to keep an eye on him as she reinforces his strength in a time of crisis."

"I didn't think the Kanzi tolerated 'religious outsiders,'" Rolfson rumbled.

"The fact that the Emancipator movement *exists* suggests otherwise, now that I have to think about it," she admitted. "According to Cawl, if you push far enough to get declared a heretic, it ends *very* badly, but there's a degree of tolerance for some deviation."

She snorted.

"Presumably alongside a significant amount of social ostracization and disapproval." Which made the Kanzi sound more like her Japan back on Earth in many ways. That was a disturbing thought.

"So, we're not certain of her competence," Tidikat noted. "Against this enemy, I find that more concerning than helpful."

"Competence be damned," Division Lord Iffa stated, the rippling multi-voiced sound of their voice echoing around the translation. "She has thirty battleships and ten super-battleships. Even with the Taljzi's superior weapons, that is a force to make them hesitate."

"Except it's a weaker force than Fleet Master Cawl's," Rolfson pointed out. "And they had good-enough intelligence to locate a Frontier Fleet squadron none of us knew existed."

"And she's short on escorts," Fo Nadit warned them all. "She only has twenty regular cruisers from the Theocracy Navy, not even attack cruisers. She's making up the numbers by drafting local Clan ships, which has given her another fifty regular and attack cruisers, but..."

"But they're Clan, and they intentionally cripple the Clan fleets,"

Harriet finished for her intelligence officer. "Those ships are worth maybe half their tonnage versus modern units.

"We cannot assume that Alstroda will hold," she told her people. "We are at least seven cycles away. The Taljzi may have already arrived, we won't hear for almost twenty hours after they do. We can do nothing to change Fleet Master Oska's fate that we haven't already done.

"The question, officers, is what we do if Alstroda falls."

THERE WAS no point in trying to send a message to Captain Leeare. The Rekiki destroyer commander was in position to watch what happened in Alstroda, but there was no way his single destroyer could change what was going to happen.

Plus, Harriet was certain that any message she sent Leeare would arrive after the Taljzi. There was nothing anyone in Xīn Táiwān could do for Alstroda—and the necessity of remaining linked into the hyperfold relay network meant she couldn't even take her fleet into hyperspace.

She didn't know where the Taljzi would go from Alstroda. She wouldn't know until they *left*, at which point Leeare would update her and she and Cawl would scramble to get their fleets into position to stop the bastards.

Their only real advantage was that the Taljzi seemed to be moving relatively slowly. They had no evidence that the Taljzi ships were slower than theirs, in or out of hyperspace. In fact, *Bellerophon*'s encounters with the Taljzi suggested that they were roughly equal for strategic mobility.

But it seemed that they were pulling back to rendezvous points between attacks and slowly working their way down a list. That left her nervous in presuming that Oska could defeat the fleet heading toward Alstroda, but it gave them time.

This time, there were destroyers scattered around Alstroda, too.

Peeah's entire squadron was moving in to keep an eye on the hyperspace around the system. They would give Oska a few hours' warning, and they might, just might, allow Harriet and Cawl to track the bastards back to somewhere worth hitting.

Or get in front of them. One way or another, this "Return" needed to be stopped. Harriet was grimly certain there'd be more to come, but she didn't know where the Taljzi were coming from.

All she could do was find the fleet they had moving around and smash it into pieces.

CHAPTER THIRTY-FIVE

YOU AND THE KANZI CAN FIGHT TOGETHER? WORK TOGETHER?

Morgan considered the message from Coraniss with one eye as she kept another on the space around *Bellerophon*. There were a *lot* of starships around them now, and while no one was supposed to be moving much, it didn't take much of a mistake to cause trouble.

She and Victoria Antonova were sharing the midnight watch, at this point a silent vigil waiting for the news from Alstroda. Coraniss, it seemed, was also awake and was asking questions.

Morgan wasn't sure if the Mesharom was as young as they occasionally felt, or was simply inexperienced in dealing with other races. To be an Interpreter, Coraniss had to have some experience...but it quite possibly wasn't very much at all.

Yes, she finally replied. *We don't trust each other and there are definitely people on both sides who hate each other, but these Taljzi are worse. We know the Kanzi. All we know about these Taljzi is that they keep blowing up planets.*

She realized Antonova was watching her, and flashed the other blonde woman a smile.

"Coraniss is asking questions," she told the com officer. "As they do. I think they may be starting to feel lonely."

"I didn't think Mesharom could do that," Antonova said.

"Oh, they can," Morgan disagreed. "It's a very different thing for them than for us, but it's good for Coraniss to have someone to talk to. They don't really want to have anyone *around*, but they want someone to talk to.

"Sometimes." She smirked, checking for a new response from the Mesharom.

"How is Coraniss handling being aboard? They're basically imprisoned in their pod."

"That's their choice and preference," Morgan explained. "Coraniss doesn't *want* to be aboard *Bellerophon* any other way. That pod has everything they need. So long as we keep sending over water, power and Universal Protein, they're fine."

A new message had appeared on her screen, and the young woman sighed as she read it.

So much death. So many potentialities ended. Can we stop them?

"Well, I guess 'we' is promising when we're talking to a Core Power," Morgan said. "I'm pretty sure that Core Fleet detachment they have heading our way is a sufficient answer to the Taljzi. Before that..."

"Us and the Kanzi," Antonova agreed. "No update from Leeare yet. Last word had Oska pre-placing missiles under the command of her defensive platforms."

"I guess she's studied the Fleet Lord's file." Morgan chuckled. "That was one of her tricks at Centauri."

She turned her attention back to the messaging program.

If anyone can stop them out here with this fleet, it's Tanaka.

This time, the response was almost instant.

Can I help?

Morgan shook her head with a sigh.

Unless you have a superweapon hidden in that pod, you're already doing all you can, she told the alien. *Your people are coming. Every-*

thing we do right now is buying time for our reinforcements, including your Core Fleet.

Coraniss didn't respond. Morgan enjoyed her conversations with the alien, but this time, she was glad for it to end.

There was, after all, only one currency available to Fleet Lord Tanaka to buy time with.

TIME SEEMED to tick by like molasses. They were now in the window where they might get an update informing them the Taljzi had arrived—twenty hours before—but they weren't in the most likely time frame.

Captain Vong and Commander Masters were planning to be on duty for that time frame. Right now, Morgan had orders to buzz them immediately if word arrived. Otherwise, it was her watch, and the bridge was empty except for her and Antonova.

"So, I heard a certain Marine got himself shot down in flames," the com officer mentioned as the silence stretched on. "I'm surprised."

Morgan snorted. She'd long since learned that warships and high schools had a great degree of resemblance when it came to relationship drama and rumors.

"Hardly in flames," she pointed out. "More shut down than shot down. Rumor, as always, exaggerates things."

"But still! You said you thought he was pretty."

Morgan shook her head, somewhat repressively, at the other woman.

"I think a *lot* of people are pretty without leaping into bed with them, Victoria," she pointed out. "I also got dumped by videomail when we shipped out from Earth."

"Ouch." Antonova winced sympathetically. "That sucks. He wasn't okay with a service tour of unknown length?"

"She'd probably have been okay with it with a heads-up," Morgan admitted. "Or if it had been the first time I'd told her I was going to be unavailable for an extended period with twelve hours' notice."

She sighed.

"Or the second. Or the third," she confessed. "I'm not a great girl-friend. It wasn't always my fault, I'm a Militia officer and my parents' daughter, but...that many short-notice screw-ups was *definitely* my fault."

Antonova, she noted, perked up slightly at the mention of "she" with regards to Morgan's ex, though her enthusiasm dimmed a bit with Morgan's description of *why* she'd been dumped.

That was something that Morgan needed to very specifically *not* notice, she was sure. They weren't in each other's direct chain of commands, but, unlike Major Phelps, she did work with Antonova.

"Not many people handle dating military people well," the other woman finally said. "My dad left my mom over it, way back. It wasn't a pretty scene."

"Pretty sure dad knew *exactly* what he was getting into when he married the Duchess of Terra," Morgan said with a chuckle. "Mom pretty much beat him over the head with it a few times."

"What did you think?" Antonova asked.

"I was...four? Maybe five, when they got together? I thought it was the best thing ever. I *loved* my 'Auntie Annette.'" Morgan smiled. "Loved her more as my mom, for all of the usual teenage BS along the way."

"My mom never asked my opinion," the Russian admitted. "Just... decided not to remarry in case I hated them."

Morgan's response was cut off as a light flashed up on Antonova's console.

"Victoria?" she asked quickly.

"Wake the Captain," her friend replied. "The Taljzi are arriving at Alstroda."

CHAPTER THIRTY-SIX

IT WAS EASY TO FORGET THAT THE RELAY FROM *U*NDERWATER *Shining* wasn't live. The level of detail wasn't perfect, but the destroyer had scattered hyperfold-equipped drones throughout the Alstroda System.

Harriet had a low-resolution view, but everything *Shining* had seen had been in real time.

Then, of course, Captain Leeare had transmitted it via hyperfold to a relay station nine light-years away, which had taken nine hours. That relay station had transmitted to another relay station eight light-years from it, which had taken eight hours, which had then transmitted to Harriet's fleet three light-years away.

If they could have sent the message directly, they would have saved six hours. But the hyperfold communicator had a maximum range, and they had to work with it.

"One of Peeah's ships dropped out of hyperspace to advise Leeare the Taljzi were coming approximately an hour before what we're seeing now," Sier told her. "It was a large anomaly signature, too close together and too powerful for Division Lord Peeah's people to be able to identify individual ships."

Harriet nodded, her gaze riveted to the holographic display of the Alstroda System. She and the Kanzi with her would know the system's fate before anyone else outside Alstroda. Like Asimov for the Imperium, the Kanzi's forward fleet base in this area was slated to receive a starcom. Eventually.

What Alstroda *had* received was the infrastructure to maintain five squadrons of capital ships and a defensive constellation to make some racial homeworlds green with envy.

Fleet Master Oska was keeping her fleet tight in to the planet, Clan auxiliaries and Theocracy Navy alike. She was risking the asteroid miners and cloudscoops and much of the system's space-borne industry—but there were eighty million people on the planet behind her and only four in the part of the system she'd abandoned.

Harriet couldn't disagree with the Kanzi officer's judgment. She'd have made the same call, terrible as it was.

"Hyper portal," Sier murmured next to her. They studied the metrics the nearby drone fed them, and Harriet shivered.

Fleet hyper portals were always mind-boggling. Even a destroyer would normally generate a portal a few kilometers across; the energy investment in doing so was minuscule compared to the risk of half-missing your portal.

The Taljzi portal was over a thousand kilometers across, and their entire fleet entered the system in a single mass, fifteen super-battleships wide.

The portal slowly flickered closed behind them, but Harriet's attention was on the Taljzi fleet.

"I make it fifteen super-battleships, ten battleships and thirty destroyers," she said aloud. "I see they're still using the same squadron size as the Kanzi."

"Interesting breakdown, that," her chief of staff replied. "No cruisers and heavily overweight at the top end. Matches up with what we've seen, though, assuming they found some more super-battleships somewhere."

Harriet nodded. The force was lighter than they'd feared, if still more powerful than they might have hoped. She had, in fact, been hoping that the five super-battleships that had escaped the Mesharom and *Bellerophon* were the only ships of that size this Return had possessed.

Leeare was relaying his data to the Kanzi via a carefully positioned drone—one refitted with an even more-hair-trigger-than-usual self-destruct—and Oska had seen the enemy with as much detail as Harriet was seeing.

"The catch to all of this," Harriet murmured, "is that we *know* they have stealthed battleships and cruisers. It's not a perfect system, though... Could Leeare's sensor drones pick them up?"

Sier pulled the data from the stealth ship *Bellerophon* had encountered and looked it over thoughtfully.

"Potentially, if we'd calibrated them *very* carefully," he said slowly. "As it is...the drone would need to stumble over the ship. *Underwater Shining* could pick them up at about a light-minute, further if she was coordinating with other ships."

"And we wouldn't dream of giving that much access to the Kanzi —or vice versa," the Fleet Lord concluded. "If I wasn't thinking about stealth ships, though, I'd see..."

The Kanzi fleet was moving. The Taljzi had five more super-battleships than Oska did, but her thirty battleships should even the odds. It wouldn't have been an easy fight, but Oska could take on the Taljzi fleet—and in doing so, save an extra four million people.

Even half-expecting a trap, Harriet wasn't sure she'd have chosen differently.

AT THE SPEEDS available to ships with modern interface drives, it took barely twenty minutes for the two fleets to come together and reach weapons range of each other. The Taljzi missiles were clearly superior, with longer flight times and higher velocities.

The Kanzi missiles, however, were better than Harriet had been expecting. Point eight cee weapons with two-minute flight times, they were equal to the modern missiles in her own magazines.

She was expecting the active missile defenses the Kanzi fleet deployed, though their effectiveness was a surprise again. Without hyperfold communications, their decoys and missile defense platforms had to be kept in close to the hull, like the original Buckler drones.

They still made a mess of the Taljzi salvos, superior missiles or not. Neither side did noticeable damage with their long-range bombardment, but the Taljzi turned to keep the range open.

"Still no communication?" Harriet asked.

"Nothing. Leeare had drones close enough that we'd have picked up anything they sent to Oska. Not a word from these bastards since the first system they entered."

Cawl was right, she reflected. There was no way that ship had escaped Kanda on her own. They'd let her go to make sure the Kanzi heard the one thing they had to say.

"The Taljzi have about a point oh five cee edge over the Kanzi for shipboard drives as well," Sier noted. "They're in control of the range." The Yin clacked his beak. "They can't hurt Oska's ships at that range, though; they have to close into her range to actually get missiles through her defenses."

"They learned from some of the best," Harriet said with a sad smile. "No, Sier, they're not going to close the range. Whoever is in charge of the Taljzi is *playing* with her."

"Fleet Lord?"

The Taljzi answered before Harriet could. Their stealth fields might suck compared to Mesharom or Laian technology, but they were far beyond anything the Kanzi or the Imperium possessed. Oska had seen what she'd been shown, a powerful force but one she could defeat in open combat to save the system.

She *hadn't* seen the other fifty battleships and hundred cruisers that had approached under stealth.

There was a limit to even the Taljzi tech. They didn't get close enough to fire their godawful energy guns from stealth. The Kanzi picked them up at ten light-seconds, dodging away from the fresh icons and opening fire with everything they had.

That point oh five cee advantage Sier had noticed made all of the difference there. The Taljzi lunged into the teeth of Fleet Master's Oska's fire. They *didn't* have active missile defenses, and shields went down across their fleet.

Proton beams from the Kanzi ships tried to take advantage of the openings, only to dissipate into nothingness well short of the Taljzi hulls. Missiles made it through but hammered into compressed-matter armor.

The battle lasted barely two minutes after that. The Taljzi lost ships—they *were* sailing into the teeth of an entire battle fleet—but by the time they reached one light-second of Oska's fleet, it was already over.

The massed salvo of their hyperspace disruption guns was overkill. Nothing survived of the Kanzi fleet except debris, and Harriet forced herself to be calm as she assessed the Taljzi losses.

"Their super-battleship strength is intact, but I'd say at least a squadron of their battleships are either gone or mission-killed," she concluded aloud, her voice level. "That still leaves them with sixty-five capital ships."

"We can take them," Sier said, his voice equally level, equally forced. "Between us and Cawl? We have them outnumbered and outgunned."

"And we need to," Harriet said as she watched the Taljzi battle-ships turn toward the planet, massive salvos of missiles beginning to spill out toward the badly outranged defenders.

"Because I swear to you, Division Lord Sier, that is the *last* fucking world I intend to watch die."

CAWL LOOKED like he'd aged a century in a few hours. The old Kanzi officer was alone in his office when Harriet finally got in touch with him, all of the screens in the room dark and his eyes glazed as he looked at the pickup.

It took Harriet a moment to recognize what the snapped object lying on his desk was. Cawl had broken his cane in half, and the pieces now sat in front of him. Almost hidden amidst the broken pieces of his walking aid was the matte-black shape of a Theocracy Navy service pistol.

"Fleet Lord," he greeted her. Even through the translator he sounded wooden, broken. There was no tone to what she picked up of his actual voice.

"Fleet Master. *Underwater Shining* has been forced to withdraw from Alstroda and destroy her drones," she told him gently. "Our destroyer squadron is maintaining their picket around the system. We *will* know when they leave."

"Twenty hours too late to do anything," he said. "Even if I'd been able to jump my entire fleet there when we got the message, we'd have been twenty hours too late. I failed my oaths."

And where Harriet was mourning hundreds of thousands of Imperial citizens, Cawl was mourning tens of millions. The Taljzi had come after their old kindred, and everyone else had been incidental.

She was honest enough to admit that if the Taljzi had been able to bring themselves to bypass the Imperium's human colonies and only attack the Kanzi, the Imperium wouldn't be involved yet. They would have regretted the deaths of millions of slaves, but even now, many of her people were somewhat gleeful at the deaths of the Kanzi themselves.

"Does blowing your brains out with that gun un-fail them?" she finally asked harshly. She didn't know Cawl. Hell, she didn't even know Kanzi psychology outside of combat interactions.

He stared silently at the weapon for several seconds, then swept all of the debris off his desk with a violent gesture.

"No. His Light consume me, I don't know what would," he told her. "Alstroda was supposed to be our bulwark, the fortress from which we secured our Rimward flank. The people there *knew* they were safe."

Well, the Kanzi *there knew they were safe. The slaves probably thought differently.* Harriet shivered. *Not that it saved anyone.*

The last footage they had from Alstroda was the Taljzi ships spreading out around the planet to launch kinetic bombardments. Their track record suggested their destroyers would already be moving on to take out the cloudscoops and mining stations.

There was nothing Captain Leeare could do to save anyone. There was even less that Harriet or Cawl could do to save anyone.

"We'll know where the bastards go next," she told him. "The currents are with us, not them. We can beat them to whichever one of your systems they head to. We *will* catch them, Fleet Master. This Return will end."

"Will it?" he asked softly. "Even if we defeat this fleet, I don't know where our old enemies found the strength for one assault. Who knows what else they may have in reserve?"

If they'd spent the centuries since the civil war cloning workers and building ships, the Taljzi could have a *lot* in reserve. This Return was likely only the first, but Harriet didn't have it in her to tell Cawl that.

Not right now. Not when she suspected she'd literally interrupted him about to blow his brains out.

She needed Cawl. She needed his fleet. She could *probably* stop the Return with just her fleet...but that was what Fleet Master Oska had thought.

CHAPTER THIRTY-SEVEN

Harold Rolfson was drunk. Normally, he was exactly the kind of loud, friendly drunk people expected from his size and coloring, but there were also times when all he wanted was a locked office and a bottle of vodka.

There was probably some Russian in his background somewhere. Who knew? Twenty-third century humanity was pretty intermingled at the best of times.

It was hard to hate the Kanzi right now. He wanted to. He had years of practice; it should have been easy to just keep hating the blue-furred bastards.

But the truth was that only a portion of any race could actually be slaving, murdering assholes. Most of the tens of millions of dead Kanzi had been shopkeepers, accountants, wait staff...ordinary people who happened to have blue fur and be under a meter and a half tall.

It was impossible to watch anyone die in those numbers and still hate them. The feeling was rippling through Seventy-Seventh Fleet, a hard-won sympathy for the people they'd regarded as the devil.

They would have tried to stop this kind of mass murder anyway, but they understood what Fleet Master Cawl and his people had to be feeling.

So, Rolfson was a third of his way into a bottle of vodka, ignoring coms that weren't flagged as urgent by his secretary, and morosely staring at the astrographic chart of the region.

The message that was actually flagged as urgent earned a disgruntled growl from him, and he checked to make sure it was actually a message—as opposed to a live com request—before hitting Play.

He didn't check *who* it was from, so he was surprised when Ramona Wolastoq appeared above his hologram projector.

"Hey, you," she greeted him. "I haven't heard anything from you in a while. I know you're wandering through hell, but some reminder that you're alive would be nice. There's not a lot of news being released to the public, but, well, I'm not the public."

She smiled wickedly, but the smile faded as quickly as it appeared.

"Even what I'm getting isn't pretty at all, so I can't imagine what it's like out there. If I know you—and I do—there's either a bottle of vodka on your desk or in your near-term plans. Won't tell you not to remake that friend's acquaintance, but watch for the demon that comes with him, love."

Ramona reached out toward him and sighed.

"Asimov is a fleet base, so people are used to knowing more than most about what's going on, and rumors are flying. Everyone is terrified. I'm not, not really." She smirked. "I know you're between me and whatever might threaten us.

"I've sent my staff back to Earth, though. With Lelldorin gone, well, my Arend expedition is a bust. I'm researching new destinations from here. Most archeologists don't have my level of access to the hyperfold relay network, so it could be worse.

"I'm just not going anywhere until I see you, Admiral. Take care of yourself. I know what your job is like, but you're no good to anybody drunk, unconscious or heartbroken."

She smiled to soften the blow.

"I love you. I'll see you soon. Hopefully, I'll *hear* from you sooner."

The transmission ended and Harold sighed. He was already farther down the bottle of vodka than he should have let himself get, and he swept it into his desk. An inhaler was already in the drawer, and he studied the white device balefully for a moment.

He wasn't going to record a message to his wife while drunk, however, so he picked it up.

Self-pity hour was over. Time to call his wife...and then get back to work.

THE INHALER DID its job exactly as it was supposed to, and by the time Harold returned to his bridge, the last vestiges of the alcohol, the hangover and the nausea from the inhaler itself were gone.

He strode onto his flag bridge once again projecting full control and dominance of the situation, taking his seat and studying the screens and holograms showing *President Washington's* surroundings.

"Any update from Division Lord Peeah?" he asked.

"Nothing so far," Ling Yu replied. She'd barely moved from where he'd left her, standing beside the main holographic projector. Her black braid was showing signs of wear where she'd been pulling on it.

"I'll keep an eye on things, Nahid," he told her gently as he looked around the bridge. "You're the last person who hasn't had a break on this deck since the feed from Alstroda. Go rest."

"Can't, sir," she said quietly. "Can barely blink. All I see is—"

"Then go see the ship's doctor," he replied. "You're no good to anybody, staring blankly at a tactical plot because you're too tired to think straight, and if you're having waking nightmares, you need to talk to the doctor."

Ling Yu was silent, and he rose and crossed the couple of meters between them to lay his hand on her shoulder.

"Nahid, I'll make it an order if I need to," Harold said. "These are terrible times to live through, but we have to be able to do our jobs to make sure that doesn't happen again. Do you understand me?"

His operations officer shivered under his hand and then suddenly had her face buried in his shoulder as she broke down into tears. He had twenty years and six inches on Ling Yu, and he gently held her as she sobbed.

"All we could do was *watch*."

"I know," he murmured. "Revenge won't bring them back. Honor won't bring them back. All we can do is make sure it never happens again."

It took a few more seconds for her to regain her composure and realize she was crying into her flag officer's shoulder. She pulled back and he let her go, leveling his best smile on her.

"That wasn't appropriate, sir, sorry," Ling Yu admitted.

"Nobody is going to hold it against you, Captain," he told her formally. "But I'm going to reiterate my suggestion."

"Yes, sir. I'll make my way to Dr. Lehman's office and check in."

"Good," Harold said. "Take care of my ops officer, Captain Ling Yu. She's good people."

She gave him a weak snort in response, then saluted and left the flag deck in crisp step.

The Vice Admiral continued to focus on the tactical plot, carefully not registering the junior officers and technicians around him.

"I don't think I need to remind you that no one saw that," he said conversationally, not really addressed to anyone. "But if *anyone* here needs to talk to Dr. Lehman's people, flag your relief and go.

"There will never be a time we'll need it more...and I'd take the time while we have it, people."

SOME OF HIS people drifted out. Replacements drifted in, and Harold very specifically did not pay attention. The last thing his people needed was to be shamed for getting the medical help that all too many of them were going to need.

The best example he could set, he supposed, was to go talk to one of Dr. Lehman's people himself. There'd be time for that once they were in hyperspace, though. Right now, the Admiral was On Duty, and he was watching for the next stage in this nightmare.

He was unsurprised, somehow, when Fleet Lord Tanaka appeared on his personal com screen.

"Do I need to send you to a counselor, Fleet Lord?" he said with an only mostly forced smile.

"It's on my to-do list once we're in hyperspace," Tanaka replied, echoing his own thoughts. "Our medical teams are doing a brisk business today—and it's definitely better than the alternative."

"I can think of one alternative that would be better," Harold said darkly, then shook himself. "Apologies, Fleet Lord. There was nothing any of us could have done. These...*people* knew what they were doing from the beginning."

"They got Cawl well out of position, that's for sure," she agreed. "Though I suspect their trap would have easily taken his fleet combined with Oska's. I don't think he'd have been able to let the outer system platforms burn either."

Tanaka sighed.

"*I* wouldn't have been able to let the space stations burn. These *kusottare-me* know where to hit our buttons."

Harold snorted. His translator earbud was off, but he could guess the meaning of the Japanese curse from context.

"Kanzi think more like us than I would have figured," he said.

"Not really a surprise, when you think about it," Tanaka replied. "The A!Tol are amphibious ocean predators with a parasitical reproductive cycle, and they think much like we do. Civilization and sentience seem to have a shaping effect on the mind.

"And god knows humanity has produced enough religiously

motivated slaver cultures," she concluded. "Some of both of our ancestors among them."

"If you'd asked me two months ago what my reaction to Alstroda being obliterated would be, I probably would have said *good riddance*," Harold said. "Now I realize that would have been wrong regardless. But this mess..."

"You could argue it's their own fault. They did attempt to *exterminate* the Taljzi, after all. Don't cry too many tears for our blue-furred friends."

"No one deserves to see their worlds blown apart around them," he replied. "Whatever the Theocracy did three hundred years ago, there's no one left alive on either side who was involved. And these Taljzi make my skin crawl.

"They couldn't just attack the Kanzi worlds. They could have easily passed by our systems, and it would have taken a lot longer for the Imperium to get involved. Instead, they attacked. They sacrificed a strategic advantage to do...what?"

"To meet a religious imperative, so far as I can tell," Tanaka told him. "They believe their god has commanded them to destroy all other races. So long as they believe that, I hesitate to blame the Kanzi for what they did to get rid of the Taljzi.

"I don't know what we might have to do before this is done."

Harold winced at the thought, but before he could reply, a new alert flashed up on his console.

"Sir," Commander Yong Xun Huang interrupted, his coms officer looking pale. "We just got an update from Division Lord Peeah. *Dark Sun* dropped out of hyperspace twenty hours ago to update us."

Harold traded a glance with Tanaka, who was getting the same report on her bridge, and left the channel open.

"What do we know?"

"He lost three destroyers tailing the Taljzi, but he's confirmed their vector," Xun Huang told him. "They're heading for current LKI-651-V8."

"That crosses the border, doesn't it?" Harold demanded.

"Yes, sir. Their only likely target from that current is Asimov."

Harold felt the ground fall out from underneath him and met Harriet Tanaka's horrified gaze for several seconds before he turned to study the astrographic plot.

There were no major Kanzi systems in the area that the Taljzi could have reached except by brute-forcing their way through hyper-space. Between currents and geometry, the Kanzi and Imperial fleets could have met them at any major Kanzi system nearby.

There was no current between them and Asimov. The Talzji had a six-to-eight-day flight to the Imperial fleet base—five to seven now, with the time delay from Peeah's transmission.

Seventy-Seventh Fleet and Alstroda Fleet were at least seven days away. Possibly as much as ten. There were a hundred million Imperial citizens, over three-quarters human, in Asimov.

Including Vice Admiral Rolfson's wife.

CHAPTER THIRTY-EIGHT

HARRIET TOOK A SINGLE LONG MOMENT TO CLOSE HER EYES AND breathe, collecting her thoughts as she processed the geometry, the timing...the absolute disaster and horror show staring down at her.

Those few seconds were all she could afford.

"Orders to the fleet," she snapped. "All ships are to set course for Asimov, maximum speed. Sier—I need you to coordinate cycling the sprint modes. The escorts can't carry what's coming on their own, so we *need* the capital ships there as soon as possible."

Every capital ship in her fleet could make point five lightspeed. They could all sprint to at least point five five cee, but that wasn't sustainable for seven days.

"We won't save that much time," her chief of staff noted. "But a few hours could make all of the difference. I will make it happen."

Her single set of orders set her entire staff into motion. There were support sections located around her flag bridge, and every one of them was now linking into squadron and individual ship communication networks.

"Harold," she turned back to the channel to Admiral Rolfson. "*Thunderstorm*-Ds. What's their sustained top speed?"

"Point five seven," he said instantly. "The rest of the *Thunder-storms* are point five five—which is the *Bellerophon*'s flank speed." He shook his head. "The *Vindications* and *Manticores* are all point five cee ships."

One of her Imperial squadrons was made up of *Thunderstorms*. A second squadron was a different design of the same vintage, same point five five cee engines. All of her destroyers could match that speed, and the Duchy of Terra Militia ships were all *Thunderstorms*.

Eighty-eight cruisers. Two Imperial squadrons, three and a half Terran squadrons. Plus three battleships that could punch well above their weight.

"We'll hold half the Imperial destroyers back to escort the main fleet," she finally ordered. "The other half, plus all of the Militia destroyers, will form on the *Bellerophons* and all point five five cee–rated cruisers.

"Vice Admiral Rolfson, get your butt and your flag staff aboard one of the *Bellerophons* ASAP. You're taking command of our new Task Force Seventy-Seven–One. You've got a ten percent speed edge on the rest of the fleet, which means you'll get there at least sixteen hours ahead of the rest of us."

She grimaced.

"That makes you the *only* ships we have that have any chance in hell of beating the Taljzi to Asimov. You'll need to hold them, Harold. At any cost. Do you understand me?"

He nodded slowly, and his eyes told her he understood exactly what she was ordering. The destruction of the entirety of TF 77–1 and the deaths of the over eighty thousand sentients aboard those ships were an entirely acceptable price to buy those sixteen hours.

"My staff and I will be moving over to *Bellerophon* in the next ten minutes," he promised. "77–1 will be on our way within twenty."

"The rest of the fleet will be behind you," Harriet told him. "We will relieve you, Admiral. You just have to hold until we get there."

He saluted.

"I've got half the S-HSM launchers in the universe, sir," Rolfson pointed out. "If anyone can hold them, it's these ships, these crews."

"God speed you, Harold. We'll see you in Asimov."

———————

HARRIET MADE sure everything was arranged for Harold's task force and the movement of the rest of her fleet before she checked in on the Kanzi.

"Sier, what is Fleet Master Cawl up to?" she asked after the seventh—possibly eighth; she wasn't sure anymore—round of reassignment and movement orders had been transmitted.

"Not much," her chief of staff admitted, the blue Yin snapping his beak as he studied the screen. "He started preparing his ships to move about five thousandth-cycles after we did, but they haven't said anything. I'd guess he's waiting for you."

For a moment, she was tempted to let the Kanzi wait. That wasn't *entirely* fair, though. Cawl had made the first serious efforts towards peace between the Imperium and the Theocracy in decades, and he'd been relatively straightforward with her.

"Get me a channel," she ordered with a sigh. "I owe the smurf an explanation."

Sier might have lacked the cultural context behind the slur, but it had managed to infiltrate large swathes of the Imperial Navy—especially units like Seventy-Seventh Fleet that had been positioned in Sol for extended periods. He knew who she meant.

When the channel opened, she found herself looking at the Kanzi's flag deck. The layout and design philosophy were very different—her staff's sections were in separate spaces detached entirely from the flag bridge, where the Kanzi put them in pits around the raised central area occupied by the commander, for example—but the function was clear.

Cawl was seated in the hologram, showing no sign of his usual infirmity or his earlier brush with depression. Activity swirled around him, but he met her gaze calmly.

"Fleet Lord Tanaka," he greeted her. "I presume you have identified the Taljzi's destination. May I ask where we are headed?"

That was...not quite what she'd expected.

"The Taljzi are crossing the border into Imperial space," she told him. "We believe they are headed for our equivalent of Alstroda."

"Ah. That would be Asimov, correct?" he asked. "We have the coordinates, of course, but I wonder if we should move our fleets together to avoid confusion and make certain we deliver the strongest blow possible to the Taljzi."

"I..." Harriet swallowed, refocusing her thoughts. "They are not heading toward a Kanzi world. Asimov is my responsibility, not yours."

"These Taljzi are my responsibility," Cawl told her. "They were forged by my ancestors, and any measure they take today, even if it is against the Imperium, is targeted at my people. Regardless of where they go or who they attack, I will fight them. We share an enemy, Fleet Lord Tanaka. I will not ask you to face them alone."

She bowed her head and realized she'd done the alien in the projection a disservice. She'd had every intention of deploying to defend Kanzi worlds—and yet it hadn't even *occurred* to her that the Kanzi fleet would deploy to defend Imperial worlds.

"Most of my fleet can pull half of lightspeed," she told him finally. "A small portion can sustain point five five cee. I'm sending them ahead. If you have any capital ships that can keep up with Admiral Rolfson's Task Force, their assistance would be invaluable."

He shook his head, a very human gesture for all that he was blue.

"My capital ships can match yours, but only my escorts could sustain that speed," he admitted. "And, well..." He shrugged. "Our drones aren't as good as yours, and it has been easier to update the missile defenses on our destroyers than our battleships. My missile-defense doctrine relies more on my escorts than yours. I can't really afford to send them ahead."

"Then we move together, Fleet Master, and we bring the largest hammer we can when we catch the bastards."

"We do what we can," he agreed, a shadow crossing his eyes. "I wish I could send more ahead, Fleet Lord. I know what we're asking of Admiral Rolfson."

"So does he," Harriet said quietly. "So does he."

CHAPTER THIRTY-NINE

"Task Force Seventy-Seven–One, arriving!"

Morgan snapped to attention amidst the honor guard. Normally, greeting the Admiral and his staff would be a job for a more-senior officer, but every member of *Bellerophon*'s crew was straining to the limit to get the battleship ready for a multi-day sprint at maximum flank speed—and to receive a new flag officer.

Vice Admiral Rolfson and his staff clearly weren't expecting even this much ceremony. The drop-dead gorgeous Persian woman leading the way off the ship almost stumbled at the sight of the Guard lined up to greet them.

She recovered herself quickly, however, and promptly saluted Morgan.

"Lieutenant Commander Casimir," she said swiftly, demonstrating that Morgan's attempts at anonymity had, as usual, failed. "The whole task force is in a hurry. Can you let us know where the flag bridge and our quarters are?"

"That's why I'm here, Captain," Morgan replied. "We have a team going through the flag deck like a hurricane right now, but *Bellerophon*'s flag control systems haven't been brought online since initial testing. Captain Vong doesn't expect any problems, but my orders are to show you to your quarters and let you drop off your things first."

The giant that emerged behind the Captain chuckled loudly.

"Far be it for me to argue with my new flag captain," Harold Rolfson told Morgan.

The last time she'd seen Rolfson, Morgan had been fifteen and he'd towered over her. She wasn't that much taller at twenty-five, but somehow, she'd expected the red-bearded Admiral to tower less now.

She'd been wrong.

"This is Captain Nahid Ling Yu," he continued, introducing Morgan to the woman who'd led the way. "My operations officer and chief of staff. All of my senior officers are with me, but I've two more shuttles of support staff on their way."

Morgan checked the communicator she had nestled in her left arm.

"They're in a holding pattern while we clear the boat bay," she reported. "If everyone you have can grab their things, I can show you to your quarters and leave the next wave to Chief Eliza."

Chief Andrea Eliza was the boat bay NCO of the deck, and she was only barely managing to *not* actively shoo the Admiral out of her boat bay.

"Of course," Rolfson agreed genially. "We're all under time pressure here. We have seven minutes left to leave this system, per the orders *I* gave, so I have no problems getting out of the way!"

MORGAN LED the collection of officers to the section of the ship reserved for the flag officer and their staff. It was on the "flag officer's deck", but not actually part of the flag deck itself—a block of quarters of various scales wrapped around the working flag deck.

Like the flag deck, the quarters hadn't been used before. Unlike the flag deck, the rooms didn't have electronics and complex systems to review. Sweeping the spaces to make sure they were usable had taken a team of stewards and techs under ten minutes.

That team was now helping others work through the flag deck systems. Morgan didn't expect those to be fully online until the Task Force was well on their way to Asimov.

"Nahid," Rolfson addressed his chief of staff as Morgan pointed out the flag officer's own quarters. "Can you download the map and room assignments from the ship's computers? I need to borrow Commander Casimir for a few minutes."

"Of course," Ling Yu confirmed, slicing off the rest of the staff and leading them away with practiced skill before Morgan could say a word.

"Now, unless we built *Bellerophon* to completely different standards than every other capital ship we ever designed, there's an office in here," Rolfson told Morgan with a grin. "I'll need to impose on a few minutes of your time."

"You're the Admiral, sir," Morgan allowed. Her codes opened the door and assigned the room to Rolfson.

The suite was far larger than hers and, as Rolfson had predicted, had a good-sized office right next to the main entrance. The big Admiral led the way in and slotted his communicator into the desk computer systems.

"That'll take a few minutes to update and get everything loaded from my backups," he said. "You're live on the ship's systems, Commander. How long until we get moving?"

Morgan checked her communicator.

"The last of your people have boarded and we've finished shaking the new task force out of the main fleet," she reported. They were leaving with most of the Imperial escorts, though she was already missing the fifty super-battleships they were leaving behind.

"Without being on the bridge or having the squadron systems fully online, I'd say we'll be underway for your deadline. Our coms officer will relay any questions or concerns to you directly. She's good at her job."

"I've heard generally good things about this ship," Rolfson told her. "You were the first to meet these Taljzi in battle and win. You're still the only people in the Imperium who have—and the only ship in the universe, so far as we know, to fire S-HSMs in combat."

Ah. Now Morgan understood why she'd been pulled in.

The Admiral gestured her to a seat and searched for the coffee machine. It turned up relatively quickly and he got it whirring away.

"Coffee, Commander?"

"I don't know if we'll have time, sir."

"Take the damn coffee, Morgan," he ordered, somehow managing to disturbingly mix Vice Admiral Rolfson, her boss, with Uncle Harold, her family friend—and both of them in full command mode.

She took the coffee.

"What's your assessment of the HSMs?" He paused thoughtfully. "Both versions."

"The D-HSM is simply too big to be useful," Morgan said instantly. "It's relatively reliable for taking down targets with minimal shields or armor—we took out Taljzi transports and destroyers with two apiece—but the ammunition limit is unsustainable.

"They help with the alpha strike, but if I had any say, the future *Bellerophon*s will trade their Golf battery D-HSMs for another set of S-HSM launchers. There isn't enough space to add another four full batteries, but we could probably bring the new ships up to six batteries and double the munition allotment."

"You have notes on this somewhere?" Rolfson presumed aloud.

"Commander Masters and I have a file with a list of suggestions," Morgan told him. "I would assume every other department on all three ships has done the same."

"We'll need to make sure those make it home. Your mother has ordered that every slip that can hold a *Bellerophon* or a *Thunderstorm*-D is being reprioritized to build those ships. All evidence we've seen is that the S-HSMs outweigh anything else in our line of battle."

Morgan considered.

"Yes and no," she concluded. "As far as single-weapon mounts go, they're our most powerful system, yeah. But even with the upgrades we're discussing, we're talking battleships with thirty-six S-HSM launchers. Right now, while we're facing enemies that aren't expecting that? That's a one- or two-shot kill, even on Taljzi super-battleships.

"They're going to *learn*, however, and the S-HSMs have the same core weakness as the Mesharom system: you can't reprogram the emergence point.

"With tachyon scanners and hyperfold-equipped drones, you know where they are when you fire. But at maximum range, there's as much as a ten-second gap between firing and emergence. The S-HSMs have slightly better maneuverability after terminal emergence than the Mesharom version, but they're still range-limited and slow at that point in the envelope."

"So, we want more of them, but we don't want to dedicate entire platforms to them," Rolfson concluded. "That's what I was planning towards, so it's good to hear my ideas validated."

"I can understand why the Mesharom carry conventional missiles and hyperfold cannons as well," she confirmed. "I'm not sold on giving up my plasma lance yet, but we already know proton beams are almost useless against the Taljzi."

"I suspect that we'll be seeing a B variant of the *Bellerophon* design out of DragonWorks quickly," Rolfson told her. "I'll put Ling Yu on making sure we have everyone's notes to them as soon as we arrive in Asimov."

They could transmit the data before they went into battle. Morgan shivered at the likely result of that battle.

"Are the odds as bad as I think, sir?" she asked quietly.

"You're the only person who's ever fired single-portal hyperspace missiles, Commander," Rolfson noted. "The *only* one. They're our ace in the hole, so you tell me, Lieutenant Commander Casimir.

"Are the odds as bad as *I* think?"

Morgan was spared from answering by the tremor of the interface drive coming online. A quick glance at her communicator confirmed what she expected: every ship in TF 77–1 had lit off their drives within a few seconds of each other, exactly on Admiral Rolfson's deadline.

"That's it, then," he said softly. "Hyperspace in thirteen minutes. A bit over six days to Asimov where, if we're *very* lucky, we'll arrive at the same time as the Taljzi."

She didn't know the Admiral well, but he had been a friend of her parents, and she realized he was letting his guard down around her more than he should. Rolfson was worried.

"The good news for the odds," she finally said, "is that our HSMs of both varieties outrange the Taljzi by two light-minutes. Their birds have a range of about one point seven LM, but our HSMs can hit almost as far as four.

"Our accuracy sucks at that range, but our first salvo is going to be a sucker punch that they're not expecting. After that, it'll get harder, but with this many launchers and the D-HSMs, we should be able to hammer their super-battleships to debris before they can engage us."

She shook her head.

"After that, though, it's down to that we have active missile defenses and they don't. Their shields are a bit tougher and I think their compressed-matter armor is a bit tougher as well, but we have to stop fewer missiles."

"And their hyperspace disrupters have a far more limited range than anything in our arsenal," he agreed, then sighed. "The hyperfold cannons will hopefully be a surprise as well. The Kanzi didn't have those, either; all they had were proton beams."

"I don't think we can stop them on our own, sir," Morgan admitted quietly. "But I think we can damn well bloody their noses hard enough to make them back off and reconsider. And the rest of the fleet are only, what, three days behind us?"

"If we're lucky, less, with hyperspace being what it is," he agreed. "And it's not just Fleet Lord Tanaka, either."

"Sir?" He couldn't possibly mean what she thought he did.

"I received confirmation from her just before I came aboard. The Kanzi are coming with her. I'd give a lot to be a fly on the wall of the Taljzi flag deck when, after having their asses kicked for days by three battleships, Cawl and Tanaka come through a hyper portal with eighty *super*-battleships."

CHAPTER FORTY

"The Alstroda System has been leveled."

Admiral Patrick Kurzman's words were flat, calm, a stark counterpoint to the content of his short report to the Ducal Council.

His husband, General Arthur Wellesley, sat at Annette's right hand as Kurzman's bombshell dropped.

"Fleet Master Oska met the Taljzi Return with ten super-battleships, thirty battleships, and assorted escorts drawn from both the Theocracy Navy and the local Clan forces," he continued. "The Return used stealth fields to conceal the majority of their forces, including their entire battleship strength.

"They ambushed the Kanzi fleet at near-point-blank range and wiped them out. The last reports we have from the system show them bombarding the planet at long range with specially designed munitions. Most recent estimates of the Alstroda System's population were between eighty-four and eighty-six million people."

"Kanzi," Takuya Miyamoto said in sharply accented English. The old Japanese electronics tycoon's English was perfect most of the time, his accent only slipping in when he was stressed. "Do we weep now for those who would enslave us?"

"Only thirty-two million of those sentients were Kanzi," Kurzman said quietly. "The remaining fifty-plus million *people* were slaves of various degrees of status. And even the Kanzi, I will remind the Councilor, have their dissidents. It is only a tiny portion of even the Kanzi population that can be argued to seek to enslave us."

"And right now, their entire population realizes their back is against the wall," Wellesley added. "I'll admit that leaves me with enough satisfaction to allow me to sympathize with their losses. The deaths of millions of innocents are not something I'm prepared to celebrate."

"These Taljzi are a nightmare made flesh," Annette concluded aloud. "While their main efforts are pointed at the Kanzi Theocracy, let's not forget that they lost their war with the Kanzi because the Imperium blew up their main star system. They may be coming for the Kanzi *first*, but they'll come for the A!Tol...and if they come for the A!Tol, Sol is directly on their course."

"The kind of mass cloning our intelligence suggests is terrifying," An Sirkit noted.

"There have to be some limits to it," Miyamoto argued. "Nothing is magic."

"I would have placed the limits to it well below what we *know* they have achieved," the doctor replied. "Once they have passed the difficulties in parallel cloning, rapid growth acceleration and high-speed education that they *must* have passed for our autopsies to find *six-year-old starship technicians...*"

She let that hang over them all.

"Once they have passed those difficulties, it is only a question of scaling up. Our only true hope, Councilor, is that they cannot duplicate whatever Precursor technology is allowing them to clone themselves.

"Even so, however, if they have sustained mass cloning of new individuals for three centuries..." An Sirkit shivered. "The greatest limitation of any galactic-level civilization is birth rates. Our own has slowed dramatically over the last twenty years, but we remain the most rapidly growing member race of the Imperium.

"If they don't have that limitation, thirty thousand could have easily become thirty billion."

"Or thirty trillion," Annette added. "If they can duplicate the Precursor tech they are using, they could have built an empire beyond our known universe to rival the Kanzi and A!Tol combined. Or larger."

The Duchess of Terra rose to her feet and surveyed her people.

"We must prepare for war like we have never seen before," she warned them. "Even in the most optimistic scenarios that Admirals Kurzman and Villeneuve and I have worked through, this Return is only the first fleet of several—or many.

"Fleet Lord Tanaka and Fleet Master Cawl will deliver victory this time, but I suspect this attack is only a test. A calibration, if you will, of the level of force the Taljzi must bring to bear to avenge their long-dead."

"So, we have to make peace," Zhao told them all. "A!Shall has a plan. We're waiting to hear back from the Kanzi on whether they're prepared to meet her price."

"They're against the wall and they know it," Wellesley said with a snort. "What else can they do?"

"Die."

Jean Villeneuve's single word hung in the air. "They can choose to die rather than change. The High Priestess knows that alliance with us will destroy the Theocracy as it currently exists. Faced with one death or another, she may well choose to sacrifice her people instead of their culture."

Annette grimaced.

"Let's hope it doesn't come to that," she replied. "For now, regardless of whether we fight alongside the Kanzi, we need to make sure the Imperium can fight the Taljzi. Elon—how goes the switchover to *Bellerophon* construction?"

THE COUNCIL DISPERSED as their meeting concluded, holo-grams—including Annette's husband—winking out of existence all around her and leaving her alone in the big conference room except for Zhao and Wellesley.

"The Empress and the High Priestess *do* both have starcoms, correct?" Wellesley asked.

"They do. The High Priestess isn't sure if she's prepared to release *every* member of an Imperial subject species her people hold as slaves," Annette replied. "With the raids they've done over the years—the *centuries*—that's got to be hundreds of thousands of people. Perhaps millions."

"Some of whom were born into slavery in the Theocracy," Zhao agreed. "They're going to have a rough time of it if the Kanzi do turn them over. Some of the slave groupings are *very* well treated. They do use them for everything except soldiers, after all."

"Like the inverse of the Ottoman Janissaries," Wellesley said. "Slaves are what, fifty percent of the population? Sixty?"

"Around there," Annette confirmed. "I'm not sure anyone outside the Theocracy even knows how many species they've enslaved, but they fill a *lot* of roles in Kanzi society. It literally can't function the way we envision it, with half-dressed slaves being driven by whip-wielding overseers."

"It's still slavery," her Guard commander replied. "I don't have much sympathy for any loss of 'culture' they suffer in losing it."

"No one does," she agreed. "And that's part of why the High Priestess is hesitating. Even the mass release of slaves required as our precondition to talks sets a precedent that risks her power base and the structure of her government."

Annette grinned coldly.

"That, of course, is part of why we made it a condition. The other part is to get our people home. Right now, for the first time, we have the leverage to make it a possibility, so A!Shall is going to hammer it home.

"Make no mistake: the temporary agreement we have in place thanks to Fleet Master Cawl is enough that Seventy-Seventh Fleet will assist in fighting off the Taljzi. We'll use our leverage to force change in the Kanzi and to rescue our people, but we're not going to knowingly watch worlds burn."

"I didn't think we were," Zhao said. "Should I be planning for us to absorb a large portion of these slaves?"

"Prepare for some," Annette instructed. "Most likely the bulk will go from their core systems to our core systems. I'm not even the logical person to send to meet with the High Priestess. I'm not sure why A!Shall is sending me."

"Because she trusts you," an oddly modulated, clearly translated voice interjected into the conversation. Annette looked up sharply to see who had bypassed all of the security around the main conference room of the Ducal Council, then relaxed when she saw the familiar big A!Tol standing there.

Ki!Tana was an oddity of her race, an A!Tol female that had survived the "breeding madness" that drove most of her kin to suicide at the end of their lives. Given the immense healing capability of females of the species, an A!Tol who survived their bodies' demand to breed could live nearly forever.

Breeding, sadly, was an inherently fatal process for the A!Tol. They were leaders in artificial reproductive technology in the galaxy for the simple reason that they didn't have wombs. Their young literally ate their mothers from the inside out.

The Ki!Tol, the ones who survived the madness, were regarded as a mix between trickster demons and wise advisors. Ki!Tana had been a pirate when she'd fallen into Annette's orbit, and had been instrumental in the success of the Duchy of Terra.

She'd moved on over a decade ago, and Annette had never expected to see her again.

"Now I *know* it's a crisis," Annette declared as she smiled at the big alien. "You never do show up unless everything is going to hell."

"I'd have been here sooner, but I was busy," Ki!Tana replied, a flush of red pleasure suffusing her skin at the sight of the humans. "The Mesharom updated me. These are murky waters you have swum into, Duchess Bond."

"The entire Imperium is trapped in them," Annette said. "If you've any advice or help to give, I'll gladly take it."

"And I'll gladly give it," Ki!Tana told her. "This seems to be the consequences of my own actions coming home to roost, after all."

Annette glanced at Wellesley and Zhao. She'd never told them what Ki!Tana had once told her about herself. The red in the A!Tol's skin flushed deeper as she clearly realized that.

"You honor my trust beyond reason, Annette Bond," she said. "Councilor Zhao, General Wellesley."

"If you do not wish to explain that, I can forget I ever heard it," Zhao said dryly.

Ki!Tana's beak snapped in harsh A!Tol laughter.

"No, I know you two of old and trust your winds," she replied. "Before I was Ki!Tana. Before I was Ki!Tol at all...I was Empress A!Ana. I remember little of that life—but believe me, my friends, I remember firing a star killer."

The A!Tol Imperium held the questionable honor of being one of a bare handful of nations to fire the galactic weapons of mass destruction known as star killers. The weapons did exactly what the name implied, so few of the galactic-level powers had ever actually used one.

"It was done to destroy a Precursor facility the Taljzi were studying," she continued. "The Mesharom provided us the technology, to make sure that whatever Precursor tech they'd acquired was destroyed.

"It seems we failed—or at the very least, they extracted a map of other Precursor facilities. Which means we now face the consequences of the harsh duty the Mesharom imposed on me."

"They're coming," Annette replied. "A detachment of the Core Fleet has already been dispatched, but...they're months away."

"Darkest waters," Ki!Tana swore. "They're sending Core Fleet ships?"

"They didn't tell you?" Annette asked.

"They interrupted a fascinating archeological investigation on a world you've never heard of and told me to get my tentacles to Sol," the Ki!Tol explained. "They told me enough to get me moving; they didn't tell me they were sending war spheres."

"War spheres," Wellesley echoed. "Do I dare ask?"

"I've never seen one," Ki!Tana replied. "What little I have heard suggests a warship that no other power in the galaxy could match one on one—or even three on one. Something to put even Laian war-dreadnoughts or Wendira star hives to shame."

Annette winced.

She'd seen both of those ships, each of which massed around a hundred million tons and could fight most Arm Power fleets to a standstill on their own.

"They could be gods forged in steel and fire, and they still won't be here for almost six months," she said harshly. "We need to act today. We need to concentrate every ship we can in Sol and upgrade their systems. We need a fleet of hyperspace missile–armed warships that can meet these bastards in battle at ten-to-one odds and win."

"Tell me everything," Ki!Tana instructed. "It seems I wasn't as up to date as I hoped."

CHAPTER FORTY-ONE

THE GRAY VOID SWAM AROUND *BELLEROPHON* AND MORGAN found herself counting ships as if a new run through the numbers would increase them.

Three battleships, all *Bellerophon*-class. Sixteen *Thunderstorm-D*–class cruisers.

That was every ship they had with S-HSM launchers. One hundred and sixty-eight launchers. That many regular missiles wouldn't even make most capital ships blink, but the hyperspace missiles had some terrifying advantages that might make up the difference.

Fifty-six *Thunderstorm*-Bs and -Cs, plus sixteen *Abrasion*-class cruisers. Powerful, capable units. All of them had plasma lances and hyperfold communicators, but only the *Thunderstorm*-Cs had hyperfold cannons.

All of them were currently carrying two dual-portal hyperspace missiles strapped to the outer hulls, and the sixty-four destroyers that made up the rest of the task force were carrying one apiece.

They had just over two hundred of the D-HSMs mounted externally, and the *Bellerophon*s carried another thirty-six in their one-shot cell launchers. Their opening salvo would be their strongest, their Sunday punch.

It would also be the only clean shot they got. After they'd landed one hit with FTL missiles, the Taljzi would adapt.

And even that plan was assuming they beat the genocidal bastards to Asimov. There was no way the eight *Thunderstorms* and sixteen destroyers guarding the system could hold the fleet that had taken Alstroda for even ten minutes.

Maybe if they'd left *Thunderstorm*-Ds behind they'd have had a better chance, but Rear Admiral Sun had sent all of his most modern warships to Xīn Táiwān. Morgan agreed with the decision, but it still left the planet swinging in the breeze.

Asimov was decently fortified, but those defenses were equipped with proton beams and point eight cee missiles. They weren't worthless, even against this enemy, but they couldn't hold a fleet of super-battleships off for long.

She counted the ships and the hyperspace missiles again, seeking some solution that had evaded her. The map gave the mockery to any calculation around ships and weapons, though. Morgan Casimir wasn't a navigator, but she'd trained to be able to do every job on a starship's bridge to at least a basic degree.

She could do the math on the travel times and probabilities. There was only one chance in three they'd beat the Taljzi to Asimov. Two chances in three that everything they were doing was for naught and all TF 77–1 would be able to do was mourn the dead—because Morgan knew that Vice Admiral Rolfson wouldn't be able to justify committing the Task Force to a suicide charge to avenge the system they'd willingly die to protect.

When the notification system on her shipboard messenger program popped up a notification, she latched on to the distraction like a drowning woman grabbing a piece of floating debris.

The message was from Coraniss.

Come to my pod. Now. It's important.

CHIEF ELIZA INTERCEPTED Morgan at the edge of the bay they'd tucked the Mesharom escape pod into. The dark-haired, stocky noncom towered over Morgan, but her tight bun was starting to fray and she looked like she was about to start chewing on deck plates.

"I haven't managed to so much as sit down in fourteen hours, and now your *friend* in there has robots all over *my* deck!" she snapped. "I didn't think there was enough *space* in that damn pod for all those metal worms. Can you find out just what the *hell* it thinks it's doing?"

"*They* are not an *it*, Chief," Morgan said bluntly. "But yes, I'm here to talk to Coraniss. What do you mean by 'robots all over the deck'?"

"Take a look," Eliza replied with an expansive gesture.

Morgan stepped past her into the boat bay and swallowed.

It was one thing to *know* that a Mesharom space vessel was a swarm of microbots attached to a frame. It was quite another thing to see the vessel reduced to not much more than the frame and the microbots spread out all over a sixty-meter-wide-boat bay. The segmented robotic worms that served as extra hands aboard Mesharom ships seemed to be everywhere, organizing microbots and moving cabling.

Some of the cabling was from Coraniss's ship. Much of it, though, was definitely from *Bellerophon*. Morgan was reasonably sure that *most* of the cabling was supposed to be movable, intended for interfacing with shuttles and such. Several open panels along the boat bay wall suggested that at least some of it wasn't.

"We weren't using this boat bay, anyway," she pointed out to Chief Eliza in a voice that sounded far calmer than she felt. "Not with the pod here. We'd already have to move craft to the other bays for deployment before this."

"So, what, we just let the Mesharom eat an entire boat bay?" the noncom demanded.

"Exactly, Chief," Morgan replied, her voice hardening into command tones. "Coraniss is an ally, and if properly treated and taken care of, a potentially extraordinarily valuable one. If they want to turn our boat bay into an extension of their ship, I'm going to trust that they have a reason.

"So, yes, we'll mark the boat bay as off limits for now, and I'll go ask Coraniss what's going on. Is that understood, Chief Eliza?"

"Yes, sir. Of course, sir."

Morgan knew *those* tones from an NCO as well as she knew command tones from a senior officer. She shook her head.

"I'll go see what Coraniss wants," she repeated. "Keep an eye on things for me, Chief."

DESPITE THE SWARMING microbots and robots, there was still a clear pathway to the entrance to the pod. Morgan walked along it carefully but quickly realized the robots were leaving the path for her.

The pod airlock slid open as she approached, and she realized that the *entire* interior of the craft had been made out of microbots. The space she stepped into was at least twice the size of the room she'd met Coraniss in before, and there clearly was still a small bedroom tucked away against the side of the ship.

Otherwise, though, the entire interior of the ship was now open. Cabling and ducts and technology that the Mesharom normally concealed behind the stark white cover of their intelligent and moving walls and floors were fully visible.

Buried in the middle of the visible tech was Coraniss, their body extended to its full height as they dug deep into a strange technological artifact quite unlike anything Morgan had seen before.

A moment's study, however, showed at least part of the answer: the large cylinders on either side of the device Coraniss was working on were the emitters of a hyperdrive. Morgan could *feel* the odd pushing sensation of being close to charged exotic matter.

"You had a hyperdrive," she said in surprise. "I thought you had to wait for us to rescue you."

"No," Coraniss confirmed. "Was *ordered* to wait for you. Now... may be able to make a difference at last."

"I don't understand," Morgan admitted.

The Mesharom reared back and gestured towards the device with several limbs.

"This is a hyperspace density modulator," they explained. "It creates what you call a hyperspace current. Without systems the pod does not carry, it can only create a current toward the galactic core, the central gravity source of our galaxy."

Morgan stared at the machine in awe. She'd always wondered how the Mesharom could get around faster than anyone else. She'd known hyperspace grew denser as you approached the Core, which was why the Core Powers could interfere in Arm Power affairs more easily than the other way around, but she didn't know that density could be manipulated.

On the other hand, a path toward the Core didn't help them right now.

"So, what are you doing?" she asked carefully.

"If I can link into *Bellerophon*'s hyper-portal emitters, I believe I can use them to replicate the functionality I do not have. I need you to tell your engineers to assist me instead of slowing my efforts by attempting to block my access to your computer systems."

Morgan managed not to visibly react to that admission.

"You're hacking our systems," she checked.

"I need full access," Coraniss said reasonably. "I need to adjust your hyper emitters."

"Will we still be able to open a hyper portal if you do that?" Morgan asked.

"No, but you have one hundred and fifty-four other vessels capable of doing so," the alien replied. "If your engineers will assist rather than hinder, I believe I can have the modulator online and fully functional within six hours."

Morgan swallowed.

"How...fast a current?"

"It's weaker out here than it would be closer to the core, and directing it away from the core weakens it again," Coraniss admitted. "Perhaps a...sixty-three percent increase in pseudo-velocity."

That would carve days off the trip. It would guarantee TF 77–1 arrived in Asimov before the Taljzi.

"Why didn't you tell us before we left?" Morgan asked. "We could have moved the whole fleet!"

"Won't be able to create a large-enough effect for the entire fleet. Should be able to move entire Task Force." Coraniss paused. "May have to leave behind some smaller ships," they confessed. "Definitely battleships, almost certainly all cruisers."

That...was a trade Morgan was sure they'd take, but it wasn't her call.

"Are you allowed to share this technology?" she asked. This was something even the other Core Powers didn't have, and she knew the Imperium had demonstrated the ability and will to duplicate Mesharom technology from scans before.

"Asked permission. Was not refused before we left Xīn Táiwān."

For the first time since coming aboard, Coraniss lowered themself and looked Morgan directly in the eyes. The Mesharom had large, multi-faceted eyes in a dark sapphire blue.

"No one denied me and I saw my fellows die," Coraniss said flatly. "We Mesharom are slow of thought, cautious of temperament, and hesitant to action...but we understand *revenge*."

Those jewel-like eyes closed for several seconds, then reopened.

"Talk to your engineers, my friend. I will deliver your fleet in time to save your people."

CHAPTER FORTY-TWO

"You want us to do *WHAT*?"

Harold was quite sure he'd heard Casimir's request perfectly clearly, but he was still surprised. He'd figured there had to be something going on when the young officer had requested a meeting with her entire chain of command.

Commander Masters sat next to his subordinate on one side of the table in the flag conference room, and Captain Vong sat next to Harold. The Admiral didn't even need to look at his new flag captain to know that Vong was horrified by the concept...and was considering it anyway.

"Coraniss believes they have the ability to interface their hyperspace density modulator with *Bellerophon*'s exotic-matter emitters and create a current that should be large enough to move most of the task force to Asimov at an increased pseudo-velocity," Morgan Casimir repeated.

"To do so, they need full access to our computer and engineering systems, which our cyberwarfare and engineering teams are currently fighting them over," she continued.

"This ship is the culmination of everything the Gold Dragon

Protocols were about," Vong noted. "The entire purpose of those Protocols was to conceal the existence of much of this ship's technology from the Mesharom.

"If we give Coraniss full access to our systems, they will learn things that they cannot learn any other way. It is not, for example, obvious that we are using a microbot matrix to support our compressed-matter plates. That is a technology we have not admitted we have. There are others as well, Lieutenant Commander.

"Are we prepared to completely abandon that attempt at secrecy? There is Precursor tech embedded in this ship's systems—something the Mesharom do *not* permit."

"Technically, there isn't," Harold pointed out. "There is technology *based on* Precursor systems in *Bellerophon*'s construction, but for reasons I'm not cleared to explain—or indeed, to fully understand —DragonWorks was strictly forbidden from attempting direct duplication of any of the Precursor technology we have scans and samples of.

"It's a flimsy shield against fifty millennia of Mesharom tradition and law, but it's the truth as well."

"And frankly, sirs, I don't think it should matter," Commander Masters interjected. *Bellerophon*'s tactical officer gave his subordinate a look that Harold hoped was supportive. There were some undercurrents there, and Harold didn't think Casimir had expected the tactical officer to back her.

"The question is whether or not we value that secrecy, those Protocols, above a hundred million sentient lives. If we do not, sirs, then this is not the service I volunteered for."

Harold smiled.

"That does put it all in perspective, doesn't it? Thank you, Commander Masters." He turned to Vong. "Captain, it's your ship. I'd hate to order you to let an alien reengineer your primary FTL systems."

Bellerophon's Captain laughed aloud.

"But you'd do it anyway," he pointed out. "Because anything less would be a dereliction of duty. No, sir, I won't pretend I'm comfortable with it—but I agree completely that it needs to be done.

"Let secrecy hang. If we're prepared to sacrifice this ship to protect Asimov, we cannot then refuse to sacrifice her secrets."

Harold turned back to Casimir, who was trying *not* to look like she was about to melt into her seat in relief. Unfortunately for the young officer, however, Harold had known her on and off since she was barely more than a toddler.

Almost as importantly, Harold Rolfson knew Morgan Casimir's parents. He could see through her attempts at controlling her emotions.

"Vong will talk to Engineering and get everything in place. You're temporarily reassigned as liaison between Coraniss and *Bellerophon*'s engineers until this is done."

He held up a hand to forestall her superior's complaint.

"Don't worry, Commander Masters; you can have her back as soon as she's helped get us to Asimov in time. We need the Lieutenant Commander at the tactical console when we get there."

Harold grinned.

"After all, no one *else* has fired these hyperspace missiles at a live target before. We'll all need her experience before this is over."

"IT'S DONE."

Bellerophon's Chief Engineer, Commander Batari Made, sounded exhausted. Harold felt a twinge of guilt over that—the battleship's engineering team had gone from a rush job to prepare to move out to a rush job to try and get the task force to Asimov in time.

While he was certain that the junior officers and techs had been given the breaks they needed, Harold was grimly certain that Made had been up and working for at least thirty hours at this point.

"Will it work?" Harold asked.

The Indonesian engineer snorted an exhausted excuse for a laugh.

"Ask the Mesharom," she suggested. "I don't understand half of what we've done. All I can tell you is that our exotic-matter emitters are now arranged in a pattern that definitely won't open a hyperspace portal, linked directly to the matter-conversion plants, and under Coraniss's control.

"If the modulator does what they say it does, I *think* it will work. It's a rush job, but I've built in breakers and safety measures. If it doesn't work, we'll wreck the hyperdrive but the ship will be fine."

"Well done, Commander," Captain Vong told her. "I'd love to tell you to go sleep, but I need you to stick around for another half-hour or so while we bring this monster online. Are you going to be okay?"

"I'm going to sleep until we reach Asimov once this is done, but yeah, I can stand up for a while yet," Made responded.

Harold noted that she did *not* say she was actually okay or able to contribute usefully. Hopefully, the woman would get the day or so of sleep she was going to need after this.

"Lieutenant Commander Casimir." He brought the assistant tactical officer into the channel. "Does Coraniss think we're good to go?"

There was a few seconds' pause.

"Yes," Casimir confirmed. "They're prevaricating now, but that's because parts of this are as far beyond them as they are beyond us. It should work. If it doesn't..."

"Commander Made has secured the ship against failure of the device," Harold told her. "If Coraniss has done everything they think they can, we may as well fire it up. If you'd like the honors?"

"I think I'll leave that to Coraniss," the Lieutenant Commander confirmed. "Hold on."

Harold waited, watching the hologram at the heart of the flag deck patiently until it lit up with power signatures.

"Whoa," Made breathed. "We're live. Power is flowing to the

exotic-matter emitters... Damn, I didn't think those arrays were rated for this much power."

They probably weren't, Harold reflected, which meant there was a decent chance that even if this worked, *Bellerophon* was about to destroy her hyperdrive.

"I have a gravitational singularity forming at the edge of the visibility bubble," Ling Yu reported.

Sensors could only see about one light-second in hyperspace, and gravity was a rare thing to see as anything except the point sources of stars and black holes.

"Vong?" Harold asked quietly.

"We've never seen anything like it, but I'm vectoring towards it... dear gods."

"Captain?"

"I honestly wasn't sure it was going to work, but our sensors confirm it. We have a new hyperspace current, heading directly towards Asimov." Vong paused. "Do we know how long it will last?"

"Casimir?"

"Coraniss says we're projecting it ahead of us and it will collapse behind us," the Lieutenant Commander replied. "They're estimating that the current is only ever going to be about sixty thousand kilometers long and roughly two thousand across."

Ling Yu tossed a model of that into the hologram before Harold could even ask and he studied it for a long moment.

"It'll be tight, but we should be able to fit everyone in. Captain Ling Yu, I suggest you get on issuing movement orders."

"Yes, sir."

Harold considered the situation for a moment, then turned to the channel linking him to Casimir as he made a decision.

"And Lieutenant Commander Casimir?"

"Sir?"

"You're back on bridge duty, but stop by the quartermaster on your way up."

"Sir?" It was amazing how much confusion a single word could convey.

"You'll need to get your uniform updated...*Commander* Casimir."

Her willingness to listen to and ability to talk to Coraniss might have just saved a hundred million lives. That was worth an early promotion to Rolfson.

CHAPTER FORTY-THREE

THE SILVER OAK LEAF ON MORGAN'S COLLAR FELT LIKE IT WAS stabbing into her neck far more than the bronze one it had replaced. So far as she could tell, they were the same size, so that was impossible, but it still felt that way.

She hadn't even been a Lieutenant Commander for two months, though her lack of seniority as a Commander meant she still reported to Commander Masters for now. She'd probably get moved to another ship as soon as they had time.

Right now, however, the promotion didn't really change anything. Her date of rank would be on record as of the impromptu promotion, though, which would impact her seniority and salary. It hadn't even increased the number of shifts she was on watch—though previously, her watches would have specifically excluded having even non-line Commander-ranked officers on duty while she held the command.

Of course, right now, she wasn't sure the navigator had left the bridge since Coraniss's device was turned on.

"We will be arriving within the next half-hour," Commander Kumari Hume reported. "Modulator is holding steady."

"Guesses on whether or not we get our hyperdrive back after

this?" Morgan asked.

"From the feed I'm getting from Engineering? Not a bloody chance," Hume told her. "They're barely holding everything together back there. I think Dr. Lehman might have slipped the Chief a medical mickey, too, since she only just got back on duty."

"Her team seems to have managed well enough without her," Morgan noted. "We're still here, after all."

They'd managed to cram a hundred and fifty-five warships into the artificial current Coraniss's bastard hybrid device had created. Every ship on Morgan's plot was marked with flashing orange icons denoting that they were violating their recommended interface-drive safety distances, but they were all still there.

"You're running the numbers on our genocidal acquaintances, Casimir," Hume pointed out. "Are we going to beat them?"

Morgan had been running a constantly updated plot of the likely location of the Taljzi Return for days now. She didn't even need to look at it to answer the navigator's question.

"The most likely worst case, where hyperspace decided that it liked them or they suddenly turn out to have modulators of their own, is that they arrive a little over five hours after us," Morgan told the other woman. "I won't taunt Murphy; they *could* get there as we do or even be a bit ahead of us.

"But if they're far enough ahead of us that we can't ram an entire fleet's worth of hyperspace missiles up their tailpipes to get their attention, I'll have to reassess my whole stance on God—because she'd *definitely* be on the Taljzi's side!"

Hume forced a small laugh, but the thought clearly bothered her.

Which was fair. It bothered Morgan, too. They'd just done everything they could.

CAPTAIN VONG REJOINED them on the bridge a few minutes later, and Morgan moved back to the main tactical console. Masters, it seemed, was leaving this to her for now. He was apparently in his office, which meant he was actively and intentionally trying to show trust.

It was better than half-consciously undermining her, that was for certain.

"Emergence in five minutes, flag is advised," Hume reported. "We are relying on *Perseus* to open the portal. Vice Admiral Rolfson sends his regards and we are to shut down the modulator."

"Understood," Vong replied. "Made, did you get that?"

"On the ball, skipper," the chief engineer replied. "Stand by. We're coordinating with Coraniss."

The entire ship suddenly *jerked*, as if it had collided with a brick wall, and the lights flickered. Then the lights went down and Morgan could *feel* the interface drive go offline.

They had just enough time to start to panic before the lights and the interface drive came back up. Morgan's sensors showed them badly out of position with the fleet but still inside the visibility bubble.

Barely.

"Commander Made?" Vong asked, his voice sounding somewhat strained.

"We're still here," the engineer replied. "But remember those safety cutouts I told you I'd put in?"

"I'm guessing I'm very grateful for them."

"Yeah." The engineer paused.

Morgan had access to the damage reports, and she could guess what was coming next as the automated systems calmly updated their data codes and internal scans.

"We no longer have a hyperdrive," Made finally told the bridge. "Or exotic-matter emitters, for that matter. We had to eject them as part of the safety measures—the final overload triggered every single failsafe I included and *still* forced a hard reboot of the ship's main power systems."

"Can we fight?" Vong demanded.

"That's why I had failsafes, skipper," the engineer replied. "Our hyperdrive is trash and space debris, but that's it. You've got engines, guns, power, coms. Everything. You just can't open a hyper portal yourself anymore."

"What about the Hotel batteries?" Morgan asked. "I'm getting some odd warning reports flashing in from my systems."

"*Ngentot*," Made swore. "That has to be some kind of harmonic interference with their exotic-matter emitters. We'll get on it."

"We need those launchers, Commander," Vong said calmly. "But that said, well done. I know we made a mess of your engineering spaces, but unless something's gone very wrong, it was worth it."

"You carved two and a half days off our trip, chief. That's going in your record. Now go make sure I still have my superweapons, will you?"

HERAKLES WENT through the hyper portal first as *Perseus* slowed in space to let her abused sister catch up. Cruisers and destroyers streamed through into reality in a steady line as *Bellerophon* caught up with the task force and made her own transition into the Asimov system.

Perseus was the last ship out of hyperspace, but even by the time *Bellerophon* made transition, they knew they'd beaten the Taljzi there. Hyperfold communications were flying back and forth with Rear Admiral Sun as TF 77–1 inserted themselves into orbit above Isaac.

Morgan's main focus was on linking in to the sensor network laced throughout the system. Her drones weren't really necessary there, but she allocated several of them to fill in gaps she noticed as she went over Asimov's data.

Sublight civilian ships were streaming toward the planet from the various spaceborne industry platforms, and dozens of stations that Morgan remembered from *Bellerophon*'s brief stopover there were now dark. With power and life support systems shut down and the stations placed in hibernation, the hope was that the Taljzi would miss them.

Their crews were either evacuating to Isaac or evacuating the system entirely. New hyper portals were opening for civilian ships every few minutes as the last ships still in the system took the arrival of Vice Admiral Rolfson's fleet as a sign it was time to be somewhere else.

Anywhere else.

Updated information from Division Lord Peeah's squadron fed into Morgan's calculations. The most recent data was two days old—and including the note that *Dark Sun* itself had been destroyed, with the Division Lord aboard.

With only two ships left to shadow the Taljzi fleet and the Taljzi's course nailed down, the remaining captains had chosen to withdraw toward Sol. Morgan didn't blame them. Fourteen ships and over three thousand sentients had given their lives to get Asimov the warning and the data they had.

It was enough.

"Captain, I've got a time locus," she announced. "We've got fourteen hours. The Taljzi will arrive at some point in a six-hour window starting then." She shrugged. "That's the ninety-nine percent probability interval, anyway. Small chance we'll see them before or after that, but...most likely within the next twenty hours."

Vong nodded slowly, closing his eyes.

"Make sure you've passed that on to the Admiral's staff," he ordered. "We were hoping for more time, but we'll make do."

The rest of Seventy-Seventh Fleet was at least two days out. Possibly as much as five—and there was no way for Fleet Lord Tanaka to update them and let them know where she was.

Their task force would have to hold the line for at least thirty-six hours.

"We'll be ready, sir," Morgan promised.

CHAPTER FORTY-FOUR

Vice Admiral Harold Rolfson was not a happy husband. He wasn't a particularly *surprised* husband, not really, but he wasn't going to pretend he was happy to see Ramona Wolastoq on the planet the Taljzi were expected to attack.

Or, as was actually the case, walking onto his new flagship from the orbital station refueling the warship.

"Shouldn't you have been on the first transport out?" he asked bluntly. "Or the second? Or the third? Or even the *last* goddamn transport?"

Said last transport was still close enough that he could, he supposed, recall her and throw his wife aboard. Assuming his Ducal Guards were stupid enough to obey the Admiral's orders to do so, anyway.

"There are a lot of people who needed to be off-planet more than I did," Ramona said cheerfully with a smile. "Plus, you should have *seen* the rates some of the ship captains were charging to haul people off-world. I hope they won't get away with that!"

"They won't," Harold said grimly. "The last half-dozen transport captains were spoken to by Rear Admiral Sun *personally*."

With Ducal Guards looming behind the Admiral. In power armor.

For some reason, the captains had been more than willing to listen to the Admiral's impassioned pleas to their compassion and better nature.

And to give the merchant captains credit, the extortionate rates had been a minority. Many captains whose ships had not been designed to carry passengers at all had opened up their cargo bays for a pittance per person that probably didn't even cover fuel and a sleeping bag.

"There are," he continued, "at least three organizations that had a moral, legal and contractual obligation to get you out of this star system. Do you really mean to tell me that neither the University of Asimov, the planetary government nor the Militia got you a ticket out-system?"

His wife shrugged.

"I stopped paying attention to who had bought the tickets after the third or fourth," she admitted. "People kept buying me tickets out-system. I gave them to my students. Even grad students couldn't afford the rate to get out-system on anything more than cold floor."

Harold stared at Ramona for several long seconds in sheer shock.

"How..." He coughed. "How many of your students did you get out?"

"Both of the students left over from my expedition, all twelve of the grad students in the xenoarchaeology department at U of A, and about a third of the impromptu five hundred–level course I was teaching. So, um, thirty or so?"

He took a second to make sure they were alone in the corridor as they headed to his quarters, and then face-palmed.

"The Militia and others bought you *thirty* tickets out-system...and you gave them all away?"

"Something like that, yeah," she admitted.

"Why?!"

"Love, I'm sixty," she pointed out. "The oldest of those students was thirty-two. I've lived a damn successful life—yeah, I've got another couple of centuries in me, best case, but those kids haven't even started.

"If I could evacuate every kid in the system, I would."

"Fair enough," Harold admitted, shaking his head. "God knows I'd give a good bit to be able to spare my crews what's coming."

"Plus, well, I'm an Admiral's wife," Ramona said quietly. "Sun gave me a pretty detailed rundown of where we stood, and I don't care *what* comes next, Harold Rolfson. If you're making a suicide stand, I'm right here with you. Nowhere else I'd want to be."

They entered his quarters and she almost charged into his arms. They held each other silently for a long time.

"Ramona...my mission amounts to 'die standing,'" he admitted. "We need to buy days. *Days.* I can give the bastards a bloody nose, but the only way to delay them that long is to get them to take the time to kill us."

"I know," his wife said levelly, without letting him go. "And you'll do your job. But I'm here and I'm not going anywhere. Together, Harold Rolfson. No matter what. No matter where. I won't let you die alone, hear me?"

He was sure there was *something* wrong with her argument, but he wasn't going to fight her. Not tonight.

REAR ADMIRAL SUN saluted as Harold entered the room, the older Chinese officer looking clearly relieved to finally be able to hand his impossible burden to someone else.

If only the burden that was falling to Harold was less impossible.

"How are we doing for supplies and logistics, Admiral?" Harold asked.

"We emptied our logistics ships as soon as we got the warning," Sun told him. "All of their cargos are in a holding orbit above Isaac.

That let us put all of the Militia support personnel and their families aboard the ships and evacuate them to Sol."

"Makes sense," Harold agreed. "Do we have an inventory?"

"Of course," the older officer said sharply. "We have everything flagged and tagged. There are about a dozen containers labeled GOLD DRAGON that we didn't open, but otherwise, we know what's out there: fuel, missiles, food, spare parts, the works."

"We'll want to crack open those Gold Dragon containers ASAP," Harold ordered. "They either contain hyperspace missiles or tachyon scanners, and either of those will come in handy."

"I take it the secrecy on those protocols is being somewhat relaxed?" Sun asked.

"*Bellerophon* had a Mesharom escape pod aboard when she went up against a Taljzi super-battleship," the Vice Admiral replied. "We'll still try and keep the Gold Dragon gear under wraps, but it was the Mesharom we were worried about—and we'd be derelict in our duty if we didn't go all out to protect this system, Sun."

"Agreed. That's not my call to make, though," the other Admiral pointed out. "I wasn't actually cleared for Gold Dragon beyond the tachyon scanners."

"I saw that those had been deployed into the sensor network," Harold said. "Good work. Even a few seconds' reduction in time delay on our data may make all of the difference, especially when we're firing hyper missiles."

"We don't have very many of those." Sun brought up a list of data on the screens. "I'm hoping the containers have D-HSMs, though S-HSMs would be handy too."

"Reloads are good, but our alpha strike is going to be the best hit we get," Harold agreed. "The only Taljzi ships that have met our hyperspace missiles are dead. We have a decent chance of sucker-punching a good chunk of their capital ships before they even realize they should be dodging."

"That sounds like the best chance we have. Fifteen-to-one odds aren't my favorite."

"Oh, I love fifteen-to-one odds. When I have the fifteen," the senior Admiral said. He stepped over to the screens, bringing up the positions of his ships. Right now, everything was closed in tightly around the planet.

"We'll hold a flag officers' planning session in four hours," Harold continued. "A lot of this is going to come down to whether or not we can make the Taljzi blink. We don't have the firepower to actually *hold* them for three days."

"Any chance for reinforcements before that?" Sun asked.

"Tanaka and Cawl are the only forces remotely close. There's a new fleet mustering at Sol, but they're ten to fourteen days away. The next-nearest Kanzi concentration died at Alstroda, and anyone else is weeks and weeks away."

"The Mesharom?"

"Months," Harold confirmed. "They're involved, the Interpreter aboard *Bellerophon* is why we got here in time, but they're redirecting from other sectors and the Core itself. They won't be here soon."

"So, we hold for Tanaka."

"We hold for Tanaka. One way or another."

CHAPTER FORTY-FIVE

EIGHTY SUPER-BATTLESHIPS REQUIRED A *LOT* OF SAFETY
distance between them. That was before you even factored into play
the fact that while the Imperials were trusting the Kanzi enough to
bring them along, no one wanted to be the ship right next to their
once and future enemies.

Harriet couldn't even see the entirety of the combined fleet from
Justified. Half of the fifty Kanzi capital ships were outside the visibility bubble from *Justified*'s position at the head of the formation.
There were over two hundred starships, a hundred-plus of those
capital ships, trailing her super-battleship flagship.

She had no confidence they would arrive in time and kept
studying the formation and comparing it to the maps of the Asimov
System.

Seventy-Seventh Fleet and her Kanzi allies could *probably* defeat
the Taljzi Return, presuming they hadn't been reinforced and didn't
have more ships they'd been concealing at Alstroda.

Her math said that they were rapidly approaching the earliest
time period the Taljzi might arrive at Asimov, though, and they were

still over a day away from the soonest Rolfson and his task force could arrive.

"Sir."

Harriet looked up, realizing she'd been humming thoughtfully to herself and her A!Tol coms officer had interrupted her.

O!Kan was an A!Tol male, small even for males of his race in that he towered only twenty centimeters or so above Harriet at his full height. He had none of the self-control of older A!Tol and he wore his emotions on his skin without even the slightest filter.

The blueish-pink tinge his skin was currently wearing was a surprise to Harriet, though. That was...relief?

"What is it, Lesser Commander O!Kan?" she asked gently.

"We have a starcom transmission from Sol," the A!Tol reported. "They're relaying a hyperfold transmission from Admiral Rolfson."

There was no way to send a hyperfold transmission from hyperspace. If Rolfson was sending her a message—had sent it over sixteen hours before, if it had already reached Sol for them to relay to her—he'd either failed or somehow pulled off a miracle.

O!Kan's skin did not suggest that they were too late.

"He got there in time," she said aloud.

"They got there in time," O!Kan confirmed. "Details are in the message, but it looks like their Mesharom passenger helped them pull together some kind of hyperspace accelerator. Thanks to Peeah, they know when the Taljzi will arrive."

That was less reassuring.

"When?"

"Their estimate was twenty hours from when they sent the message."

"So, four hours or so from now," Harriet said quietly. "Thank you, O!Kan."

The A!Tol saluted, manipulator tentacle to central torso, and drifted away from her command seat as she considered the situation.

"Sier." She gestured the Yin over to her.

"Your orders, Fleet Lord?"

"Rolfson beat the Taljzi to Asimov," she told him. "They'll be there in about four hours, though. What can we do?"

The blue-feathered avian winced.

"The currents have been helpful, we're only two cycles away, but... the Kanzi don't have sprint modes on their drives, and we can't sustain sprint on our ships that long."

"And it would only buy us a few hours," she said slowly. "But those hours might make all of the difference."

"If I thought we could buy them, I would pass the orders myself, Fleet Lord," Sier told her. "But the attempt would lose us ships...and gain nothing, in the end."

"See if you can get details on what Rolfson did to *Bellerophon*," Harriet finally ordered. "I doubt it's anything we can duplicate, but at this point I'm grasping at anything."

"I don't know if that would be included in the message, and we cannot reply," her chief of staff pointed out. "I will see what I can find. There must be some wind we can lay beneath our wings for this."

She nodded and dismissed him with a wave.

There wasn't. Not really. It was all down to Harold Rolfson and the three terrifyingly capable battleships he commanded.

CHAPTER FORTY-SIX

"WELL, COMMANDER CASIMIR, IT SEEMS WE FOUND SOME more goodies for you in the logistics orbit," Captain Vong told Morgan as he stepped back onto the bridge. "Turns out that the Duchess decided to send every spare HSM of both varieties forward to Asimov to resupply us.

"We'll need you to go through the numbers and coordinate with Engineering," he continued. "I want every D-HSM in those boxes deployed and ready to launch for our sucker punch."

"I'll make it happen," Morgan promised, only half-looking up from the console where she was laying in fire plans for the task force's hyperspace missiles. "Who's running logistics for the fleet base?"

Most of the fleet base personnel had been shipped back to Sol. Despite the limited transportation available, they'd managed to evacuate over two million people.

Of course, that meant there were still over ninety-eight million people left, but it was more than she'd expected.

"Looks like a Commander Karl Rogers," Vong told her. "We're running against the clock here, Casimir. What can we pull off your plate?"

"If we're including new missiles, I need those numbers before I can finalize these firing plans," she admitted. "I'm working with *Herakles'* tactical officer on using our sensor drones to patch the gaps in Asimov Control's tachyon-scanner coverage, but I think I can push that all onto her."

"That's no fairer to Commander Gisarme than it is for us to expect you to handle everything," Vong told her. "Forward everything you have on that to my console. Masters and I will take it over."

"Neither of you have slack either," Morgan pointed out.

"Yes, but we're the ones in charge, which means we get to *make* slack," the Captain replied with a smile. "Regardless of whether or not it's actually possible.

"Now get on those missiles, Commander. They're your number one priority."

THE MISSILES WERE STILL LOCKED down under a Gold Dragon security code, so Morgan's initial attempt to just pull the data from the local systems before she started arranging movement orders came to a short and unsatisfying halt.

With a concealed sigh and a moment of sympathy for Coraniss's attitude toward talking to people, she linked into the coms systems and reached out to Commander Rogers on the main orbital station.

It took a surprisingly long time for Rogers to respond to her call, given that she was hailing from the flagship of the task force.

When the pasty-faced officer finally appeared on her screen, he seemed unimpressed.

"What is it?" he snapped. "We're rather busy here."

"Commander Rogers," she said politely. "This is Commander Casimir aboard *Bellerophon*."

"I know who you are," he responded. "And I don't have a great deal of time for you, so why don't you tell me what you think is so important so I can get back to real work?"

She blinked. She was junior to Commander Rogers, yes, but they now held the same rank and she was the ATO on the flagship, backing up the Admiral's staff. That was *not* the response she was expecting.

"Excuse me, Commander, I'm not sure that came out the way you intended," she said, the temperature of her voice sliding toward freezing. "We have a job to do here."

"Yes, and it'll get done better if I'm not coddling the Duchess's over-promoted daughter, so either get off my screen or tell me what you want," he barked.

"Well, Commander Rogers," she told him, her voice hovering somewhere around absolute zero. "I need access to all of the information you have on the Gold Dragon munitions containers you have in orbit of Asimov, and once I've confirmed what's in them, I'm going to need priority time on your cargo-handling teams to make sure their contents are where they need to be."

"I'll make a note and get back to you," he snapped. "You're not on my priority list, 'Commander.'"

The air quotes around her rank were audible, and Morgan swallowed her anger again.

"I suggest you check again, under the section listed as 'the Vice Admiral's direct orders,' Commander," she told him icily. "Or do I need to bring this conversation to both Vice Admiral Rolfson and Rear Admiral Sun's attention before you, say, *do your damned job?*"

"Watch yourself, Casimir. You're talking to a superior officer," he snapped. "Regardless of what insignia you hang on your collar."

"I don't give two shits what your date of rank is, so long as you do your job," Morgan replied. "Right now, I need to know how many hyperspace missiles we have access to. Whether or not I get those deployed in time will decide whether you and the poor bastards on the planet below get to live through the next twenty-four hours.

"So, either you can give me the authorizations and data I need, or I *will* take this to Vice Admiral Rolfson. How do charges of 'impeding the common defense' sound to your 'superior officer' self...*sir?*"

He was speechless for several seconds, staring at her in shock.

"You wouldn't dare," he hissed.

"One hundred million civilians," Morgan said quietly. "Do you really think I'll stack your offended sense of propriety against their lives? Are *you* really going to put that above their lives?"

Her voice had edged back up to somewhere around freezing, but she was holding his gaze now. She didn't want to ruin the man's career because he was stressed and overreacting—but she also needed those missiles.

"I'll..." He coughed, then swallowed. "I'll have the files on those containers over to you in a couple of minutes and let my tug crews know to expect to hear from you."

"Thank you, Commander Rogers." She smiled. "Given the stress we're all under, I don't think this needs to be mentioned to anyone, do you?"

THE SHIPMENT from Earth was better than Morgan had dared hope. It looked like basically every hyperspace weapon that wasn't currently loaded aboard a warship or defense platform had been stuffed into the sealed containers and shipped to Asimov.

It wasn't a lot in the grand scheme of things—there was, for example, a single manufacturing line for S-HSMs in the entire Imperium, hidden inside DragonWorks bubble in Jupiter—but it was enough to make a difference.

A full reload for all the battleships' S-HSM launchers and another two hundred D-HSMs. That was easily four or five times as many weapons as she'd expected.

She sent orders out to the tug crews to open up the containers. The D-HSMs would get added to the floating array of prepared missiles in Isaac orbit, almost doubling the number of the massive missiles they'd deploy in their first salvo.

The S-HSMs were hopefully already in the reload-packs of five that would drop easily into the *Bellerophons'* magazines. That would allow them to rearm the battleships in under ten minutes, doubling the Task Force's sustained long-range fire.

She noted up everything she'd found and forwarded it to the Admiral's staff, and went back to her fire plans. The Taljzi didn't know what was waiting for them, and if the humans were very lucky, that might be enough.

She was still updating her primary fire plan when everything went to hell and the battle stations alert went off.

"Hyper portal!" Masters snapped from the main command seat. "We have multiple hyper portals on the system perimeter. Fleet orders to battle stations!"

Morgan was left hoping the tugs could work quickly as she turned her console to its battle configuration.

They were out of time.

CHAPTER FORTY-SEVEN

"What am I looking at?" Rolfson demanded as he barged onto his flag bridge.

"Well, I'm pretty sure 'nothing' isn't the right answer," Ling Yu told him drily. "So, I'm guessing we're looking at the Taljzi playing clever buggers. We had at least five separate portals opening. None were large enough for significant formations, but all were big enough for a cruiser or battleship to come through.

"And since we can't see *anything*, tachyon scanners or no, I'm guessing the buggers have stealth fields."

"We learned at Xīn Táiwān that their stealth fields suck," Rolfson replied. "Is that data enough for us to pick them up?"

"We're working on it," she replied. "The call is yours, though: do we want to reveal that we can see through their invisibility cloak just yet?"

"That'll depend on how many damn ships they have in my system, Captain," he told her. "Find me some Taljzi."

He settled into his seat, pulling data onto his personal repeaters while he studied the main tactical plot. All five of the hyper portals were flagged on the big hologram, but that didn't tell them much.

Even under stealth, the Taljzi were maneuvering at half the speed of light. The potential area they could be hiding in was growing almost exponentially with each passing second.

"And...there we go," Ling Yu reported. "Casimir flagged a battleship here. Hold on." She held up a hand. "Yup, battleship by portal three. Gisarme has dialed in a pair of cruisers by portal five. We're relaying the data to the other ships; that should help us..."

Eight more red icons appeared on the screen, and Rolfson grunted in satisfaction. Five hyper portals had thrown out two battleships and eight cruisers, reinforcing the theory that only the Taljzi battleships and cruisers had stealth.

"So, two choices now, I suppose," he murmured aloud. "Do we let them scout around so the Taljzi think they can hide from us later, or do we kick their asses now and leave the rest of the Return wondering?"

"I can't guarantee we've got them all, sir," Ling Yu pointed out. "Plus, we can only hit them with hyper missiles at this range, and if we miss even one..."

"Then our sucker punch gets undermined," he agreed with a sigh. "Hold the task force in position in Isaac orbit. Move ships as needed to make sure the bastards do *not* get a clean line of sight on the D-HSM swarm.

"Let them see what they expect to see: a desperately rushed and thrown-together defence force." Rolfson grinned coldly. "And then when they bring their friends, well, we'll show them how effective their invisibility cloak really is."

THE TALJZI WERE CLEARLY MORE confident in their stealth screens than Harold's experience with the aliens suggested they should be. The battleships hung back, well away from his fleet, but the cruisers swept their way around the system with an almost-complete disregard for the defenders.

If they hadn't already evacuated all of the space stations, there were several points where Harold would have ordered the cruisers destroyed regardless. As it was, they just "accidentally" kept destroyers between the Taljzi ships and the floating swarm of over four hundred dual-portal hyperspace missiles.

The tactical teams of the three battleships had each assembled firing plans, and they were now running them against each other, taking into account the new boxes of missiles that Commander Casimir had managed to identify and get opened up.

No plan would survive contact with the enemy, and the presence of the stealth ships swanning around the Asimov System was a potential roadblock. Once their sucker punch connected, the follow-up was going to be critical, and Harold wasn't even sure what that was going to be just yet.

"Well, I suppose the good news is that they've used up two hours dancing around the system waiting to see what we do," Ling Yu said philosophically. "We're now three hours into their window, so I'm guessing the big boys are hanging out in hyperspace either on a specific timetable or waiting for their scouts to report back in."

"I'd have a timetable, personally," Harold admitted. "Gives the scouts more time to pick up data and, well, doesn't leave me waiting for them to come back if something goes wrong. Depending on how much I trust my scanners and stealth systems...at least two, more likely four or five hours."

"And it's going to wear down our crews," Ling Yu warned him.

"Agreed." He studied the holographic plot, wishing he knew what his enemy was thinking. Right now, he didn't even know who his counterpart was—presumably someone was in command on the other side.

But was that someone who'd earned their rank through battle or through seniority? Or, even stranger to Harold's mind, through being cloned from the stock some scientist had labeled "fleet commander" and stuffed full of someone else's knowledge?

The possibility existed that every fleet commander they'd meet among the Taljzi could be, in some ways, the exact same person. He didn't know if they'd faced enemies out in the dark stars beyond civilized space.

His counterpart could be a clone, running with theoretical training and downloaded memories of a three-century-old war. Or they could be a hardened veteran who'd fought their way up the ranks against enemies unknown to the A!Tol Imperium.

Or possibly both.

"We really don't know enough about these people," he said aloud. "I can't guess which way they're going to jump."

"Well, they are Kanzi. If we were facing a Kanzi Fleet Master, what would you expect?" Ling Yu asked.

Harold snorted.

"I'd ask to see their file," he admitted. "In the main, though…I'd expect them to try and wear us down, and I'd be looking for at least one more feint to try and make us overreact."

He sighed.

"Orders to the fleet: two-thirds of all ships will drop to status two while the remaining vessels remain at battle stations. We will rotate every two hours until every Alpha Team has had a break, then we'll reconsider."

"Or the Taljzi will reconsider for us," Ling Yu pointed out as she began to open the communications link.

"Or maybe the horse will learn to sing and they saw Tanaka coming and ran scared," Harold countered. "But most likely, yes. I don't expect to complete that cycle of stand-downs."

But at least some of his crews would be better rested. It was all he could do for now.

HAROLD DIDN'T LEAVE the bridge for the following hours. Even when *Bellerophon* stood down to status two, letting most of her crew take at least a quick break, the Admiral remained on the bridge. A steward brought him coffee and a sandwich, and he ate and drank quickly, barely registering the food.

Every hour that the Taljzi decided to scout the system was an hour less he had to wait for Tanaka to arrive. The earliest she was due was forty hours after the stealthed ships arrived. The latest was over a hundred hours. A three-day window for how long he had to hold.

He wasn't going to complain if the enemy spent four hours dancing around the system. Or ten. Hell, if they wanted to spend a *week* wandering around, poking at the shadows to find his secrets, he'd cheer.

He knew he wasn't going to get that, so he'd count every minute, every hour, they were prepared to give him as precious.

But in the end, they had to have a decent idea of the time constraint he was under.

"We're about to cycle over," Ling Yu told him quietly. "That'll bring *Perseus* back to battle stations and take *Herakles* back to status two." She shook her head. "You said six hours if they were Kanzi, huh?"

"If they were Kanzi, I'd have expected at least one more play at psychological warfare," he admitted. "Even if it was just opening up hyper portals without sending anyone through, just to see what we—"

"Hyper portal!"

He and Ling Yu turned to look at the holographic plot in sync, looking for the icon they both knew would be there.

There was only one portal, but it was huge. The Taljzi had ripped a hole in space a thousand kilometers across, and their super-battleships led the way in pentagonal "walls" of five apiece.

He'd been expecting fifteen of the massive warships, so the first three formations didn't surprise him. The fourth did. The *fifth* sent a chill down his spine.

The sixth set of capital ships terrified him. That was *thirty* super-battleships. If the rest of their fleet had been equally augmented, his stand went from "suicide to achieve the objective" to merely suicide.

Then the destroyers started coming through, in a widely dispersed cylindrical formation he could guess the purpose of.

"Get me sensor resolution on the inside of that cylinder," he ordered. "I'm going to guess that's where they're hiding the battleships and cruisers."

The smaller ships kept coming, circles of ten at a time emerging every few seconds from the portal. Easily two hundred destroyers, double the number that had been at Alstroda, emerged.

Lastly, a wall of ten battleships that weren't in stealth emerged. Clearly, they were the ones who'd been holding the portal open, as the gap into hyperspace collapsed behind them.

"We think we've nailed down the stealth ships," Ling Yu said from behind him, her voice small.

"How bad?"

"Thirty super-battleships. Sixty battleships and sixty cruisers, including our ghosts. Two hundred destroyers. Three hundred and fifty warships, all basically Core Power ships."

"So are the *Bellerophon*s now," he said grimly. "We have the super-battleships dialed in?"

"The plan called for fifteen, sir," Ling Yu reminded him. "We think we can kill fifteen. I don't know about..."

"We can't kill thirty," Harold told her. "Target the leading fifteen. Let's bloody their noses."

He studied the red icons speckling his plot. They didn't know he could see them in real time. They didn't know he could *hit* them at this range. They were sorting out their formations, flying in nice, predictable patterns.

"The order is *hakkaa päälle!*"

Cut them down.

CHAPTER FORTY-EIGHT

"THE ORDER IS *HAKKAA PÄÄLLE!*"

Morgan had spent the entire time since they'd arrived in Asimov preparing for this moment. Since she was the only one who'd fired hyperspace missiles before, controlling their entire salvo of dual-portal missiles had fallen to her.

She was also controlling *Bellerophon*'s missiles and had helped write the fire-pattern plan for everyone else. More than any other individual in the task force, the sucker punch they were trying to land was her responsibility.

And the moment she hit the button in response to Vice Admiral Rolfson's command, there was no longer anything she could do. Hundreds of hyperspace portals opened across Isaac's orbit and missiles disappeared.

Bellerophon, however, *screamed*. Two of her four S-HSM batteries responded to Morgan's commands, generating their portals as expected and flinging their missiles through them. The other two...did not.

"Hotel One, report," she snapped. "Hotel Four, report. What's your status?"

"This is Hotel One. The portal destabilized; we were forced to shut it down. Two of our emitters just *disintegrated*. Sir...we can't fire. We don't have a portal."

That was six launchers rendered useless—bad-enough news. Worse news, however, was the automated report from Hotel Four.

Hotel Four was *gone*. The hyper portal hadn't been shut down by a vigilant gun crew. It had been shut down by emergency failsafes... too late.

"Sir, Hotel One is disabled and Hotel Four is destroyed," Morgan reported grimly. "We lost Four's portal, launchers, and crew."

That was at least fifty people dead, torn apart by the suddenly untamed vortex into hyperspace that had been the core of their weapon system.

She hated herself for what she had to do, but she focused her gaze on her systems as she pulled the data.

"Hotel One's magazines are intact; I'll get the crew on transferring the weapons," she continued. "Hotel Four's magazines are wrecked. I'm going to have to eject them to protect us from the warheads."

Unlike most of the other weapons aboard *Bellerophon*, the hyper missiles carried warheads. Big, nasty antimatter warheads. The ninety missiles in Hotel Four's magazines represented almost two *teratons* of explosive power.

"Do it!" Vong ordered.

Morgan already had...and only then turned her attention to the enemy.

The salvo might have been twelve missiles short, but the rest of the *Bellerophon*s and the *Thunderstorm*-Ds had done them proud. Four hundred-plus dual-portal missiles had launched independently from Isaac orbit, and the antimatter explosions were only fading now as she looked.

They'd targeted fifteen super-battleships. The Taljzi ships were bigger than any Kanzi or A!Tol warship ever built, clad in the heavy shields and compressed-matter armor the A!Tol vessels commanded and the Kanzi couldn't yet match.

They were both unimaginably immense and unimaginably tough.

Two of them survived, reeling wrecks spewing atmosphere from gaping wounds in their sides.

"Orders from the flag, all S-HSM batteries are to continue firing," Antonova relayed. "They're not dodging hard enough yet, and every ship we kill in this pass is one we don't have to fight later!"

"Continue fire with Hotel Two and Three, if you please, Commander Casimir," Captain Vong ordered calmly. "I'd like to add some super-battleship kills to our list that no one is going to argue with."

"Yes, sir." Her attention focused on the task ahead, retargeting her launchers on the remaining super-battleships.

Her people were wounded and dying. Many had died instantly when Hotel Four's hyper portal had lost control. But if she focused on that, the civilians behind her would pay the price.

Morgan Casimir was Annette Bond's daughter in every way that mattered. That would *not* happen.

IT TOOK ALMOST a full minute for the Taljzi force to even begin to react—a minute in which a second salvo of hyperspace missiles from the internal launchers claimed another five super-battleships.

Then the aliens started maneuvering, initiating what had to be their standard evasive patterns to reduce missile and beam hits at range. They hadn't known they were in the defenders' range, but now that they did, they reacted to it.

Ten super-battleships survived at that point, two-thirds of their heavy capital ship strength smashed before the battle had even begun. The third salvo of hyper missiles was less effective even than the second. The evasive maneuvers meant that none of the missiles emerged inside Taljzi shields.

Even the S-HSM missiles were slow in real space, only having seconds of endurance left on their interface drives at that point. The need to make an easy emergence from hyperspace kept their velocity down, and they closed with the Taljzi ships at a mere fifteen percent of lightspeed.

Heavy antimatter warheads erupted throughout the enemy formation, but they'd spread their fire too much, hoping for the shield-penetrating kills of the first two salvos.

Shields flickered across the Taljzi fleet, but only one super-battleship's shields fell. Data streaming into Morgan's display told her they'd breached the ship's compressed-matter armor, but she remained in the fight.

"Focus fire on single targets," Captain Ling Yu's voice murmured in her headset. "Flagging SB-22, we already tagged him, let's drown him in fire."

They were firing at a relatively slow pace for the launchers they had available, waiting to see the results of each batch of missiles before opening fire again. That let them recalibrate, and their fourth salvo went entirely at the super-battleship whose armor they'd cracked.

She writhed in the fire as hundreds of missiles emerged from hyperspace around her, twenty-gigaton warheads igniting new suns as the super-battleship tried desperately to survive.

She failed. The Taljzi warship's shields collapsed once more, and at least a dozen missiles hammered into her armor. Mighty as she was, that was more than she could take.

"Target SB-25," Ling Yu ordered. "Take her."

Morgan was already flagging the remaining ships in sequence. A single tap directed *Bellerophon*'s remaining S-HSM batteries towards the designated target.

A few seconds later, SB-25 shared her sisters' fate. Twenty-two of the Taljzi super-battleships were destroyed or crippled.

The Militia ships had spent half of the cruisers' missiles, though, and *Bellerophon*'s damage was undermining the salvos.

They had five more solid hits, and then they were going to have to see what the Taljzi did when the long-range bombardment stopped.

"Hostiles are moving towards us, point six cee," Masters reported. Morgan's boss was handling the sensors while she managed the hyperspace missiles. "If their missiles line up with previous encounters, range in five minutes."

"Minimum-sequence fire," Ling Yu ordered. "SB-26 and work your way up to 30. Hack them down, people."

Morgan smirked at the Iranian-Chinese officer's translated repetition of the Scandinavian Admiral's order, but the sequence was already in play in her computers. Five more salvos until the cruisers ran dry.

Those salvos would take them just over three minutes to fire. Then they'd get to see what the Taljzi were going to bring to bear on Asimov.

A SUPER-BATTLESHIP DIED. Then another. And another. The lead elements of the Taljzi Return were melting away as Morgan and her fellows hammered their hyperspace missiles into the charging fleet.

The Taljzi couldn't know that the Militia were going to run out of ammunition, and Morgan couldn't help but wonder just what they *were* thinking. Even with their losses, over three hundred ships were still charging toward the planet.

"That's the last salvo from the cruisers," she reported as the tenth salvo of S-HSMs shot out. "I don't think the battleships can put enough fire on target for guaranteed kills."

When the last full salvo cleared, only five super-battleships remained from thirty. An entire battle fleet's worth of warships was wreckage and cripples in the wake of the charging Taljzi, and they were *still* coming.

"No, we'll need the rest of the weapons," Vong agreed. "Hume, prepare to take us forward. Combat maneuvers online now."

The icons on Morgan's screen began to shift as the warships began their own evasive maneuvers.

"All right, people," Ling Yu's voice sounded over her earbud. "We're down to sixty launchers now and no idea if *Bellerophon* is getting her surviving damaged battery back online. Target is SB-18. Hammer her to pieces. Continue minimum-sequence fire."

Sixty missiles against a maneuvering target wasn't enough for a guaranteed kill, but a salvo every thirty seconds was enough to leave the Taljzi super-battleship desperately maneuvering to try and avoid the explosions and keep intact shields between her and the incoming fire.

She dodged *into* a cruiser, the smaller ship's shields flickering under the impact—and then vanishing as two hyperspace missiles hit the wrong ship. The cruiser imploded, the gravitational singularity that fed her power system breaking containment...in contact with the super-battleship.

Half of SB-18 was sucked into the temporary black hole. The other half took most of a salvo of twenty-gigaton hyper missiles and disappeared.

"Enemy range in twenty seconds," Masters reported. "All Bucklers deployed."

"For what we are about to receive, may the divine make us truly thankful," Vong snarked from the center chair. "That's it for hyper missiles, folks. It's time for the old-fashioned part of this brawl."

Morgan shivered as her portals slowly powered down. They hadn't expected to get to a straight missile duel this quickly. The *plan* had been for the Taljzi to pause after taking this bad of a bloody nose.

They'd underestimated how much their enemy simply did not care about losses.

And that was terrifying.

CHAPTER FORTY-NINE

"They have to break."

Ling Yu's almost-prayerful mutter echoed loudly in *Bellerophon*'s flag bridge, and Harold wished he could agree with her.

In his opponent's place, he'd have withdrawn to hyperspace after the first couple of salvos to reassess the situation. Instead, they'd simply taken the fire and were now closing with his fleet.

Assuming the Taljzi ran similar crews to the Kanzi, over a *hundred thousand* sentients had already died in this battle, and they were barely getting started.

"Are they maneuvering to stay out of our missile range?" he asked.

"No, they are heading straight towards us at what we believe is their maximum speed," Ling Yu reported after a moment. "Thirty seconds to our range. Thirty-five to the range of the orbital defenses."

His ships were armed with the latest and greatest sublight missiles the Duchy of Terra Militia had access to. Given the role of the Terran Militia as the testing bed for the Imperial Navy, that meant they had the best missiles the A!Tol Imperium had access to.

The orbital defenses were, at least, equipped with point eight cee missiles. They were the first generation of missiles the Imperium had built with that capability, and they had several critical seconds' less endurance than his task force's missiles.

"Hold fire until they're in range of the defenses," he ordered. "I'm not passing up another couple of hundred launchers in the teeth of this."

"Enemy is launching."

Harold's calm determination to play the battle by his rules took a hard hit as the enemy fleet disappeared behind the wall of red icons. His enemies carried fewer varieties of weapons than his own ships, and while the Taljzi battleships lost some of the advantage from carrying the stealth systems, they had far more launchers per ton than he did.

And they had sixty battleships to his three. They might have shattered the Taljzi's super-battleship strength, but they hadn't even touched the smaller capital ships.

"We need to buy time to rearm the hyperspace launchers," Ling Yu told him. "I don't suppose you have any clever ideas?"

"Move the Bucklers forward and pull the escorts back behind them," Harold ordered, his voice far calmer than he expected. "The new Bucklers have hyperfold coms; we can control them at range. Also, release all hyperfold cannons to the point-defense role and integrate them with the tachyon scanners."

He watched the tsunami rushing toward his task force and forced a grin.

"They may *think* they have the technology advantage here, but we need to teach them how wrong they are."

There was a continuing debate on whether or not the next generation of Buckler drones and Sword turrets should mount light hyperfold cannons instead of lasers. So far, the desire to keep the tachyon scanners secret had helped keep the argument in favor of the existing system.

Task Force 77–1's defense against the Taljzi Return was probably going to change that.

Even at point eight five cee, tachyon scanners gave the Buckler's lasers time to adjust and assess. Speed was far less of a defense against sensors that picked up the missiles in real time. Hundreds of missiles died to the lasers of the first line of defense.

Then the Sword turrets on the escorts opened up—and the hyperfold cannons on the later-model *Thunderstorms* and the *Bellerophons* lit up as well. The space around Harold's fleet was glittering with the light of destroyed missiles, and he almost held his breath, waiting for the damage report.

"Sixty hits across the battleships," Ling Yu finally told him. "Shields are holding. None of the escorts were hit."

"That's it?" he replied, stunned. "I saw the Mesharom do the hyperfold cannon-tachyon scanner combination at Centauri. I still didn't expect it to be *this* effective."

"Again, I think, with the enemy not expecting it," his ops officer told him. "It won't be as effective in the future...but now it's *our* turn."

Three battleships and over a hundred and fifty escorts opened fire as one. Two hundred defensive platforms, each holding a single automated missile launcher, joined the salvo.

It was a tiny response to the tsunami the Taljzi had just unleashed on them, but their enemy didn't have active missile defenses. The Taljzi could dodge or rely on their shields...but they couldn't shoot down missiles in their hundreds and thousands.

"Second enemy salvo incoming, defenses engaging," Ling Yu reported. "They haven't had a chance to adapt; I think we're going to gut this one, too."

Harold's eyes were on his own attack this time, the missiles slashing into the Taljzi fleet. The enemy had been evading since the third salvo of hyperspace missiles, and their ECM came online now. Ghosts and jammers lured and deluded his missiles, and their systems were better than he'd expected.

A *lot* better, in fact. Better than his.

But not good enough. Decoyed missiles slammed into escorts.

Unaffected missiles slammed into battleships. Half a dozen cruisers blew apart, their shields overwhelmed. A battleship's shields flickered, her armor seeming to hold...and then the singularity at her core collapsed.

As the one battleship disappeared, shields dropped on two more and their own salvo melted away in the teeth of the hyperfold cannons defending the Militia fleet.

"Hyper portal!" Ling Yu barked. "What the hell? They can't open one that..."

It seemed the Taljzi could. Exotic-matter emitters tore a hole through reality far closer than any Imperial ship could manage, and the Return was suddenly gone, their remaining ships fleeing into hyperspace.

The flag bridge was silent.

"We took no losses, sir," Ling Yu finally said. "A few shield failures. *Perseus* took a hard knock, but nothing that made it through the armor. Our worst damage was the hyper portal failures on *Bellerophon*."

"They had no idea what they were facing," Harold pointed out grimly. "They'll know next time."

And he still had to hold for at least thirty more hours.

"SO, that went better than we were afraid of, but I'm not liking what it's telling me for round two," Harold said grimly to the conference of his flag officers a few minutes later. "How long to rearm the battleships with S-HSMs?"

"Already underway," Ling Yu replied. "Casimir drew up a plan for what to do with our extra missiles from her Hotel One magazine and the missiles that would have gone to her two missing batteries.

"That's three full loads for a battleship battery's magazines, which means four and a half for the cruisers—she's suggesting we give each of the cruisers a half-load for each launcher. That'll reduce our firepower for the trailing salvos from the battleships, but it'll give us five solid salvos from everything."

"It's a good suggestion," Harold allowed. "Make it happen. With a full salvo from all nineteen ships with S-HSM launchers, we have a near-guaranteed kill on anything in their order of battle. The same is not true with only sixty missiles from the battleships."

"I'm almost more concerned about the way they ran," Division Lord Iffa pointed out. The Frole commanded Harold's sixteen *Abrasion*-class cruisers from the Imperial Navy. "If they can come out of hyperspace as close to the planet as they went in, they can emerge inside weapons range."

"That's what they did to the Mesharom," Rear Admiral Sun agreed. "But the Mesharom were in deep space. Can they pull the same trick on us?"

"I've put that question to our engineers," Harold told them. "I don't know. We're going to need to watch for it regardless, as the Taljzi have once again demonstrated that just because *we* think something is a hard and fast rule doesn't mean it applies to them."

"I wish some of those discoveries were in our favor," Iffa complained.

"At least one has been," the Admiral argued. "We would assume that a ship with compressed-matter armor and heavy shielding would also have active missile defense. The Taljzi don't have those systems, which is the only reason this task force held our own in the actual missile exchange.

"The closer they get, however, the less that matters," he continued grimly. "Demonstrably, we have no defenses that can stop the hyper disruptors they use as energy weapons, and our proton beams are all but useless.

"Our hyperfold cannons and plasma lances are our only hope when the bastards close." Harold shook his head, studying the screen listing their strength and the armaments of each vessel.

"Make no mistake, people, if the Taljzi decide they are prepared to take the losses a direct charge would inflict, they can get enough capital ships to disruptor range to end this battle," he said. "Against any other opponent, I'd say they wouldn't be willing to make that trade. They've already lost over ten times our total tonnage.

"But one of the reasons they lost that much was that they pressed the attack long after anyone else would have. They are not *completely* insensitive to losses, clearly, but they also don't put the same value on their crews' lives as we do."

"So, what do we do?" Sun asked.

"We keep smashing them in the nose for at least three more days. Under no circumstances do we withdraw. One way or another, we keep these sons of bitches out of Isaac orbit until Fleet Lord Tanaka arrives."

"And what do we do if they get more reinforcements?" someone else asked.

Harold smiled coldly.

"What part of 'under no circumstances' wasn't clear?"

CHAPTER FIFTY

THE GENERAL QUARTERS ALERT JERKED MORGAN AWAKE FROM the first sleep she'd had in over a day. She hadn't even bothered to get out of her combat uniform with its emergency vacuum gear before falling over.

They'd had twelve hours of silence from their enemies, and Morgan had finally managed to get back to her quarters. Her communicator told her she'd managed four hours of sleep, which meant that it had taken the Taljzi sixteen hours to decide what the hell they were planning on doing.

The screen on her communicator wasn't large enough for her to get a good idea of what that plan was, especially given that she was trying to read it while moving. Her quarters were exactly ninety seconds' brisk walk from her battle station on the bridge.

She made it in just over a minute, slightly out of breath as she dropped into her seat and brought up her console to see if she could make sense of the enemy.

Commander Masters gave her a firm nod.

"What do you make of it, Casimir?" he asked with a gesture toward the plot.

"Well, firstly, they apparently can't leave hyperspace as close to the star as they can enter it," she replied. The new hyper portal was at the same distance as the Taljzi's original arrival, not at the range where they'd fled into hyperspace.

That distance, she realized, was actually *farther* than an Imperial drive or current-generation Kanzi drive. The Taljzi, it seemed, had taken a different route in developing their hyperdrives over the last three hundred years.

"Also, they still think their stealth fields work on us," she continued. None of the super-battleships or destroyers were on her screens. Their scanners were still resolving the numbers hidden inside the enemy stealth screens, but the Taljzi's version of the device was vastly inferior to the Core Powers'.

"According to the files on Centauri, it's unusually effective in atmosphere," Masters replied. "But yes, our tachyon scanners can resolve through it significantly more reliably than we can resolve through the other stealth fields we've encountered."

Twenty battleships and forty cruisers had emerged from the hyperspace portal, but they'd done so under stealth and were approaching the joint Terran-Imperial task force at barely a quarter of the speed of light.

"They're trying to be sneaky," Morgan concluded. "They've learned that we have a massive advantage at long range, so they're using their stealth fields—which we don't have and they haven't realized we can see through—to try and get into at least missile range before engaging."

"Agreed. I figure they'll try and sneak all the way into range of their disruptors." *Bellerophon*'s tactical officer smirked. "If they were Mesharom, I'd be worried. As it is, we could start picking them off right now."

"Are those our orders?" she asked.

"No. They're well out of regular missile range, so we're waiting on orders from the flag. Someone actually managed to convince the Admiral to go take a nap."

Morgan chuckled. Masters had basically ordered her to go sleep, but there wasn't anyone aboard who could do that to Admiral Rolfson.

"How'd they manage that?" she asked.

"No one is saying, but reading between the lines, Ling Yu got his wife involved."

"So, we wait for orders," Morgan confirmed, still chuckling as she studied the screen. "Can we take them if we let them get closer?"

"It depends on what range we let them get to, I suppose," Masters admitted. "I kind of want to shoot them to hell right now...but I suspect the Admiral is going to want to hold on to the hyper missiles for a bit longer."

Morgan's fingers flew over her console, drawing in various weapon ranges for the fleet.

"Ten light-seconds," she suggested.

"Commander?" Masters sounded confused.

"I'm guessing we open fire at ten light-seconds. Far enough out that they might buy we didn't see them yet and might still be holding their fire and, well..." She gestured at the spheres on her console. "Inside range for our hyperfold cannons and plasma lances."

"ALL RIGHT, everyone, this is Vice Admiral Rolfson."

The Admiral's voice was as bright and cheery as always over the shipwide PA, presumably on every ship in the task force.

"The enemy thought they had enough of an advantage that they could just roll over us. That didn't work out so well for them, and they've already lost more in Asimov than they have in their whole campaign so far.

"Now they want to be sneaky, and we're getting the payoff for ignoring their scout ships. They think they have a cloak of invisibility but we...we, my fellow spacers, know that the emperor is naked."

Morgan snorted. There were probably a lot of confused nonhumans in the task force now, but they probably got the gist from context.

"We're going to let them close. The moment they launch, we launch...but if they're brave enough and confident enough to get to ten light-seconds, then we give them everything we've got.

"Now, there's a risk to this, people. The closer they get, the less time our missile defenses have to shoot down their missiles, and if we have the hyperfold cannons tasked for offensive fire, our defenses are weaker than they were before.

"But if we pull this off, we wipe out a third of their remaining ships and we make the bastards think twice before sticking their noses in this system again.

"Remember: Fleet Lord Tanaka is on her way. We don't have to wipe these Taljzi out. We don't even have to drive them off. We just need to make them hesitate enough that when they finally go all out, they're doing it into the teeth of over fifty super-battleships.

"I don't know you all as well as I'd like, but I know enough of you. And I know the traditions of the Imperial Navy and the Duchy of Terra Militia.

"And I know there are a hundred million civilians behind us," the Admiral concluded grimly, as Morgan saw every spine in the room straighten.

"I will not fail them. I know that *you* will not fail them. Godspeed and shoot straight, people."

WATCHING an enemy flotilla approach and doing nothing was harder than Morgan would have expected. *Bellerophon*'s bridge grew quieter with each passing moment, until it reached absolute silence at around five million kilometers.

Both sides were so far inside each other's missile ranges, it was insane. At point eight cee, it would take barely twenty seconds for the defenders' missiles to arrive. The Taljzi weapons would arrive even faster.

But eighty warships continued their steady, deliberate advance underneath their stealth fields. Seconds ticked away and Morgan passed a course correction over to Hume at navigation. Their hyperfold cannons could target anything in the enemy force, but the plasma lance had a limited firing arc.

They needed to make sure the battleships were in it.

"Ten seconds."

Masters's words echoed in the dead silence of the bridge.

"I have the lance," Morgan confirmed, her voice also quiet, as if the enemy could hear them.

Part of her screen was showing her her superior's targeting of the hyperfold cannons. Each of the battleships was targeting two battleships, one with their lance and one with their cannons. All of the cruisers had plasma lances, but theirs didn't match the power a matter-conversion plant could feed into a battleship-sized weapon.

Only about half the cruisers had hyperfold cannons. All told, however, every single Taljzi battleship was being targeted with enough firepower for what *should* be an instant kill.

"Hakkaa päälle!"

Morgan didn't bother to establish if the harsh Finnish phrase was from the Admiral or not. The ten-light-second mark was crossed and her plasma lance came eagerly to life at her command.

Unlike the hyperfold cannon, it was "merely" a lightspeed weapon. A magnetic channel flashed across space to lock on to her target, and then hundreds of kilograms of superheated plasma flashed down that channel at nearly the speed of light.

The Taljzi battleship's shields could have taken the lesser bolts unleashed by the cruisers. Its armor could absorb even those mighty blows.

Against the might of *Bellerophon*'s plasma lance, those defenses failed and plasma gutted the ship. The implosion of her gravitic singularity contained the explosion and compressed the heavy armor into a crumpled ball.

A single cruiser lance couldn't duplicate that impact—but that was why TF 77–1's cruisers had fired their lances by eight-ship echelon. Eight cruiser lances were more than enough to obliterate even the mightiest Taljzi warship.

The problem, Morgan realized, was that the lances were light-speed weapons, invisible before they arrived...but the hyperfold cannons were *faster*-than-light weapons. They'd arrived instantly, a cascade of energy fire that had washed over the Taljzi fleet, demonstrating they'd been seen but wrecking only half the battleships.

None of the battleships that survived the hyperfold-cannon bombardment survived the plasma lance fire, but all of them lived long enough to launch missiles.

As did the cruisers. Thousands of missiles were now in space, charging toward TF 77–1. More plasma fire and hyperfold beams lashed the Taljzi fleet, and the defenders' missiles were also on their way. Cruisers started to die, and not a single Taljzi ship retreated. Even without the battleships they'd come in to escort, the cruisers charged forward.

Stealth fields dropped and a second salvo of missiles lashed out. Cruisers passed into the firing arc of Morgan's plasma lance, and even a *glancing* blow from *Bellerophon*'s spinal cannon was enough to obliterate the lighter Taljzi ships.

The Imperial and Terran destroyers did what they had to do, flinging themselves forward into the teeth of the missile storm as it passed through the shield of Buckler drones. Sixty destroyers backed up almost a thousand drones, but they had only fractions of a second to stop the Taljzi missiles.

It wasn't enough time.

Destroyers burned in the fire, but they weren't the targets. Cruisers interposed themselves, taking hits meant for the *Bellerophon*s. The escorts flung themselves between the battleships and the incoming fire.

It was...enough. All three battleships took hits. *Herakles'* shields collapsed and missiles hammered into her armor, but she was intact.

The Taljzi were not. Eighty warships had tried to sneak up on TF 77–1 and none of them had survived. Almost half of the Return's initial capital ship strength was gone, a stunningly lopsided victory by any calculation.

Except Morgan was grimly certain that the Taljzi weren't done yet and the Imperial losses were now being tallied on her screen.

Eighteen destroyers and six cruisers had died to save the battleships, including one of the precious *Thunderstorm*-Ds. They'd taken a hundred times their tonnage and firepower with them, but it wasn't going to be enough.

Morgan wasn't sure that *anything* was going to be enough.

CHAPTER FIFTY-ONE

TWENTY-FOUR SHIPS GONE IN A BLINK. AS MANY DAMAGED, AND Harold was getting no information on whether some of them would be able to fight again.

In fact...

"Nahid," he addressed Ling Yu. "Inform Captain Ngo that if she *doesn't* get me a detailed status report on *Fēngbào Yún*'s status in the next five minutes, I'm going to assume that she's not combat-capable and order her to withdraw."

He didn't *want* to lose a *Thunderstorm*-D from the order of battle, but if Kimberly Ngo wasn't telling him whether or not her ship could fight, his suspicions went the wrong way.

"I'll tell her," his chief of staff confirmed.

Harold shook his head and returned his attention to the holographic plot. Regardless of *Fēngbào Yún*'s status, he was down at least ten cruisers. He had five good salvos of hyper missiles left to open up the battle with, and then they were down to fighting the Taljzi in their range.

And they still had over ten times as many capital ships as he did. They'd tested his people, then they'd tried to sneak up on his people.

The next step was to line up forty-odd capital ships and clobber his people. There wasn't much else they could do...and there really wasn't a need *for* them to do more. The sneak attack would have worked if their stealth fields were effective against his people, but the Taljzi would figure out that the attempt hadn't worked.

If anything, Harold was curious as to how long the Taljzi would wait for their stealthed force to report back. Presumably, there had been a time limit. At some point, the Return would have to send new scouts through.

Which left him with an idea.

"Nahid." He gestured his chief of staff over. "How many more hyper missiles than the cruisers do the battleships have?"

"Cruisers are carrying five rounds per launcher. Battleships have ten apiece."

"Make sure the battleship tactical officers know they are authorized to fire at enemy scout ships that come through," Harold ordered. "They're to maintain a five-missile reserve per launcher, but I want the Taljzi completely uncertain what's happening here."

"I'll pass it on."

Ling Yu had barely returned to her console when the first hyper portal opened. A stealthed cruiser slipped through, the portal closing behind her as she tried to get into the system to see what had happened to her sisters.

Bellerophon might have been missing twelve launchers, two full batteries, but Casimir and Masters had received the orders first. Twelve hyper missiles bracketed the cruiser moments after the hyper portal closed, making sure that stealth ship wasn't going to report back to the Return.

"My compliments to Captain Vong's tactical officers," Harold said with a smile. "I suggest that the battleships take turns. Let's blind these people."

THREE MORE SCOUT ships followed over the next two and a half hours, each cruiser creeping out of hyperspace slower than the last. Each cruiser was allowed to enter the system and close their hyper portal behind them, and then Harold's people blew them to hell.

"That's our time window," Ling Yu murmured to him. "Tanaka could be here anytime now."

"Anytime in the next two days," he replied. "We still need to hold."

"Then it's a good thing they're still wondering what the hell happened to their scout ships, isn't it?" she said. "How long before they try something more significant?"

"We might be lucky and get another hour so before—"

"Hyper portal! Big one."

"Never mind," Harold said with a wry smile as he studied the hologram. The Taljzi had apparently guessed roughly what was happening and were *damned* determined to find out what had happened to their fleet.

Sixty destroyers screened the remaining super-battleships, and Harold considered for several long seconds.

"All ships with hyper missiles are to target the super-battleships," he ordered. "They're going to learn what they came here for. Let's bleed them for the privilege."

His battleships and remaining *Thunderstorm*-D's obeyed instantly. The first super-battleship died quickly, their initial evasive maneuvers only enough to drag two Taljzi destroyers into the Imperial fire with her.

The second died almost as quickly, but the rest of the Taljzi ships evaded, diving back into hyperspace and wasting one of Harold's precious salvos of faster-than-light missiles.

"How long were they in for?" he asked.

"Seventy-six seconds," Ling Yu confirmed. "Enough. They know we got hurt; they know they lost their entire fleet. Everyone knows all of the pieces now."

He grunted and brought up an estimate of the enemy strength.

"We've got two salvos of S-HSMs left?" he asked.

"Two salvos on the cruisers, nine on the battleships," she confirmed. "It won't be enough."

"No." He looked at the timer for their estimate of Tanaka's arrival as it flipped into the green zone. "We might be able to throw back one more attack. *Maybe.* But it's down to Fleet Lord Tanaka now."

MINUTES BLED into other minutes and then into hours as time passed without anything changing. Harold remained on his bridge, watching the plots and waiting for the final hammer to drop.

Somehow, he wasn't entirely surprised when someone linked his wife into his communicator earbud.

"So, Harold, your staff is calling me again," Ramona said with a throaty chuckle. "Are you zombie-pacing around your bridge, scaring them?"

"Not this time," he told her, keeping his voice quiet so his flag bridge crew couldn't really hear him. "Mostly zombie-staring at the main tactical plot. I can't be anywhere else at this point."

"Your quarters are literally seconds from the flag bridge. You can *sleep*, love."

"Not without medication," Harold admitted. "And we can't afford that, not at this point. No, Ramona, at this point, all I can do is stand the watch."

"Sir." Xun Huang approached him. "I don't want to interrupt, but our damaged ships are loaded up with their new cargo. They're ready to make their run."

"Thank you, Yong," Harold told him. He checked the screens, then turned his attention back to his wife.

"I don't suppose I could convince you to get on one of those ships?" he asked his wife.

"Your very kind staff already tried," Ramona said brightly. "I don't think it would be right to stick the Admiral's wife on the last convoy out, not when the governor's people pulled together a lottery for those few spaces at such short notice."

"That's what they did?" Harold asked in surprise. "I just told them to stick as many people as they could fit onto our cripples before they ran."

"I don't think anything else would have been fair," his wife admitted. "Are...are they going to be safe, Harold?"

"There's no guarantees at this point," he reminded her. "I'm sending extra ships with them to keep an eye on them, but that's all we can do."

"I know. I'm staying," Ramona told him firmly. "I can't make you rest, but know that I'm here. To the end."

"Thank you, love."

She dropped the call and he turned back to Xun Huang.

"How many people did we get on the new convoy?" he asked.

"Three thousand on the cripples. Another eight hundred on the escort squadron."

Harold snorted.

"I *don't* recall telling Commodore Huber she could load civilians onto her destroyers," he pointed out. Sixteen of his *Bonnie Tyler*-class destroyers, the latest out of the Militia's non-DragonWorks design crews, made up Commodore Hillary Huber's command. Their role in the battle to come would be minimal, so he'd assigned them to make sure his crippled cruisers and destroyers made it back to Sol.

"I don't believe the Commodore asked permission," Xun Huang replied. "She's waiting on orders to get underway."

Harold checked the time. Six hours since the last scouting wave. Those six hours had let them pull almost four thousand people off the planet.

It was all they were going to get.

"Tell her to get underway," he ordered.

As his coms officer moved away, Harold studied the tactical plot once more.

The Taljzi had made their scouting run. They knew what he had left, that stealth had failed them. The only option left to them was to repeat their initial charge, a plan that Harold was grimly certain would work.

So...where were they?

CHAPTER FIFTY-TWO

Harriet glared at her screens and holographic plot, as if her angry half-muffled hum could accelerate starships faster than all the artifice of over two dozen species. They'd gained a couple of hours on their original estimate, but it had still been sixteen tenth-cycles—over thirty-six hours—since they believed the Taljzi would have arrived.

Even with the Gold Dragon tech and the supplies and defenses in Asimov, Harriet saw no way that Rolfson could have held for thirty-six hours. Not against ten times his numbers and a dozen times his tonnage.

Her fleet was still a full tenth-cycle away. Even if a miracle had preserved TF 77–1 this long, could they hold another two and a half hours?

"Fleet Lord, we've got something on the anomaly scanners. Heading our way, fast."

She turned to face the Indiri officer speaking.

"How many signatures, Commander Ilaize?" she asked.

"Perhaps two squadrons' worth, moving at point five five cee," she replied. "The anomaly scanner doesn't give us much more."

Anomaly scanners were the only thing that could see through hyperspace beyond the one-light-second visibility bubble. Given that bubble translated to light-weeks to light-months of real space, depending on the current hyperspace density, anomaly scanners could sometimes see light-years away.

But all they could see was interface drives, and only interface drives in hyperspace. They couldn't tell Harriet, for example, if she was looking at two squadrons of destroyers—or two squadrons of Laian war-dreadnoughts.

Two squadrons totaled thirty-six ships. Most likely they weren't a threat, but...she couldn't take anything for granted.

"My compliments to Rear Admiral Jung-Hee Rhee," she said after a moment. "Her *Manticore*s have a full point six sprint capability. I want her to use every scrap of it to get to the one-light-second range of those ships."

"Yes, sir," Commander Miril Ilaize responded. She shook slightly, scattering water droplets from her damp red fur. "What if they're Taljzi?"

"Rhee is authorized to use whatever force is necessary to protect her command," Harriet replied. "I trust her discretion."

HARRIET WATCHED the icons representing Rhee's understrength battleship echelon leap ahead of the fleet. If she'd judged wrong, she'd just sent six battleships of her home star's Militia to their deaths.

It was unlikely, though. Thirty-odd ships was unlikely to be a major force, no matter who it belonged to.

She hadn't given orders to keep communications open, but Admiral Rhee had assumed that was part of her orders. A coil of destroyers expanded out behind the *Manticore*s, each slightly less than one light-second from each other.

Hyperfold communications didn't work in hyperspace, but they were relaying Rhee's sensors and coms back to the fleet following in her trail.

The farther the ships moved, the older the information she was receiving from them became. Every ten seconds' flight added another second to the information delay.

By the time Rhee broke into the visibility bubble around the other ships, she was almost a full light-minute ahead of the main fleet —easily half a light-year in real space.

"Confirmation is coming back," Ilaize reported. "Admiral Rhee reports a mix of Imperial and Militia units, cripples with a destroyer escort. Commodore Huber sends her regards and reports that Admiral Rolfson was holding as of six hours ago."

"Make sure we get the Commodore's full report," Harriet ordered with a concealed sigh of relief. "I want to know everything that happened in Asimov before she left."

"The Commodore is on your wave, Fleet Lord," the Indiri replied. "Data transmission is already commencing."

Harriet nodded her thanks, her gaze still locked on to the tactical plot. Rhee had slowed her ships down and was waiting for the fleet to catch up. Huber would continue on. Harriet saw no reason to pull the destroyers off their escort duty, even if they were *probably* safe now.

Six hours. Could her people have held for six more hours?

Sier stepped up next to her, the blue-feathered chief of staff looking disturbingly refreshed and calm despite the situation.

"Admiral Rolfson bought us more time than we dared hope," he said. "I fear the price."

"There was no price we weren't prepared to pay," Harriet noted. "That he had a chance to send away his cripples tells me he's paid less than I was prepared to lose."

She shook her head.

"Rolfson understood his orders: hold at any cost. If he has lost every ship under his command, but the Taljzi have not yet bombarded Isaac when we arrive, then he completed his mission."

Harriet grimaced.

"I just hope he's still there when we arrive."

"May the wind carry your words to the sun," Sier told her, the phrase half a hope and half a prayer. "We're at least an hour away from being able to detect ships in hyperspace around Asimov."

"And then we will know," she agreed. "Let me know as soon as we have a full download of Huber's data. I need to know where we were when she left."

THE HYPERSPACE MISSILES were terrifyingly more effective than Harriet had ever predicted. She watched the battle to date on fast forward, slowing down to study the individual portions of the engagement and stunned by the sheer amount of damage Rolfson had inflicted.

Huber's report suggested that Rolfson was almost out of HSMs, but he'd *smashed* the capital ship strength of the Taljzi Return. She could understand why the aliens were hesitating. Without evidence that the defenders were low on ammunition for their weapons and without time to assess just what the hyperspace missiles were, the Return faced the distinct possibility of repeating the losses from their first attack if they charged.

In their place, she'd be going over every piece of data she had with a fine-toothed comb. Eventually, they'd come up with the conclusion that the closer they got to the Terrans, the more effective their missiles were—though without the data about what had happened to their stealth attack, they wouldn't realize there was a danger to getting too close as well.

In their place, Harriet wasn't sure she'd make the assault at all. There was nothing in Asimov worth what they'd already lost trying to attack the system. The cold calculus of war said that they could take Asimov, but at a price that was *ridiculous,* considering the mere three capital ships defending it.

A chill ran across her neck as she considered that. There *was* something worth taking in Asimov, though there was no way the Taljzi could take them intact.

Would the Return be prepared to trade another twenty or thirty battleships—*they*, after all, didn't know that Rolfson was about to run out of HSMs—just for the chance to wipe out a planet and study the wreckage of three battleships?

If they lost the majority of this force, how many reinforcements did they have? For that matter, even if they took a *Bellerophon* mostly intact, how quickly could they reverse-engineer it and get a weapons system into production?

Harriet didn't know the answer to those questions. The Taljzi, however, would—and that would decide whether the Return's commander was going to spend the ships and lives to take Asimov.

In their place, however, *she'd* be waiting for reinforcements. Even against three ships.

After all, the Taljzi had no way of knowing that those were the *only* three *Bellerophon*s in existence.

CHAPTER FIFTY-THREE

"FLEET LORD! YOU NEED TO SEE THIS!"

Harriet jerked awake from an unexpected and unplanned nap at the sound of the junior Speaker's excited chatter. Blinking away sleep she hoped nobody else had seen, she rose from her chair and crossed to the young Tosumi's station.

Sier met her halfway there, something in the birdlike alien's dark eyes suggesting he knew damn well she'd been asleep—and was more than a little frustrated with the other avian alien for waking her.

The moment she saw the Tosumi's screen, however, she stopped caring.

"That's not near Asimov, is it?" she asked softly.

"No, sir," the Tosumi replied, all four arms fluttering across the station. "Heading towards Asimov, though. Point six lightspeed. Vector is...from DLK-5539."

That was the black hole where *Bellerophon* had found a Taljzi refuelling station and destroyed the logistics ships and the super-battleship guarding them. That was not a good sign.

"Can we resolve numbers?"

"They're at our maximum scan distance and there's a *lot* of them, sir." The Speaker fluttered his arms—what had once been the supporting limbs of a remote ancestor's wings—again in discontent. "Can't resolve individual anomaly signature, but a signature this large..."

He trailed off.

"Speaker?" Sier said sharply. "That kind of estimate is your job."

"Yes, Division Lord. Apologies, Division Lord. My waters darken and—"

"Give me the clouds-shadowed estimate," Sier snapped, and Harriet shivered.

It was still *weird* to hear a species that had been born to fly and had evolved down to jumping between trees use the metaphors of an amphibious race without thinking. The Imperial Races like the Tosumi had seen their original cultures all but destroyed, replaced with A!Tol culture.

The A!Tol had learned and they had two dozen subject races they *hadn't* done that to. The Imperial Races were still weird.

This particular example was wilting in his seat, a feather dropping loose in stress-molt as Harriet watched.

"Speaker?" she asked, far more gently than Sier had.

"At least five hundred ships, Fleet Lord," the Tosumi said in a very small voice. "Possibly more. Given enemy force proportions to date, at least a hundred capital ships."

"If it's the Taljzi," Harriet noted.

"Point six lightspeed, Fleet Lord," the youth repeated. "Wrong vector for a Core Power; they're coming from beyond our Rimward borders."

"They're Taljzi," Sier finished the conclusion. "Blazing suns."

THE GOOD NEWS, pathetic as it was, was that the geometry was in their favor. The second Taljzi fleet would arrive at Asimov roughly thirty thousandth-cycles—forty-five minutes or so, Harriet automatically translated still—after they did.

They were faster but her ships were closer.

"Anomaly scanners are picking up a force in hyperspace around Asimov," Sier reported. "Two hundred–plus ships, no breakdown yet."

"That lines up with what Huber reported," Harriet said. "So, they haven't decided to suicide-charge Rolfson yet."

"Would you, if a force twice your size was on the way?" her subordinate asked. "They do not seem to care about their people's lives for any moral concern, but they still understand that ships and spacers take time to replace."

"So, we take them by formation," Harriet concluded. "Do you think the buggers are smart enough to run for their friends when they see us coming?"

"They can run the geometry just like we can," he told her. "They'll know they won't make it—plus, all they can see in hyperspace is how many hulls we have. Even the first Return outnumbers us."

Harriet hadn't even considered that. Even combined with Cawl's fleet, she had fewer ships than the force lurking outside Asimov. That force was clustered together, a tight formation they clearly hadn't even budged to chase Huber's refugee column.

What the Taljzi didn't know was that between her and Cawl, they had over a hundred capital ships. Those ships might not have hyperspace missiles or hyperfold cannons or any of the fancy toys that the *Bellerophons* had...but they had active missile defenses and the Taljzi didn't.

"We probably can't take them both combined," she noted. "But either of those fleets..."

Yin beaks didn't have the flexibility of human mouths. Sier couldn't grin. His species' equivalent gesture was a wide opening of the beak that showed its sharp, serrated edge.

"Are you ready to become a legend, Fleet Lord?" he asked. "Two hundred against eight hundred?"

"That Asimov still stands tell me that Harold Rolfson has already become a damn legend," she told him. "Again. I can't let the Norseman get *all* of the glory. My ancestors would cry with shame.

"Get me a channel to Cawl. This is going to need to be far better coordinated than I think either of us are truly comfortable with, but I don't intend to let a single one of these *bastards* get away. Let the people who sent them wonder what black hole they dropped into."

"They may still have hyperfold coms, Fleet Lord," Sier warned.

"Yes. But they have to survive leaving hyperspace to phone home with those."

"FLEET LORD TANAKA," Cawl greeted her, the old Kanzi Fleet Master looking more awake and energized than she'd seen him yet. It seemed he had more than one cane like the one he'd snapped, as he was leaning on its exact duplicate as he stood in his flag bridge, facing her image in his main hologram projector.

"Fleet Master Cawl. I presume you have also seen our enemies," Harriet told him.

The white scars around his blue-furred jaw twitched in what might have been either amusement or frustration.

"Your people have shared their scans of the force at Asimov," he replied. "The force coming from the Rim we do see ourselves. It seems that your anomaly scans are longer-ranged than ours, though, I will note, less detailed."

"Less detailed?" Harriet asked carefully.

"Yes. The force coming from the rim is five hundred and twenty ships strong. One hundred and twenty are capital ships. We cannot break it down further than that."

That was more than her people's scanners could tell her. Despite herself, she was impressed.

"That's a lot of firepower."

Cawl shrugged.

"I doubt they have eighty super-battleships, Fleet Lord," he pointed out. "Nor are they fighting to defend God and Clan-blood. They may believe God has willed them to destroy, but even fanatic belief in that cause cannot match the will of those with family and friends to protect."

"I suppose you would know," Harriet replied before she could stop herself.

The old Kanzi winced.

"I would. For both the reasons you mean and others," he agreed. "I am sworn to service, Fleet Lord. I do not choose what orders to obey, what doctrines to follow. I may only choose what I *believe*, not what I do."

"It is what we do that defines us."

He nodded.

"And what do we intend to do today, Fleet Lord Tanaka? I have watched too many of my people die to these monsters. I don't intend to add your people to that tally."

"We're going to kill them all," Harriet replied. "No runners, no escapes. There's no way for them to surrender in hyperspace, though I'd let any of them that tried. We hit each fleet in sequence and smash them to pieces."

"In hyperspace," Cawl echoed. "Have you fought a battle in hyperspace before, Fleet Lord?"

"Only skirmishes," Harriet admitted. "But I don't see a choice."

He laughed.

"Even skirmishes, I must admit, are more than I have fought in hyperspace," he told her. "It seems that even old warlords can be taught new tricks when we must learn."

"We will need to coordinate our fire closely," she stated. The thought of merging tactical networks with a Kanzi fleet made her almost physically ill—but she liked it better than the losses they'd take if they didn't.

"Of course," he agreed. "And of course, neither of us feels entirely content with this. I think our best plan is—"

CHAPTER FIFTY-FOUR

"Well, it seems the Taljzi aren't lacking in courage."

Harriet wouldn't have minded a cowardly enemy. It wasn't what she was expecting, of course. The Taljzi's errors tended to be in the other direction, a callous disregard for losses that made no sense to her.

Even if you could produce infinite ships and soldiers and attached no moral value to them, you only had so many at the point of contact. Every ship and soldier lost was a ship and soldier that couldn't press the current campaign.

Her plan hadn't really relied on the Taljzi doing anything in specific, but their charge out to meet her definitely worked in her favor. The Taljzi missile-range advantage was still meaningful in hyperspace, but Harriet was counting on her layered defenses to make up the difference.

She had the data on Rolfson's defense with hyperfold cannons, but that ran into the same problem as her communicators: they didn't work in hyperspace. Tachyon scanners did, if not as efficiently as in normal space, but the hyperfold cannons and communicators didn't.

This was going to be a more traditional battle, missile against missile. No energy weapon could function at a range above a light-second, so her range advantage over the Taljzi's guns didn't matter.

Her engineers were still arguing over whether they thought the hyperspace disruptors would work inside hyperspace. Harriet didn't care. She wasn't courting a visibility-bubble engagement. This was going to end long before anyone got to see each other.

"They'll make their range of us in ten thousandth-cycles," Sier reported. "We'll range on them roughly two thousandth-cycles after that. The Kanzi should range at the same time."

They'd given each other far more information on their weapons systems than Harriet would have dreamed of even a few weeks before. She wasn't trusting Cawl, not really...but she needed his capital ships.

"So, what happens if Cawl betrays us?" Sier asked quietly. The Yin was closer to her than he usually came, whispering into her ear. "We're going on his word for who these people really are, after all. If he's working *with* them..."

"They didn't fake Alstroda's fate," she told him. "I believe the Kanzi are capable of many things, but destroying worlds to bait a deception?" She shook her head. "No. Not without a far larger prize on the table than Seventy-Seventh Fleet."

"What about the *Bellerophon*s?" her chief of staff said. "They'd make a pretty damn large prize."

"Not large enough for them to have murdered millions of Kanzi," Harriet replied. "Non-Kanzi? Maybe. But we'd have known if they'd evacuated fifty million of their own from Alstroda. No, someone burned that planet down and killed a *lot* of Kanzi.

"Cawl wants their blood, and we're all pretty sure it was these bastards, so I don't think he's going to turn on us."

"And if he does?" Sier pressed.

"Then we die, Sier," she admitted. "We're too close and have given him too much information. Call it necessity, call it trust...Fleet Master Cawl is in a position to kill us all. But right now, I think we all know who our real enemy is."

"I agree," the Yin told her. "I just wanted to make sure you realize how vulnerable we are."

Harriet snorted.

"The data network alone is giving me hives," she admitted. "Fortunately, it's going to give the *Taljzi* more cee-fractional missiles than their shields can handle. That's a trade I have no choice but to make."

THE TALJZI still had better missiles. There wasn't anything Harriet could do in preparation for that, and she remained still and silent in her seat as they opened fire. It took a precious handful of seconds for them to reach the range of her tachyon scanners, but *those* at least gave her useful data.

Almost six thousand missiles were screaming toward her fleet, and even as she was eyeing them, a second salvo dropped into space.

"Push the drones further forward," she ordered. She sighed. It was time. "Then activate the datanet connections."

There were a million firewalls, defenses and everything else in play, but this was still the moment of truth. Only one ship on each side, a super-battleship in both cases, was acting as the relay. They could cut that ship out of the network and cut off a cyber-attack—if they realized it was happening.

There were backup ships positioned to take over if a ship was lost, but there was only so much data flow Harriet could risk with the Kanzi.

"Network connection is live," Commander Ilaize reported. "The stream is clean and clear. Data flow is good. We are communicating."

"No sign of malware?" she asked.

"Nothing," Ilaize confirmed. "The Kanzi datafeed is clean."

It seemed Cawl was on the level. So far.

"Sier, time to weapons range?"

"One thousandth-cycle." He paused. "Their first salvo will hit ten seconds before that."

"Move the super-battleships forward," Harriet ordered. "They can't tell the difference until the last second, and the big ships can take a lot more hits before they're in danger."

Bucklers and their Kanzi equivalents swung out in front of the fleet, slightly less than one light-second away. Their relays expanded Harriet's sight and doubled the engagement time against the missiles.

Fortunately, this was an environment the antimissile systems' designers had considered. They wouldn't be as effective as they were in normal space, but the tachyon scanners gave them a few fractions of a second they wouldn't otherwise have.

The storm still smashed down on Harriet's super-battleships. Eighty of the immense warships took their place at the front line of her fleet. Normally, she'd have used destroyers to screen her capital ships—but the Taljzi missiles knew less about their enemies than hers did. The Taljzi weapons split their fire across all eighty capital ships, and her drones and antimissile turrets gutted the incoming fire.

Hundreds of missiles still made it through, and *Justified* vibrated around Harriet as near-cee hammers battered her shields.

"We have shield failures on several units," Sier reported. "No hits." He shook his head. "A good thing, since the shield failures are all Kanzi ships. Those hulls can't take a real hit."

Harriet chuckled. Twenty years before, the same thing had been true of the Imperium. As with the active missile defenses, the Imperium had learned from humanity.

Humanity had sold the Imperium compressed-matter armor—and the money from *that* had made the Duchy of Terra wealthy beyond belief.

Today, the presence of that armor was going to save a hundred million humans.

An indicator flashed green as Harriet's fleet entered their range of the enemy.

"Open fire," she ordered.

IF THE TALJZI had thought they had the advantage, that illusion was dashed when the joint Imperial-Kanzi fleet opened fire. They flung over twice as many missiles back at the Taljzi as had been fired at them, and they were targeted with deadly efficiency.

Even with the Kanzi scanners, Harriet's people could only truly distinguish "capital ship" versus "non-capital ship," but that was more than they'd expected to be able to do. There were forty-one capital ships among the two hundred and fifty enemy ships.

The allied fleet sent twelve thousand missiles at twenty of them.

"Pull the Kanzi ships that have shield failures back," Harriet ordered as their own missiles took off. "Cycle in battleships to fill their places until their shields are back up. Keep the line at eighty ships, but do *not* hold anything in the line whose shields are failing."

They only had twenty-six battleships, including the *Manticores*, and most were Kanzi. Untouched super-battleships, however, could bring their shields back up far faster than ships under fire.

She had the ships to rotate and the knowledge that the enemy would only barely be able to see what she was doing.

It took two minutes for their first missiles to arrive, and they had lost six Kanzi battleships by then. Over a dozen of her Imperial and Terran super-battleships had taken hits, but their armor could *take* hits.

The Kanzi ships couldn't.

When their missiles crashed down on the Taljzi, it was all worth it. They hit twenty ships with thousands of missiles. Sixteen of the anomaly icons blinked out—and the next salvo was only a few seconds behind them.

Only five of the Talzji capital ships survived that second salvo, and the third salvo had been sent in specifically to clean up any surviving heavy warships.

The follow-on salvos worked their way through the escorts with brutal precision, hammering individual ships that could have survived perhaps two hundred missiles in a salvo with four hundred at once.

Ten salvos was all it took. When the eleventh salvo arrived to clean up, there were only a handful of scattered cripples left from the fleet that had leveled Alstroda and Lelldorin and other worlds.

Three super-battleships and twelve battleships didn't survive from the Kanzi fleet. They didn't die alone, though, and Harriet saluted the brave search-and-rescue crews who swarmed *Indira Gandhi*'s shattered hull.

They didn't get everyone off before the antimatter cores failed, and *Gandhi*'s chief engineer was there to the end...but they got over two-thirds of the damaged super-battleship's crew clear before she went up.

The two Imperial super-battleships she'd lost hadn't been as lucky. They'd come apart under the bombardment, and other search ships were sweeping hyperspace for escape pods. It wasn't a hopeless task...but with only a light-second of visibility, it was an extraordinarily dangerous one.

"Detach a squadron of destroyers to back up the search-and-rescue," Harriet ordered. "Then send a courier into Asimov. I need Rolfson's ships."

"And then, Fleet Lord?" Sier asked.

She gestured at the tactical plot.

"Then I have another five hundred Taljzi warships to take out, and this time, they know what we have to fight them with."

CHAPTER FIFTY-FIVE

"Hyper portal!"

Harold almost sighed in relief at the report. The continually passing hours were starting to stretch his nerves to the breaking point. He didn't believe, not for one moment, that the Taljzi had just up and left.

That meant that they were waiting for something, and now, it seemed, the other shoe was dropping.

"What have we got?" he asked.

"Single portal, small ship...waiting on tachyon scanners." Ling Yu shook her head as a wide grin spawned on her face. "It's a *Wet Marsh*–class destroyer, Imperial design and IFF."

"Seriously?" Harold demanded.

"Incoming hyperfold communication," Xun Huang reported. "It's flagged to your attention, sir!"

"Link me up," he ordered, rotating the screens on his seat to show him the comm channel.

A tall and hairless humanoid with double-jointed arms and legs filled his screen, the Commander bowing as he saw Rolfson's return channel.

"Warm waters greet you, Vice Admiral. I am Commander Stiroth of *Small Amphibious Mammal Nest*."

Stiroth was an Ivida, one of the Imperial Races. His people had evolved on the desert plains of a homeworld that was about as dry as a habitable world could get. The A!Tol phrasing sounded strange coming from him—but not nearly as strange as the ship name after the translator was done with it.

"Commander," Harold greeted him. "I take it Tanaka will be here shortly?"

"Not exactly," Stiroth admitted. "The waters are murky. The initial Taljzi Return that you engaged has been destroyed, but a second, larger, fleet has been detected. I have encrypted orders for you, but my understanding is that the Fleet Lord intends to engage the enemy in hyperspace once more."

Once more. Which meant that Tanaka had taken on the Taljzi Return in hyperspace already. Victoriously, from the sound of it.

"The news is never entirely good or bad, is it?" he asked, somewhat whimsically. "Send me the encrypted messages, Commander, then make for rendezvous with the Task Force. I suspect we'll be returning to the Fleet Lord soon enough, and I'd hate to let you wander into trouble on your own when I have battleships to protect you with."

Ivida faces were motionless, a hard shield against the weather of their homeworld. Their *eyes*, however, were surprisingly readable, even to an alien.

Fortunately, it seemed that Commander Stiroth also had a sense of humor.

HARRIET TANAKA, thankfully, hadn't changed noticeably in the days since Harold had left the rest of Seventy-Seventh Fleet behind to charge ahead to Asimov. Maybe a new worry line or two, but her dark complexion concealed them, to his eyes at least.

"Vice Admiral," she greeted him. "We're in hyperspace near Asimov, but it doesn't look like I'm going to be able to join you in the system anytime soon. We took lighter losses against the first Return than I would have dared hope, but we're still sweeping for escape pods and survivors—and with hyperspace being what it is, if we leave them behind, they're gone forever."

He nodded. There was a very short window to try and find anyone who'd ended up lost in hyperspace. Once you'd left the visibility bubble of an object without an interface drive, it was unlikely you'd ever find it again.

"There is a second Taljzi fleet headed our way as well," she continued. "Five hundred and twenty ships, one hundred and twenty of them capital ships. It turns out that Kanzi anomaly scanners get more information on the anomaly than ours do."

Which was useful information all on its own, really.

"Your orders are to refuel and rearm—which, frankly, I'm assuming you've already done—and join us in hyperspace. We desperately need your cruiser screen. I just wish we could duplicate your hyperfold antimissile defenses in hyperspace."

To do that, they'd have to lure the enemy into normal space, which Harold didn't see a way to do without exposing the rescue operation already going on in hyperspace.

"It's also my unfortunate duty to report the loss of *Indira Gandhi* to the enemy," Tanaka told him. "We've confirmed the rescue of over two-thirds of her crew, but exact names and numbers are still uncertain.

"I wish I had better news for you, Admiral, but that's the news I've got. I need your ships and their defense drones. This is going to be a nightmare either way, but even seventy cruisers and three battleships could make the difference between victory or defeat out here."

The image of the Fleet Lord froze and Harold stroked his beard as he considered.

Tanaka was right in that his ships were fully fueled and armed.

Once he pulled out, however, Asimov only had its orbital defenses for protection.

He trusted Tanaka, but they'd still have to be careful. He hadn't fought as hard as he had for Asimov to lose the system and its hundred million souls by rushing.

PERSEUS AND *HERAKLES* opened the hyper portal once again. Cruisers led the way, the *Abrasion*-class ships of Division Lord Iffa's command. Destroyers and more cruisers followed, but the battleships remained in Asimov for several long minutes.

A plot on Rolfson's flag bridge showed the telemetry being relayed from the escorts he'd sent into hyperspace, showing the unfolding tentacle of ships reaching out toward Tanaka's fleet.

Someone over there had clearly recognized what he was doing, as a matching tentacle of hyperspace anomalies reached out from the fleet of unknown icons until a full chain of ships, each one light-second from the next, reached between the two fleets.

"We have a live link with Seventy-Seventh Fleet," Xun Huang confirmed. "Thirty-second delay each way, though. Hold on. Message incoming from Fleet Lord Tanaka."

"All right, Admiral Rolfson, you've got a link all the way home. I don't blame you, not with Isaac's population on the line, but we only have so much time. Can we get this show on the road?"

Harold laughed aloud.

"The Fleet Lord certainly knows how to make her point, doesn't she?" he said aloud. "Orders to the task force: we will make rendezvous with Seventy-Seventh Fleet at maximum velocity."

Bellerophon led the way, her hyperspace emitters unreplaced so far. The damage to her S-HSM batteries was looking permanent too. Harold's new flagship was going straight into a shipyard when this was over.

For now, however, she had almost a hundred conventional missile launchers and a *lot* of missiles for those launchers. Everything else was pointless in a hyperspace fight.

"We're getting the relay from the Kanzi anomaly scanners," Xun Huang reported. "Looks like we've got better range, but they've got better resolution. I don't think I knew that."

"I don't think any of us knew that," Harold replied. "Please tell me we're better once we're in tachyon-scanner range?"

"Honestly? In hyperspace, they have about the same resolution as we get with the tachyon scanners. We just have real-time data at thirty hyperspace light-seconds. They don't."

Harold shook his head.

"Nice to know we have some advantages, though gods know we may have to share some tech if this war drags on."

Several of his officers looked at him in horror.

"If we become full military allies against the Taljzi? We'd need them to be able to keep up with us, at least, and preferably be nearly as survivable."

His ships shot over toward Seventy-Seventh Fleet at point five five cee, and he studied the telemetry stream coming in along the chain.

Tanaka's calm list of losses had failed to mention that her super-battleships might be *intact*, but they'd taken a massive beating. It didn't look like a single Imperial or Terran ship had managed to go undamaged.

All were combat-capable—but *Bellerophon* wasn't going to be the only ship going into this fight who should have been going into a shipyard.

"I never thought I'd say this, but I hope the Kanzi are in better shape than we are," he muttered.

The data he had suggested that the Kanzi ships that were left had taken fewer hits...mostly because the Kanzi ships that had *taken* hits weren't around anymore.

Their tentative allies didn't have compressed-matter armor. Once their shields went down, they were gone.

Which left Harold with some fascinating questions. The biggest one, of course, was just where the Taljzi had acquired their technology.

Somehow, he didn't think they were going to have prisoners to interrogate. The Taljzi didn't strike him as the surrendering sort.

CHAPTER FIFTY-SIX

MORGAN WATCHED THE ICONS GROW ON HER SCREEN AS *Bellerophon* rejoined Seventy-Seventh Fleet. The Terran and Imperial ships were marked in green. The Kanzi were marked in the gold of allied units, *probably* friendly but still marked distinctively on the screens.

As her battleship joined the line, a sparkle of new green and gold icons shot out from the formation as defensive drones, the Imperial Bucklers and their Kanzi equivalents, were launched to fill in the gaps.

Cruisers and destroyers passed through the line of capital ships, moving forward a quarter million kilometers, just inside the visibility bubble. The defensive drones moved farther out, stretching out as far as they could while remaining linked to the screening warships.

She checked her systems. A two-second communication delay each way meant she couldn't usefully provide information from her tachyon scanners to the drones. A quick interrogation confirmed what she suspected: only the *Bellerophons* were carrying the Buckler-GD with an integrated tachyon-sensor array.

The rest of the defensive drones were using normal scanners.

They didn't even have the anomaly scanners that would give them a basic warning of incoming fire; the escorts would be relaying them that information.

The drones could function in that environment, but it wasn't effective. A handful of tachyon scanner–equipped drones were slotting into the formation, but the tactics Morgan and Commander Masters had developed required hyperfold coms to relay the starships' tachyon scanners to the drones.

Time and distance were both evaporating with disturbing swiftness as the two fleets moved toward each other. The Taljzi were adjusting their formation, not that the defenders could see any useful details of it.

"Division Lord Sier." Morgan opened a communications link to the main operations officer. She was jumping at least three layers of chain of command, but there was no *time*. "The *Bellerophon*s are carrying Buckler-GD drones with built-in tachyon scanners. We need to disperse those through the drone screen and use them as master sensor controls. It'll buy the drones at least four or five seconds to aim."

The drones would still only have about a third of a second to actually *fire* at the missiles, but those seconds of aiming could make all of the difference.

"Commander Casimir," the Yin replied. "You know there's a chain of command for this sort of suggestion, yes?"

"There's no time, sir."

"Agreed." Even as they were talking, Morgan saw the orders going out and her drones being taken over by fleet command in exchange for regular Buckler drones from the rest of the fleet.

"I'm just reminding you," Sier continued. "In case someone in that chain decides to complain later. It's a good call, Commander, and I forgot the GD units had that. Thank you."

Morgan looked up from her console to meet Masters's gaze. Her superior shook his head and wagged a finger at her—and then went right back to targeting his missiles.

It was almost time.

THE MOMENT the Taljzi opened fire, Morgan realized they'd misjudged their new enemy once again. The data feed she'd been receiving from *Justified* included their estimate of the breakdown of the enemy's hundred and twenty capital ships: roughly half and half super-battleships and battleships.

Those hundred and twenty capital ships, however, launched *sixteen thousand* missiles. It wasn't half and half super-battleships —*every one* of the Taljzi capital ships was a super-battleship.

"Well, that's going to get rough," Masters grumped. "The computers don't even want to resolve individual anomalies. What's your guess on the escorts, Casimir?"

Morgan ran the numbers. Her boss was right: once the escorts had added their contribution to the tsunami of missiles the super-battleships had launched, the computers simply stopped being able to break down individual launches. Their anomaly scanners hadn't been designed for major fleet actions in hyperspace.

"I'd guess we've got another eight to nine thousand missiles in play from the escorts," she told him. "That gives us about twenty missiles per ship, so I'd guess a pretty even split between destroyers and cruisers."

And almost twenty-five *thousand* missiles headed toward Seventy-Seventh Fleet that they couldn't respond to yet. It had been over a century since an Imperial fleet had seen that kind of firepower in play.

Over a *hundred* super-battleships. The Imperium only had about four hundred total, and that was including the several Duchies, like Terra, that had super-battleship squadrons of their own. The Kanzi had fewer.

The eighty super-battleships gathered around Morgan represented a significant portion of the type available to the Theocracy and the Imperium...and the Taljzi had sent over a hundred and fifty, including the ships the Mesharom and TF 77–1 had previously destroyed, against them.

"Clones only buy them so much," Masters muttered as a second immense salvo tore into space. "You can't clone super-battleships!"

"But you can clone construction workers and miners and crews," Morgan reminded him. "The biggest weakness of any galactic power is population...and if they have mass-produced clones, well..."

"Yeah," he admitted. "Good call on the tachyon scanners, Casimir. You may have just saved the fleet."

Morgan didn't think it was going to make that much difference... but then the missiles cascaded down on the drone screen. Three hundred–plus defending starships had deployed almost two thousand defensive drones.

Her computer projections said they'd stop about a missile each on average, and the main defense was going to fall on the screening cruisers and the capital ships' shields. A lot of cruisers were going to die, but Morgan's screens told her why they were in front.

The capital ships had shielded the escorts to preserve their launchers in the first battle, but they'd paid for it. None of the Imperial capital ships were undamaged. No one wanted to lose the cruisers and destroyers screening the big ships, but given the choice between losing a ship with thirty launchers and a ship with a hundred...

"Bucklers engaging," she announced. By the time she'd finished speaking, the missiles were already through the line of drones—but they'd paid for passing and flashed into the firing paths of the cruisers as an already much-reduced force.

Firing through two visibility bubbles wasn't an entirely practical option. The refraction caused by crossing through hyperspace was weird. *Not* attempting to protect the screen with the capital ships' defensive turrets would have been untenable, however, and hundreds of laser beams cut through space.

Many missed. More hit cruisers and destroyers and were shrugged aside by shield segments that weren't facing the enemy.

The escorts were far from defenseless themselves. The *Thunderstorm-* and *Abrasion*-class cruisers actually carried more defenses, ton per ton, than Imperial capital ships. Their Kanzi counterparts carried even more again, their systems updated far more readily and thoroughly than their bigger sisters'.

Thousands of missiles made it through, but they flung themselves at over two hundred escorts. Like the battleships in the battle before, the cruisers put themselves between the incoming fire and the destroyers. A hundred and fifty cruisers weathered the storm, each of them taking dozens of missiles against their shields—but this was the environment they'd been designed for.

And it turned out the Kanzi had a few surprises of their own.

"I've got at least three Kanzi light cruisers whose shields went down," Masters declared. "All of them took solid hits to the hull—and they're still with us."

"Compressed-matter armor?" Vong asked.

"Not sure," Morgan's boss replied. Even as they were speaking, a second immense salvo hit the outer limit of the Bucklers. "If it isn't CM, it's something equally effective. They haven't rolled it out to the bigger ships, whatever it is."

The second salvo had no more luck getting through the interlacing fields of laser fire than the first, but the cruisers' shields hadn't had time to recover. More shields went down across the screen, and this time, ships began to die.

Morgan consciously tried not to read ship names. She had friends in the screen, and some of them weren't going to come back from this. Ships from both fleets died, and she focused on trying to cover their sisters.

"Range," Masters said calmly, as if announcing the weather. The salvo that blasted out from the Kanzi-Imperial joint fleet didn't match the tsunamis the Taljzi were unleashing on them, but the Taljzi had yet to demonstrate anything resembling active missile defense.

Morgan just didn't know if that would make the difference against a hundred and twenty super-battleships.

ANOTHER DOZEN CRUISERS died as the two fleets continued to close, new salvoes joining the first wave of the defenders' missiles on their suicide course for the enemy. Morgan's fingers flew across her console as she loaded up ECM programs, evasion patterns... anything she could think of to try and save more of her comrades.

The attack wasn't her responsibility, but she was keeping an eye on it. The ability to distinguish between capital ship and escort was disturbingly valuable in a hyperspace engagement. Like the defenders, the Taljzi had put their escorts out in front.

Imperial commanders would argue with the knowing sacrifice of the lighter ships but accept the cold calculus of war. From what Morgan had seen, the loss of the lighter ships barely even occurred to the Taljzi's commanders as a concern.

Unfortunately for the Taljzi, Seventy-Seventh Fleet and their Kanzi allies could see exactly what they were doing, and the vast majority of their missiles completely bypassed the screen—a screen that had no ability to shoot down those missiles.

Tanaka's orders had erred on the side of caution. That entire twelve-thousand-plus missile salvo was targeted on a mere ten ships. Super-battleship or not, their shields couldn't stand under that fire. Their compressed-matter armor couldn't stand under that fire.

Ten icons disappeared from the screen and Morgan saw Masters shake his head.

"I wish I could say that was overkill, but we fought one of these bastards head-on," he admitted. "Twelve hundred or so missiles apiece sounds about right."

The second salvo repeated the first's success. Another ten super-battleships disappeared—but the Imperial and Kanzi screening units were getting hammered. Missiles were leaking through and the capital ships were taking hits.

"Move the capital ships forward," Morgan heard Tanaka order. "We'll cycle off, relieve the escorts while keeping the majority of the fleet protected. Keep hammering the—"

The Fleet Lord stopped in mid-word as a sudden flash lit up their screens. Hyper portals tore through reality, ripping an entire salvo of missiles to pieces—and then the Taljzi were gone.

They'd dropped back into normal space, rendering the salvos still heading toward them harmless.

Unfortunately, the same wasn't true for the Taljzi salvos heading toward Morgan.

CHAPTER FIFTY-SEVEN

"OH, YOU CLEVER KUSOTTARE-ME," HARRIET MURMURED AS SHE watched her enemy disappear. She'd hammered a sixth of their capital ships into debris, but now her missiles were useless and she was still facing down over a hundred thousand incoming weapons of her own.

Except...

"All ships, adjust course to zero by ninety and go to maximum velocity," she barked. "If you've got a sprint mode, *use it*. Move!"

"What about the Bucklers?" Sier asked.

"Leave them," she ordered. "Let's give the missiles something to look at while *we* get out of the way!"

The entire combined fleet moved, every single ship pitching "up" ninety degrees and using every scrap of the impossible maneuverability the interface drive gave them to move away from where the missiles were expecting them.

The missiles didn't change course to match. About half of the closest salvo tried, but they handed the Buckler drones a perfect extended targeting period and died in their thousands.

The rest charged past the Bucklers and attacked suddenly empty space, tens of thousands of missiles flinging themselves pointlessly into the void.

"Sun's last shadow," Sier hissed. "How?!"

"Hyperspace anomaly scanners are *huge*, Division Lord," Harriet reminded him. "We don't even have them mounted on the Bucklers. We're feeding our missiles targeting data up to the last second or so, making sure they get into the visibility bubble of their targets."

She gestured to the now-harmless missiles as their interface drives flickered out and they disappeared from their screens.

"Theirs are the same. They were counting on there being *enough* missiles in hyperspace with us that it wouldn't matter."

Harriet shook her head.

"Detach our destroyers to retrieve the escape pods and search for survivors," she ordered. "They're to sweep back and find everyone they can. Hell, if they can find any of the *Taljzi* alive, I'll take them."

"What are the rest of us going to be doing?" her chief of staff asked carefully.

"Every ship *bigger* than a destroyer in Seventy-Seventh Fleet has been refitted with at least ten hyperfold cannons, Sier," Harriet pointed out. "Calculate me an emergence point that will be within two million kilometers of the bastards—and preferably more than half a million kilometers away from them.

"Two can play the close-range-ambush game—and they sure as hell aren't going anywhere without us seeing them."

THERE WERE days Harriet Tanaka hated hyperspace. It wasn't the best way to travel faster than light, just the only way anyone knew of.

It took almost ten minutes for them to calculate the emergence point of the Taljzi fleet and move into position to duplicate it, and her staff was still looking nervously at her.

"It all depends on what they did after they went through," Sier reminded her. "We're dropping in about two million kilometers from where they came out, we *think*, but they could be as much as six or seven light-minutes away from there."

"Then we chase them, whatever it takes," she told them. "We can skip through hyperspace after them and use Rolfson's hyperspace missiles on the bastards. For that matter, all of Seventy-Seventh's capital ships are currently carrying at least two D-HSMs. If we're at long range, we'll be able to use them."

"And if we get this all right?"

"Then they'll be losing super-battleships before they even know we're there," Harriet said with satisfaction. "So, I'll take the risk, Sier. These bastards have killed entire *worlds*. They don't get to go home. Not today. Not ever."

They were reasonably sure, in truth, that the *first* fleet they'd destroyed had been responsible for that. No one decided to point that out to Harriet, however, which was probably a good thing.

"Portal formation in twenty seconds," Sier told her with a sigh. "Vice Admiral Tidikat's squadron is leading the way."

The second Taljzi fleet probably hadn't had a chance to communicate with the fleet that had attacked Asimov. If they had, they'd have realized the last thing they wanted to do was fight the Imperial Navy in normal space before they'd had a chance to build countermeasures.

"Portals open," Sier reported, and sixteen super-battleships vanished through it in a moment. More ships followed, a steady stream of massive warships as Harriet Tanaka fed her fleet into the fire.

The telemetry coming back was a chaotic mess, and she barely had time to see it before *Justified* flung herself through the portal held open by the Kanzi battleships. She had enough time to realize they'd got it *almost* right before her flagship joined the maelstrom.

They'd emerged just over *one* million kilometers from the Taljzi, and the aliens had responded immediately. By the time Harriet's flagship was in normal space, the Taljzi had already closed most of the gap to bring their disruptors into range.

It took them precious seconds to do so. Seconds the knife fight Harriet had chosen to court didn't give them. Super-battleships died by the dozen as massed hyperfold cannon fire bypassed their shields and compressed-matter armor alike. Only a tiny portion of her fleet's weaponry was striking inside the enemy ships...but only a tiny portion of it needed to.

"Hit them," Harriet snapped, watching as plasma lances and proton beams added their fire to the fray. Even at this range, missiles were flashing out of both sides as the distance dropped.

At three hundred thousand kilometers, Vice Admiral Tidikat's flagship lurched. *Vindication* reeled out of formation as her entire front quarter *disappeared*, torn to debris as random pieces of it were flung into hyperspace.

A second Imperial super-battleship died. Then a third. A fourth.

But there were no Taljzi capital ships left to face them. The cruisers' disruptors were bad enough, but they struggled against super-battleship shields—and their antiproton curtains were failing in the face of the massed proton-beam fire of two entire battle fleets.

One moment, Harriet was holding on to the arms of her seat with white-clenched fingers.

The next, it was over, the last Taljzi cruiser ripped apart by point-blank fire from a Kanzi battleship before it could ram Tidikat's crippled flagship.

Silence hung over her flag bridge like a fog as she rose, studying the display. The butcher's tally for this was going to take hours, even days, to total. Harriet Tanaka had just led tens of thousands of sentients to their deaths.

But the Taljzi Return had been stopped.

"Did any of them get away?" she asked softly.

"I can't be sure," Sier admitted. "We'll have to go over the data in detail; with the hyperfold cannons overwhelming our anomaly scanners, it's *possible* they opened a portal and got a handful of their ships out without us seeing." He paused. "None of the capital ships. We got all of those."

She nodded slowly.

"It will have to do."

CHAPTER FIFTY-EIGHT

Annette Bond massaged her temples slowly as the hologram played in front of her. The recording had winged its way through the hyperfold relay network to her from Asimov, where Harriet Tanaka's flagship now hung in orbit of the no-longer-threatened planet of Isaac.

"We confirmed it in the end," Tanaka said in a tired voice. "Four of their destroyers ran during the final clash. We didn't make it into hyperspace in time to catch them, so they got away. I don't know where the logistics elements of either fleet were, but they were definitely around, since the bastards never seemed to run out of ammunition.

"I've sent a squadron of super-battleships, with your *Manticores* and the *Thunderstorm*-Ds for escort, to check out black hole DLK-5539," she continued. "I don't expect them to find much, but I'm guessing that was a rendezvous point for them, since the second fleet seemed to be coming from there.

"Our alliance with Fleet Master Cawl, tentative as it has to be, is holding for now. He's pulling most of his ships back to Kanzi space, but I sent a squadron of cruisers with him. They have hyperfold coms, so we can keep in coordination with him.

"I can't help but fear that this is only the beginning. We know *nothing* about these Taljzi except that they fled Kanzi space almost six hundred long-cycles ago. The size of their industrial base, their population, hell, even how they're cloning their soldiers. We know nothing."

The petite Japanese officer sighed and shrugged.

"I don't have the ships to spare for scouting expeditions beyond DLK-5539," she admitted. "Part of my message to the Empress is requesting more reinforcements. *Not* Ducal ships," Tanaka added. "We've already asked more of your Militia than is appropriate, and lost too many of your ships.

"They made all the difference, though. Without the *Bellerophon*s, Asimov would have fallen. Without Tidikat and Rolfson, we'd have lost the hyperspace battle." She snorted. "Notably, without your stepdaughter, I think we would have still lost the battle. She has an eye for the chink in the armor that will serve her well. Today, it was the chink in our armor, and she probably cut our losses in half.

"Tomorrow, it may be the chink in *their* armor and turn the tide of a battle we won't be able to afford to lose."

Annette studied the weary face of the other woman. Tanaka had been the first human to put on an Imperial officer's uniform, and Annette Bond had been the woman who'd given up the last fight humanity had against the Empire. They understood each other better than many did.

"We're sending our cripples back to Sol, with our Mesharom rescuee," the Fleet Lord concluded. "*Vindication* is going to need to be towed. In different times, I might have ordered her abandoned and scuttled, but I have this sinking feeling we'll need every ship we can get in the days to come.

"Seventy-Seventh will hold at Asimov until further orders. Annette..." Tanaka paused, considering her next words. "Annette, I need you to convince the Empress. Everything we can spare. Every ship, every portable surface-to-space battery, every defense platform we can box up: we need it on the Rim.

"We just smashed half the navy of a decently sized Arm Power and they didn't blink. Didn't flinch. The only way that even begins to make sense is if there are *far* more of them to come."

"TAN!SHALLEGH has left the Sontar System."

Annette bowed her head in silence as A!Shall spoke.

"I have received Fleet Lord Tanaka's message. You agree with her assessment, I would guess?" the A!Tol Empress asked.

"I am biased, but yes," Annette confirmed. "Those are human-colonized worlds at risk. If we can put the Grand Fleet between them and this enemy, we should."

"We will," A!Shall said flatly. "Tan!Shallegh is already on his way. When these Taljzi come again, they will not meet a scratch force of hesitant allies. They will meet the Grand Fleet of the A!Tol Imperium."

"We are beginning a refit program on the ships that have already arrived," Annette told her Empress. "Full Gold Dragon technology, hyperfold cannons, tachyon scanners and S-HSM launchers."

"I wish, now, that we had never tried to hide those developments," the Empress replied. "I need an entire Navy armed with the weapons the *Bellerophons* took into battle."

"I do not think the Mesharom will lightly forgive us for our transgressions," the human noted. "They have accepted it as done now that these Taljzi are coming, but Adamase is furious."

"Let the deep abysses swallow his anger," A!Shall snapped, her beak clacking together with harsh finality. "If we had done as they willed, millions upon millions of *my* subjects would be dead. You say they are human worlds, Dan!Annette Bond, but you forget yourself."

Annette kept her head bowed. It was rare for the A!Tol monarch to show anger.

"They are *my* people. I do not care what world they were born on or how many limbs they have. *They are my people.* The Imperium stands guard. We always have. We always will. That was the deal, was it not?"

"It was," Annette agreed. "It is...easy to fear that one's own race will be forgotten, when there is an Imperium to watch."

"The swords of the Duchy of Terra have stood side by side with the Imperial Navy," A!Shall said, her tone calming again. "This will not be forgotten. The families of the fallen will receive full Imperial Pensions as well as whatever benefits your Duchy lays upon them. We will pay for the replacement ships.

"I must, however, ask two things of you I have never asked before, and you must obey."

Annette winced. She knew what at least one of those things would be.

"The full files from DragonWorks and the *Bellerophon* and *Thunderstorm*-D designs must be forwarded to the Imperial Navy," A!Shall ordered. "In the past, I have allowed you to keep a hold on the technologies you have provided the Navy, to help support your Duchy's economy.

"Now every shipyard in the Imperium must bend their limbs to the construction of a new war fleet. Licensing and control of the designs and the technology must lie with the Imperium."

That was going to hurt Earth. A lot. They didn't *need* that extra support, not now that they were roughly the fourth-largest shipbuilding complex in the Imperium, but it was still going to hurt the Ducal economy.

"I understand."

"Your companies will be compensated and you can be assured that the Imperium will continue to expand the Sol shipyards," A!Shall told her. "But we need that new fleet if we are to face the storm to come."

"So be it. And the second?"

The A!Tol's skin flashed from her usual gray to a flushed bright blue of pleased success.

"The Kanzi have met my price," A!Shall told her. "They are collecting a convoy at Arjzi of ships loaded with the slaves they are to release. *You* will take your *Tornado* and a squadron of super-battle-ships under Fleet Lord !Olarski to Arjzi, where !Olarski will send half of her ships back to Sol with the slaves.

"You, however, will remain in Arjzi. I will send more detailed instructions as you prepare for the trip, but you carry full plenipotentiary authority and my full faith.

"It will fall to you, Duchess Dan!Annette Bond of Terra, to negotiate the end to a cold war we can no longer afford.

"The future of over fifty species will rest in our hands, my dear Annette. Tan!Shallegh will see the Taljzi stopped.

"*You* must make sure we have the strength to see them ended."

JOIN THE MAILING LIST

Love Glynn Stewart's books? Join the mailing list at

GLYNNSTEWART.COM/MAILING-LIST/

to know as soon as new books are released, special announcements, and a chance to win free paperbacks.

ABOUT THE AUTHOR

Glynn Stewart is the author of *Starship's Mage*, a bestselling science fiction and fantasy series where faster-than-light travel is possible– but only because of magic. His other works include science fiction series *Duchy of Terra, Castle Federation* and *Vigilante,* as well as the urban fantasy series *ONSET* and *Changeling Blood.*

Writing managed to liberate Glynn from a bleak future as an accountant. With his personality and hope for a high-tech future intact, he lives in Kitchener, Ontario with his partner, their cats, and an unstoppable writing habit.

VISIT GLYNNSTEWART.COM FOR NEW
RELEASE UPDATES

 facebook.com/glynnstewartauthor

OTHER BOOKS
BY GLYNN STEWART

For release announcements join the
mailing list or visit **GlynnStewart.com**

STARSHIP'S MAGE
Starship's Mage
Hand of Mars
Voice of Mars
Alien Arcana
Judgment of Mars
UnArcana Stars
Sword of Mars
Mountain of Mars
The Service of Mars
A Darker Magic
Mage-Commander (upcoming)

Starship's Mage: Red Falcon
Interstellar Mage
Mage-Provocateur
Agents of Mars

Pulsar Race: A Starship's Mage Universe Novella

DUCHY OF TERRA
The Terran Privateer
Duchess of Terra
Terra and Imperium
Darkness Beyond
Shield of Terra
Imperium Defiant
Relics of Eternity
Shadows of the Fall
Eyes of Tomorrow

SCATTERED STARS
Scattered Stars: Conviction
Conviction
Deception
Equilibrium
Fortitude (upcoming)

PEACEKEEPERS OF SOL
Raven's Peace
The Peacekeeper Initiative
Raven's Course
Drifter's Folly (upcoming)

EXILE
Exile
Refuge
Crusade
Ashen Stars: An Exile Novella

CASTLE FEDERATION
Space Carrier Avalon
Stellar Fox
Battle Group Avalon
Q-Ship Chameleon
Rimward Stars
Operation Medusa
A Question of Faith: A Castle Federation Novella

SCIENCE FICTION STAND ALONE NOVELLA
Excalibur Lost

VIGILANTE
(WITH TERRY MIXON)
Heart of Vengeance
Oath of Vengeance

**Bound By Stars: A Vigilante Series
(With Terry Mixon)**
Bound By Law
Bound by Honor
Bound by Blood

TEER AND KARD
Wardtown
Blood Ward

CHANGELING BLOOD
Changeling's Fealty
Hunter's Oath
Noble's Honor
Fae, Flames & Fedoras: A Changeling Blood Novella

ONSET
ONSET: To Serve and Protect
ONSET: My Enemy's Enemy
ONSET: Blood of the Innocent
ONSET: Stay of Execution
Murder by Magic: An ONSET Novella

FANTASY STAND ALONE NOVELS
Children of Prophecy
City in the Sky

Made in the USA
Middletown, DE
21 June 2023

33040856R00239